LE

COSÌ FAN TUTTE

In the same series

MOZART

Don Giovanni
Idomeneo

MOZART

Die Zauberflöte
Die Entführung aus dem Serail

UNIVERSE OPERA GUIDES

W. A. MOZART

Le Nozze di Figaro

*

Così fan tutte

Introduction by Dennis Arundell

UNIVERSE BOOKS
New York

Published in the United States of America in 1971 by Universe Books, 381 Park Avenue South, New York, N.Y. 10016

Library of Congress Catalog Card Number: 74-162691

ISBN 0-87663-149-9

Devised and produced by Norton Bailey Ltd., 103 Lonsdale Road, London, S.W.13
Printed in Great Britain

CONTENTS

Introduction

For the first thirteen years of his life Mozart, in spite of being made to work hard, was fêted and petted and made to believe that life was fun, though according to his father he was always too serious to be childish, especially where music was concerned.

Before he was six years old he had taken part in a comedy called *Sigismund, King of Hungary* set to music by the court organist of Salzburg and performed in the University Hall in September 1761, and by the time he was eleven he and his sister Marianne had been taken by their father on a grand tour all over Germany and to Brussels, Paris, London, Holland and Switzerland, playing the violin, harpsichord and organ and advertised as 'prodigies of nature'.

At that time the career of any artist, especially a musician, depended on the support of influential patrons, and this journey was well calculated by Leopold Mozart, their father, to teach the young Mozarts the value of publicity—they played to, among others, the Empress Maria Theresa, Louis XV, George III and Queen Charlotte, the Prince of Orange and John Christian 'London' Bach. This had little effect on Marianne, and although the amazing technique of her baby brother, both as composer and performer was everywhere admired, the admiration in no way turned his logically clever head.

At the end of 1766 the family returned to Salzburg where the Archbishop, doubting young Mozart's skill, made him compose part of a sacred cantata, *The Obligation of the First Commandment,* which was performed the following spring in the University Hall, where the eleven-year-old composer's Latin comedy *Apollo et Hyacinthus* was given a month later.

These two works 'may be dismissed at once' wrote E. J. Dent in his famous book on Mozart, and the two operas which followed were remarkable only for having been written by a twelve-year-old: they were *La finta semplice,* composed for the new Emperor Joseph II in 1768, but not immediately performed because of intrigues, and *Bastien und Bastienne.* The latter was a parody of Rousseau's opera *Le Devin du Village* and was acted in the garden of Doctor Mesmer, the famous hypnotist whose methods were introduced in *Così fan tutte* twenty-two years later.

Mozart's first stage compositions were notably comedies, doubtless the influence of the operas he had seen on his childhood travels, which included Piccini's universally famous *La buona figliuola* (based on Richardson's *Pamela*), Gassmann's *La notte critica*, Monsigny's *Rose et Colas* and Philidor's *Le Sorcier.* All these operas, it should be noted, were contemporary works treating their subjects with a lightly comic touch rather than grand or heroic dramas in the serious vein favoured by earlier composers.

But for the next eight years Mozart, though still fêted, was chiefly concerned with serious opera, or *opera seria* as the genre was known. At the end of 1769 he went for two years with his father to Italy, the land of opera.

In Milan he met the most famous of male sopranos, Farinelli, and was commissioned to write an *opera seria* for the following season; in Bologna he studied under the great teacher Padre Martini; in Mantua he heard Hasse's *Il Demetrio*, and in Cremona the same composer's *Tito Vespasiano, ossia, La clemenza di Tito,* written thirty-five years before. The libretti for both works were by the recognised master librettist of *opera seria,* Metastasio (Mozart himself was to set an adaption of *La clemenza di Tito* at the end of his life).

In Naples he saw Jomelli's *Demofoönte* and the first production of the same composer's *Armida abbandonata.* Of the latter the fourteen-year-old Mozart said: 'Beautiful, but too meticulous and old-fashioned for the theatre'. As Dent wrote:

> the stately elegance of Metastasio, Jomelli and Hasse belonged to a past generation, and the sentimental humour of Piccini's *Buona figliuola* had set a fashion destined to rule the musical world until Mozart himself was in a position to lead a new movement.

Mozart might have heard the first performance of Gluck's *Orfeo* in Vienna in 1762, and works by Rameau in Paris, but until he went to Italy he had chiefly heard only lighter works in Paris and London, including perhaps some by Monsigny and Arnold, both composers of light comedy operas.

Back in Milan, Mozart composed the serenade *Ascanio in Alba* for the marriage of the Archduke Ferdinand. Among the singers was Manzuoli, whom he had met in London, and the piece was performed together with *Ruggiero,* the last opera by the old composer Hasse, who remarked, 'this boy will throw us all in the shade'.

He then started on a commissioned opera, *Mithridates, King of Pontus.* As he was only fourteen, it is not surprising that he was hardly ready for such a serious work; nevertheless it was performed twenty times running from 26 December, 1770, and conducted by the young composer with Manzuoli singing. After some eight months at home in Salzburg, Mozart went once more to Milan in 1772 and finished *Lucio Silla,* his second *opera seria,* which was produced that winter.

In 1773 he was back in Austria and happy to be with German musicians again. While there, he wrote entractes and choruses for Gebler's heroic drama *Thamos, King of Egypt,* but he could not forget the lighter operas he had tried to imitate or the Italian style he had absorbed.

When his *La finta giardinera* was performed in Munich in 1775, the editor of the *Deutsche Chronik* wrote that 'unless Mozart should prove to be a mere overgrown product of the forcing house, he will be the greatest composer that ever lived'.

For a time, however, he turned to whatever composition seemed most in demand, and his next dramatic work was a cantata based on Metastasio's *Il re pastore.* He spent the year 1776 in polishing his style in music other than opera.

From this time on, Mozart showed that he was no longer a spoiled darling and became enthusiastic for the promotion of German music, serious or otherwise. On a visit to Mannheim he told the Elector that his most anxious wish was to write an opera and said he 'could write a German one, God be praised', though privately he thought the German singers were not very good. He knew that the Emperor was planning to establish German opera in Vienna and, though he realised he would not be put in charge, he hoped he might be given the opportunity to compose an opera 'and as to what may occur hereafter I care not'. In spite of this great ambition, he felt strongly that Italian was the language for singing, and wrote to his father:

> Don't forget my wish to write an opera; I envy every person who writes one; I could almost weep from vexation when I hear or see an aria. But Italian, not German–*seria,* not *buffa*!

So for the moment he was veering between serious and comic opera, between German and Italian.

After an abortive visit to Paris in 1778 ('that confounded French language . . . so detestable for music'), Mozart returned to Mannheim, where the Elector was doing his best to establish German opera. The composer's enthusiasm for German melodrama, and in particular those melodramas he saw on the subjects of *Medea* and *Ariadne on Naxos,* with speech over music, led him to undertake the music for *Semiramis;* in addition the director of the theatre considered him for the composer of his opera *Cora*, but nothing came of either scheme.

Mozart maintained that he had long wanted to write music for melodramas, and thought 'most operatic recitatives should be treated in this way and the recitatives only sung when *the words can be thoroughly expressed by the music*'. So on his return to Salzburg early in 1779 he enthusiastically rewrote and added music for the melodrama *Thamos*, which he had set six years previously, encouraged in this by the success of the German dramatic companies of Böhm and Schikaneder–he was to collaborate with the latter on *Die Zauberflöte* twelve years later. He subsequently started to set the German opera *Zaide*, but never finished it.

The following year he wrote *Idomeneo*, an Italian *opera seria*, for the Munich carnival of 1781, and the success of the first performance finally established him as an opera composer.

Mozart's enthusiasm for German opera led him to obey the Emperor's express command to compose music to Bretzner's libretto of *Die Entführung aus dem Serail*, which had already been performed with music by André in Berlin in May 1781. It was of this opera that Mozart wrote:

> In an opera the poetry must be the obedient daughter of the music. For why do the Italian comic operas succeed everywhere with all the wretched nonsense of their libretti . . . ? Because the music has the upper hand completely.

He ignored the fact that the best Italian operas had well-made plots, so perhaps, since in his later and greater operas words and music are admirable partners, at this stage in his career Mozart found it easier, eager though he was to establish German opera, to force German words to fit his Italianate music rather than vice versa.

This German comic opera, or *Singspiel*, produced in Vienna on 16 July 1782, was Mozart's first popular stage success. It was performed seventeen times in six months to packed houses, and in over thirty other cities in the next twenty years. It was much admired by Gluck, but the Emperor thought 'it was no great thing', for he preferred Italian opera, especially as written by Salieri.

In February 1783 Mozart wrote to his father:

> I do not believe that the Italian opera will be long carried on; for my part I prefer the German; even though it may cost me more trouble, still I like it best. Every nation has an opera of its own; why should not the Germans have one also? Is not German as well adapted for singing as French or English and more so than the Russian? I am at present writing a German opera *for myself* . . . Goldoni's comedy, *The Servant of Two Masters* . . . Baron Binder is the translator; but I keep it a profound secret till it is quite finished.

But it never was finished, even if it was started.

Some time before 1783 Mozart and his wife were staying in Vienna with the rich Baron Wetzlar, a converted Jew. At his house they met the dramatic poet of the Imperial Theatre, Lorenzo da Ponte, whose Jewish father had had his whole family baptised when he married his second wife, a Catholic.

Da Ponte, an expert in Latin and Italian poetry, after many disreputable adventures in Venice, arrived in Vienna in about 1779 and there, after four years of poverty, received his Imperial appointment and wrote libretti for Salieri and the Spanish composer Martin y Soler.

Wetzlar undertook to pay for the production of an opera in London or Paris, if Vienna proved impossible, with music by Mozart to a libretto by Da Ponte, who promised he would write it. But, as Mozart confided to his father on 7 May 1783:

> Who can tell whether he will or can keep this promise? You are aware that these Italian gentlemen are very civil to your face.

Well, we know them! If he is in league with Salieri, I shall never while I live get a libretto from him. I should so like to show what I can do in an Italian opera!

In the same letter Mozart rather hopelessly asked his father to approach Varesco, the librettist of *Idomeneo,* for a comic libretto; and a year later started work on the ludicrous result, *L'Oca del Cairo.* But the librettist disagreed with Mozart's suggested changes, and the music was never finished. By 1785, however, Salieri had turned against Da Ponte, declaring he would rather cut off his fingers than set another line of Da Ponte's to music, so it is not surprising that Mozart and Da Ponte got together. Both of them being ambitious and practical, they hit on the idea of making an opera out of a notorious contemporary play, Beaumarchais's *La Folle Journée, ou, le Mariage de Figaro (The Crazy Day,* or, *The Marriage of Figaro).*

Beaumarchais, though never an active revolutionary, had been a champion of popular rights since 1770, and following the success of *The Barber of Seville* five years later, he produced a sequel, the plain-speaking *Marriage of Figaro.*

This play, which showed up the unscrupulousness of the aristocrats of the old regime (epitomised by the use of the already lapsing 'droit du seigneur'–the right of the Lord of the Manor to sleep with any new bride from his estate on her wedding night), had been accepted by the Théatre Francais in 1781. But Louis XVI had the play read to himself and Marie Antoinette in private and forbade its performance, strangely adding, 'It would be necessary to destroy the Bastille in order to prevent the representation of this piece from being a dangerous anomaly'.

Strangely enough, however, the Duke of Fronsac, who had not been friendly with the author, asked his permission to have the play given privately, the Queen having told him that the King acquiesced: so it was performed in September 1783 before the whole court, but without the King or Queen being present. As a result it was played in public in the following year, on 27 April, though the King demanded certain cuts.

The audiences packed the theatre for sixty-eight performances, and Beaumarchais, who had been imprisoned by the King for four days after replying vigorously to a printed attack on the play, was received with acclamation on his next appearance at the theatre. Louis XVI then ordered the earlier *Barber of Seville* to be acted at court, where the Count of Artois (afterwards Charles X) played Figaro and Marie Antoinette herself appeared as the heroine.

It is surprising that the successful presentation of *The Marriage of Figaro* was the result of intervention by that aristocratic class which was attacked in the play, because, as Napoleon later said, it was 'the Revolution already in action', though the Revolution proper did not begin till the Bastille was stormed in the summer of 1789.

It does not matter who first suggested turning this notoriously successful play into an opera, whether it was Da Ponte, as he himself claimed, or Mozart, as the Irish singer Michael Kelly maintained in his *Reminiscences.* Da Ponte was cunning enough and Mozart had so absorbed his father's eagerness for publicity that the choice of subject was by no means surprising, especially as Paisiello's operatic version of *The Barber of Seville*, first produced in Russia in 1782, had already been a great success the following year in Vienna; besides, the play of *Figaro* was still forbidden in Vienna and, as Dent wrote in the foreword to the vocal score with his translation:

> There can be no doubt that the political sympathies of both Da Ponte and Mozart were with the ideas that found vent in Paris in 1789 and that they deliberately chose this unusual subject for their opera with a view to popular success. It may be pointed out here that their two subsequent operas, *Don Giovanni* and *Così fan tutte* both make fun of the privileged classes and present them in ridiculous situations, while *The Magic Flute* . . . bids a definite farewell to the ideas of the eighteenth century and opens the door to the doctrines of Liberty, Equality and Fraternity.

Mozart began composing the music for *Le Nozze di Figaro* in the autumn of 1785, in spite of intrigues against it (though Da Ponte claimed that he and Mozart agreed to keep the opera secret). Two other operas were in preparation - Righini's *Il Demogorgone* and Salieri's *La Grotta di Trifonio* - and the story goes that Mozart swore he would put the score of his opera into the fire if it was not produced first (in actual fact Salieri's was the first to be performed in October of that year).

Unfortunately there is a gap in Mozart's letters at this time, but he certainly did not put the *Figaro* score in the fire. On 11 November

1785 Leopold Mozart wrote to Marianne explaining why her brother had not written letters lately:

> His excuse for not writing is that he has been over head and ears at work on his opera, *Le Nozze di Figaro.* He has put off all his pupils to the afternoon, so that he may have his mornings free. I have no fear as to the music, but there will no doubt be much discussion and annoyance before he can get the libretto arranged to his wish; and having procrastinated and let the time stop after his usual fashion, he is obliged now to set to work in earnest, as Count Rosenberg [the Oberstkämmerer, or Lord Chamberlain] insists upon it.

No doubt this was by command of the Emperor, because Rosenberg was apparently a sworn enemy of Germans, who would listen to nothing that was not Italian.

At the same time the Emperor, who also preferred operas sung in Italian, was not absolutely against either German opera or Mozart, (though he had said a Mozart opera was no great thing), because on 7 February 1786 the Emperor's garden party held in the Orangery at Schönbrunn was entertained by Mozart's one-act opera (or, as he called it, comedy with music) *Der Schauspieldirektor (The Impresario),* a burlesque of operatic life, as well as by Salieri's theatrical amusement *Prima la musica e poi le parole (First the music and then the words).* Mozart's one-acter was publicly performed at the Kärntnertor Theatre eleven days later and in March *Idomeneo* was privately performed under his own supervision and with two new numbers for the aristocratic cast at Prince Auersperg's in Vienna.

No doubt encouraged by this sudden interest in Mozart and in view of the dearth of new operas, Da Ponte told the Emperor about *Figaro.* Joseph II sent for Mozart to bring the score to him and, after hearing some of it, ordered it to be put into rehearsal at once, much to the displeasure of Mozart's opponents, who included Casti, the librettist of Salieri's garden-party amusement, and Count Rosenberg.

According to Da Ponte the manager of the Burgtheater, Bussani, told Rosenberg of the scene in the opera when, during a short ballet at the wedding festivities, Susanna secretly slips a note into the Count's hand, with the result that Rosenberg not only reminded Da Ponte that the Emperor disliked the inclusion of ballet in opera but even tore the scene out of the book. Mozart, it seems, was so furious that he wanted to challenge Rosenberg, horsewhip Bussani, appeal to the Emperor and take back the score, and was only pacified with difficulty.

The Emperor, however, seeing at a full rehearsal, with the ballet omitted, Susanna and the Count making meaningless gestures in silence, was puzzled and, hearing the explanation, immediately ordered the ballet to be performed as written. Incidentally the music for this scene was imitated by Mozart for local Spanish colour from a fandango adapted by Gluck for his ballet of *Don Juan* in 1761, which Dent suggests may still have been known in Vienna twenty-five years later.

In April 1786 Leopold Mozart wrote to his daughter with the news that *Figaro*

> is to be produced on the stage for the first time. It will say much for the work if it be successful, for I know that some very strong cabals have been formed against it. Salieri and all his satellites will again move heaven and earth to ensure its failure.

He adds that Duschek, a composer and pianist from Prague (he and his wife were old friends of Mozart)

> recently told me that your brother was the object of so many hostile intrigues, solely owing to his remarkable talents and genius obtaining for him so great a reputation.

Da Ponte said that Mozart wrote the score in six weeks, which seems to be contradicted by Leopold's letter of November 1785 (unless, as is more than possible, the score was completed that winter and then shelved until the Emperor approved of it); in any event *Le Nozze di Figaro* by Mozart and Da Ponte was produced at the Burgtheater in Vienna on 1 May 1786.

To appreciate *Figaro* fully (though the twists and turns of the apparently farcical but quite possible true-to-life story are brilliantly amusing in themselves) it is necessary to understand the relationships and past history of the chief characters. These are established in the first Figaro story, *The Barber of Seville*, which was already well-known to most contemporary Viennese theatre-lovers.

In the earlier play, as in Paisiello's opera, Count Almaviva has fallen in love with Rosina, the ward of Doctor Bartolo, and she with him. Doctor Bartolo plans to marry Rosina himself, though he has an unofficial attachment to his housekeeper Marcellina (she is mentioned several times in the first play, but does not appear). Figaro has the entrée to Bartolo's house as his barber and surgeon, and disables the whole household, giving a sleeping-powder to one of the Doctor's valets and a sneezing mixture to another, as well as drawing blood from Marcellina's foot. Almaviva puts on various disguises, bribes the scandal-mongering Don Basilio, Rosina's singing teacher, and succeeds in marrying the girl who, it must be stressed, is under-age.

At the start of *Le Mariage de Figaro* the Count, who now employs Figaro as his general factotum and has Doctor Bartolo and Don Basilio as part of his household, has found that three years of marriage 'makes hymen so respectable' (as Beaumarchais puts it) that he is therefore ready to add to his conquests Susanna, the Countess's maid and niece of Antonio, the gardener. Susanna, who today is to marry Figaro, warns her future husband (who is clever at getting out of scrapes but not clever enough to avoid getting into them) of the situation and he at once schemes to put the Count in the wrong.

His first idea is to ask the Count in front of village friends as witnesses to perform the betrothal ceremony now that the 'droit du seigneur' has been abolished, and the Count is forced to appear to agree. Then, on hearing that the Count is forcing the thirteen-year old page, Cherubino, to join his regiment in Seville and having discovered he was a witness to the Count's approaches to Susanna, Figaro ends the first act by promoting the delightful dangers of battle to the boy; but he is not serious, as is shown by his asking the page to have a word with him in private (a point that is almost always understressed in performance).

Figaro's next plan (in the second act) is to let Basilio know (he is sure to tell the Count) that the Countess is to meet an admirer in the garden that night but to send in her place Cherubino dressed as a woman, with the intention of catching the Count when he goes to surprise the supposed lovers. Susanna and the Countess, who hopes to win back her husband's waning affection, start to dress Cherubino as a girl, but the Count arrives unexpectedly and Cherubino only escapes by jumping out of the window of the Countess's boudoir, while the Count is abashed at finding only Susanna with the Countess.

Figaro is able to explain away the gardener's story that he saw a man jump out of the window by claiming that he himself had jumped out on hearing a noise and convincingly insists that the papers dropped by the page and found by Antonio under the window were the Count's commission documents left for Figaro to get signed and sealed while Cherubino rode away to Seville; but he is put on the spot when Marcellina comes to claim him as her husband-to-be in accordance with an agreement he signed when she lent him some money.

When in the third act the Count and the stuttering lawyer, Don Curzio, support Marcellina's claim, Figaro insists he must have the consent of his unknown parents, from whom he was stolen as a baby, and the Count's attempt to stop Figaro's marriage to Susanna is thwarted when the evidence quoted by Figaro proves that Marcellina is his mother and Bartolo his father; so now there can be a double wedding. During the official celebrations, the Count pardons Cherubino, and when the dancing begins, Susanna secretly slips the Count a note confirming what she has already told him—that she will meet him in the garden later, though the Countess has assured her that she herself will go instead.

The fourth act takes place in the pine-grove of the Count's garden with a pavilion, or arbour, on each side of the stage. Figaro, furious at finding out that the note he saw the Count read was from Susanna, brings Basilio, Antonio and some workmen with torches to watch in hiding for her meeting: Susanna and the Countess arrive, each dressed as the other, while Barbarina, looking for Cherubino, and Marcellina hide in the left-hand pavilion. The disguised Susanna leads the listening Figaro to think she is excited at the thought of soon being with her lover; Cherubino tries to kiss the Countess, thinking she is Susanna, and to escape the blow the Count would deal him, also goes into the left-hand pavilion, while the Count gives the supposed Susanna a ring as token of his favour. Seeing lighted torches approaching the Count hides and so does not see the real Countess go into the right-hand pavilion, but on his return he does see the supposed Countess (whose voice Figaro has recognised as that of Susanna) run away from Figaro into the left-hand pavilion. The Count, calling for the torch-bearing men (those Figaro had collected) to witness his triumph over the pretendedly frightened Figaro, shouts for the Countess to come out. Instead out come Cherubino, Barbarina, Marcellina and lastly Susanna, still dressed as the Countess, hiding her face with a handkerchief as if ashamed. All beg forgiveness, which the Count refuses until unexpectedly from the right-hand pavilion there comes the Countess herself to ask him to relent. Realising his mistake the Count begs his Rosina to forgive him and all ends happily.

From the play we learn that Barbarina is only twelve and Cherubino thirteen, but more especially that Rosina became Almaviva's bride when she was under age and has only been married for three years at the start of the play–facts which the audience of the day would have known but which are usually disregarded in modern productions of the opera.

All performers in the first production seem to have been absolutely right for their respective parts. Michael Kelly wrote in his *Reminiscences* (or rather Theodore Hook probably wrote for him):

> Never was opera stronger cast. I have seen it performed at different periods in other countries, and well too, but no more to compare with its original performance than light is to darkness. All the original performers had the advantage of the instruction of the composer, who transfused into their minds his inspired meaning. I never shall forget his little animate countenance, when lighted up with the glowing rays of genius;–it is as impossible to describe it, as it would be to paint sun-beams.

It is also remarkable how near in age the performers were to the characters they played, and it should be remembered that all Mozart's juvenile characters should be really young and not middle aged, as Patti was when she still kept on singing, for instance, Zerlina in *Don Giovanni.*

The original cast in order of singing was:

Figaro .... Francesco Benucci
Susanna .... Anna Storace
Dr Bartolo .... Francesco Bussani
Marcellina .... Maria Mandini
Cherubino .... Dorotea Sardi Bussani
Count Almaviva .... Stefano Mandini
Don Basilio .... Ochelly (*that is,* Michael Kelly)

The Countess .... Luisa Laschi
Antonio .... Francesco Bussani
Don Curzio .... Ochelly
Barbarina .... Nannina Gottlieb

Anna, or Nancy Storace as she was usually called, of an Italian family in London sometimes named Sorace, was just twenty and had sung in Italy since she was fourteen, moving to Vienna in 1784 for the then unprecedented sum of £500 for the season; Mozart's biographer Jahn tells us she 'possessed in a degree unique at that time, and rare at any time, all the gifts, the cultivation, and the skill which could be desired for Italian comic opera'.

Signora Laschi, who was married to the singer Domenico Mombelli in the year of Mozart's *Figaro*, cannot have appeared older on the stage than Beaumarchais's Rosina, because she and Susanna must look sufficiently alike to make their exchange of costume in the last act deceptive and they must both be young enough to play such tricks as they do; if the Countess were–as she is often played in the opera–a more mature figure like Strauss's *Rosenkavalier* Feldmarschallin, she would never change clothes with her maid to trick her husband in the darkness. It is partly Mozart's fault for giving her two such lovely arias that singers are tempted to sing them too richly and emotionally, and too slowly–especially 'Dove sono' thereby making the character more staid than the Countess should be*.

Another frequent misinterpretation is made by those who maintain that Susanna's aria in the garden, 'Deh vieni', is an expression of her true self and her love for Figaro, thereby following Otto Jahn who ends his excessively ecstatic discourse over this presumed transfiguration of Susanna by stating that Mozart has turned her necessary sensuality 'into a noble purity which may fitly be compared with the grandest achievement of Greek sculpture'! Is it likely that the down-to-earth Susanna would ever seriously think of crowning Figaro with roses (as she sings in the aria)? She nowhere else indulges in poetic metaphors: and surely the pattering music

*Mozart's marking for 'Dove sono' with two crotchets to the bar is either Andante (Kochel) or the slightly faster Andantino (Einstein), and his father explained Andante as 'going. This word itself tells us that one must give the piece its natural gait' (which Dent explained as 'keep it going'); de Brossard's earlier dictionary describes it as 'to stroll with even steps'. Perhaps the best explanation nowadays would be 'don't drag'.

between the lines of her introductory recitative suggests her tip-toeing to make sure that Figaro is listening. He certainly must be listening, because at the end of her aria* he calls her 'Traitress', She is of course disguised as the Countess, but surely in either character she is putting on an act (apparently seriously) to hoodwink Figaro.

Dorotea Sardi married Francesco Bussani, the manager of the Burgtheater, in 1786: she must have made a charming 'boy', for a Berlin paper wrote that she was admired for her lovely figure and unreserved acting; Da Ponte mentions her *'smorfie e pagliacciate'* (roughly translated as 'twinkling expressiveness and sense of fun'). Bussani's debut was in 1763 and so he was in his forties.

Nannina Gottlieb, who later created Pamina in *Die Zauberflöte,* was, like Barbarina herself, only twelve years old.

Stefano Mandini, whose younger brother was born in 1757, must have been about thirty, and Benucci, who Mozart agreed was one of the best comedy baritones when he first heard him some years before, was just about forty. These two men, according to Kelly, were the best comic singers in Europe, and had been engaged with Nancy Storace and Kelly for the Italian opera in Vienna in 1783†.

Michael Kelly himself, who was later a prolific composer of light stage-works, was only twenty-four. His doubling of the parts of Don Basilio and Don Curzio was easy to manage as in early editions of the opera Don Curzio has only his one scene in the third act and does not appear in the finale of the last: in modern editions, allowing for one singer per part, Curzio sings the same notes as Basilio at the end.

The other doubling of Doctor Bartolo and Antonio by Bussani at first sight seems more difficult, though again Bartolo does not appear in the last act according to earlier scores and in more modern scores he sings the same notes as Antonio (incidentally earlier scores give nothing for Marcellina to sing in the finale, maybe because Bartolo was not there). But in the third act Antonio has only some fifty-five

*This aria is also marked Andante (i.e. for each dotted crotchet) but the pace of four recordings vary between a metronome mark per quaver of 96 (Lotte Lehmann), 100 (Elizabeth Schumann), 108 (Kleiber complete recording) and 120 (Mignon Nevada), the last of which seems more in key with Susanna's ever-sparkling character.

†Details about the singers in *Figaro* and *Così fan tutte,* some of whom have been wrongly identified even in fairly recent books of reference, have been supplied by Harold Rosenthal.

bars, lasting about one minute, in which to become Bartolo—though this need not be difficult if Antonio in shirt-sleeves and breeches with a scratch wig and a gardener's apron removed the last two and put on waistcoat, coat and a grey tie-wig as well as a hat to become Bartolo (the change back to Antonio is easy).

In his *Reminiscences* Kelly, who played Don Curzio as a stutterer (as Beaumarchais's lawyer Brid'oisin, was known to be), writes that he was forbidden by Mozart to stutter in the sextet that begins with Marcellina's recognition of Figaro as her son, and which according to Kelly was Mozart's favourite piece in the whole opera. Mozart said he would spoil the music if he did so, but Kelly politely disagreed, saying 'besides, it certainly was not in nature, that I should stutter all through the part, and when I came to the sestetto speak plain' and he added:

> (apologising at the same time for my apparent want of deference and respect in placing my opinion in opposition to that of the great Mozart) that unless I was allowed to perform the part as I wished, I would not perform it at all.

Mozart dubiously agreed and, said Kelly, in performance

> the audience were convulsed with laughter, in which Mozart himself joined. The Emperor repeatedly cried out Bravo! and the piece was loudly applauded and encored. When the opera was over, Mozart . . . shaking me by both hands, said 'Bravo! young man I feel obliged to you; and acknowledge you to have been in the right, and myself in the wrong'. There certainly was a risk run, but I felt within myself I could give the effect I wished, and the event proved that I was not mistaken.

He played the part as a stupid old man, though at the time he was 'a bearded stripling'.

Kelly has recorded that at the first full rehearsal, conducted *from the stage* by Mozart 'with his crimson pelisse and gold-laced cocked hat', Benucci sang Figaro's military song 'Non piu andrai' 'with the greatest animation and power of voice and gave out the fine passage, "Cherubino, alla vittoria, alla gloria militar" with stentorian lungs', so that 'the effect was electricity itself'; everyone shouted 'Bravo! Maestro!' and 'Viva, grande Mozart!', while the orchestra, Kelly thought, 'would never have ceased applauding, by beating the bows of their violins against the music desks' and 'the little man acknowledged, by repeated obeisances, his thanks for the distinguished mark of enthusiastic applause bestowed upon him'.

Before the first rehearsal Kelly was, he claimed (but it must be remembered his *Reminiscences* were written many years after the dead Mozart's fame was admitted), the only member of the company who did not join the cabal against *Figaro* organised by Salieri.

He gives his account of the first performance:

> I thought the audience would never have done applauding and calling for Mozart, almost every piece was encored, which prolonged it nearly to the length of two operas, and induced the Emperor to issue an order on the second representation, that no piece of music should be encored. Never was any thing more complete, than the triumph of Mozart, and his *Nozze di Figaro,* to which numerous overflowing audiences bore witness.

Unfortunately Kelly's memory of *Figaro's* success, though not entirely untrue, may have been coloured by later reactions, because the report of the opera in the *Wiener Realzeitung* gives a different picture:

> 'What is not allowed to be said these days, is sung', one may say with *Figaro*. This piece, which was not allowed to be performed here as a comedy, we have at last had the felicity to see represented as an opera.
>
> The public, however (and this often happens to the public), did not really know on the first day where it stood. It heard many a bravo from unbiassed connoisseurs, but obstreperous louts in the uppermost storey exerted their hired lungs with all their might to deafen singers and audience alike with their St! and Pst!; and consequently opinions were divided at the end of the piece.
>
> Apart from that, it is true that the first performance was none of the best, owing to the difficulty of the composition. But now, after several performances, one would be subscribing either to the Cabal or to tastelessness if one were to maintain that Herr Mozart's music is anything but a masterpiece of art. It contains so many beauties, and such a wealth of ideas, as can be drawn only from the source of innate genius.

It is quite clear from this report that though there was indeed 'many a bravo', the applause was not as frequent or as full as Kelly implies, and that there was a claque in the cheaper parts of the house paid to do their best to cause a disturbance. Dent wondered why the famous German singers of Vienna, some of whom had previously sung in Mozart's *Entführung*, did not sing in *Figaro* and it is quite possibly for the reason that the German singers, urged on by Salieri, tried to wreck the performance through the interruptions of hired labour, a practice that has not been unknown even in recent years.

Niemetschek, the Bohemian author of *Reminiscences of Mozart*, tells the unlikely story that the singers in *Figaro* did all they could to ruin the opera by intentional mistakes, so that they had to be sternly reminded of their duty by the Emperor, to whom Mozart is said to have appealed in despair at the end of the first act. Singers, however much they may bear a grudge against a composer or conductor, are never likely to spoil their own performances (though they have often been known to distract attention from the performances of others), especially at a time when their whole career and their engagement for the season depended on the Emperor who had favoured that very opera; quite possibly Niemetschek, having heard that singers, including the great Cavalieri, who was intimate with Salieri, had done their best to ruin the performance (maybe by hiring a claque to boo and hiss), misunderstood and presumed it was the *Figaro* singers the story referred to.

Kelly's allusion to 'numerous overflowing audiences' is also misremembered by him: there were only nine performances in Vienna in 1786 (though these may have been well attended) and none in 1787 or 1788, partly perhaps because of the great success in November 1786 of *Una cosa rara* by Martin y Soler (with a libretto by Da Ponte).

But in the winter of 1786 *Figaro* was given in Prague where its instant success immediately established it as a masterpiece. A correspondent in the *Prager Oberpostamtzeitung* wrote on 12 December:

> No piece (so everyone here asserts) has ever caused such a sensation as the Italian opera *Le Nozze di Figaro*, which has already been given several times here with unlimited applause by Bondini's resident company. The music is by our celebrated

Herr Mozart. Connoisseurs who have seen this opera in Vienna are anxious to declare that it was much better here. Our great Mozart must have heard about this himself, for there is a rumour since that he will come here in person to see the piece.

Rumour was correct. On 11 January 1787, Mozart and his wife arrived in Prague and that very night (as he wrote to a friend four days later) he went to a ball which was attended by 'the flower of the Prague beauties'. He added:

> I neither danced nor flirted with any of them, the former because I was too tired, and the latter from my natural bashfulness. I saw, however, with the greatest pleasure, all these people flying about with such delight to the music of my *Figaro,* transformed into quadrilles and waltzes; for here nothing is talked of but *Figaro,* nothing played but *Figaro*, nothing whistled or sung but *Figaro*, no opera so crowded as *Figaro,* nothing but *Figaro*—very flattering to me, certainly.

Mozart gave a concert in Prague on 19 January at which he extemporised on themes from *Figaro*, which showed he was obviously glad to have written such a popular opera of light music. Years later Rossini was to say that *Figaro* was a true *dramma giocosa* (humorous play), whereas he and other Italians only wrote comic operas.

On 22 January Mozart conducted *Figaro* to tumultuous applause and in February 1787 he left Prague with a commission from Bondini, the theatre director, to write an opera (it was to be *Don Giovanni*) for that year's winter season and, naturally eager to collaborate with Da Ponte again, he returned to Vienna.

Soon after the brilliant reception of *Don Giovanni* in Prague on 14 October 1787, Mozart returned to Vienna, where Gluck, the Court Conductor and Composer for thirteen years, died on 15 November. As his British friends Nancy Storace, her brother Stephen, Michael Kelly and Thomas Attwood (Mozart's favourite pupil) had returned to England the previous February and had promised to try to get him some appointment there, Mozart seriously considered following them; but—maybe partly because of this and also in recognition of his successes in Prague—the Emperor appointed him Court Composer in Gluck's place at a salary of 800 gulden (about £80).

His new position prevented Mozart's possible return to London, but his financial situation was so poor and his Court duties seemed only to entail composing dance music for the royal balls, so that when he had to make a return of his income he wrote 'Too much for what I produce; and too little for what I could produce'.

The production of *Don Giovanni* in Vienna on 7 May 1788 was not a great success: according to Da Ponte the Emperor said, 'The opera is divine, finer perhaps than *Figaro*, but it is not the meat for my Viennese', which prompted Mozart to declare, 'We must give them time to chew it'. Besides, the production did not aid his finances, and so in June he had to ask his musical merchant friend and fellow Freemason, Puchberg, for a loan (by no means for the last time) and was grateful to receive from him 200 gulden.

During six weeks that summer Mozart wrote his last three symphonies, and later that year took an active part in oratorio performances given through the amateur enthusiast, Van Swieten, director of the Court Library, and added wind-parts to Handel's *Acis and Galatea* in November and to the *Messiah* in March 1789.

In April 1789, at the invitation of his pupil and patron Prince Karl Lichnowsky, Mozart accompanied him in his comfortable travelling carriage to Berlin. They stopped for a day in Prague, where Mozart was nearly offered another opera commission; he performed in Dresden, and in Leipzig he played Bach's own organ in the St Thomas Church.

He was well received by the King of Prussia, Frederick William II, who loved music, though he annoyed the Court Conductor Reichardt and Duport, the King's violoncello teacher, by giving His Majesty an honest opinion of the Court orchestra: 'It contains great virtuosi but if the gentlemen would play together, they would make a better effect'. He was equally outspoken when he made audible criticisms near the orchestra during a performance of his *Entführung*.

He played before the Queen, and the King gave him 100 Friedrichs d'or, which Mozart disappointedly wrote to his wife were worth only 700 gulden ('at least so I am told here'): this present was an advance for a commission for Mozart to write some quartets for the King. There is also a story, probably apocryphal, that His Majesty offered Mozart the post of Court Conductor in Berlin at a salary of 3,000 thalers (about £600) but that he declined, saying 'How could I desert my good Emperor?' Anyway, by June he was back in Vienna, where he wrote the first quartet for the King of Prussia, who at once sent him a second 100 Friedrichs d'or and a gold snuff-box.

Mozart's popularity as a composer outside Austria was now established; apart from the success of *Figaro* and *Don Giovanni* in Prague, *Figaro* had been given in 1787 both in Prague and at the Prince of Fürstenberg's private theatre in Donaueschingen in German, in Italian at Monza (though with the third and fourth acts rewritten by Angelo Tarchi); in 1788 in Italian at the Pergola Theatre, Florence (attributed to Paisiello in Morini's book on that theatre) and in German at Frankfurt and Graz; in May 1789 at Hanover, where the German translation included portions from Beaumarchais's play that had been omitted by Da Ponte.

Whether or not Mozart, as has been said, turned down the King of Prussia's offer and had a conversation with the Emperor in Vienna, the Royal Court there must have thought they ought to recognise his fame as it was recognised abroad and so had *Figaro* revived in Vienna on 29 August 1789.

For this revival Mozart wrote two new arias for the new Susanna, Adrianna Ferrarese del Bene: the first, 'Al disio di chi t'adora' ('At the desire of one who adores you'), is for the garden scene and is better suited to the Countess, so it was apparently intended, as Jahn says, to strengthen Figaro in his delusion that it was the Countess he saw in the pine-grove—a further proof that the original 'Deh vieni' was a deliberate spoof love-song and not a revelation of the true Susanna.

This time Vienna received *Figaro* with enthusiasm (it was performed twelve times in about two months), and the now emphatic and general recognition of Mozart (though financially he was still in such a bad way that he again had to borrow from Puchberg) led the Emperor to order him to write a new comic opera—but this time it was to be on a subject of the Emperor's own choosing, so it was said later, and Da Ponte had to write a libretto based on scandalous events which gossip reported had recently taken place in Viennese society.

There is no evidence (certainly not in the score) that Mozart, as has been stated, disliked the subject and wrote the music very much against his will, and there is little known of how and when he wrote it. Certainly both the libretto and the music must have been written in great haste for the autograph score is full of abbreviations, which is not at all typical of Mozart's way of composing.

He cannot have started before September 1789, but on 29 December, when writing again to his friend Puchberg asking for a loan of 400 gulden until he got paid 200 ducats for his new opera, he invited him to hear a rehearsal of it, stressing that he was inviting only him and Haydn.

Then on 26 January 1790 the Burgtheater of Vienna saw the first performance of the new opera, *Così fan tutte, ossia la scuola degli amanti* (*So do all Women, or, the School for Lovers*).

The original cast in order of singing was:

Ferrando	Vincenzo Calvesi
Guglielmo	Francesco Benucci
Don Alfonso	Francesco Bussani
Fiordiligi	Adrianna Ferrarese del Bene
Dorabella	Louise Villeneuve
Despina	Dorotea Sardi Bussani

Nothing is known of Calvesi except that he first appeared in April 1785; Benucci was the original Figaro and Bussani, the theatre manager, the original Doctor Bartolo and Antonio in *Figaro* (they were also the Leporello and the Commendatore-Masetto of the Viennese premiere of *Don Giovanni*).

Adrianna Ferrarese del Bene and her sister Louise Villeneuve have until recently often been confused with Francesca and Caterina Gabrielli, the daughters of Prince Gabrielli's cook (hence the latter's nickname La Cochetta or La Cocchettina, the little cook) who, because they also came from Ferrara, were also known as Ferrarese. Adrianna, whose married name was del Bene, was Da Ponte's mistress. This is no doubt the reason why she sang in both the Vienna revival of *Figaro* and in *Così fan tutte,* because Mozart certainly did not think much of her singing. He wrote on 16 April 1789 about the Dresden prima donna, Madame Allegrandi, that she 'is far better than Ferrarese, but that is not saying much'. Still, according to Jahn, Adrianna, though an indifferent actress and without a good figure, did have a beautiful eye and a charming mouth and was a popular favourite.

Louise Villeneuve was well-known for her pleasing appearance, expressive acting and artistically beautiful singing.

Dorotea Bussani, the original Cherubino, probably had a chance to use her roguish face and sense of fun to more advantage as Despina than as the boyish page in *Figaro*, and therefore probably played Despina as a youngish woman. Indeed all three women must have appeared on the stage as younger, rather than older, as they are often played today (so that students have been known to think that the two sisters were about forty to forty-five): both the story and the music show they should be quite young.

The scandalous story, whether founded on fact or not, is about the attempt by two young officers to disprove an old cynic's statement that their two betrothed sweethearts, 'like all women', are ready to be unfaithful. This they do by appearing in the disguise of two rich Albanian noblemen and making love to each other's girl with such success that betrothals are prepared for the wrong couples. When, however, the officers return as themselves all is put right, though Alfonso has won his wager.

The libretto, as Dent said,

> has almost invariably been denounced as intolerably stupid, if not positively disgusting, and various attempts have been made . . . to improve it, or even to provide Mozart's music with an entirely fresh libretto on a totally different subject.

There were new versions as early as 1813 in Paris (*The Chinese Labourer*), 1826 in Copenhagen (*Flight from the Cloister*), 1863 in Paris (founded on Shakespeare's *Love's Labour's Lost*) and as recently as 1909 in Dresden (*The Goblin Lady*, from a comedy by Calderon).

But, as Dent also said, there is no need for this. Da Ponte merely followed the laws of farce by starting with one improbability (in this case that the girls cannot see through disguises–the same as in *Charley's Aunt* when the disguised undergraduate is accepted as the rich widow from Brazil, where the nuts come from): then all follows logically, if not naturally. If it is accepted as a logical farce, *Così fan tutte* is a most amusing opera with music which may be, as Jahn said, deficient in the delicate detail of *Figaro* and

Don Giovanni, but is in other respects fuller, more brilliant and richer in separate instrumental effects. If the music to the earlier operas expresses character, the music to *Così fan tutte* not only gives character to the stage-figures but almost seems to suggest the necessary movements made by them.

Originally, Otto Jahn says, the scene was to be set in Trieste (which makes the arrival of 'Albanians' more likely), though in the early published libretti it was in Naples, and finally in the original printed score it was set in Venice, where all nations were likely to meet; but nowadays Naples is the accepted setting.

The overture, with at the start and at the end the musical phrase that is later connected with the motto 'Così fan tutt-e' sparkles with the bubble of gossip. The two young men in the opening scene sing their music in a self-satisfied way, while Don Alfonso at the start of the trio lays down the law good-humouredly, betting that before tomorrow his belief in the unreliability of women will be proved correct.

Similarly the duet that introduces the two girls bubbles over with happiness*. As a test of this try speaking the opening words of the girls, who are showing off to each other the portraits of their respective lovers, first slowly as if by two bored *soignée* women, and then excitedly as if by two eager young girls: as sung in full, they read: 'Ah, look, sister! Ah, look, sister! Look! Look!'–and this surely only makes sense if said or sung with youthful exuberance (though obviously it can be taken only as fast as the singers can sing their demisemiquavers). The trouble is that singers love to spread their voices on Mozart's good tune, forgetting that he could have more easily written the same music with three crotchets (i.e. twelve semiquavers) to the bar, as every music-copyist knows, had he wished a slower pace.

It is also often disregarded (or misunderstood by English audiences if sung in Italian) that Dorabella is so 'modern' and outspokenly young as to say after the duet 'But what the devil do our fiancés mean by this delay in coming here?' (not the politer versions such as 'why in the world' or 'it seems').

*It is marked three quavers to the bar, but is usually played as if it were elongated into three crotchets (there is no doubt that contemporaries were right when they implied that 3/8 tends to be twice as fast as 3/4). For confirmation of this and other points concerning Mozart's tempi see the quotations from eighteenth-century writers cited in *The Interpretation of Early Music* by Robert Donnington.

Similarly, the Quintet of farewell should not be sung slowly but with urgent sobs so that the men sing broken sentences ('I feel, O God . . . that this foot . . . is stopped from moving forward!' and 'My lip . . . all aquiver . . . cannot pronounce it!')–it is an overacted heartbreak, not a funeral, while the pace of the soldiers' march that follows can be tested by marching on the crotchets (which is right) or the minims (which is wrong), and the wavering thirds in the little trio for the girls and Don Alfonso after the officers have gone should be thought of as ripples on the calm water and not as semiquavers. Dorabella's 'tragic' aria 'Smanie implacabili', an overdramatic *allegro agitato*, is obviously a burlesque, sung as it is over cups of chocolate.

When the disguised officers come in as Albanians, Despina laughs at their grotesque appearance, a 'true antidote of love' (but they are rich!), yet they are usually made handsomely smart. 'Come scoglio', the 'insulted' aria of Fiordiligi (Flower of duty)–a burlesque name if ever there was one–with its wild leaps and twirls of the voice is also a burlesque of outraged innocence.

Ferrando's aria about the 'amorous aura' is sincere, but it is lightly romantic and not an expression of long-drawn-out passion, so that he and Guglielmo can later rush on to take arsenic and 'die' quickly.

Despina, disguised as a doctor, cures them with the contemporary invention, the magnet developed by Doctor Mesmer (in whose garden the boy Mozart's opera had been performed). This grotesque revival of the Albanians could surely be accepted only by silly young girls in a farce and not by the usual sincerely devoted sentimental women of the average modern *Così* production, especially when they are nearly won over by the young men's pretence that they are among the classical deities and want to kiss the goddesses they see before them, Pallas Athene and the Cytherean Venus. The act ends, like all farcical first acts, with a rough and tumble of chasing and avoiding being caught, not an elegant series of society bows and protesting hands.

At the start of the second act Fiordiligi shows that she too is not a sentimental romantic when she swears 'By Bacchus!' in a most unmaidenly fashion–an oath that only a 'modern' girl would use; and indeed Despina then implies that they are not grown-ups when she says to them that every fifteen-year-old young lady ought to know, for instance, where the devil keeps his tail—very plain speaking, though not necessarily implying that they are only fifteen. At once the girls decide to 'have a go': Dorabella chooses the dark one and Fiordiligi the blond (showing that Guglielmo is dark and Ferrando fair), and unhesitatingly they tell the men to say frankly what is in their minds, while the men now pretend to be shy and have to be shown by Alfonso and Despina how to make up to young ladies (as if Albanians need telling!).

There follows the amusing flirtation scene starting (like the scene in *The Pirates of Penzance*) by talk about the weather—again a burlesque of social conversation that leads Fiordiligi to show Ferrando the garden and Dorabella, as hot, she says unabashed, as Vesuvius, to give the locket she is wearing to Guglielmo.

Ferrando pretends to be in despair and Fiordiligi, left alone, begs her absent lover to forgive her for even having thought of faithlessness.

Ferrando is angry that Guglielmo has made headway with Dorabella, but Guglielmo amusedly cannot make out why all men are swayed by women who treat them so badly. The officers claim they have won the wager, but Don Alfonso reminds them that the time is not up yet and they must do as he says till tomorrow.

Dorabella seems to be acting on Despina's advice by falling for 'that little devil', as Dorabella calls Guglielmo (which surely described the appearance of Benucci—and therefore of Figaro, whom he played in the earlier opera), and it is noticeable that Despina does not mind swearing 'By the body of Satan', which she would do only in the presence of a 'modern' young lady, while Dorabella even tries to persuade her sister to give way to Ferrando. Fiordiligi, however, much to Guglielmo's delight, refuses and prepares to make Dorabella join her in going to find their lovers, wearing the uniforms they have left in the girls' apartments (which cannot be explained away if the women are respectably faithful at heart), but the disguised Ferrando threatens to kill himself if Fiordiligi goes away and she falls into his arms, much to the wrath of Guglielmo. Alfonso then tells them that they must accept his dictum 'So do all women', and insists that they carry on with their cross-purpose flirtations.

So the last scene celebrates the betrothal of the wrong pairs of lovers: it was originally intended to be longer so that Guglielmo could have a show-down scene with Dorabella (which probably explains the quotation he makes later, the original of which has not been heard in the opera), but Mozart is said to have cut it out, probably realising correctly that all that is now needed is to bring the farce to an end. This is done when Despina, disguised as a lawyer, produces the marriage contracts, only to be interrupted by the sound of the returning soldiers' march (it is never explained how the soldiers connive at the tricking of the girls, nor does it matter—the effect is enough); Alfonso pretends alarm at the return of the officers and the 'Albanians' hide in another room but return as themselves to confront the girls; they discover the marriage contracts and rush out to challenge the 'Albanians'. The girls wait, terrified, but back come the officers with part of their Albanian disguises, they explain the trick and are happily reunited, all joining in the final ensemble with its moral that things in life must not be taken too seriously, for a sense of humour can bring peace of mind.

The production was only moderately successful. The *Wiener Zeitung* merely announced it had taken place, without comment, and the *Journal des Luxus und den Moden* wrote that 'The opera in question is the most absurd stuff in the world, and only sought after on account of the excellence of the music!' But the opera had soon to be taken off because the Emperor, Joseph II, died twenty-five days after the first performance on 22 February 1790 and the theatres of Vienna were closed for two months: even after that *Così fan tutte* had only five more performances.

But the last word can be left to the *Journal's* writer:

'That the music is by Mozart says, I believe, everything'.

DENNIS ARUNDELL

Le Nozze di Figaro

libretto by

Lorenzo da Ponte

Dramatis Personae

THE COUNT ALMAVIVA, *a Spanish nobleman*
THE COUNTESS ALMAVIVA, *his wife*
SUSANNA, *the Countess's maid, promised in marriage to*
FIGARO, *the Count's servant*
CHERUBINO, *the Count's page*
MARCELLINA, *housekeeper*
BARTOLO, *a Doctor from Seville*
BASILIO, *a music teacher*
DON CURZIO, *a lawyer*
BARBARINA, *a daughter of*
ANTONIO, *the Count's gardener and Susanna's uncle*

CHORUS of country people and peasants

The opera is set in Count Almaviva's country house near Seville, and the action is contained within one day.

Synopsis

ACT 1

A partly furnished room. It is Figaro's wedding day. While he is measuring the room that has been set aside for their use, Susanna points out to him that it is dangerously close to the Count's, and that the latter, a notable womanizer, intends to revive the 'droit du seigneur', which he has officially abolished on his estates, in the case of this particular marriage. Figaro determines to lead his master a dance.

Marcellina tells Bartolo that she has a contractual hold over Figaro and is set on marrying him herself, and Bartolo is delighted at the prospect of revenge on the man who helped trick him out of marrying his former ward, now the Countess. Marcellina and Susanna indulge in polite backbiting, and Marcellina, getting much the worst of it, retires.

Cherubino comes to tell Susanna that he has been dismissed after the Count found him alone with Barbarina, but their conversation is interrupted by the arrival of the Count himself. Cherubino hides behind a chair while the Count tries to persuade Susanna to meet him alone that evening. This conversation is in turn interrupted by Basilio, the Count's go-between. The Count hides behind the chair while Cherubino manages to slip into it, covered by a dress. Basilio hints at the attentions Cherubino is paying to both Susanna and the Countess, among others, and the jealous Count emerges from hiding to hear more. While describing how he caught Cherubino with Barbarina, he accidentally reveals the page in the chair, much to everyone's confusion.

Figaro brings in a group of villagers to sing the praises of the Count for abolishing 'droit du seigneur' and asks him to perform the betrothal ceremony at once. The Count, not so easily caught, promises to do it later with due ceremony. In the face of Susanna's pleadings (and a touch of blackmail from Cherubino, who could not help overhearing the Count propositioning Susanna) the Count commutes the page's dismissal to a commission in his regiment in Seville. He is to leave immediately. Figaro sings ironically of the delights of military life.

ACT II

A handsome room with closet, alcove and two doors. The Countess, saddened by the loss of her husband's affections, is prepared to join in Figaro's plots aimed at discomforting the Count in general, and in particular distracting him from his designs on Susanna. Figaro has already sent an anonymous note to the Count via Basilio warning him that the Countess is to meet a lover in the garden that evening, and he now proposes that Susanna should make an assignation with the Count for the same time, which Cherubino, dressed as a girl, would keep.

As the Count is out hunting, there is plenty of time to devise Cherubino's costume, but the mild flirtation between Cherubino and the Countess that ensues while Susanna has gone to her room is interrupted by the Count's sudden return. Cherubino hides in the closet and the Countess locks him in, concealing the key. When he knocks a chair over, the Count's suspicions, already aroused by the locked outer door and by Basilio's letter, seem to be confirmed. The Countess refuses to open the closet door, saying that only Susanna is in there, and Susanna herself, returning from her room, accurately sums up the situation and hides in the alcove. The Count prepares to force the closet door, and retiring with the Countess to fetch the appropriate tools, locks the other doors. Susanna releases Cherubino from the closet, and there is only one escape for him–through the window. He jumps. Count and Countess return. The Countess admits that Cherubino is in the closet, gives the key to the Count who unlocks it and reveals–Susanna. The Countess, recovering quickly, says that she was only testing the Count's affections, and admits that Figaro wrote the letter via Basilio with the same idea in mind. Figaro then enters to tell the Count that all is prepared for the wedding, and despite much prompting will not admit to the letter.

The gardener Antonio arrives to describe how he saw a man jumping from the window. He thinks it was Cherubino (greatly to the Count's interest) but Figaro swears it was he himself. What then is the paper, swiftly seized by the Count from Antonio, that was dropped in the garden? While playing for time, the Countess and Susanna manage to see that it is Cherubino's commission, which is unsealed and could have been left for Figaro to get the Count's seal. They accordingly prompt Figaro, but their success is shortlived. Bartolo, Marcellina and Basilio enter flourishing a contract promising Figaro in marriage to Marcellina in the event of non-payment of a debt. The marriage of Figaro is postponed.

ACT III

A large hall, decorated for a wedding. The Countess and Susanna now get together: Susanna is to make an assignation with the Count for that evening, but the Countess will go in her place. The Count is delighted, but a chance remark overheard renews his suspicions. In the course of an examination of Marcellina's contract, a tell-tale birthmark reveals that Figaro is the long lost illegitimate son of Marcellina and Bartolo. The surprised parents decide to do the decent thing, and nothing now stands in the way of a double wedding.

The Countess dictates to Susanna a note for the Count fixing the place for their meeting, adding that the Count should return the pin used to seal the note as a sign of his assent.

At the start of the wedding celebrations, the Count, prompted by Antonio, discovers Cherubino dressed as a girl alongside Barbarina. The latter forestalls the Count's anger by innocently hinting at startling revelations. During the ceremony itself Susanna slips the Count her note, but having pricked his finger he angrily throws the pin on the floor. Figaro is amused to see him searching for it–but he does not know whom the note is from.

ACT IV

The garden. Figaro and Marcellina come upon Barbarina searching for a pin she has lost. She ingenuously tells Figaro that the Count asked her to return it to Susanna. Figaro, in despair at Susanna's supposed instant faithlessness, rushes away, leaving Marcellina to muse on the sadness of woman's lot.

Another part of the garden, with two pavilions, one on the left and one on the right. Barbarina enters the left-hand pavilion, where she has arranged to meet Cherubino. Figaro brings Bartolo and Basilio to witness his bride's perfidy, curses the wiles of womankind and retires to await developments. Marcellina warns the disguised Susanna that Figaro is lurking somewhere before going herself to hide in the left-hand pavilion.

The plot is complicated by the appearance of Cherubino, coming to keep his appointment with Barbarina in the pavilion. He sees the Countess, thinks it is Susanna, seizes her hand and tries to kiss her. The Count arrives, thinks he sees Cherubino kissing Susanna, and, while Cherubino escapes into the left-hand pavilion, Figaro comes forward to see what is going on and receives the blow the Count intended for Cherubino. As Figaro retires mystified, the Count makes advances to the woman that both he and Figaro think is Susanna but who is of course the Countess. He gives her a ring as a token of his affections. Disturbed by someone approaching, he says he will rejoin her in a moment, and retires, while the Countess slips into the right-hand pavilion.

Susanna and Figaro now come forward. Taking her at first for the Countess, Figaro soon discovers who it really is and pretends to make passionate advances. Susanna, before she realises that he is making fun of her, is furiously jealous. The Count too, on returning, thinks he sees his servant making love to his wife and summons the company to witness her disgrace. Susanna escapes into the left-hand pavilion. When Bartolo, Basilio, Don Curzio and others have run on, from the left-hand pavilion come Cherubino, Barbarina, Marcellina and Susanna, who holds a kerchief to her face, as if from shame. While the Count berates her, the Countess enters calmly from the right, and her husband is forced to beg her forgiveness in public. The company remarks that a day of folly may be brought to a happy end by the power of love.

ATTO PRIMO

ACT I

SCENA PRIMA

Camera non affatto ammobiliata, una sedia d'appeggio in mezzo

Figaro con una misura in mano, e Susanna allo specchio, che si sta mettendo un cappellino ornato di fiori

1. DUETTINO

FIGARO
Cinque . . . dieci . . .
trenta . . . trenta sei . . .
quaranta trè

SUSANNA
(fra se stessa, guardundosi nello specchio)
Ora sì ch'io son contenta;
Sembra fatto inver per me.
(seguitando a guardarsi)
Guarda un po', mio caro Figaro
Guarda adesso il mio cappello.

FIGARO
Sì, mio core, or è più bello:
Sembra fatto inver per te.

SUSANNA E FIGARO
Ah, il mattino alle nozze vicino
Quanto è dolce al mio (tuo)
tenero sposo,
Questo bel cappellino vezzoso
Che Susanna ella stessa si fè

SCENE 1

A partly furnished room, with an easy chair in the centre

Figaro with a measure in his hand, Susanna at the mirror, trying on a hat decorated with flowers

1. DUET

FIGARO
Five . . . ten . . . twenty . . .
thirty . . . thirty-six . . . forty-
three . . .

SUSANNA
(to herself, gazing into the mirror)

Yes, I'm very pleased with that;
it seems just made for me.
(she continues to gaze at herself)
Take a look, dear Figaro
just look at this hat of mine.

FIGARO
Yes, my dearest, it's very pretty;
it looks just made for you.

SUSANNA AND FIGARO
On this morning of our wedding
how delightful to my (your)
dear one
is this pretty little hat
which Susanna made herself.

RECITATIVO	RECITATIVE
SUSANNA Cosa stai misurando, Caro il mio Figaretto?	SUSANNA What are you measuring, my dearest Figaro?
FIGARO Io guardo se quel letto Che ci destina il Conte Fara buona figura in questo loco.	FIGARO I'm seeing if this bed which the Count has put aside for us will go well just here.
SUSANNA In questa stanza?	SUSANNA In this room?
FIGARO Certo, a noi la cede Generoso il padrone.	FIGARO Of course; his lordship's generously giving it to us.
SUSANNA Io per me te la dono.	SUSANNA As far as I'm concerned, you can keep it.
FIGARO E la ragione?	FIGARO What's the matter?
SUSANNA *(toccadosi la fronte)* La ragione l'ho qui.	SUSANNA *(tapping her forehead)* I've my reasons in here.
FIGARO *(facendo lo stesso)* Perchè non puoi Far che passi un po' qui?	FIGARO *(doing the same)* Why can't you let me in on them?
SUSANNA Perchè non voglio. Sei tu mio servo, o no?	SUSANNA Because I don't choose to. Are you my slave, or not?
FIGARO Ma non capisco Perchè tanto ti spiace La più comoda stanza del palazzo.	FIGARO But I don't understand why you so dislike the most convenient room in the palace.
SUSANNA Perchè io son la Susanna e tu sei pazzo.	SUSANNA Because I'm Susanna and you're a dolt.
FIGARO Grazie, non tanti elogi: guarda un poco	FIGARO Thanks, you're too flattering: just see

Se potriasi star meglio in altro loco.

if it could be better anywhere else.

2. DUETTINO

2. DUET

FIGARO
Se a caso madama
La notte ti chiama:
Din din: in due passi
Da quella puoi gir.
Vien poi l'occasione
Che vuolmi il padrone,
Don don: in tre salti
Lo vado a servir.

FIGARO
Supposing my lady
calls you at night:
ding ding: in two steps
you can be there from here.
Or if it should happen
that his lordship should want me,
dong dong: in three bounds
I'm there at his service.

SUSANNA
Così se il mattino
Il caro Contino,
Din din, e ti manda
Tre miglia lontan.
Don don; e a mia porta
Il diavol lo parta
Don don, e in tre salti . . .

SUSANNA
And supposing one morning
the dear Count should ring,
ding ding, and send you
three miles away,
dong dong, and the devil
should lead him to my door–
dong dong, in three bounds . . .

FIGARO
Susanna, pian pian.

FIGARO
Stop, stop, Susanna.

SUSANNA
Ascolta.

SUSANNA
Listen.

FIGARO
Fa presto

FIGARO
Quick, tell me!

SUSANNA
Se udir brami il resto
Discaccia i sospetti
Che torto mi fan.

SUSANNA
If you wish to hear the rest,
banish those suspicions
which do me wrong.

FIGARO
Udir bramo il resto:
I dubbi, i sospetti
Gelare mi fan.

FIGARO
I burn to hear the rest:
doubts and suspicions
freeze my blood.

RECITATIVO

RECITATIVE

SUSANNA
Or bene, ascolta, e taci

SUSANNA
Well then, keep quiet and listen.

FIGARO
Parla, che c'è di nuovo?

FIGARO
Speak: what's there to tell?

SUSANNA
Il signor Conte,
Stanco d'andar cacciando le straniere
Bellezze forestiere,
Vuole ancor nel castello
Ritentar la sua sorte;
Nè già di sua consorte, bada bene,
Appetito gli viene.

FIGARO
E di chi dunque?

SUSANNA
Della tua Susannetta.

FIGARO
(con sorpresa)
Di te?

SUSANNA
Di me medesma, ed ha speranza
Ch'al nobil suo progetto
Utilissima sia tal vicinanza.

FIGARO
Bravo! Tiriamo avanti.

SUSANNA
Queste le grazie son, questa la cura
Ch'egli prende di te, della tua sposa.

FIGARO
Oh, guarda un po'che carità pelosa!

SUSANNA
Chetati: or viene il meglio.
Don Basilio, mio maestro di canto e
suo factotum, nel darmi la lezione
Mi ripete ogni di questa canzone.

FIGARO
Chi? Basilio? oh birbante!

SUSANNA
E tu credevi
Che fosse la mia dote
Merto del tuo bel muso?

FIGARO
Me n'ero lusingato.

SUSANNA
The noble Count,
tired of scouring the
countryside for fresh beauties,
wants to try his luck again
in his own palace,
though, let me tell you
it's not his wife
who whets his appetite.

FIGARO
Well, who then?

SUSANNA
Your little Susanna.

FIGARO
(astonished)
You?

SUSANNA
The very same, and he's hoping
that being so close will be most useful
to his noble project.

FIGARO
Bravo! Go on.

SUSANNA
This is the gracious favour, this the care
he bestows on you and on your wife.

FIGARO
Have you seen such condescension!

SUSANNA
Wait though: there's better to come.
Don Basilio, my singing teacher and his
factotum, repeats this same theme daily
when he gives me my lesson.

FIGARO
What, Basilio? The scoundrel!

SUSANNA
Did you imagine he gave me a dowry
for the sake of your beaux yeux?

FIGARO
So I'd flattered myself.

SUSANNA
Ei la destina
Per ottener da me certe mezz'ore . . .
Che il diritto feudale . . .

SUSANNA
He intends it
to obtain from me certain half hours . . .
which feudal privilege . . .

FIGARO
Come! ne' feudi suoi
Non l'ha il Conte abolito?

FIGARO
What! Didn't the Count
abolish that in his domain?

SUSANNA
Ebben, ora è pentito e par che tenda
Riscattarlo da me.

SUSANNA
He did, but now he regrets it, and it seems
he wants to bring it back for me.

FIGARO
Bravo! mi piace:
Che caro signor Conte!
Ci vogliam divertir: trovato avete . . .

FIGARO
Well! very pretty:
how charming of his lordship!
He wants some fun: he'll get it . . .

(Si sente suonare un campanello).

(A bell rings).

FIGARO
Chi suona? La Contessa.

FIGARO
Who's ringing? The Countess.

SUSANNA
Addio, addio, Figaro bello.

SUSANNA
I must go. Goodbye, dear Figaro.

FIGARO
Coraggio, mio tesoro.

FIGARO
Courage, my dearest.

SUSANNA
E tu, cervello.

SUSANNA
And you be wary.

(parte)

(exit)

SCENA SECONDA

SCENE 2

Figaro solo, passeggiando con fuoco per la camera, e fregandosi le mani

Figaro alone, feverishly pacing up and down the room, rubbing his hands

FIGARO
Bravo, signor padrone! Ora
incomincio a capir il mistero . . .
e a veder schietto tutto il vostro
progetto: a Londra, è vero?
Voi ministro, io corriero, e la
Susanna . . . secreta ambasciatrice . . .
Non sarà, non sarà, Figaro il dice.

FIGARO
Well done, my noble master! Now I
begin to understand the secret . . .
and to see your whole scheme clearly:
to London, isn't it you go as minister,
I as courier, and Susanna . . .
confidential attachée . . .
It shall not be: Figaro has said it.

3. CAVATINA

3. CAVATINA

FIGARO
Se vuol ballare,
Signor Contino
Il chitarrino
Le suonerò.
Se vuol venire
Nella mia scola,
La capriola
Le insegnerò.
Saprò . . . ma piano
Meglio ogni arcano
Dissimulando
Scoprir potrò.
L'arte schermendo,
L'arte adoprando,
Di qua pungendo,
Di là scherzando,
Tutte le macchine
Rovescierò.

FIGARO
If, my dear Count,
you feel like dancing,
it's I
who'll call the tune.
If you'll come
to my school,
I'll teach you
how to caper.
I'll know how . . . but wait,
I can uncover
his secret design
more easily by dissembling.
Acting by stealth
or openly,
here stinging,
there mocking
all your plots
I'll overthrow.

(parte)

(exit)

SCENA TERZA

SCENE 3

Bartolo e Marcellina con un contratto in mano

Bartolo and Marcellina with a contract in her hand

RECITATIVO

RECITATIVE

BARTOLO
Ed aspettaste il giorno
Fissato alle sue nozze
Per parlami di questo?

BARTOLO
And you waited until the day
appointed for his wedding
to tell me this?

MARCELLINA
Io non mi perdo,
Dottor mio di coraggio:
Per romper de' sponsali
Più avanzati di questo
Bastò spesso un pretesto, ed egli ha meco,
Oltre questo contratto, certi impegni . . .
So io . . . basta: conviene
La Susanna atterrir; convien con arte
Impuntigliarla a rifiutare il Conte.
Egli per vendicarsi
Prederà il mio partito
E Figaro cosi fia mio marito.

MARCELLINA
Oh, my dear doctor,
I'm not giving up:
to break off engagements
even later than this
a pretext has often sufficed, and besides
this contract he has certain pledges
to me I could mention . . .
but enough:
we must frighten Susanna;
we must somehow
make her reject the Count's advances.
To revenge himself,
he'll take my part,
and so Figaro will become my husband.

BARTOLO
Bene, io tutto farò, senza riserve.
(prende il contratto dalle mani di Marcellina)
Tutto a me palesate.
(tra sè)
Avrei pur gusto
Di dar per moglie la mia serva antica
A chi mi fece un dì rapir l'amica.

BARTOLO
Well, I'll do all I can, without reserve.
(taking the contract from Marcellina's hand)
Tell me everything.
(aside)
I'd enjoy
giving him my old servant for a wife for having stolen my intended from me.

4. ARIA

BARTOLO
La vendetta, oh, la vendetta
È un piacer serbato ai saggi;
L'obliar l'onte, gli oltraggi,
Èbassezza, è ognor viltà.
Coll'astuzia, coll'arguzia
Col giudizio, col criterio
Si potrebbe . . . Il fatto è serio;
Ma credete, si farà.
Se tutto il codice dovessi volgere
Se tutto l'indice dovessi leggere,
Con un equivoco, con un sinonimo
Qualche garbuglio si troverà.
Tutta Siviglia conosce Bartolo:
Il birbo Figaro vinto sarà!

(parte)

4. ARIA

BARTOLO
Revenge, yes, revenge
is a pleasure meant for the intelligent;
to forget insults and outrages
is always low and base.
With astuteness and acuteness,
with judgement and discernment,
I can do it . . . The case is serious;
but, believe me, I'll bring it off.
If I have to search the legal code,
if I have to read through the whole statute book;
with a quibble or a paraphrase
I'll find some obstacle.
All Seville knows Dr.Bartolo:
that rascal Figaro will lose the day!

(exit)

SCENA QUARTA

Marcellina, poi Susanna, con cuffia da donna, un nastro ed un abito da donna

RECITATIVO

MARCELLINA
Tutto ancor non ho perso:
Mi resta la speranza.
Ma Susanna si avanza: io vo' provarmi.
Fingiam di non vederla.
(tra sè, forte)
E quella buona perla
La vorrebbe sposar!

SCENE 4

Marcellina, later Susanna, carrying a lady's cap, a ribbon and a dress

RECITATIVE

MARCELLINA
All is not lost yet:
I still have hopes.
But here comes Susanna; I'll make a start.
Let's pretend not to see her.
(aside, loudly)
And that's the pearl of virtue
he intends to marry!

SUSANNA
(resta indietro, tra sè)
Di me favella.

SUSANNA
(holding back, aside)
She's talking of me.

MARCELLINA
Ma da Figaro alfine
Non può meglio sperarsi:
L'argent fait tout.

MARCELLINA
But, after all, from Figaro
one can't hope for anything better:
money means everything.

SUSANNA
(tra sè)
Che lingua! manco male
Che ognun sa quanto vale.

SUSANNA
(aside)
A spiteful tongue! It's lucky
everyone knows the worth of
what she says.

MARCELLINA
Brava! questo è giudizio!
Con quegli occhi modesti,
Con quell' aria pietosa,
E poi . . .

MARCELLINA
Bravo! such discretion!
And those modest eyes
and demure expression,
as well as . . .

SUSANNA
(tra sè)
Meglio è partir.

SUSANNA
(aside)
I'd better go.

MARCELLINA
Che cara sposa!

MARCELLINA
What a charming bride!

*(vanno tutte e due per partire
e s'incontrano alla porta)*

*(both make as if to leave, and
meet at the doorway)*

5. DUETTINO

5. DUET

MARCELLINA
(facendo una riverenza)
Via, resti servita,
Madama brillante.

MARCELLINA
(curtseying)
Your humble servant,
gracious lady.

SUSANNA
(facendo una riverenza)
Non sono si ardita,
Madama piccante.

SUSANNA
(curtseying)
I'd not be so bold,
worthy ma'am.

MARCELLINA
(facendo una riverenza)
No, prima a lei tocca.

MARCELLINA
(curtseying)
No, you go first, pray.

SUSANNA
(facendo una riverenza)
No, no, tocca a lei.

SUSANNA
(curtseying)
No, no, after you.

SUSANNA E MARCELLINA
Io so i dover miei,
Non fo inciviltà.

SUSANNA AND MARCELLINA
I know my place,
I'd not so presume.

MARCELLINA
(facendo una riverenza)
La sposa novella.

MARCELLINA
(curtseying)
A bride-to-be first.

SUSANNA
(facendo una riverenza)
La dama d'onore.

SUSANNA
(curtseying)
A lady in waiting.

MARCELLINA
(facendo una riverenza)
Del Conte la bella.

MARCELLINA
(curtseying)
The Count's favourite.

SUSANNA
Di Spagna l'amore

SUSANNA
The toast of Spain.

MARCELLINA
I meriti.

MARCELLINA
Your qualities.

SUSANNA
L'abito.

SUSANNA
Your bearing.

MARCELLINA
Il posto.

MARCELLINA
Your position.

SUSANNA
L'età!

SUSANNA
Your age!

MARCELLINA
(tra sè)
Per bacco, precipito
Se ancor resto qua.

MARCELLINA
(aside)
I'll fly into a rage
if I stay here any longer.

SUSANNA
(tra sè)
Sibilla decrepita,
Da rider mi fa.

SUSANNA
(aside)
Decrepit old witch,
she's a laughing stock.

(Marcellina parte infuriata)

(Exit Marcellina in a fury)

SCENA QUINTA

SCENE 5

Susanna, e poi Cherubino

Susanna, later Cherubino

RECITATIVO

RECITATIVE

SUSANNA
Va là, vecchia pedante,

SUSANNA
Get away, you old frump!

Dottoressa arrogante,
Perchè hai letti due libri,
E seccata madama in gioventù . . .
(mette il vestito sopra il seggiolone)

Putting on high and mighty airs
because you've read a couple of books
and used to torment my lady in her youth . . .
(putting the dress on the easy-chair)

CHERUBINO
(esce in fretta)
Susannetta, sei tu? . . .

CHERUBINO
(entering hurriedly)
Susanna dear, is it you?

SUSANNA
Son io, cosa volete?

SUSANNA
Yes, it's me. What do you want?

CHERUBINO
Ah, cor mio, che accidente!

CHERUBINO
Oh my dearest, what a misfortune!

SUSANNA
Cor vostro! cosa avvenne?

SUSANNA
Your dearest! What's happened?

CHERUBINO
Il Conte ieri
Perchè trovommi sol con Barbarina,
Il congedo mi diede:
E se la Contessina,
La mia bella comare,
Grazia non m'intercede, io vado via,
(con ansietà)
Io non ti vedo più, Susanna mia!

CHERUBINO
Yesterday the Count,
because he found me all alone
with Barbarina, dismissed me:
and if the Countess,
my lovely godmother,
doesn't intercede to get me pardoned,
I'll have to go away
(anxiously)
and never see my
dear Susanna again!

SUSANNA
Non vedetete più me! bravo! ma dunque
Non più per la Contessa
Secretamente il vostro cor sospira?

SUSANNA
Never see me again! Well then!
But isn't your heart secretly sighing
any longer for the Countess?

CHERUBINO
Ah, che troppo rispetto ella m'ispira!
Felice te che puoi
Vederla quando vuoi!
(con un sospiro)
Che la vesti al mattino,
Che la sera la spogli,
Che le metti gli spilloni, i merletti . . .
Ah, se in tuo loco . . .
Cos'hai lì? dimmi un poco . . .

CHERUBINO
Ah, she fills me with too much respect!
How lucky you are, to be able
to see her whenever you wish!
(sighing)
You dress her in the morning
and undress her at night,
you put on her pins and laces.
If only I could be in your place . . .
What have you got there? Let me see . . .

SUSANNA
(imitandolo)
Ah il vago nastro, e la notturna cuffia
Di comare sì bella . . .

CHERUBINO
Deh, dammela, sorella,
(Cherubino toglie il nastro di mano a Susanna)
Dammela, per pietà.

SUSANNA
Presto, quel nastro.
(Susanna vuol riprenderglielo; egli si mette a girare intorno alle sedia)

CHERUBINO
O caro, o bello, o fortunato nastro!
Io non tel renderò che con la vita.
(bacia e ribacia il nastro)

SUSANNA
(seguita a corrergli dietro, ma poi si arresta come fosse stanca)
Cos'è quest'insolenza?

CHERUBINO
Eh via, sta'cheta!
In ricompensa poi
Questa mia canzonetta io ti vo'dare.
(cava di tasca una canzone)

SUSANNA
E che ne debbo fare!
(gliela prende)

CHERUBINO
Leggila alla padrone,
Leggila tu medesma,
Leggila a Barbarina, a Marcellina,
(con trasporto di gioia)
Leggila ad ogni donna del palazzo.

SUSANNA
Povero Cherubin, siete voi pazzo?

SUSANNA
(imitating him)
Oh what a pretty ribbon, and the nightcap
of so lovely a godmother . . .

CHERUBINO
Oh give me it, my dear.
(He snatches the ribbon from her hand)
Give me it, I beg.

SUSANNA
Give it back at once.
(She tries to take it back: he dodges round the chairs)

CHERUBINO
O dear, sweet, fortunate ribbon!
I'll not give it up except with my life.
(kisses the ribbon again and again)

SUSANNA
(begins to run after him, but then stops as if tired)
What is this insolence?

CHERUBINO
Go on, don't be angry!
In exchange for it I'll give you
this little song of mine.
(taking a song from his pocket)

SUSANNA
And what am I to do with it?
(taking it)

CHERUBINO
Sing it to my lady,
sing it for yourself,
sing it to Barbarina, Marcellina,
(in a transport of joy)
sing it to every woman in the palace.

SUSANNA
Poor Cherubino, have you gone mad?

6. ARIA

CHERUBINO
Non so più cosa son, cosa faccio,
Or di fuoco, ora sono di ghiaccio,
Ogni donna cangiar di colore,
Ogni donna mi fa palpitar.
Solo ai nomi d'amor, di diletto
Mi si turba, mi s'altera il petto
E a parlare mi sforza d'amore
Un desìo ch'io non posso spiegar!
Parlo d'amor vegliando,
Parlo d'amor sognando,
All'acqua, all'ombra, ai monti,
Ai fiori, all'erbe, ai fonti,
All'eco, all'aria, ai venti,
Che il suon dei vani accenti
Portan via con sè . . .
E se non ho chi m'oda
Parlo d'amor con me.

SCENA SESTA

Cherubino, Susanna e poi il Conte

Cherubino vedendo il Conte da lontano, si nasconde dietro una sedia

RECITATIVO

CHERUBINO
Son perduto!

SUSANNA
Che timor . . . Il Conte!
(Susanna cerca mascherar Cherubino)
Misera me!

CONTE
Susanna, tu mi sembri
Agita e confusa.

6. ARIA

CHERUBINO
I no longer know what I am
or what I'm doing,
now I'm burning, now I'm made of ice;
every woman makes me change colour,
every woman makes me tremble,
At the very word love or beloved
my heart leaps and pounds,
and to speak of it fills me
with a longing I can't explain!

I speak of love when I'm awake,
I speak of it in my dreams,
to the stream, the shade, the mountains,
to the flowers, the grass, the fountains,
to the echo, the air, the breezes,
which carry away with them
the sound of my fond words . . .
And if I've none to hear me
I speak of love to myself.

SCENE 6

Cherubino, Susanna, later the Count

Cherubino, seeing the Count approaching, hides behind the armchair

RECITATIVE

CHERUBINO
I'm lost!

SUSANNA
Heavens . . . the Count!
(She tries to conceal Cherubino)

Woe is me!

COUNT
Susanna, you seem to be
agitated and confused.

SUSANNA
Signor . . . io chiedo scusa . . .
Ma . . . se mai . . . qui
sorpressa . . .
Per carità, partite.

CONTE
(si mette a sedere sulla sedia, prende Susanna per mano, ella si distacca con forza)
Un momento e ti lascio.
Odi.

SUSANNA
Non odo nulla.

CONTE
Due parole. Tu sai
Che ambasciatore a Londra
Il re dichiarò; di condur meco
Figaro destinai . . .

SUSANNA
(timida)
Signor, se osassi . . .

CONTE
(alzandosi)
Parla, parla, mia cara, e con quel dritto
Ch'oggi prendi su me finchè tu vivi,
Chiedi, imponi, prescrivi.
(con tenerezza, e tentando riprenderle la mano)

SUSANNA
(con smania)
Lasciateme, signor; dritti non prendo,
Non ne vo', non ne intendo . . .
oh me infelice!

CONTE
Ah no, Susanna, io ti vo'far felice!
Tu ben sai quanto io t'amo:
A te Basilio
Tutto già disse, or senti.
Se per pochi momenti

SUSANNA
My lord . . . pray excuse me . . .
but . . . suppose someone caught
us . . .
I beg you to leave.

COUNT
(seating himself in the armchair and taking Susanna's hand, which she withdraws with an effort)
One moment and I'll leave you.
Listen.

SUSANNA
I mustn't listen.

COUNT
Just two words. You know
that the king has appointed me
ambassador in London: I planned
to take Figaro with me . . .

SUSANNA
(timidly)
My lord, if you'd allow me . . .

COUNT
(rising)
Speak, my dear, speak, and with that right
which today you may assume of me as long
as you live, ask, demand what you will.
(tenderly, trying to take her hand again)

SUSANNA
(agitatedly)
Let me go my lord; I claim no right,
nor wish to, nor intend to . . .
I'm so unhappy!

COUNT
But no, Susanna, I want to make you happy!
You well know how much I love you:
Basilio has already told you; now listen.
If you'll give me a few minutes
in the garden at dusk . . .

Meco in giardin sull'imbrunir del giorno . . .
Ah, per questo favore io pagherei . . .

for that favour I'd pay . . .

BASILIO
(dentro le quinte)
È uscito poco fa.

BASILIO
(off-stage)
He's just gone out.

CONTE
Chi parla?

COUNT
Who spoke?

SUSANNA
Oh Dei!

SUSANNA
O Heavens!

CONTE
Esci, e alcuno non entri.

COUNT
Go out, and see no one comes in.

SUSANNA
(inquietissima)
Ch'io vi lasci qui solo?

SUSANNA
(very anxiously)
I'm to leave you here alone?

BASILIO
(come sopra)
Da madama sarà, vado a cercarlo.

BASILIO
(as before)
He'll be with my lady: I'll go and look for him.

CONTE
(addita la sedia)
Qui dietro mi porrò.

COUNT
(indicating the armchair)
I'll get behind here.

SUSANNA
Non vi celate.

SUSANNA
Do not hide there.

CONTE
Taci, e cerca ch'ei parta.

COUNT
Hush, and get rid of him.

(Il Conte vuol nascondersi dietro il sedile: Susanna si frappone tra il paggio e lui. Il Conte la spinge dolcemente. Ella rincula; intanto il paggio passa al davanti del sedile, si mette dentro in piedi. Susanna il ricopre colla vestaglia)

(The Count goes to hide behind the chair: Susanna interposes herself between the page and him, the Count pushes her gently aside. As she moves, the page steals in front of the chair and curls up inside it: Susanna covers him with the dress)

SUSANNA
Ohimè! che fate?

SUSANNA
Alas! What's going on?

SCENA SETTIMA

SCENE 7

I suddetti e Basilio

Basilio and the above

BASILIO
Susanna, il ciel vi salvi; avreste
Acaso veduto il Conte?

SUSANNA
E cosa deve far meco il Conte?
Animo, uscite.

BASILIO
Aspettate, sentite,
Figaro di lui cerca.

SUSANNA
(tra sè)
Oh cielo!
(forte)
Ei cerca
Chi dopo voi più l'odia.

CONTE
(tra sè)
Vediam come mi serve.

BASILIO
Io non he mai nella moral sentito
Ch'uno ch'ama la moglie odii il marito.
Per dir che il Conte v'ama . . .

SUSANNA
(con risentimento)
Sortite, vil ministro
Dell'altrui sfrenatezza: io non ho d'uopo
Della vostra morale,
Del Conte, del suo amor . . .

BASILIO
Non c'è alcun male,
Ha ciascun i suoi gusti: io mi credea
Che preferir dovreste per amante,
Come fan tutte quante,
Un signor liberal, prudente e saggio,
A un giovinastro, a un paggio . . .

SUSANNA
(con ansietà)
A Cherubino?

BASILIO
Susanna, Heaven be with you:
have you by any chance seen the Count?

SUSANNA
What should the Count be doing here with me? Please go away.

BASILIO
Just a moment, listen;
Figaro's looking for him.

SUSANNA
(aside)
Oh dear!
(aloud)
He's looking for the one
who, after you, hates him most.

COUNT
(aside)
We'll see how I am served.

BASILIO
I've never heard the proposition
that one who loves the wife must hate the husband.
To tell you how the Count loves you . . .

SUSANNA
(indignantly)
Begone, base agent
for another's lust: I don't need your propositions,
your Count and his love . . .

BASILIO
There's no harm done: everyone
to his own taste: I'd have thought
that for a lover you'd prefer,
like any other woman,
a generous, prudent and discreet nobleman
to a youngster, a pageboy . . .

SUSANNA
(nervously)
To Cherubino?

BASILIO
A Cherubino. Cherubin d'amore
Ch'oggi sul far del giorno
Passeggiava qui intorno
Per entrar . . .

SUSANNA
(con forza)
Uom maligno!
Un'impostura è questa!

BASILIO
È un maligno con voi chi ha gli occhi in testa.
E quella canzonetta?
Ditemi in confidenza: io sono amico
E ad altrui mulla dico;
E per voi, per madama . . .

SUSANNA
(mostra dello smarrimento, tra sè)
Chi diavol gliel'ha detto?

BASILIO
A proposito, figlia,
Istruitelo meglio;
Egli la guarda a tavola si spesso,
E con tale immodestia,
Che se il Conte s'accorge . . .
e su tal punto,
Sapete, egli è una bestia.

SUSANNA
Scellerato!
E perchè andate voi
Tai menzogne spargendo?

BASILIO
Io! che inguistizia! quel che compro io vendo.
A quel che tutti dicono
Io non ci agguingo un pelo.

CONTE
(sorte dal loco)
Come, che dicon tutti!

BASILIO
Oh bella!

BASILIO
To Cherubino, that amorous cherub
who at daybreak this morning
was prowling about here
trying to get in . . .

SUSANNA
(vehemently)
Slanderer!
It's an invention!

BASILIO
To you, anyone who keeps his eyes open is a slanderer.
And that little song?
Tell me in confidence: I'm a friend
and won't let it go any further;
was it for you, or for my lady . . .

SUSANNA
(bewildered, aside)
Who on earth told him about that?

BASILIO
By the way, my daughter,
it would be wise to warn him:
at table he gazes at her so often
and with such avidity,
that if the Count noticed . . .
On that point you know, he's ferocious.

SUSANNA
You wretch!
Why do you go around
spreading such lies?

BASILIO
I? You wrong me: I sell only what I buy.
I don't add a jot
to what everyone is saying.

COUNT
(emerging from his hiding place)
Really, what everyone is saying?

BASILIO
Very pretty!

SUSANNA
Oh cielo!

SUSANNA
O Heaven!

7. TERZETTO

7. TRIO

CONTE
(a Basilio)
Cosa sento? tosto andate,
E scacciate il seduttor.

COUNT
(to Basilio)
What do I hear? Go at once
and send the seducer packing.

BASILIO
In mal punto son giunto!
Perdonate, o mio signor.

BASILIO
My presence is ill-timed.
Pray excuse me, my lord.

SUSANNA
(quasi svenuta)
Che ruina, me meschina!
Son oppressa dal dolor.

SUSANNA
(almost fainting)
Unhappy me, I'm ruined!
I'm overcome with misery.

BASILIO E CONTE
(sostenendo Susanna)
Ah, già svien la poverina!
Come, oh dio! le batte il cor!

BASILIO AND COUNT
(supporting Susanna)
Ah! the poor child's fainted!
Lord, how her heart is beating!

BASILIO
Pian pianin su questo seggio.

BASILIO
Gently, gently, on to this seat.

(approssimandola al sedile in atto di farla sedere)

(they draw her towards the chair to let her sit down)

SUSANNA
(rinviene)
Dove sono? cosa veggio?
Che insolenza, andate fuor.
(si stacca da tutti e due)

SUSANNA
(reviving)
Where am I? What's going on?
How dare you! Go away!
(She repulses them both)

CONTE
Siamo qui per aiutarti
Non turbarti, o mio tesor.

COUNT
We're only helping you;
do not be alarmed, my dear.

BASILIO
(con malignità)
Siamo qui per aiutarvi,
È sicuro il vostro onor.
(al Conte)
Ah del paggio quel ch'ho detto
Era solo un mio sospetto!

BASILIO
(sardonically)
We're only helping you;
your honour is quite safe.
(to the Count)
What I said about the page
was only my suspicion.

SUSANNA
E un'insidia, una perfidia,

SUSANNA
It's a plot, it's quite untrue;

Non credete all'impostor.

CONTE
Parta, parta il damerino.

SUSANNA E BASILIO
Poverino!

CONTE
(ironicamente)
Poverino!
Ma da me sorpreso ancor.

SUSANNA
Come!

BASILIO
Che!

CONTE
Da tua cugina
L'uscio ier trovai rinchiuso,
Picchio, m'apre Barbarina
Paurosa fuor dell'uso,
Io dal muso insospettito,
Guardo, cerco in ogni sito,
Ed alzando pian pianino
Il tappeto al tavolina
Vedo il paggio!
(imita il gesto colla vestaglia, e scopre il paggio)
(con sorpresa)
Ah, cosa veggio!

SUSANNA
(con timore)
Ah, crude stelle!

BASILIO
(ridendo)
Ah, meglio ancora!

CONTE
Onestissima signora!
Or capisco come va.

SUSANNA
Accader non può di peggio;
Giusti Dei! che mai sarà?

don't believe this deceiver.

COUNT
That young fop must go.

SUSANNA AND BASILIO
Poor boy!

COUNT
(ironically)
Poor boy!
I've found him out again.

SUSANNA
How so!

BASILIO
What?

COUNT
Yesterday I found
your cousin's door locked;
I knocked, and Barbarina opened it
more flustered than usual.
My suspicions aroused by her appearance,
I looked and searched in every corner,
and very, very softly lifting the tablecloth, there I saw the page!
(He illustrates his actions with the dress and discovers the page)
(with amazement)
Ah, what do I see?

SUSANNA
(fearfully)
All is lost! .

BASILIO
(laughing)
Better and better!

COUNT
You paragon of virtue!
Now I see how it is.

SUSANNA
Nothing worse could come about,
Heavens above, what's to happen?

BASILIO
Così fan tutte le belle!
Non c'è alcuna novità.

BASILIO
Every woman's alike!
There's nothing new about it.

RECITATIVO

RECITATIVE

CONTE
Basilio, in traccia tosto
Di Figaro volate,
Io vo'ch'ei veda . . .
(additanto Cherubino, che non si move dal loco)

COUNT
Basilio, go off
to Figaro at once.
I want him to see . . .
(pointing to Cherubino, who does not move)

SUSANNA
(con vivezza)
Ed io che senta: andate.

SUSANNA
(with spirit)
And I want him to hear: go on.

CONTE
Restate: che baldanza! e quale scusa
Se la colpa è evidente?

COUNT
Wait! What assurance! What's your excuse when your guilt is obvious?

SUSANNA
Non ha d'uopo di scusa un' innocente.

SUSANNA
Virtue has no need of excuses.

CONTE
Ma costui quando venne?

COUNT
But when did he come in?

SUSANNA
Egli era meco
Quando voi qui giungeste, e mi chiedea
D'impegnar la padrona
A intercedergli grazia: il vostro arrivo in scompiglio lo pose,
Ed allor in quel loco si nascose.

SUSANNA
He was with me
when you came in here,
and was asking me
to beg my lady
to intercede for him; your
arrival threw us into confusion,
and so he hid himself in there.

CONTE
Ma s'io stesso m'assisi
Quando in camera entrai!

COUNT
But I sat down there myself
when I came into the room!

CHERUBINO
(timidamente)
Ed allora di dietro io mi celai.

CHERUBINO
(timidly)
Then I hid myself behind it.

CONTE
E quando io là mi posi?

COUNT
And when I placed myself there?

CHERUBINO
Allor pian io mi volsi, e qui
M'ascosi.

CHERUBINO
Then I quietly crept round and hid
here.

CONTE
(a Susanna)
Oh cielo! dunque ha sentito
Quello ch'io ti dicea?

COUNT
(to Susanna)
Heavens! then he heard
all that I was saying to you?

CHERUBINO
Feci per non sentir quanto potea.

CHERUBINO
I did everything I could not to hear.

CONTE
Oh perfidia!

COUNT
Deceitful boy!

BASILIO
Frenatevi: vien gente.

BASILIO
Restrain yourself: someone's coming.

CONTE
(lo tira giù dal sedile)
E voi restate qui, picciol serpente!

COUNT
(dragging Cherubino out of the chair)
And you're still there, you little viper!

SCENA OTTAVA

Figaro con bianca veste in mano. Contadini e Contadine vestite di bianco che spargono fiori, raccolti in piccoli panieri, davanti al Conte

SCENE 8

Figaro with a white veil in his hand: villagers dressed in white scatter before the Count flowers arranged in little baskets

8. CORO

Giovani liete,
Fiori spargete
Davanti al nobile
Nostro signor.
Il suo gran core
Vi serba intatto
D'un più bel fiore
L'almo candor.

8. CHORUS

Blithe maids
scatter flowers
before our
noble lord.
His generous heart
has preserved intact for you
the chaste purity
of a still fairer flower.

RECITATIVO

CONTE
(a Figaro con sorpresa)
Cos'è questa commedia?

FIGARO
(a Susanna, piano)
Eccoci in danza,
Secondami, cor mio.

RECITATIVE

COUNT
(in surprise to Figaro)
What's all this nonsense?

FIGARO
(aside to Susanna)
Here we go:
back me up, my dear.

SUSANNA
(piano a Figaro)
Non ci ho speranza.

FIGARO
Signor, non disdegnate
Questo del nostro affetto
Meritato tributo. Or che aboliste
Un diritto sì ingrato a chi ben
ama . . .

CONTE
Quel diritto or non v'è più; cosa
si brama?

FIGARO
Della vostra saggezza il primo frutto
Oggi noi coglierem: le nostre nozze
Si son già stabilite: or a voi tocca
Costei, che un vostro dono
Illibata serbò, coprir di questa,
Simbolo d'onestà, candida vesta.

CONTE
(tra sè)
Diabolica astuzia!
Ma fingere convien.
(forte)
Son grato, amici,
Ad un senso sì onesto,
Ma non merto per questo
Nè tributi, nè lodi;
E un diritto ingiusto
Nè miei feudi abolendo
A natura, al dover lor dritti io
rendo.

TUTTI
Evviva, evviva, evviva,

SUSANNA
(malignamente)
Che virtù!

FIGARO
Che giustizia!

CONTE
(a Figaro e Susanna)
A voi prometto

SUSANNA
(aside to Figaro)
I'm not hopeful.

FIGARO
My lord, do not disdain
this humble expression of our affection,
Now that you've abolished
a privilege so painful to
lovers . . .

COUNT
That privilege exists no more: what
now?

FIGARO
Today we've come to gather the first
fruit of your generosity: our wedding
is already arranged: may it please
you to crown her, whom this gift
of yours has preserved spotless, with
this white veil, symbol of virtue.

COUNT
(aside)
Devilish sly!
But I must dissemble.
(aloud)
My friends, I thank you
for your honest feelings,
but for this I do not deserve
any tribute or praise;
it was an unjust privilege,
and by abolishing it in my domain
I have restored to nature and duty
their rights.

ALL
Hurrah! Hurrah! Hurrah!

SUSANNA
(sourly)
What nobility!

FIGARO
What justice!

COUNT
(to Figaro and Susanna)
To you I promise

Compier la cerimonia,
Chiedo sol breve indugio. Io voglio in faccia
De' miei più fidi, e con più ricca pompa
Rendervi appien felici.
(Marcellina si trovi.) Andate, amici.

8a. CORO

(spargendo il resto dei fiori)
Giovani liete,
Fiori spargete
Davanti al nobile
Nostro signor.
Il suo gran core
Vi serba intatto
D'un più bel fiore
L'almo candor.

(partono)

RECITATIVO

FIGARO
Evviva!

SUSANNA
Evviva!

BASILIO
Evviva!

FIGARO
(a Cherubino)
E voi non applaudite?

SUSANNA
È afflitto, poveretto,
Perchè il padron lo scaccia dal castello.

FIGARO
Ah, in un giorno sì bello!

SUSANNA
In un giorno di nozze!

to perform the ceremony,
but give me leave
awhile. I wish to complete your happiness
before my closest friends and in richest style.
(Marcellina must be found.) Leave me, friends.

8a. CHORUS

(scattering the remaining flowers)
Blithe maids,
scatter flowers
before our
noble lord.
His generous heart
has preserved intact for you
the chaste purity
of a still fairer flower.

(exeunt)

RECITATIVE

FIGARO
Hurrah!

SUSANNA
Hurrah!

BASILIO
Hurrah!

FIGARO
(to Cherubino)
And you're not cheering?

SUSANNA
He's unhappy, poor boy,
because my lord has dismissed him from the palace.

FIGARO
On this happiest of days!

SUSANNA
On a wedding day!

FIGARO
(al Conte)
Quando ognun v'ammira!

CHERUBINO
(s'inginocchia)
Perdono, mio signor . . .

CONTE
Nol meritate.

SUSANNA
Egli è ancora fanciullo.

CONTE
Men di quel che tu credi.

CHERUBINO
È ver, mancai; ma dal mio labbro alfine . . .

CONTE
(lo alza)
Ben, ben; io vi perdono.
Anzi, farò di più: vacante è un posto
D'uffizial nel reggimento mio;
Io scelgo voi; partite tosto; addio.
(Il Conte vuol partire, Susanna e Cherubino l'arrestano.)

SUSANNA E FIGARO
Ah! fin domani sol . . .

CONTE
No, parta tosto.

CHERUBINO
(con passione e sospirando)
A ubbidirvi, signor, son già disposto.

CONTE
Via, per l'ultima volta
La Susanna abbracciate.
(Cherubino abbraccia Susanna che rimane confusa.)
(tra sé)
Inaspettato è il colpo.

FIGARO
(to the Count)
When everyone applauds you!

CHERUBINO
(kneeling)
Forgive me, my lord . . .

COUNT
You don't deserve it.

SUSANNA
He's still a child.

COUNT
Less so than you think.

CHERUBINO
I did wrong, I know; but I'll never mention . . .

COUNT
(raising him)
Enough, enough: I pardon you.
Nay, I'll do more: there is a vacancy
for an officer in my regiment;
I nominate you; go at once; goodbye.
(He turns to go: Susanna and Cherubino stop him.)

SUSANNA AND FIGARO
Ah! just until tomorrow . . .

COUNT
No, he must go at once.

CHERUBINO
(passionately, sighing)
I'm ready, my lord, and will obey you.

COUNT
Then embrace Susanna
for the last time.
Cherubino embraces Susanna, who stands confused.)
(aside)
That took them by surprise.

FIGARO
(a Cherubino)
Ehi, capitano, a me pure la mano.
(piano)
Io vo' parlarti
Pria che tu parta.
(con finta gioia)
Addio, picciolo Cherubino,
Come cangia in un punto il tuo destino!

FIGARO
(to Cherubino)
Well, captain, won't you give me your hand?
(aside)
Before you go
I want a word with you.
(with assumed joy)
Goodbye, master Cherubino!
How your fate changes in a moment!

9. ARIA

9. ARIA

FIGARO
Non più andrai, farfallone amoroso,
Notte e giorno d'intorno girando,
Delle belle turbando il riposo,
Narcisetto, Adoncino d'amor.
Non più avrai questi bei pennacchini,
Quel cappello leggiero e galante,
Quella chioma, quell'aria brillante,
Quel vermiglio, donnesco color.
Tra guerrieri, poffar bacco!
Gran mustacchi, stretto sacco,
Schioppo in spalla, sciabla al fianco,
Collo dritto, muso franco,
Un gran casco, o un gran turbante,
Molto onor, poco contante,
Ed invece del fandango,
Una marcia per il fango.
Per montagne, per valloni,
Con le nevi e i sollïoni.
Al concerto di tromboni,
Di bombarde, di cannoni,
Che le palle in tutti i tuoni
All'orecchio fan fischiar.
Cherubino, alla vittoria,
Alla gloria militar.

(partono tutti al suono d'una marcia)

FIGARO
No more, you amorous butterfly,
will you go fluttering round by night and day,
disturbing the peace of every maid,
you pocket Narcissus, you Adonis of love.
No more will you have those fine feathers,
that light and dashing cap,
those curls, those airs and graces,
that roseate womanish colour.
You'll be among warriors, by Bacchus!
Long moustaches, knapsack tightly on,
musket on your shoulder, sabre at your side,
head erect and bold of visage,
a great helmet or a headdress,
lots of honour, little money,
and instead of the fandango,
marching through the mud.
Over mountains, through valleys,
in snow and days of listless heat,
to the sound of blunderbusses,
shells and cannons,
whose shots make your ears sing
on every note.
Cherubino, on to victory,
on to military glory!

(Exeunt omnes to the sound of a march)

ATTO SECONDO ACT II

SCENA PRIMA

Magnifica camera, con un' alcova, la porta d'entrata alla destra, un gabinetto alla sinistra, una porta in fondo – che dà adito alle stanze della cameriere – un finestra a lato

La Contessa, sola

10. CAVATINA

CONTESSA
Porgi, amor, qualche ristoro
Al mio duolo, a' miei sospiri:
O mi rendi il mio tesoro,
O mi lascia almen morir.

SCENE I

A handsome room with an alcove, the entrance on the right, a closet on the left, upstage a door which leads to the maids' rooms, a window on one side

The Countess, alone

10. CAVATINA

COUNTESS
O love, bring some relief
to my sorrow, to my sighs;
o give me back my loved one
or in mercy let me die.

SCENA SECONDA

La Contessa, Susanna, poi Figaro

RECITATIVO

CONTESSA
Vieni, cara Susanna
Finiscimi l'istoria.

SUSANNA
È già finita.

CONTESSA
Dunque volle sedurti?

SUSANNA
Oh, il signor Conte

SCENE 2

The Countess, Susanna, later Figaro

RECITATIVE

COUNTESS
Come in, dear Susanna,
and tell me the rest.

SUSANNA
There's no more to tell.

COUNTESS
So he tried to make love to you?

SUSANNA
Oh, his lordship

Non fa tai complimenti
Colle donne mie pari:
Egli venne a contrattar di denari.

CONTESSA
Ah, il crudel più non m'ama!

SUSANNA
E come poi
È geloso di voi!

CONTESSA
Come lo sono
I moderni mariti: per sistema
Infedeli, per genio capricciosi,
E per orgoglio poi tutti gelosi.
Ma se Figaro t'ama,
Ei sol potria . . .

FIGARO
(incomincia a cantare entro le quinte)
La la la . . .
La la la . . .

SUSANNA
Eccolo; vieni, amico:
Madama impaziente . . .

FIGARO
(con ilare disinvoltura)
A voi non tocca
Stare in pena per questo.
Alfin di che si tratta? Al signor Conte
Piace la sposa mia.
Indi secretamente
Ricuperar vorria
Il diritto feudale:
Possibile è cosa e naturale.

CONTESSA
Possibil!

SUSANNA
Natural!

FIGARO
Naturalissima!
E, se Susanna vuol, possibilissima.

doesn't pay such compliments
to girls like me;
he came to offer me money.

COUNTESS
Cruel man, he loves me no longer!

SUSANNA
Yet how
can he be jealous of you?

COUNTESS
That is the way
of modern husbands: on principle
unfaithful, by nature fickle,
and by pride all jealous.
But if Figaro loves you,
only he could . . .

FIGARO
(singing off-stage)
La la la . . .
la la la . . .

SUSANNA
Here he is! Come in, friend:
my lady's getting anxious . . .

FIGARO
(with gay coolness)
You've no call
to be worried about that.
After all, what's it all about?
My bride attracts
his lordship.
And so he'd like
secretly to revive
his feudal right:
it's all possible and natural.

COUNTESS
Possible!

SUSANNA
Natural!

FIGARO
Very natural!
And if Susanna consents, very possible.

SUSANNA
Finiscila una volta.

SUSANNA
Have done with you!

FIGARO
Ho già finito.
Quindi prese il partito
Di sceglier me corriero, e la Susanna
Consigliera segreta d'ambasciata:
E perch'ella ostinata ognor rifiuta
Il diploma d'onor ch'ei le destina,
Minaccia di protegger Marcellina.
Questo è tutto l'affare.

FIGARO
I've done.
That's why he decided
to choose me as courier, and Susanna
as confidential attachée to the embassy;
and because she persistently refuses
the post of honour he had planned for her,
he threatens to favour Marcellina.
That's the whole story.

SUSANNA
Ed hai coraggio di trattar scherzando
Un negozio sì serio?

SUSANNA
And you're so bold as to treat lightly
so serious a matter?

FIGARO
Non vi basta
Che scherzando io ci pensi? Ecco il progetto.
(alla Contessa)
Per Basilio un biglietto
Io gli fo capitar che l'avvertisca
Di certo appuntamento
Che per l'ora del ballo
A un amante voi deste.

FIGARO
Aren't you glad I can
treat it lightly? Here's my plan.
(to the Countess)
By Basilio I've sent a letter
warning his lordship
about an assignation
which you've made with a lover
for the time of the ball.

CONTESSA
O ciel! che sento!
Ad un uom sì geloso! . . .

COUNTESS
Great Heaven! What do I hear?
To so jealous a man! . . .

FIGARO
Ancora meglio,
Così potrem più presto imbarazzarlo,
Confonderlo, imbrogliarlo,
Rovesciargli i progetti,
Empierlo di sospetti, e porgli in testa
Che la moderna festa
Ch'ei di fare a me tenta, altri a lui faccia;
Onde quà perda il tempo, ivi la traccia.
Così quasi *ex abrupto,* e senza ch'abbia
Fatto per frastonarci alcun disegno
Vien l'ora delle nozze, e in faccia a

FIGARO
All the better;
the more easily can we harass him,
confuse him, embroil him
foil his designs,
fill him with suspicions, and make him
realise that this new game which
he's trying to play on me can be played on him.
So let him waste his time in fruitless search.
Then, without him having made any plan
to prevent us, the time of our wedding
will suddenly be upon us, and in your

lei
(segnando la Contessa)
Non fia ch'osi d'opporsi ai voti
miei.

presence
(indicating the Countess)
he'd not dare to
oppose it.

SUSANNA
È ver, ma in di lui vece
S'opporrà Marcellina.

SUSANNA
That's true, but in his stead
Marcellina will oppose it.

FIGARO
Aspetta: al Conte
Farai subito dir che verso sera
Attendati nel giardino:
Il picciol Cherubino,
Per mio consiglio non ancor partito,
Da femmina vestito,
Faremo che in tua vece ivi sen vada:
Questa è l'unica strada
Onde monsù, sorpreso da madama,
Sia costretto a far poi quel che si
brama.

FIGARO
Wait: quickly let the Count know
that towards evening
you'll be waiting in the garden:
we'll get young Cherubino,
whom I advised not to leave just yet,
to go there in your place,
dressed as a woman.
If monsieur is caught by milady,
this is the only way by which
he can be made to grant her
wishes.

CONTESSA
Che ti par?

COUNTESS
What do you think?

SUSANNA
Non c'è mal.

SUSANNA
Not bad.

CONTESSA
Nel nostro caso . . .

COUNTESS
In our situation . . .

SUSANNA
Quand'egli è persuaso . . .

SUSANNA
When he's determined . . .

CONTESSA
E dove è il tempo?

COUNTESS
Have we time enough?

FIGARO
Ito è il Conte alla caccia, e per
qualch'ora
Non sarà di ritorno:
(in alto di partire)
Io vado e tosto
Cherubino vi mando: lascio a voi
La cura di vestirlo.

FIGARO
The Count has gone out
hunting,
and won't be back for some hours;
(He is about to go.)
I'll go and send Cherubino
to you at once; I leave to you
the task of disguising him.

CONTESSA
E poi?

COUNTESS
And then?

FIGARO
E poi . . .

FIGARO
And then . . .

Se vuol ballare, Signor Contino, Il chitarrino Le suonerò. *(parte)*	if, my dear Count, you feel like dancing, it's I who'll call the tune. *(exit)*
SCENA TERZA	SCENE 3
La Contessa, Susanna, poi Cherubino	*The Countess, Susanna, later Cherubino*
RECITATIVO	RECITATIVE
CONTESSA Quanto duolmi, Susanna, Che questo giovinotto abbia de Conte Le stravaganze udite; ah tu non sai! . . . Ma per qual causa mai Da me stessa ei non venne? . . . Dov'è la canzonetta?	COUNTESS I'm grieved, Susanna, that that youth should have overheard the Count's follies: you just don't know . . . But why ever did he not come straight to me? Where's his song?
SUSANNA Eccola: appunto Facciam che ce la canti; Zitto: vien gente: è desso: avanti, avanti, *(Cherubino entra)* Signor uffiziale.	SUSANNA Here it is: and when he comes let's make him sing it. Hush, someone's coming: it's he. *(enter Cherubino)* Come in, my gallant captain.
CHERUBINO Ah, non chiamarmi Con nome sì fatale! ei mi rammenta Che abbandonar degg'io Comare tanto buona . . .	CHERUBINO Oh don't call me by that horrid title! It reminds me that I am forced to leave a godmother so kind.
SUSANNA E tanto bella!	SUSANNA And so beautiful!
CHERUBINO *(sospirando)* Ah . . . sì . . . certo . . .	CHERUBINO *(sighing)* Ah . . . . yes . . . indeed!
SUSANNA *(imitandolo)* Ah . . . sì . . . certo . . . ipocritone! Via, presto, la canzone Che stamane a me deste, A madama cantate.	SUSANNA *(imitating him)* Ah . . . yes, . . . indeed . . . You hypocrite! Make haste, sing to my lady the song you gave to me this morning.

CONTESSA
(aprendola)
Chi n'è l'autor?

SUSANNA
Guardate: egli ha due braccia
Di rossor sulla faccia

CONTESSA
Prendi la mia chitarra
E l'accompagna.

CHERUBINO
Io sono sì tremante . . .
Ma se madama vuole . . .

SUSANNA
Lo vuole, sì, lo vuol . . . manco parole.
(Susanna fa il ritornello sulla chitarra.)

11. CANZONA

CHERUBINO
Voi che sapete
Che cosa è amor,
Donne, vedete
S'io l'ho nel cor.
Quello ch'io provo
Vi ridirò;
È per me nuovo,
Capir nol so.
Sento un affetto
Pien di desir,
Ch'ora è diletto,
Ch'ora è martir.
Gelo, e poi sento
L'alma avvampar,
E in un momento
Torno a gelar.
Ricerco un bene
Fuori di me,
Non so chi'l tiene,
Non so cos'è.
Sospiro e gemo
Senza voler,
Palpito e tremo
Senza saper.
Non trovo pace
Notte, nè di,

COUNTESS
(taking the sheet)
Who wrote it?

SUSANNA
Look: he's blushing
all over his face.

COUNTESS
Take my guitar
and accompany him.

CHERUBINO
I'm all a-tremble . . .
but if my lady wishes . . .

SUSANNA
Yes, indeed she does . . . don't keep her waiting.
(She plays the introduction on the guitar.)

11. CANZONA

CHERUBINO
You ladies
who know what love is,
see if it is
what I have in my heart.
All that I feel
I will explain;
since it is new to me,
I don't understand it.
I have a feeling
full of desire,
which now is pleasure,
now is torment.
I freeze, then I feel
my spirit all ablaze,
and the next moment
turn again to ice.
I seek for a treasure
outside of myself;
I know not who holds it
nor what it is.
I sigh and I groan
without wishing to,
I flutter and tremble
without knowing why.
I find no peace
by night or day,

Ma pur mi piace
Languir così.
Voi che sapete
Che cosa è amor
Donne, vedete
S'io l'ho nel cor.

but yet to languish thus
is sheer delight.
You ladies
who know what love is,
see if it is
what I have in my heart.

RECITATIVO

RECITATIVE

CONTESSA
Bravo! che bella voce! io non sapeä
Che cantaste sì bene.

COUNTESS
Bravo! a charming voice!
I didn't know you sang so well.

SUSANNA
Oh, in verità
Egli fa tutto ben quello ch'ei fa
Presto, a noi, bel soldato:
Figaro v'informò . . .

SUSANNA
Oh, I must say
everything he does, he does well.
Come along, handsome soldier;
Figaro will have told you . . .

CHERUBINO
Tutto mi disse.

CHERUBINO
He's told me everything.

SUSANNA
Lasciatemi veder: andrà benissimo.
Siam d'uguale statura . . . Giù quel manto.
(gli cava il manto)

SUSANNA
Let me see: this will do splendidly.
We are of equal height . . . Off with that mantle!
(She takes off his mantle)

CONTESSA
Che fai?

COUNTESS
What are you doing?

SUSANNA
Niente paura.

SUSANNA
There's nothing to fear.

CONTESSA
E se qualcuno entrasse?

COUNTESS
But if someone should come in?

SUSANNA
Entri, che mal facciamo?
La porta chiuderò.
(chiude la porta)
Ma come poi
Acconciargli i capelli?

SUSANNA
Let him; what harm are we doing?
But I'll lock the door.
(She does so.)
But how am I
to dress his hair?

CONTESSA
Una mia cuffia
Prendi nel gabinetto.
Presto. Che carta è quella?
(Susanna va nel gabinetto a pigliare una cuffia; Cherubino si accosta alla Contessa, e le lascia vedere

COUNTESS
Take one of my caps
from my dressing room.
Quickly! What is this paper?
(Susanna goes into the closet to get a cap: Cherubino approaches the Countess and shows her his commission, which is

la patente che terrà in petto; la Contessa la prende, la apre e vede che manca il sigillo)

sticking out of his breast pocket. The Countess takes it, opens it and notices that the seal is missing)

CHERUBINO
La patente.

CHERUBINO
My commission.

CONTESSA
Che sollecita gente!

COUNTESS
They're in a hurry!

CHERUBINO
L'ebbi oror da Basilio.

CHERUBINO
I've just had it from Basilio.

CONTESSA
Dalla fretta obliato hanno il sigileo.

COUNTESS
In their haste they've forgotton the seal.

SUSANNA
(tornando)
Il sigillo di che?

SUSANNA
(coming back)
What seal?

CONTESSA
Della patente.

COUNTESS
Of his commission.

SUSANNA
Cospetto! che premura!
Ecco la cuffia.

SUSANNA
What, so soon!
Here's the cap.

CONTESSA
Spicciati: va bene.
Miserabili noi, se il Conte viene.

COUNTESS
Hurry! That's right.
Woe betide us if the Count should come.

12. ARIA

SUSANNA
Venite . . . inginocchiatevi . . .
Restate fermo lì . . .
Pian piano, or via giratevi . . .
Bravo . . . va ben così.
La faccia ora volgetemi,
Olà! quegli occhi a me . . .
Drittissimo . . . guardatemi . . .
Madama qui non è.
Più alto quel colletto,
Quel ciglio un po' più basso.
Le mani sotto il petto . . .
Vedremo poscia il passo
Quando sarete in piè.
(piano alla Contessa)
Mirate il bricconcello,
Mirate quanto è bello,
Che furba guardatura,

12. ARIA

SUSANNA
Come . . . kneel down . . .
stay still here . . .
keep quiet; now turn round . . .
bravo . . . that's very good.
Now turn and face me,
here! your eyes towards me . . .
look straight in front at me . . .
my lady isn't here.
That collar a bit higher,
those eyes cast down,
your hands folded before you . . .
then let's see how you walk
when you're on your feet.
(aside to the Countess)
Look at the little rascal,
isn't he handsome?
What roguish glances,

Che vezzo, che figura!
Se l'amano le femmine,
Han certo il lor perchè.

what airs, what graces!
If women fall in love with him,
they have good reason why.

RECITATIVO

RECITATIVE

CONTESSA
Quante buffonerie!

COUNTESS
This is too silly!

SUSANNA
Ma se ne sono
Io medesma gelosa:
(prende pel mento Cherubino)
Ehi, serpentello,
Volete tralasciar d'esser sì bello!

SUSANNA
I'm almost inclined
to be jealous myself.
(taking Cherubino by the chin)
You little scamp,
you've no right to look so pretty!

CONTESSA
Finiam le ragazzate;
Or quelle maniche
Oltre il gomito gli alza,
Onde più agiatamente
L'abito gli si adatti.

COUNTESS
No more of this nonsense!
Now pull these sleeves up
above the elbow,
then the dress will go on
more comfortably.

SUSANNA
(eseguisce)
Ecco.

SUSANNA
(does so)
There!

CONTESSA
Più indietro.
Così . . .
(scoprendo un nastro onde ha fasciato il braccio)
Che nastro è quello?

COUNTESS
Still higher,
like that . . .
(She discovers a ribbon tied round his arm.)
What's this ribbon?

SUSANNA
È quel ch'esso involommi.

SUSANNA
That's the one he stole from me.

CONTESSA
E questo sangue?

COUNTESS
And this blood?

CHERUBINO
(turbato)
Quel sangue . . . io non so come . . .
Poco pria sdrucciolando
In un sasso la pelle io mi sgraffiai,
E la piaga col nastro io mi fasciai.

CHERUBINO
(confused)
Blood? I don't know how . . .
I slipped a little while ago
and grazed myself against a stone,
so I tied up the scratch with this ribbon.

SUSANNA
Mostrate: non è mal! Cospetto! ha il braccio
Più candido del mio! Qualche

SUSANNA
Let's see: it's nothing much.
Look!
His arm's whiter than mine!

ragazza . . .

CONTESSA
E segui a far la pazza?
Va nel mio gabinetto, e prendi un un poco
D'inglese taffetà, ch'e sullo scrigno.
(Susanna parte, La Contessa osserva attentamente Cherubino inginocchiato)
In quanto al nastro . . . inver . . .
(guarda un poco il suo nastro)
Per il colore . . .
Mi spiacea di privarmene . . .

SUSANNA
(le dà il taffetà e le forbici)
Tenete:
E da legargli il braccio?

CONTESSA
Un altro nastro
Prendi insiem col mio vestito.
(Susanna parte per la porta ch'è in fondo e porta seco il mantello di Cherubino)

CHERUBINO
Ah! più presto m'avria quello guarito.

CONTESSA
Perchè? Questo è migliore!

CHERUBINO
Allor che un nastro
Legò la chioma, ovver toccò la pelle . . .
D'oggetto . . .

CONTESSA
(interrompendolo)
. . . Forestiero,
È buon per le ferite, non è vero?
Guardate qualità ch'io non sapea!

CHERUBINO
Madama scherza ed io frattanto parto.

Like a girl's . . .

COUNTESS
Are you still chattering?
Go into my room, and fetch a piece
of plaster which is on my desk.
(Exit Susanna. The Countess looks hard at the kneeling Cherubino)
As for this ribbon . . . I'd say . . .
(examining the ribbon)
By the colour . . .
I'm sorry to have lost it . . .

SUSANNA
(bringing the plaster and scissors)
Here it is.
Now what to tie his arm with?

COUNTESS
Bring another ribbon
along with my dress.
(Exit Susanna by the rear door, taking with her Cherubino's mantle)

CHERUBINO
Ah! that one would have healed me faster.

COUNTESS
Why? A new one will be better.

CHERUBINO
But when a ribbon
has bound the hair, or touched the skin
of some . . .

COUNTESS
(interrupting him)
. . . other person,
it's good for wounds, is that it?
That's a virtue I was not aware of!

CHERUBINO
My lady mocks me when I must leave her.

CONTESSA
Poverin, che sventura!

CHERUBINO
Oh me infelice!

CONTESSA
Or piange!

CHERUBINO
Oh ciel! perchè morir non lice!
Forse vicino all'ultimo momento . . .
Questa bocca oseria . . .

CONTESSA
Siate saggio: cos'è questa follia?
(gli asciuga gli occhi col fazzoletto)
Chi picchia alla mia porta?

SCENA QUARTA

CONTE
(fuori della porta)
Perchè chiusa?

CONTESSA
Il mio sposo: Oh Dei! son morta!
Voi qui senza mantello!
In questo stato, un ricevuto foglio . . .
La sua gran gelosia!

CONTE
(con più forza)
Cosa indugiate?

CONTESSA
Son sola, sì, son sola.

CONTE
Ed a chi parlate?

CONTESSA
A voi . . . certo . . . a voi stesso . . .

CHERUBINO
Dopo quel ch'è successo, il suo furore . . .
Non trovo altro consiglio!

(Cherubino entra nel gabinetto,

COUNTESS
Poor boy, it's hard!

CHERUBINO
I'm so unhappy!

COUNTESS
What, crying?

CHERUBINO
O Heaven! would that I could die now!
Perhaps near the final moment
these lips would dare . . .

COUNTESS
Be sensible: what is this nonsense?
(She wipes his eyes with her handkerchief.)
Who's knocking at the door?

SCENE 4

COUNT
(outside the door)
Why is this locked?

COUNTESS
My husband! O Heavens, I'm lost!
You here without a coat on!
In this state; he'll have had that letter . . .
and he's so jealous!

COUNT
(more loudly)
What is delaying you?

COUNTESS
I'm alone, all alone.

COUNT
To whom were you talking?

COUNTESS
To you . . . of course, to you.

CHERUBINO
After what's happened, he'll be furious . . .
I don't know what to do!

(He goes into the closet and locks the

chiude la porta; la Contessa prende la chiave e corre ad aprire al Conte)

CONTESSA
Ah, mi difenda il cielo
in tal periglio!

SCENA QUINTA

La Contessa ed il Conte vestito da cacciatore

CONTE
Che novità! non fu mai vostra usanza
Di richiudervi in stanza!

COUNTESSA
È ver; ma io . . .
Io stava qui mettendo . . .

CONTE
Via, mettendo . . .

CONTESSA
Certe robe . . .
Era meco la Susanna . . .
Che in sua camera è andata.

CONTE
Ad ogni modo,
Voi non siete tranquilla:
Guardate questo foglio.

CONTESSA
(tra sè)
Numi! è il foglio
Che Figaro scrisse!
(Cherubino fa cadere un tavolino e una sedia, in gabinetto, con molto strepito)

CONTE
Cos'è questo strepito? in gabinetto
Qualche cosa è caduto.

CONTESSA
Io non intesi niente.

CONTE
Convien che abbiate i gran pensieri
in mente.

door: the Countess takes the key and runs to admit the Count)

COUNTESS
Heaven protect me in
this danger!

SCENE 5

The Countess and the Count in hunting clothes

COUNT
What does this mean? You never used
to lock yourself in your room!

COUNTESS
I know; but I . . .
I was in here trying . . .

COUNT
Go on, trying . . .

COUNTESS
. . . some clothes on . . .
Susanna was with me . . .
but now she's gone to her room.

COUNT
In any case,
you seem perturbed:
look at this letter.

COUNTESS
(aside)
Heavens! it's the letter
Figaro wrote!
(Cherubino noisily knocks over a table and chair in the closet)

COUNT
What is that noise?
Something fell in the closet.

COUNTESS
I heard nothing.

COUNT
You must have weighty matters on your
mind.

CONTESSA
Di che?

COUNTESS
Of what?

CONTE
Là v'è qualcuno.

COUNT
There's someone there.

CONTESSA
Chi volete che sia?

COUNTESS
Who do you think it could be?

CONTE
Lo chiedo a voi . . .
Io vengo in questo punto.

COUNT
I'm asking you . . .
I've only just come in.

CONTESSA
Ah sì, Susanna . . . appunto . . .

COUNTESS
Ah yes, Susanna . . . of course.

CONTE
Che passò, mi diceste, alla sua stanza.

COUNT
But you told me she went to her room.

CONTESSA
Alla sua stanza, o qui, non vidi bene . . .

COUNTESS
To hers or mine, I didn't notice . . .

CONTE
Susanna! E d'onde viene
Che siete sì turbata?

COUNT
Then why, if it's Susanna,
are you so agitated?

CONTESSA
(con un risolino sforzato)
Per la mia cameriera.

COUNTESS
(with a forced smile)
About my maid.

SCENA SESTA

I suddetti

SCENE 6

The above

CONTE
Io non so nulla:
Ma turbata senz'altro . . .

COUNT
I don't know;
but certainly you're agitated . . .

CONTESSA
Ah quella serva
Più che non turba me, turba voi stesso.

COUNTESS
Rather than agitating me,
which she doesn't, my maid is agitating you.

CONTE
È vero, è vero, e lo vedrete adesso.
(Susanna entra per la porta ond'è uscita, e si ferma vedendo il Conte, che dalla parte del gabinetto sta favellando)

COUNT
That's true indeed, as you'll see.
(Susanna enters by the door through which she went out, but stops on seeing the Count, who is talking by the door to the closet)

13. TERZETTO

CONTE
Susanna, or via, sortite,
Sortite, così vo'.

CONTESSA
(al Conte, affannata)
Fermatevi . . . sentite . . .
Sortire ella non può.

SUSANNA
(tra sè)
Cos'è codesta lite?
Il paggio dove andò?

CONTE
E chi vietarlo or osa? Chi?

CONTESSA
Lo vieta l'onestà.
Un abito da sposa
Provando ella si sta.

CONTE
(tra sè)
Chiarissima è la cosa:
L'amante qui sarà.

CONTESSA
(tra sè)
Bruttissima è la cosa:
Chi sa cosa sarà.

SUSANNA
(tra sè)
Capisco qualche cosa:
Veggiamo come va.

CONTE
Dunque, parlate almeno,
Susanna, se qui siete . . .

CONTESSA
Nemmen, nemmen, nemmeno,
Io v'ordino, tacete.
(Susanna si nasconde entro l'alcova.)

SUSANNA
Oh cielo! un precipizio,

13. TRIO

COUNT
Susanna, come out of there,
come out, I command you.

COUNTESS
(distressed, to the Count)
No, stop . . . listen . . .
she can't come out.

SUSANNA
(aside)
What's this row about?
Where has the page got to?

COUNT
And who dares forbid it? Who?

COUNTESS
Decency forbids it.
She's in there
trying on her wedding dress.

COUNT
(aside)
It's all too plain:
there's a lover in there.

COUNTESS
(aside)
It's all too horrible:
whatever will happen?

SUSANNA
(aside)
I think I understand:
let's see how things work out.

COUNT
Well, at least speak,
Susanna, if you're there . . .

COUNTESS
No, no, you're not to.
I order you, be silent.
(Susanna hides in the alcove.)

SUSANNA
Oh Lord! There's bound to be

Un scandalo, un disordine
Qui certo nascerà.

a catastrophe,
an open scandal.

CONTESSA E CONTE
Consorte mio (a), giudizio!
Un scandalo, un disordine
Schiviam, per carità.

COUNTESS AND COUNT
Be careful, pray!
Try to avoid
an open scandal.

RECITATIVO

RECITATIVE

CONTE
Dunque, voi non aprite?

COUNT
Then you won't open it?

CONTESSA
E perchè deggio
Le mie camere aprir?

COUNTESS
Why do I have
to open my own room?

CONTE
Ebben, lasciate . . .
L'aprirem senza chiavi . . . ehi gente . . .

COUNT
Very well then; as you please . . .
we'll open it without the key . . .
Ho there!

CONTESSA
Come?
Porreste a repentaglio
D'una dama l'onore?

COUNTESS
What!
Would you hazard
a lady's reputation?

CONTE
È vero, io sbaglio.
Posso senza rumore,
Senza scandalo alcun di nostra gente
Andar io stesso a prender l'occorrente:
Attendete pur qui . . . ma perchè in tutto
Sia il mio dubbio distrutto
Ancor le porte io prima
Chiuderò.
(chiude a chiave la porta di fondo che conduce alle stanze delle camieriere)

COUNT
That's true; I was in error.
I can go myself and bring the tools
without any outcry
or scandal before the servants.
Kindly remain here . . .
But so that my suspicions
shall be completely quieted,
first of all I'll lock the other doors.
(He locks the door upstage leading to the servants' quarters)

CONTESSA
(tra sè)
Che imprudenza!

COUNTESS
(aside)
What folly!

CONTE
Voi la condiscendenza
Di venir meco avrete.
(con affettata ilarità)
Madama, eccovi il braccio. Andiamo.

COUNT
You will have the goodness
to come with me.
(with assumed gaiety)
Let me offer you my arm. Let's go.

CONTESSA
(con ribrezzo)
Andiamo.

CONTE
(accenna il gabinetto)
Susanna starà qui finche torniamo.

(partono)

SCENA SETTIMA

Susanna esce dall'alcova in fretta, poi Cherubino

14. DUETTINO

SUSANNA
(alla porta del gabinetto)
Aprite, presto, aprite:
Aprite, è la Susanna.
Sortite, via, sortite . . .
Andate via di quà.

CHERUBINO
(uscendo, confuso e senza fiato)
Ahimè, che scena orribile!
Che gran fatalità!
(Si accostano ora ad una, ora ad un'altra porta, e le trovano tutte chiuse)

SUSANNA E CHERUBINO
Le porte son serrate.
Che mai sarà!

CHERUBINO
Qui perdersi non giova.

SUSANNA
V'uccide, se vi trova.

CHERUBINO
Veggiamo un po' qui fuori.
(s'affacia alla finestra che mette in giardino)
Dà proprio nel giardino.
(fa un moto come per voler saltarvi giù; Susanna lo trattiene)

COUNTESS
(with a shiver)
Let's go.

COUNT
(indicating the closet)
Susanna will have to stay there till we return.

(exeunt)

SCENE 7

Susanna hurries out of the alcove; later Cherubino

14. DUET

SUSANNA
(at the door of the closet)
Open quickly, open;
open, it's Susanna.
Come out of there . . .
you must get away at once.

CHERUBINO
(coming out, confused and breathless)
Oh dear, what a terrible scene!
What a dreadful thing to happen!
(They try first one door, then another, but find them all locked)

SUSANNA AND CHERUBINO
The doors are locked.
Whatever shall we do?

CHERUBINO
We can't give up.

SUSANNA
He'll kill you if he finds you.

CHERUBINO
Just let me look outside here.
(goes to the window overlooking the garden)
It gives on to the garden.
(He is about to jump out; Susanna stops him.)

SUSANNA
(trattenendolo)
Fermate, Cherubino!
Fermate, per pietà!

CHERUBINO
Qui perdersi non giova!
M'uccide, se mi trova.

SUSANNA
Tropp'alto per un salto.

CHERUBINO
Lasciami: pria di nuocerle
Nel foco volerei.
Abbraccio te per lei.
(si scioglie da Susanna)
Addio, così si fa.

SUSANNA
Ei va a perire, oh Dei!
Fermate, per pietà.
(Cherubino salta fuori; Susanna mette un alto grido, siede un momento, poi va al balcone)

RECITATIVO

O guarda il demonietto! come fugge!
È già un miglio lontano.
Ma non perdiamci invano.
Entriam nel gabinetto:
Venga poi lo smargiasso, io qui l'aspetto.

(Susanna entra nel gabinetto e si chiude dietro la porta)

SCENA OTTAVA

La Contessa ed il Conte con l'occorente per aprire la porta: al suo arrivo esamina tutte le porte

CONTE
Tutto è come il lasciai; volete dunque
Aprir voi stessa, o deggio . . .
(in atto di aprir a forza la porta)

SUSANNA
(holding him back)
Cherubino, stop!
Don't, for pity's sake!

CHERUBINO
We can't give up.
He'll kill me if he finds me.

SUSANNA
It's too high to jump.

CHERUBINO
Let me go: rather than harm her
I'd leap into the fire.
I embrace her through you.
(freeing himself from Susanna)
Farewell; so be it!

SUSANNA
He'll kill himself, for certain.
Stop, for pity's sake!
(Cherubino jumps out: Susanna lets out a shriek, sits down for a moment, then goes to the balcony)

RECITATIVE

Just look at the little demon! how he runs!
He's a mile away already.
There's no time to lose, though.
I'll go into the closet:
let the blusterer come: I'm ready for him.

(goes into the closet and locks the door behind her)

SCENE 8

The Countess, and the Count with tools for opening the door: he examines all the doors

COUNT
All is as I left it; so will you
open it yourself, or must I . . .
(He is about to force the door open)

CONTESSA
Ahimè, fermate,
E ascoltatemi un poco.
(Il Conte getta il martello e la tenaglia sopra una sedia)
Mi credete capace
Di mancare al dover?

COUNTESS
Alas! stay
and hear me for a moment.
(The Count throws the hammer and pincers on a chair)
Do you think me capable
of failing in my duty?

CONTE
Come vi piace.
Entro quel gabinetto
Chi v'è chiuso vedrò.

COUNT
As you please.
I'm going into that room
to see who's locked in there.

CONTESSA
(timida e tremante)
Sì, lo vedrete . . .
Ma uditemi tranquillo.

COUNTESS
(fearfully)
Yes, you'll see . . .
but listen to me calmly.

CONTE
(alterato)
Non è dunque Susanna!

COUNT
(angrily)
So it's not Susanna!

CONTESSA
No, ma invece un oggetto
Che ragion di sospetto
Non vi deve lasciar: per questa sera
Una burla innocente
Di farsi disponeva . . . ed io vi giuro
Che l'onor . . . l'onestà . . .

COUNTESS
No, but it's someone else
whom you could not reasonably
allow yourself to suspect: for tonight
I was preparing a harmless
diversion . . . and I swear to you
in honour . . . in honesty . . .

CONTE
(più alterato)
Chi è dunque? dite . . .
L'ucciderò.

COUNT
(angrier still)
Who is it? Tell me . . .
I'll kill him.

CONTESSA
Sentite . . .
Ah, non ho cor.

COUNTESS
Listen . . .
Oh, I dare not.

CONTE
Parlate.

COUNT
Speak out.

CONTESSA
È un fanciullo . . .

COUNTESS
He's a child . . .

CONTE
Un fanciul?

COUNT
A child?

CONTESSA
Sì, Cherubino.

COUNTESS
Yes; Cherubino.

CONTE
(tra sè)
E mi farà il destino
Ritrovar questo paggio in ogni loco!
(forte)
Come? non è partito? scellerati!
Ecco i dubbi spiegati, ecco l'imbroglio,
Ecco il raggiro onde m'avverte il foglio.

15. FINALE

Il Conte, la Contessa, poi Susanna nel gabinetto

CONTE
(alla porta del gabinetto, con impeto)
Esci, ormai, garzon malnato,
Sciagurato, non tardar.

CONTESSA
(Ritira a forza il Conte dal gabinetto)
Ah signore, quel furore
Per lui fammi il cor tremar.

CONTE
E d'opporvi ancor osate?

CONTESSA
No, sentite . . .

CONTE
Via, parlate.

CONTESSA
Giuro al ciel, ch'ogni sospetto . . .
E lo stato in che il trovate . . .
Sciolto il collo . . . nudo il petto . . .

CONTE
Sciolto il colo? . . . nudo il petto? . . .
seguitate . . .

CONTESSA
Per vestir femminee spoglie.

COUNT
(aside)
Has destiny decreed that I'm to find that page wherever I go?
(aloud)
What! Hasn't he gone? The scoundrels!
This explains my doubts, the confusion,
the plot of which the letter warned me.

15. FINALE

The Count and Countess, later Susanna in the closet

COUNT
(vehemently, at the closet door)
Now out you come, you imp of Satan,
you villain, without delay.

COUNTESS
(restraining the Count by force)
Oh my lord, your anger
makes my heart tremble for him.

COUNT
You still dare to cross me?

COUNTESS
Only listen . . .

COUNT
Go on, speak.

COUNTESS
I swear to heaven that your suspicions . . .
the state in which you'll find him . . .
his collar untied . . . his chest bare . . .

COUNT
His collar untied? . . . his chest bare? . . .
Pray continue . . .

COUNTESS
So as to dress him up as a woman.

CONTE
Ah comprendo, indegna moglie,
Mi vo' tosto vendicar!
(s'appressa al gabinetto, poi torna indietro)

COUNT
Ah, I see; you shameless creature,
I'll punish him for this!
(goes to the closet, then turns back)

CONTESSA
(con forza)
Mi fa torto quel trasporto,
M'oltraggiate a dubitar.

COUNTESS
(firmly)
Your anger does me wrong,
your suspicion is an insult.

CONTE
Quà la chiave!

COUNT
Give me the key!

CONTESSA
Egli è innocente,
Voi sapete . . .
(La Contessa porge al Conte la chiave)

COUNTESS
He is innocent,
and you know it . . .
(She hands him the key)

CONTE
Non so niente.
Va lontan dagli occhi miei.
Un'infida, un'empia sei . . .
E mi cerchi d'infamar.

COUNT
I know nothing of the sort.
Hence from my sight!
You are faithless, wanton . . .
you've sought to disgrace me.

CONTESSA
Vado . . . sì . . . ma . . .

COUNTESS
I'll go . . . yes . . . but . . .

CONTE
Non ascolto.

COUNT
I'll not hear you.

CONTESSA
Non son rea . . .

COUNTESS
I am guiltless.

CONTE
Vel leggo in volto.
Mora, mora, e più non sia
Ria cagion del mio penar!

COUNT
I can read it in your face.
He shall die, and I'll be rid
of the source of all my torment!

CONTESSA
Oh, la cieca gelosia
Qualche eccesso gli fa far!
(Il Conte apre il gabinetto e Susanna esce sulla porta ed ivi si ferma)

COUNTESS
Oh, to what extreme will
his blind fury lead him?
(The Count opens the closet and Susanna steps out, staying in the doorway)

SCENA NONA

I suddetti, e Susanna ch'esce dal gabinetto

SCENE 9

The above, and Susanna coming out of the closet

CONTE E CONTESSA
(con maraviglia)
Susanna!

COUNT AND COUNTESS
(in amazement)
Susanna!

SUSANNA
Signore!
Cos'è quel stupore?
(con ironia)
Il brando prendete,
Il paggio uccidete,
Quel paggio malnato,
Vedetelo qua.
(ognuno tra sè)

SUSANNA
Your servant!
Why this astonishment?
(ironically)
You've drawn your sword
to kill the page.
Well, here you see
that imp of Satan.
(all speak aside)

CONTE
Che veggio, la testa
Girando mi va.

COUNT
What do I see?
My head is spinning.

CONTESSA
Che storia è mai questa!
Susanna v'è là?

COUNTESS
What can have happened?
Susanna in there?

SUSANNA
Confusa han la testa,
Non san come va.

SUSANNA
They're both baffled
and can't understand.

CONTE
(forte)
Sei sola?

COUNT
(aloud)
Are you alone?

SUSANNA
Guardate,
Qui ascoso sarà.

SUSANNA
Look and see
who can be hidden there.

CONTE
Guardiamo, guardiamo,
Qui ascoso sarà.
(Il Conte entra nel gabinetto)

COUNT
Yes, let's see
who is hidden in there.
(He goes into the closet.)

CONTESSA
Susanna, son morta:
Il fiato mi manca.

COUNTESS
Susanna, I'm fainting;
I can't breathe.

SUSANNA
(Allegrissima, addita alla Contessa la finestra ond'e saltato Cherubino)
Più lieta, più franca,
In salvo è di già.

SUSANNA
(gaily, showing the Countess the window from which Cherubino jumped)
Don't worry, take heart now,
he's already in safety.

CONTE
(esce confuso dal gabinetto)

COUNT
(comes out in confusion)

Che sbaglio mai presi!
Appena lo credo;
Se a torto v'offesi
Perdono vi chiedo,
Ma far burla simile
È poi crudeltà.

How could I make such a mistake!
I can hardly believe it.
If I did you wrong,
I beg your forgiveness;
but to play such a jest
is sheer cruelty.

SUSANNA E CONTESSA
(La Contessa col fazzoletto alla bocca per celare il disordine di spirito)
Le vostre follie
Non mertan pietà.

SUSANNA AND COUNTESS
(The Countess holds a handkerchief to her lips to cover her perturbation)
Your wild accusations
do not deserve to be pardoned.

CONTE
Io v'amo!

COUNT
I love you!

CONTESSA
Nol dite!
(rinvenendo dalla confusione a poco a poco)

COUNTESS
Do not say that!
(recovering gradually from her confusion)

CONTE
Vel giuro!

COUNT
I swear it!

CONTESSA
(con forza e collera)
Mentite!
Son l'empia, l'infida
Che ognora v'inganna.

COUNTESS
(firmly and angrily)
That is untrue!
I'm a faithless, wanton creature
who's always deceiving you.

CONTE
Quell'ira Susanna
M'aita a calmar.

COUNT
Help me, Susanna,
to calm her anger.

SUSANNA
Così si condanna
Chi può sospettar.

SUSANNA
This is the punishment
for your suspicions.

CONTESSA
(con risentimento)
Adunque la fede
D'un'anima amante
Sì fiera mercede
Doveva sperar?

COUNTESS
(agitated)
So this is the reward
I can expect
for the loyalty
of my faithful heart!

CONTE
Quell'ira, Susanna,
M'aita a calmar.

COUNT
Help me, Susanna,
to calm her anger.

SUSANNA
(in atto di preghiera)
Signora!

SUSANNA
(pleading)
My lady!

CONTE
Rosina!

COUNT
Rosina!

CONTESSA
Crudele!
Più quella non sono,
Ma il misero oggetto
Del vostro abbandono,
Che avete diletto
Di far disperar.

COUNTESS
Cruel man!
I am no longer she,
but the wretched object
of your neglect,
whom you delight
to make suffer.

SUSANNA E CONTE
Confuso, pentito,
Son (È) troppo punito;
Abbiate pietà.

SUSANNA AND COUNT
Confused and repentant,
I'm (he's) sufficiently punished;
have pity now.

CONTESSA
Soffrir sì gran torto
Quest'alma non sa.

COUNTESS
My heart cannot bear
so great a wrong.

CONTE
Ma il paggio rinchiuso? . . .

COUNT
But the page locked in there? . . .

CONTESSA
Fu sol per provarvi.

COUNTESS
It was only to test you.

CONTE
Ma i tremiti, i palpiti? . . .

COUNT
And all your trembling? . . .

CONTESSA
Fu sol per burlarvi.

COUNTESS
Only to tease you.

CONTE
Ma un foglio sì barbaro? . . .

COUNT
But this cruel letter? . . .

SUSANNA E CONTESSA
Di Figaro è il foglio,
E a voi per Basilio . . .

SUSANNA AND COUNTESS
Figaro wrote it,
and sent it by Basilio . . .

CONTE
Ah perfidi! io voglio . . .

COUNT
The traitors! I'll . . .

SUSANNA E CONTESSA
Perdono non merta
Chi agli altri non dà.

SUSANNA AND COUNTESS
He who can't forgive others
doesn't deserve to be forgiven.

CONTE
(con tenerezza)
Ebben, se vi piace,
Comune è la pace;
Rosina inflessibile
Con me non sarà.

COUNT
(tenderly)
Well then, if you will,
let's make peace all round;
Rosina, do not be
so harsh to me.

CONTESSA
Ah quanto, Susanna,
Son dolce di core!
Di donna al furore
Chi più crederà?

COUNTESS
Oh, Susanna,
how soft-hearted I am!
Who would ever believe
in a woman's fury?

SUSANNA
Cogli uomin, signora,
Girate, volgete,
Vedrete che ognora
Sì cade poi là.

SUSANNA
With men, my lady,
you turn and turn about,
but you see it always
ends like this.

CONTE
(con tenerezza)
Guardatemi . . .

COUNT
(tenderly)
Look at me . . .

CONTESSA
Ingrato!

COUNTESS
Ungrateful!

CONTE
Ho torto, e mi pento!
(Il Conte bacia e ribacia la mano della Contessa)

COUNT
I wronged you, and I repent it!
(He kisses the Countess's hand repeatedly)

A TRE
Da questo momento
Quest'alma a conoscervi (mi, la)
Apprender potrà.

ALL
From this moment
my (his) heart will learn
to know you (me, her) better.

SCENA DECIMA

SCENE 10

I suddetti e Figaro

The above and Figaro

FIGARO
Signori, di fuori
Son già i suonatori:
Le trombe sentite,
I pifferi udite.
Tra canti, tra balli
De' vostri vassalli,
Corriamo, voliamo
Le nozze a compir!
(Figaro prende Susanna sotto il braccio e va per partire, il Conte

FIGARO
My lord and lady,
the musicians are outside:
you can hear
the trumpeters and the pipers.
With the singing and dancing
of your vassals,
let us hasten
to celebrate our wedding!
(He takes Susanna by the arm and is about to lead her off:

lo trattiene.)

CONTE
Pian piano, men fretta.

FIGARO
La turba m'aspetta.

CONTE
Un dubbio toglietemi
In pria di partir.

SUSANNA E CONTESSA
La cosa è scabrosa;
Com'ha da finir?

CONTE
Con arte le carte
Convien qui scoprir.
(mostrando il foglio ricevuto da Basilio)
Conoscete, signor Figaro,
Questo foglio chi vergò?

FIGARO
(finge d'esaminare il foglio)
Nol conosco.

SUSANNA, CONTESSA E CONTE
Nol conosci?

FIGARO
No, no.

SUSANNA
E nol desti a Don Basilio?

CONTESSA
Per recarlo?

CONTE
Tu c'intendi?

FIGARO
Oibò, oibò.

SUSANNA
E non sai del damerino . . .

CONTESSA
Che stasera nel giardino . . .

the Count detains him.)

COUNT
One moment: not so fast.

FIGARO
The crowd is waiting.

COUNT
Before you go,
remove a doubt of mine.

SUSANNA AND COUNTESS
This is getting difficult;
how will it end?

COUNT
Now I must
play my cards carefully.
(showing the letter received from Basilio)
Master Figaro, do you know
who penned this letter?

FIGARO
(pretending to examine it)
I've no idea.

SUSANNA, COUNTESS AND COUNT
You've no idea?

FIGARO
No, no.

SUSANNA
Didn't you give it to Don Basilio?

COUNTESS
To deliver?

COUNT
You understand us?

FIGARO
No, no.

SUSANNA
You don't know about the gallant . . .

COUNTESS
This evening in the garden . . .

CONTE
Già capisci . . .

FIGARO
Io non lo so.

CONTE
Cerchi invan difesa e scusa.
Il tuo ceffo già t'accusa;
Vedo ben che vuoi mentir.

FIGARO
Mente il ceffo, io già non mento.

SUSANNA E CONTESSA
(a Figaro)
Il talento aguzzi invano:
Palesato abbiam l'arcano,
Non v'è nulla da ridir.

CONTE
Che rispondi?

FIGARO
Niente, niente

CONTE
Dunque, accordi?

FIGARO
Non accordo.

SUSANNA E CONTESSA
(a Figaro)
Eh via, chetati, balordo,
La burletta ha da finir.

FIGARO
(prende Susanna sotto il braccio)
Per finirla lietamente
E all'usanza teatrale,
Un'azion matrimoniale
Le farem ora seguir.

SUSANNA, CONTESSA E FIGARO
Deh! signor, nol contrastate;
Consolate i miei (lor) desir.

CONTE
(tra sè)
Marcellina, Marcellina,

COUNT
You know now . . .

FIGARO
I've no idea.

COUNT
In vain you seek a defence or an excuse.
Your very face accuses you;
I can see you're trying to lie.

FIGARO
My face is the liar, not I!

SUSANNA AND COUNTESS
(to Figaro)
You sharpen your wits in vain;
we've revealed the secret,
there's no more to be said.

COUNT
What's your answer?

FIGARO
Nothing, nothing.

COUNT
So you admit it?

FIGARO
No, I don't, sir.

SUSANNA AND COUNTESS
(to Figaro)
Hold your tongue, stupid,
this comedy must be ended.

FIGARO
(taking Susanna by the arm)
Then to end it happily
according to theatrical practice,
let a marriage ceremony
now follow.

SUSANNA, COUNTESS AND FIGARO
Oh my lord, do not refuse;
grant my (their) wishes.

COUNT
(aside)
Marcellina, Marcellina,

Quanto tardi a comparir!

how slow you are in coming!

SCENA UNDECIMA

SCENE 11

I suddetti, Antonio, giardiniere, infuriato con un vaso di garofani schiacciato

The above. Antonio the gardener comes in furiously with a broken pot of carnations

ANTONIO
Ah! signor . . . signor . . .

ANTONIO
Oh my lord . . . my lord . . .

CONTE
(con ansietà)
Cosa è stato? . . .

COUNT
(anxiously)
What's the matter?

ANTONIO
Che insolenza! chi 'l fece? chi fu?

ANTONIO
How dare he! Who did it? Who was it?

CONTESSA, SUSANNA, CONTE E FIGARO
Cosa dici, cos'hai, cosa è nato?

COUNTESS, SUSANNA, COUNT AND FIGARO
What's he saying? What's wrong? What's the matter?

ANTONIO
Ascoltate.

ANTONIO
Listen.

CONTESSA, SUSANNA, CONTE E FIGARO
Via, parla, di' su.

COUNTESS, SUSANNA, COUNT AND FIGARO
Go on, then, speak.

ANTONIO
Dal balcone che guarda in giardino
Mille cose ogni di gittar veggio;
E poc'anzi, può darsi di peggio?
Vidi un uom, signor mio, gittar giù!

ANTONIO
Every day I see all kinds of things thrown
from the balcony overlooking the garden;
but just now (it couldn't be worse)
I saw a man, my lord, thrown down!

CONTE
(con vivacità)
Dal balcone?

COUNT
(alert)
From the balcony?

ANTONIO
Vedete i garofani?
(additandogli il vaso de' fiori schiacciato)

ANTONIO
D'you see these carnations?
(showing them the broken flower pot)

CONTE
In giardino?

COUNT
Into the garden?

ANTONIO
Sì!

ANTONIO
Yes!

SUSANNA E CONTESSA
(piano a Figaro)
Figaro, all'erta!

SUSANNA AND COUNTESS
(aside to Figaro)
Figaro, think quickly!

CONTE
Cosa sento!

COUNT
What do I hear?

SUSANNA, CONTESSA E FIGARO
(piano)
Costui ci sconcerta;
(forte)
Quel briaco che viene a far qui?

SUSANNA, COUNTESS AND FIGARO
(aside)
He's taken aback.
(aloud)
What's this drunkard doing in here?

CONTE
Dunque un uom, ma dov'è gito?

COUNT
So you saw a man: where did he get to?

ANTONIO
Ratto, ratto il birbone è fuggito,
E ad tratto di vista m'usci.

ANTONIO
The scoundrel took to his heels
and was out of sight at once.

SUSANNA
(piano a Figaro)
Sai che il paggio . . .

SUSANNA
(aside to Figaro)
You must know it was the page . . .

FIGARO
(piano a Susanna)
So tutto, lo vidi.
(ride forte)
Ah, ah, ah!

FIGARO
(aside to Susanna)
I know, I saw him.
(laughing loudly)
Ha ha ha!

CONTE
Taci là.

COUNT
Be quiet, sir.

ANTONIO
Cosa ridi?

ANTONIO
What's there to laugh at?

FIGARO
Tu sei cotto dal sorger del dì.

FIGARO
You're drunk from morn till night.

CONTE
(ad Antonio)
Or ripetimi, un uom dal balcone?

COUNT
(to Antonio)
Now tell me again, a man from the balcony?

ANTONIO
Dal balcone.

ANTONIO
From the balcony.

CONTE
In giardino?

COUNT
Into the garden?

ANTONIO
In giardino.

SUSANNA, CONTESSA E FIGARO
Ma, signore, se in lui parla il vino!

CONTE
Segui pure: nè involvo il vedesti?

ANTONIO
No, nol vidi.

SUSANNA E CONTESSA
(piano a Figaro)
Olà, Figaro, ascolta.

FIGARO
Via, piangione, sta zitto una volta,
Per tre soldi far tanto rumulto!
(toccando con disprezzo i garofani)
Giacchè il fatto non può star
occulto, Sono io stesso saltato di lì.

CONTE E ANTONIO
Chi? voi stesso?

SUSANNA E CONTESSA
(piano)
Che testa! che ingegno!

FIGARO
Che stupore!

CONTE
Già creder nol posso.

ANTONIO
(a Figaro)
Come mai diventasti sì grosso?
Dopo il salto non fosti così.

FIGARO
A chi salta succede così.

ANTONIO
Ch'il direbbe?

SUSANNA E CONTESSA
(piano)
Ed insiste quel pazzo!

ANTONIO
Into the garden.

SUSANNA, COUNTESS AND FIGARO
My lord, it's the wine in him talking!

COUNT
Go on though: did you see his face?

ANTONIO
No, I didn't.

SUSANNA AND COUNTESS
(aside to Figaro)
Figaro, did you hear that?

FIGARO
You whining old fool, do be quiet,
making such a fuss over nothing!
(scornfully touching the carnations)
Since the fact can't be concealed,
it was I who jumped down from there.

COUNT AND ANTONIO
What? It was you?

SUSANNA AND COUNTESS
(aside)
What presence of mind!

FIGARO
Why so surprised?

COUNT
I just can't believe it.

ANTONIO
(to Figaro)
How have you grown so tall, then?
After the jump you weren't so big.

FIGARO
Jumping does that to one.

ANTONIO
Who'd have thought it?

SUSANNA AND COUNTESS
(aside)
The fool is persistent!

CONTE
(ad Antonio)
Tu che dici?

COUNT
(to Antonio)
You, what do you say?

ANTONIO
A me parve il ragazzo.

ANTONIO
It looked like that boy to me.

CONTE
(con fuoco)
Cherubino!

COUNT
(violently)
Cherubino!

SUSANNA E CONTESSA
(piano)
Maledetto!

SUSANNA AND COUNTESS
(aside)
Wretched man!

FIGARO
(ironicamente)
Esso appunto,
Da Siviglia a cavallo qui giunto,
Da Siviglia ov'ei forse sarà.

FIGARO
(sarcastically)
Of course, it was he,
back on horseback from Seville,
from Seville where he'd been.

ANTONIO
(con rozza semplicità)
Questo no, questo no, chè il cavallo
Io non vidi saltare di là.

ANTONIO
(with stupid simplicity)
No, that's not so.
I didn't see any horse jump down.

CONTE
Che pazienza! finiam questo
ballo.

COUNT
Give me patience! let's have done with
this nonsense.

SUSANNA E CONTESSA
(piano)
Come mai, giusto ciel, finirà?

SUSANNA AND COUNTESS
(aside)
Merciful heaven, how will this end?

CONTE
(a Figaro con fuoco)
Dunque, tu . . .

COUNT
(violently to Figaro)
So it was you . . .

FIGARO
(con disinvoltura)
Saltai giù.

FIGARO
(coolly)
. . . who jumped down.

CONTE
Ma perchè?

COUNT
What for?

FIGARO
Il timor . . .

FIGARO
I was afraid . . .

CONTE
Che timor?

COUNT
Afraid of what?

FIGARO
(additando le camere delle serve)
Là rinchiuso
Aspettando quel caro visetto . . .
Tippe tappe, un sussurro fuor d'uso . . .
Voi gridaste, lo scritto biglietto . . .
Saltai giù dal terrore confuso . . .
E stravolto m'ho un nervo del pie'!
(stropicciandosi il piede, come se si fosse fatto del male)

FIGARO
(indicating the servants' quarters)
I was shut up in there
waiting for that dear little face . . .
There was an unusual coming and going
and noise . . . you were shouting,
there was that letter . . .
I lost my nerve and jumped
down in terror–and wrenched a
muscle in my foot!
(rubbing his foot as if he had hurt it)

ANTONIO
Vostre dunque saran queste carte,
Che perdeste?
(Porge alcune carte chiuse a Figaro: il Conte gliele toglie)

ANTONIO
Then these letters which you dropped
will be yours?
(hands some folded papers to Figaro: the Count seizes them)

CONTE
Olà, porgile a me.

COUNT
Here, give them to me.

FIGARO
(piano a Susanna ed alla Contessa)
Sono in trappola.

FIGARO
(aside to Susanna and the Countess)
I'm caught in a trap.

SUSANNA E CONTESSA
(piano a Figaro)
Figaro, all'erta!

SUSANNA AND COUNTESS
(aside to Figaro)
Figaro, think quickly!

CONTE
(apre il foglio, poi lo chiude tosto)
Dite un po', questo foglio cos'è?

COUNT
(opens the paper but promptly re-folds it)
Well, tell me, what's this paper?

FIGARO
Tosto . . . tosto . . . ne ho tanti, aspettate.
(cava di tasca alcune carte, finge di guardarle)

FIGARO
Wait just a moment . . .
I've so many.
(takes some letters from his pocket and pretends to look through them)

ANTONIO
Sarà forse il sommario dei debiti.

ANTONIO
I expect it'll be a list of his debts.

FIGARO
No, la lista degli osti.

FIGARO
No, a list of the tavern-keepers.

CONTE
(a Figaro)
Parlate.

COUNT
(to Figaro)
Speak up.

(ad Antonio)
E tu lascialo.

SUSANNA, CONTESSA E FIGARO
Lascia mi (lo) e parti!

ANTONIO
Parto, sì, ma se torno a
trovarti! . . .
(parte)

FIGARO
Vanne, vanne, non temo di te.
(Il Conte riapre la carta e poi tosto la chiude; a Figaro)

CONTE
Dunque? . . .

CONTESSA
(a Susanna piano)
Oh ciel! la patente del paggio!

SUSANNA
(piano a Figaro)
Giusti Dei! la patente! . . .

CONTE
(a Figaro ironicamente)
Coraggio!

FIGARO
(come in atto di risovvenirsi d'una cosa)
Oh che testa! quest'è la patente,
Che poc'anzi il fanciullo mi die'.

CONTE
Perchè fare?

FIGARO
(imbrogliato)
Vi manca . . .

CONTE
Vi manca?

CONTESSA
(piano a Susanna)
Il suggello.

(to Antonio)
And you, let him be.

SUSANNA, COUNTESS AND FIGARO
Let him (me) be and go away!

ANTONIO
All right, I'll go, but if I catch you
again! . . .
(exit)

FIGARO
Oh go away: I'm not afraid of you.
(The Count opens the letter again and then re-folds it. To Figaro)

COUNT
Well?

COUNTESS
(aside to Susanna)
Heavens! the page's commission!

SUSANNA
(aside to Figaro)
Oh Lord! the commission!

COUNT
(ironically to Figaro)
Take courage!

FIGARO
(as if recollecting something)
Oh what a head! it's the commission
the boy gave me a while ago.

COUNT
What for?

FIGARO
(at a loss)
It lacked . . .

COUNT
It lacked?

COUNTESS
(aside to Susanna)
The seal!

SUSANNA
(piano a Figaro)
Il suggello!

SUSANNA
(aside to Figaro)
The seal!

CONTE
(a Figaro che finge di pensare)
Rispondi?

COUNT
(to Figaro, who pretends to be thinking)
Well, answer!

FIGARO
È l'usanza . . .

FIGARO
It's usual . . .

CONTE
Su via, ti confondi?

COUNT
Go on, why hesitate?

FIGARO
È l'usanza di porvi il suggello.

FIGARO
It's usual to seal it.

CONTE
(guarda che manca il suggello, lacera la carta)
Questo birbo mi toglie il cervello;
(con somma collera getta il foglio)
Tutto, tutto è un mistero per me.

COUNT
(sees the paper lacks the seal and tears it up)
This rascal's driving me mad.
(throwing the paper aside in a fury)
The whole thing's a mystery to me.

SUSANNA E CONTESSA
(tra sè)
Se mi salvo da questa tempesta,
Più non avvi naufragio per me.

SUSANNA AND COUNTESS
(aside)
If I survive this storm
I'll fear no further shipwreck.

FIGARO
(tra sè)
Sbuffa invano, e la terra calpesta,
Poverino, ne sa men di me.

FIGARO
(aside)
In vain you fume and stamp, sir,
you'll get nothing out of me.

SCENA DUODECIMA

I suddetti, Marcellina, Bartolo e Basilio

SCENE 12

The above, Marcellina, Bartolo and Basilio

MARCELLINA, BASILIO E BARTOLO
Voi signor, che giusto siete,
Ci dovete or ascoltar.

MARCELLINA, BASILIO AND BARTOLO
Oh my just and noble lord,
hear us now, we pray.

CONTE
(tra sè)
Son venuti a vendicarmi.
Io mi sento consolar.

COUNT
(aside)
They've come to work my vengeance.
I feel consoled.

SUSANNA, CONTESSA E FIGARO
(tra sè)
Son venuti a sconcertarmi.

SUSANNA, COUNTESS AND FIGARO
(aside)
They've come to foil me.

Qual rimedio ritrovar?

What solution can there be?

FIGARO
(al Conte)
Son tre stolidi, tre pazzi.
Cosa mai vengono a far?

FIGARO
(to the Count)
They're three stupid blockheads.
What are they doing here?

CONTE
Pian pianin, senza schiamazzi
Dica ognun quel che gli par.

COUNT
Now quiet: without interruption
Let each say what he wishes.

MARCELLINA
Un impegno nuziale
Ha costui con me contratto;
E pretendo che il contratto
Deva meco effettuar.

MARCELLINA
This man has made a contract
promising to marry me;
and I request that the contract
shall be ratified.

SUSANNA, CONTESSA E FIGARO
Come! come!

SUSANNA, COUNTESS AND FIGARO
What's this?

CONTE
Olà, silenzio:
Io son qui per giudicar.

COUNT
I will have silence.
This is for me to judge.

BARTOLO
Io da lei scelto avvocato
Vengo a far le sue difese,
Le legittime pretese
Io qui vengo a palesar.

BARTOLO
I represent this lady
and appear here as her counsel;
I come to argue
her legitimate plea.

SUSANNA, CONTESSA E FIGARO
È un birbante!

SUSANNA, COUNTESS AND FIGARO
He's a rogue!

CONTE
Olà, silenzio,
Io son qui per giudicar.

COUNT
Keep quiet, there;
this is for me to judge.

BASILIO
Io, come uomo al mondo cognito,
Vengo qui per testimonio
Del promesso matrimonio,
Con prestanza di danar.

BASILIO
As a man of standing,
I come here as a witness
of the promised marriage,
on which she lent him money.

SUSANNA, CONTESSA E FIGARO
Son tre matti.

SUSANNA, COUNTESS AND FIGARO
They're all mad.

CONTE
Olà, silenzio! Lo vedremo:
Il contratto leggeremo,
Tutto in ordin deve
andar.

COUNT
Silence, I say! Let's see it,
let us read the contract.
Everything must be done in proper
order.

SUSANNA, CONTESSA E FIGARO
Son confusa (o), son stordita (o)
Disperata (o), sbalordita (o)!
Certo, un diavol dell'inferno
Qui li ha fatti capitar.

SUSANNA, COUNTESS AND FIGARO
I'm stunned and bewildered,
stupefied and desperate!
The devil in hell for certain
has brought them here.

MARCELLINA, BASILIO, BARTOLO E CONTE
Che bel colpo, che bel caso,
È cresciuto a tutti il naso;
Qualche Nume a noi propizio
Qui li (ci) ha fatti capitar.

MARCELLINA, BASILIO, BARTOLO AND COUNT
What a blow, what a splendid stroke,
everyone is baffled;
Providence, that smiles on us,
has brought us (them) here.

ATTO TERZO

SCENA PRIMA

Salotto, ornato per una festa nuziale

RECITATIVO

CONTE
(passeggiando)
Che imbarazzo è mai questo!
Un foglio anonimo . . .
La cameriera in gabinetto chiusa . . .
La padrona confusa . . . un uom che salta
Dal balcone in giardino . . . un altro appresso
Che dice esser quel desso . . .
Non so cosa pensar: potrebbe forse
Qualcun de' miei vassalli . . . a simil razza
È comune l'ardir . . . ma la Contessa . . .
Ah, che un dubbio l'offende . . .
Ella rispetta troppo sè stessa;
E l'onor mio . . . l'onore . . .
Dove diamin l'ha posto umano errore!

SCENA SECONDA

La Contessa, Susanna, e il Conte

La Contessa e Susanna s'arrestano in fondo alla scena non vedute

ACT III

SCENE 1

A large hall, decorated for a wedding

RECITATIVE

COUNT
(pacing up and down)
What a mix-up this is!
An anonymous letter . . .
the maid locked in the closet . . .
my lady flustered . . . a man jumping down
from the balcony into the garden . . . then
another who claims it was he . . .
I don't know what to think: it might
have been one of my vassals . . . such rabble
are bold enough . . . but the Countess . . .
No, to doubt her is an insult . . .
she has too much respect for herself
and for my honour . . . my honour . . .
in which, dammit, human frailty exists!

SCENE 2

The Countess, Susanna and the Count

The Countess and Susanna stay in the background, unseen by

dal Conte	*the Count*
CONTESSA Via, fatti core; digli Che ti attenda in giardino.	COUNTESS Go on, take courage: tell him to meet you in the garden.
CONTE *(sempre tra sé)* Saprò se Cherubino Era giunto a Siviglia: a tale oggetto Ho mandato Basilio . . .	COUNT *(to himself)* I'll find out if Cherubino went to Seville: I've sent Basilio to enquire . . .
SUSANNA Oh cielo! e Figaro . . .	SUSANNA Oh heavens! if Figaro . . .
CONTESSA A lui non dèi dir nulla, invece tua Voglio andarci io medesma.	COUNTESS Say nothing of it to him: I myself intend going in your place.
CONTE Avanti sera Dovrebbe ritornar . . .	COUNT Before this evening he should be back . . .
SUSANNA Oh Dio! non oso.	SUSANNA Oh dear! I dare not.
CONTESSA Pensa ch' è in tua mano il mio riposo. *(si nasconde)*	COUNTESS Reflect that my happiness is in your hands. *(She hides.)*
CONTE *(sempre tra sé)* E Susanna? chi sa ch'ella tradito Abbia il segreto mio . . . Oh, se ha parlato Gli fo sposar la vecchia.	COUNT *(still to himself)* And Susanna? Who knows if she has betrayed my secret? . . . If she's spoken I'll make him marry the old woman.
SUSANNA *(tra sé)* Marcellina! *(forte)* Signor . . .	SUSANNA *(aside)* Marcellina! *(aloud)* My lord! . . .
CONTE *(serio)* Cosa bramate!	COUNT *(firmly)* What do you want?
SUSANNA Mi par che siate in collera!	SUSANNA I believe you're angry!

CONTE
Volete qualche cosa?

SUSANNA
Signor . . . la vostra sposa
Ha i soliti vapori,
E vi chiede il fiaschetto degli odori.

CONTE
Prendete.

SUSANNA
Or vel riporto.

CONTE
Eh no, potete
Ritenerlo per voi.

SUSANNA
Per me?
Questi non son mali
Da donne triviali.

CONTE
Un'amante, che perde il caro sposo
Sul punto d'ottenerlo . . .

SUSANNA
Pagando Marcellina
Colla dote che voi mi
prometteste . . .

CONTE
Ch'io vi promisi? quando?

SUSANNA
Credea d'averlo inteso . . .

CONTE
Sì, se voluto aveste
Intendermi voi stessa.

SUSANNA
È mio dovere,
E quel di sua eccellenza è il mio
volere.

16. DUETTINO

CONTE
Crudele! perchè finora

COUNT
What have you come for?

SUSANNA
My Lord . . . my lady
has the vapours, as usual,
and requests your smelling salts.

COUNT
Take them.

SUSANNA
I'll bring them back at once.

COUNT
No, you may keep them
for yourself.

SUSANNA
For me?
Such ailments are not
for girls in my position.

COUNT
A girl who loses her bridegroom
on the point of winning him . . .

SUSANNA
Paying Marcellina off
with the dowry you promised
me . . .

COUNT
That I promised you? When?

SUSANNA
That's what I understood.

COUNT
Yes, if you had cared
to come to an understanding.

SUSANNA
It's my duty,
and my lord's wish is my
command.

16. DUET

COUNT
Cruel one, why have you

Farmi languir così?

caused me thus to languish?

SUSANNA
Signor, la donna ognora
Tempo ha di dir di sì.

SUSANNA
My lord, a woman always
needs time before she says Yes.

CONTE
Dunque, in giardin verrai?

COUNT
Then you'll come into the garden?

SUSANNA
Se piace a voi, verrò.

SUSANNA
If it pleases you, I'll come.

CONTE
E non mi mancherai?

COUNT
You won't fail me?

SUSANNA
No, non vi mancherò.

SUSANNA
No, I won't fail you.

CONTE
Verrai?

COUNT
You'll come?

SUSANNA
Sì.

SUSANNA
Yes.

CONTE
Non mancherai?

COUNT
You'll not fail?

SUSANNA
No.

SUSANNA
No.

CONTE
Dunque verrai?

COUNT
You'll really come?

SUSANNA
No!

SUSANNA
No.

CONTE
No?!

COUNT
No?!

SUSANNA
Sì!!
Se piace a voi, verrò.

SUSANNA
Yes!
If it pleases you, I'll come.

CONTE
Mi sento dal contento
Pieno di gioia il cor.

COUNT
In contentment I feel
my heart full of joy.

SUSANNA
(piano)
Scusatemi se mento,
Voi che intendete amor.

SUSANNA
(aside)
Forgive my deception,
you who truly love.

RECITATIVO

CONTE
E perchè fosti meco
Stamattina sì austera?

SUSANNA
Col paggio ch'ivi c'era . . .

CONTE
Ed a Basilio,
Che per me ti parlò . . .

SUSANNA
Ma qual bisogno
Abbiam noi che un Basilio . . .

CONTE
È vero, è vero.
E mi prometti poi . . .
Se tu manchi, o cor mio . . .
Ma la contessa
Attenderà il fiaschetto.

SUSANNA
Eh, fu un pretesto:
Parlato io non avrei senza di questo.

CONTE
(La prende per mano.)
Carissima!

SUSANNA
Vien gente.

CONTE
(tra sé)
È mia senz'altro.

SUSANNA
(tra sè)
Forbitevi la bocca, o signor scaltro.
(vuol partire, e sotto la porta s'incontra in Figaro)

SCENA TERZA

Figaro, Susanna ed il Conte

FIGARO
Ehi Susanna, ove vai?

RECITATIVE

COUNT
Then why were you
so distant to me this morning?

SUSANNA
With the page there . . .

COUNT
And to Basilio,
who spoke on my behalf . . .

SUSANNA
But what need have we
of a Basilio . . .

COUNT
That's true, indeed.
Promise me again . . .
If you fail me, my dear . . .
But the Countess
will be waiting for the smelling salts.

SUSANNA
Oh, that was just a pretext; I couldn't
have spoken to you without one.

COUNT
(taking her hand)
Dearest!

SUSANNA
Someone's coming.

COUNT
(aside)
She's mine, I'm sure now.

SUSANNA
(aside)
Wipe off that smile, my cunning master.
(about to exit, she meets Figaro at the door)

SCENE 3

Figaro, Susanna and the Count

FIGARO
Susanna, where are you going?

SUSANNA Taci. Senza avvocato Hai già vinta la causa. *(parte)*	SUSANNA Hush. We've won our case without a lawyer. *(exit)*
FIGARO Cosa è nato? *(la segue)*	FIGARO What's happened? *(He follows her)*
SCENA QUARTA	SCENE 4
17. RECITATIVO ED ARIA	17. RECITATIVE AND ARIA
CONTE Hai già vinta la causa! cosa sento! In qual laccio cadea! perfidi! io voglio Di tal modo punirvi! a piacer mio La sentenza sarà . . . Ma s'ei pagasse La vecchia pretendente? Pagarla! in qual maniera? . . . e poi v'è Antonio Che a un incognito Figaro ricusa Di dare una nipote in matrimonio. Coltivando l'orgoglio Di questo mentecatto . . . Tutto giova a un raggiro . . . Il colpo è fatto.	COUNT We've won our case! What do I hear! I've fallen into a trap! The traitors! I'll punish them so! The sentence will be at my pleasure . . . But supposing he has paid off the claims of the old woman? Paid her? How . . . and then there's Antonio who'll refuse to give his niece in marriage to a Figaro, of whom nothing is known. If I play on the pride of that half-wit . . . Everything favours my plan . . . The die is cast.
Vedrò mentr'io sospiro, Felice un servo mio? E un ben, che invan desìo, Ei posseder dovrà? Vedrò per man d'amore Unita a un vil oggetto Chi in me destò un affetto, Che per me poi non ha? Ah no, lasciarti in pace Non vo' questo contento! Tu non nascesti, audace! Per dare a me tormento, E forse ancor per ridere Di mia infelicità. Già la speranza sola Delle vendette mie Quest'anima consola E giubilar mi fa.	Must I see a serf of mine made happy while I am left to sigh, and see him possess a treasure which I desire in vain? Must I see her, who has roused in me a passion she does not feel for me, united by the hand of love to a base slave? Ah no, I will not give you the satisfaction of this contentment! You were not born, bold fellow, to cause me torment and indeed to laugh at my discomfiture. Now only the hope of taking vengeance eases my mind and makes me rejoice.
(Vuol partire, e s'incontra in Don Curzio)	*(About to leave, he meets Don Curzio)*

SCENA QUINTA

Il Conte, Marcellina, Don Curzio, Figaro e Bartolo

RECITATIVO

CURZIO
(entrando)
È decisa la lite.
O pagarla, o sposarla. Ora ammutite.

MARCELLINA
Io respiro

FIGARO
Ed io moro.

MARCELLINA
(tra sé)
Alfin sposa io sarò d'un uom che adoro.

FIGARO
Eccellenza, m'appello . . .

CONTE
È giusta la sentenza.
O pagar, o sposar. Bravo, Don Curzio.

CURZIO
Bontà di Sua Eccellenza.

BARTOLO
Che superba sentenza!

FIGARO
In che superba?

BARTOLO
Siam tutti vendicati.

FIGARO
Io non la sposerò.

BARTOLO
La sposerai.

CURZIO
O pagarla, o sposarla. Lei t'ha

SCENE 5

The Count, Marcellina, Don Curzio, Figaro and Bartolo

RECITATIVE

CURZIO
(entering)
The case is decided.
Pay up, or marry her. That's all.

MARCELLINA
I breathe again.

FIGARO
And I'm done for.

MARCELLINA
(aside)
At last I'll be married to the man I love.

FIGARO
My lord, I appeal . . .

COUNT
The judgement is fair.
Pay up, or marry her. Quite right, Don Curzio.

CURZIO
Your lordship is too kind.

BARTOLO
An excellent judgement!

FIGARO
In what way excellent?

BARTOLO
We are all avenged.

FIGARO
I won't marry her.

BARTOLO
Oh yes, you will.

CURZIO
Pay up, or marry her. She lent

prestati
Due mille pezzi duri.

FIGARO
Son gentiluomo, e senza
L'assenso de' miei nobili parenti . . .

CONTE
Dove sono? chi sono?

FIGARO
Lasciate ancor cercarli:
Dopo dieci anni io spero di trovarli.

BARTOLO
Qualche bambin trovato? . . .

FIGARO
No, perduto, Dottor, anzi rubato.

CONTE
Come?

MARCELLINA
Cosa?

BARTOLO
La prova?

CURZIO
Il testimonio?

FIGARO
L'oro, le gemme e i ricamati panni,
Che ne' più teneri anni
Mi ritrovaro addosso i masnadieri,
Sono gl'indizi veri
Di mia nascita illustre, e sopra tutto
Questo al mio braccio impresso geroglifico.

MARCELLINA
Una spatola impressa al braccio destro?

FIGARO
E a voi ch' il disse?

you
two thousand pieces of silver.

FIGARO
I am of gentle birth, and without
the consent of my noble parents . . .

COUNT
Where are they? Who are they?

FIGARO
Let me go on looking for them;
for ten years I've been hoping to find them.

BARTOLO
Were you a foundling? . . .

FIGARO
No, lost, Doctor, or rather stolen.

COUNT
Stolen?

MARCELLINA
What's that?

BARTOLO
Your proof?

CURZIO
Your witness?

FIGARO
The gold, the jewels and the embroidered clothes
which, in my infancy,
the bandits found upon me
are the true indications
of my noble birth, and moreover
this mark upon my arm.

MARCELLINA
A spatula on your right arm?

FIGARO
Who told you that?

MARCELLINA
Oh Dio!
È desso . . .

FIGARO
È ver, son io.

CURZIO
Chi?

CONTE
Chi?

BARTOLO
Chi?

MARCELLINA
Rafaello.

BARTOLO
E i ladri ti rapir?

FIGARO
Presso un castello.

BARTOLO
Ecco tua madre.

FIGARO
Balia?

BARTOLO
No, tua madre.

CONTE E CURZIO
Sua madre!

FIGARO
Cosa sento!

MARCELLINA
Ecco tuo padre.
(Marcellina corre ad abbracciare Figaro)

18. SESTETTO

MARCELLINA
Riconosci in questo amplesso
Una madre, amato figlio.

MARCELLINA
Great heaven!
It's he . . .

FIGARO
It's I, indeed.

CURZIO
Who?

COUNT
Who?

BARTOLO
Who?

MARCELLINA
Rafaello.

BARTOLO
And robbers stole you?

FIGARO
Near a castle.

BARTOLO
There stands your mother.

FIGARO
My nurse? . . .

BARTOLO
No, your mother.

COUNT AND CURZIO
His mother!

FIGARO
Do I hear aright?

MARCELLINA
And there stands your father.
(She runs to embrace Figaro)

18. SEXTET

MARCELLINA
Dearest son, in this embrace
recognise your mother.

FIGARO
Padre mio, fate lo stesso,
Non mi fate più arrossir.

FIGARO
Father dear, do the same,
do not leave me longer here to blush.

BARTOLO
Resistenza la coscienza
Far non lascia al tuo desir.

BARTOLO
Do not let conscience
stand in the way of your desire.

CURZIO
(tra sé)
Ei suo padre, ella sua madre:
L'imeneo non può seguir.

CURZIO
(aside)
He's his father, she's his mother:
the wedding can't go forward.

CONTE
(tra sé)
Son smarrito, son stordito:
Meglio è assai di qua partir.
(Il Conte fa per partire, Susanna l'arresta)

COUNT
(aside)
I'm astounded, I'm amazed:
to leave here would be for the best.
(He makes to leave, but Susanna detains him)

MARCELLINA E BARTOLO
Figlio amato!

MARCELLINA AND BARTOLO
My beloved son!

FIGARO
Parenti amati!

FIGARO
My beloved parents!

SUSANNA
Alto, alto, signore Conte,
Mille doppie qui son pronte.
A pagar vengo per Figaro,
Ed a porlo in libertà.

SUSANNA
Just a moment, pray, my lord.
I have the money ready here.
I've come to pay for Figaro
and set him free.

CONTE E CURZIO
Non sappiam come'è la cosa.
Osservate un poco là.

COUNT AND CURZIO
We don't know where we are.
Just look over there.

SUSANNA
(si volge e vede Figaro che abbraccia Marcellina)
Già d'accordo colla sposa?
Giusti dei; che infedeltà!
Lascia, iniquo!
(vuol partire)

SUSANNA
(turns and sees Figaro embracing Marcellina)
Already reconciled to her as wife?
Great heaven, how faithless!
Leave me, wretch!
(She starts to go.)

FIGARO
(la trattiene; ella lo forza)
No, t'arresta
Senti, o cara.

FIGARO
(detains her; she struggles)
Stay a moment.
Listen, my dearest.

SUSANNA
(dà uno schiaffo a Figaro)

SUSANNA
(boxes Figaro's ears)

Senti questa!

MARCELLINA, BARTOLO E FIGARO
È un effetto di buon core,
Tutto amore è quel che fa.

CONTE E CURZIO
Fremo, smanio dal furore,
Il destino me la (gliela) fa.

SUSANNA
Fremo, smanio dal furore,
Una vecchia a me la fa.

MARCELLINA
Lo sdegno calmate,
Mia cara figliuola,
Sua madre abbracciate,
Che vostra or sarà.
(Marcellina corre ad abbracciare Susanna)

SUSANNA
Sua madre?

TUTTI
Sua madre.

FIGARO
E quello è mio padre,
Che a te lo dirà.

SUSANNA
Suo padre?

TUTTI
Suo padre.

FIGARO
E quella è mia madre,
Che a te lo dirà.
(Corrono tutti e quattro ad abbracciarsi)

SUSANNA, MARCELLINA, BARTOLO E FIGARO
Al dolce contento
Di questo momento,
Quest' anima appena
Resistere or sa.

Listen to that!

MARCELLINA, BARTOLO AND FIGARO
It's the result of her full heart;
what she did, she did for love.

COUNT AND CURZIO
I rage, I burn with fury;
fate has overcome me (him).

SUSANNA
I rage, I burn with fury;
this old woman has overcome me.

MARCELLINA
Dearest daughter,
calm your bitterness,
and embrace his mother,
who now will be yours too.
(She runs to embrace Susanna)

SUSANNA
His mother?

ALL
His mother.

FIGARO
And this is my father,
who'll tell you it's true.

SUSANNA
His father?

ALL
His father.

FIGARO
And this is my mother,
who'll tell you it's true.
(All four embrace)

SUSANNA, MARCELLINA, BARTOLO AND FIGARO
My heart
scarcely can support
the bliss
of this moment.

CONTE E CURZIO
Al fiero tormento
Di questo momento
Quest' anima appena
Resistere or sa.

(Il Conte e Don Curzio partono)

SCENA SESTA

Marcellina, Bartolo, Figaro e Susanna

RECITATIVO

MARCELLINA
(a Bartolo)
Eccovi, o caro amico, il dolce frutto
Dell'antico amor nostro . . .

BARTOLO
Or non parliamo
Di fatti sì remoti: egli è mio figlio,
Mia consorte voi siete;
E le nozze farem quando volete.

MARCELLINA
Oggi, e doppie saranno.
(dà il biglietto a Figaro)
Prendi, questo è il biglietto
Del danar che a me devi, ed è
tua dote.

SUSANNA
(getta a terra una borsa di danaro)
Prendi ancor questa borsa.

BARTOLO
(fa lo stesso)
E questa ancora.

FIGARO
Bravi; gittate pur ch'io piglio
ognora.

SUSANNA
Voliamo ad informar d'ogni
avventura
Madama e nostro zio:
Chi al par di me contenta?

COUNT AND CURZIO
My heart
scarcely can support
the raging torment
of this moment.

(The Count and Curzio exeunt)

SCENE 6

Marcellina, Bartolo, Figaro and Susanna

RECITATIVE

MARCELLINA
(to Bartolo)
And there, my dear, is the sweet pledge
of our old love . . .

BARTOLO
Let's not talk now
of so remote a past: he's my son,
you are my consort;
and we'll get married when you wish.

MARCELLINA
Today; it can be a double wedding.
(gives the paper to Figaro)
Take this; it is the contract for the sum
you owe me; let it be your
wedding present.

SUSANNA
(throwing down a purse of money)
Take this purse too.

BARTOLO
(doing the same)
And this as well.

FIGARO
Thank you; I'll take all I'm
given.

SUSANNA
Let's go and tell my
lady
and my uncle all that's happened:
Who could be as happy as I am?

FIGARO
Io.

BARTOLO
Io.

MARCELLINA
Io.

TUTTI
E schiatti il signor Conte al gusto mio.

(partono abbracciati)

SCENA SETTIMA

Barbarina e Cherubino

BARBARINA
Andiam, andiam, bel paggio, in casa mia.
Tutte ritroverai le più belle ragazze
Del castello, di tutte sarai tu certo
Il più bello.

CHERUBINO
Ah, se il Conte mi trova, misero me!
Tu sai che partito ei mi crede per Siviglia.

BARBARINA
Oh ve' che maraviglia, e se ti trova,
Non sarà cosa nuova. Odi!
Vogliamo
Vestirti come noi, tutte insiem andrem
Poi a presentar de' fiori a Madamina.
Fidati, Cherubin, di Barbarina.

(partono)

SCENA OTTAVA

19. RECITATIVO ED ARIA

CONTESSA
(sola)
E Susanna non vien! sono aniosa

FIGARO
I am.

BARTOLO
I am.

MARCELLINA
I am.

ALL
And I don't care how furious the Count is!

(exeunt arm in arm)

SCENE 7

Barbarina and Cherubino

BARBARINA
Come, dear page, come to our house.
There you'll find all the prettiest girls
of the estate, and you shall be
the prettiest of them all.

CHERUBINO
But woe betide me if the Count should find me.
You know he thinks I've left for Seville.

BARBARINA
Oh well, if he does find you
It won't be anything new.
Listen!
We're going to dress you like one of us
and then all go to present flowers to my lady.
Cherubino, have faith in Barbarina.

(exeunt)

SCENE 8

19. RECITATIVE AND ARIA

COUNTESS
(alone)
Susanna's not come! I'm impatient

Di saper come il Conte
Accolse la proposta: alquanto ardito
Il progetto mi par, e ad uno sposo
Sì vivace e geloso . . .
Ma che mal c'è?
Cangiando i miei vestiti
Con quelli di Susanna, e i suoi co' miei,
Al favor della notte . . . oh cielo! a quale
Umil stato fatale io son ridotta
Da un consorte crudel, che dopo avermi
Con un misto inaudito
D'infedeltà, di gelosia, di sdegno,
Prima amata, indi offesa, e alfin tradita,
Fammi or cercar da una mia serva aita!

Dove sono i bei momenti
Di dolcezza e di piacer?
Dove andaro i giuramenti
Di quel labbro menzogner?
Perchè mai, se in pianti e in pene
Per me tutto si cangiò,
La memoria di quel bene
Dal mio sen non trapassò?
Ah! se almen la mia costanza
Nel languire amando ognor,
Mi portasse una speranza
Di cangiar l'ingrato cor.

(parte)

SCENA NONA

Il Conte e Antonio

RECITATIVO

ANTONIO
(con un cappello in mano)
Io vi dico, signor, che Cherubino
È ancora nel castello,
E vedete per prova il suo cappello.

CONTE
Ma come? se a quest'ora
Esser giunto a Siviglia egli dovria.

to know what the Count said
to her proposal; the plan seems to me
somewhat rash, and with a husband
so impetuous and jealous . . .
But where's the harm?
To change my clothes
with those of Susanna, and hers with mine,
under cover of darkness . . . Oh heavens!
To what humiliation am I reduced
by a cruel husband, who after
having first loved me,
then neglected and finally
deceived me, in a strange mixture
of infidelity, jealousy and disdain,
now forces me to seek help from my servant!

Where are those happy moments
of sweetness and pleasure?
Where have they gone,
those vows of a deceiving tongue?
Then why, if everything for me
is changed to tears and grief,
has the memory of that happiness
not faded from my breast?
Ah! if only my constancy
in yearning lovingly for him always
could bring the hope
of changing his ungrateful heart!

(exit)

SCENE 9

The Count and Antonio

RECITATIVE

ANTONIO
(with a cap in his hand)
I tell you, sir, that Cherubino
is still in the castle;
look, here's his cap to prove it.

COUNT
But how? By this time
he ought to be in Seville.

ANTONIO
Scusate, oggi Siviglia è a casa mia.
Là vestissi da donna, e là lasciati
Ha gl'altri abiti suoi.

ANTONIO
If I may say so, all Seville's in my house.
There he's been dressed as a girl,
and he's left his other clothes there.

CONTE
Perfidi!

COUNT
The traitors!

ANTONIO
Andiam, e li vedrete voi.

ANTONIO
Let's go, and you can see for yourself.

(partono)

(exeunt)

SCENA DECIMA

SCENE 10

La Contessa e Susanna

The Countess and Susanna

CONTESSA
Cosa mi narri!
E che ne disse il Conte?

COUNTESS
What things you're telling me!
And what did the Count say then?

SUSANNA
Gli si leggeva in fronte
Il dispetto e la rabbia.

SUSANNA
You could read in his face
his indignation and anger.

CONTESSA
Piano: che meglio or lo porremo in gabbia.
Dov'è l'appuntamento
Che tu gli proponesti?

COUNTESS
Gently now: it will be the easier to catch him.
Where is the rendezvous
that you suggested?

SUSANNA
In giardino.

SUSANNA
In the garden.

CONTESSA
Fissiamgli un loco. Scrivi.

COUNTESS
Let's fix a place for it. Write to him.

SUSANNA
Ch'io scriva? . . . ma . . .
signora . . .

SUSANNA
I write? . . . but . . .
my lady . . .

CONTESSA
Eh scrivi, dico, e tutto
Io prendo su me stessa.
(Susanna siede e scrive)
Canzonetta sull'aria . . .

COUNTESS
Write, I tell you,
and I'll take it all upon myself.
(Susanna sits down and writes)
A song to the zephyr . . .

20. DUETTINO

20. DUET

SUSANNA
Sull'aria . . .

SUSANNA
To the Zephyr . . .

CONTESSA
(detta)
Che soave zeffiretto . . .

SUSANNA
(ripete le parole della Contessa)
Zeffiretto . . .

CONTESSA
Questa sera spirerà! . . .

SUSANNA
Questa sera spirerà . . .

CONTESSA
Sotto i pini del boschetto.

SUSANNA
Sotto i pini del boschetto.

CONTESSA
Ei già il resto capirà.

SUSANNA
Certo, certo il capirà.
(piega la lettera)

RECITATIVO

SUSANNA
Piegato è il foglio . . . or come
si sigilla?

CONTESSA
(Si cava una spilla e gliela dà)
Ecco . . . prendi una spilla.
Servirà di sigillo, attendi . . . scrivi
Sul riverso del foglio:
Rimandate il sigillo.

SUSANNA
È più bizzarro
Di quel della patente.

CONTESSA
Presto, nascondi . . . io sento
venir gente.

(Susanna si mette il biglietto in seno)

COUNTESS
(dictating)
How sweet the breeze . . .

SUSANNA
(repeating the Countess's words)
The breeze . . .

COUNTESS
Will be this evening . . .

SUSANNA
Will be this evening . . .

COUNTESS
In the pine grove.

SUSANNA
In the pine grove.

COUNTESS
The rest he'll understand.

SUSANNA
I'm sure he'll understand.
(She folds the letter)

RECITATIVE

SUSANNA
The letter's folded . . . how shall
I seal it?

COUNTESS
(takes out a pin and gives it to her)
Here . . . take this pin.
It will serve as seal. Wait . . .
Write on the back of the letter,
"Send back the seal".

SUSANNA
It's stranger than
the seal on the commission.

COUNTESS
Quick, hide it . . . I hear
people coming.

(Susanna puts the note in her bosom)

SCENA UNDECIMA

Cherubino vestito da contadinella. Barbarina ed alcune altre contandinelle vestite nel medisimo modo, con mazzetti di fiori, e dette

21. CORO

CORO
Ricevete, o padroncina,
Queste rose e questi fior,
Che abbiam colti stamattina
Per mostrarvi il nostro amor.
Siamo tante contadine,
E siam tutte poverine,
Ma quel poco che rechiamo
Ve lo diamo di buon cuor.

RECITATIVO

BARBARINA
Queste sono, Madama,
Le ragazze del loco,
Che il poco ch'han vi vengono ad offrire,
E vi chiedon perdon del loro ardire.

CONTESSA
Oh brave: vi ringrazio.

SUSANNA
Come sono vezzose!

CONTESSA
(indicando Cherubino)
E chi è, narratemi,
Quell'amabil fanciulla
Ch'ha l'aria sì modesta?

BARBARINA
Ell'è una mia cugina, e per le nozze
È venuta ier sera.

CONTESSA
Onoriamo la bella forestiera.
Venite qui . . . datemi i vostri fiori.
(prende i fiori di Cherubino e lo bacia in fronte)
Come arrossì . . . Susanna, e non

SCENE 11

Cherubino dressed as a peasant girl; Barbarina and other village girls dressed in the same way, with bunches of flowers; the above

21. CHORUS

CHORUS
Accept, noble lady,
these roses and these flowers,
which we have picked this morning
to show you our affection.
We are only humble girls
from the village,
but the little that we can give
we offer with all our hearts.

RECITATIVE

BARBARINA
These, my lady,
are the girls of the district,
who have come to offer what little they have
and beg your pardon for being so bold.

COUNTESS
How kind: I thank you.

SUSANNA
Aren't they pretty!

COUNTESS
(pointing at Cherubino)
And who, tell me,
is that charming girl
who looks so shy?

BARBARINA
That's one of my cousins, who came
last evening for the wedding.

COUNTESS
We should honour this fair stranger.
Come here . . . let me have your flowers.
(takes the flowers from Cherubino and kisses his forehead)
How she blushes! . . . Susanna, don't

ti pare . . .
Che somigli ad alcuno?

you think . . .
she resembles someone?

SUSANNA
Al naturale!

SUSANNA
To the life!

SCENA DUODECIMA

SCENE 12

I suddetti, il Conte ed Antonio

The above, the Count and Antonio

Antonio ha il cappello di Cherubino, entra in scena pian piano, gli cava la cuffia da donna e gli mette in testa il capello stesso

Antonio, holding Cherubino's cap, enters very quietly, pulls off Cherubino's headdress and puts the cap on him

ANTONIO
Eh cospettaccio! è questi l'uffiziale.

ANTONIO
There you are! there's your officer!

CONTESSA
(tra sé)
Oh stelle!

COUNTESS
(aside)
Mercy on us!

SUSANNA
(tra sé)
Malandrino!

SUSANNA
(aside)
The scamp!

CONTE
Ebben! Madama . . .

COUNT
Well, madam . . .?

CONTESSA
Io sono, signor mio,
Irritata e sorpresa al par di voi.

COUNTESS
My lord, I am as annoyed
and surprised as you are.

CONTE
Ma stamane?

COUNT
But this morning?

CONTESSA
Stamane . . .
Per l'odierna festa
Volevam travestirlo al modo stesso
Che l'han vestito adesso.

COUNTESS
This morning . . .
we wanted to dress him up
as he's dressed now
for this evening's party.

CONTE
(a Cherubino)
E perchè non partisti?

COUNT
(to Cherubino)
And why have you not left?

CHERUBINO
(cavandosi il capello bruscamente)
Signor . . .

CHERUBINO
(quickly pulling off his cap)
My lord . . .

CONTE Saprò punire La tua disobbedienza.	COUNT I shall know how to punish your disobedience.
BARBARINA Eccellenza, Voi mi dite sì spesso, Qualvolta m'abbracciate e mi baciate: Barbarina, se m'ami, Ti darò quel che brami.	BARBARINA Your lordship, you've told me so often when you've kissed and caressed me, "Barbarina, if you'll love me I'll give you whatever you want".
CONTE Io, dissi questo?	COUNT I said that?
BARBARINA Voi. Or datemi, padrone, In sposo Cherubino, E v'amerò com'amo il mio gattino.	BARBARINA Yes, you did. So please give me, sir, Cherubino for a husband, and I'll love you as I love my kitten.
CONTESSA *(al Conte)* Ebbene, or tocca a voi . . .	COUNTESS *(to the Count)* Well, now it's your turn . . .
ANTONIO *(a Barbarina)* Brava, figliuola! Hai buon maestro che ti fa la scuola.	ANTONIO *(to Barbarina)* Well done, my child! You've learnt your lesson well.
CONTE *(tra sé)* Non so qual uom, qual demone, qual Dio Rivolga tutto quanto a torto mio.	COUNT *(aside)* What man, demon or god is it that turns everything I do against me?
SCENA TREDICESIMA	SCENE 13
I suddetti e Figaro	*The above and Figaro*
FIGARO Signor . . . se trattenete Tutte queste ragazze, Addio feste . . . addio danze . . .	FIGARO My lord . . . if you keep all these girls here, there'll be no party, no dancing . . .
CONTE E che! vorresti Ballar col pie' stravolto?	COUNT Indeed! You're wanting to dance with an injured foot?
FIGARO Eh, non mi duol più molto.	FIGARO Oh, it doesn't hurt any more.

(finge di drizzarsi la gamba, poi si prova a ballare)
Andiam, belle fanciulle . . .
(Chiama tutte le giovani, vuol partire, il Conte lo richiama)

(pretends to stretch his leg and try to dance)
Come, my pretty ones . . .
(calling to the girls and trying to leave, but the Count calls him back)

CONTESSA
(sottovoce a Susanna)
Come si caverà dall'imbarazzo?

COUNTESS
(aside to Susanna)
How will he get out of this predicament?

SUSANNA
(sottovoce a la Contessa)
Lasciate fare a lui.

SUSANNA
(aside to the Countess)
Leave it to him.

CONTE
Per buona sorte
I vasi eran di creta.

COUNT
By good fortune, the flower-pots
were only earthenware.

FIGARO
Senza fallo.
Andiamo, dunque, andiamo.

FIGARO
That's right, sir.
Now come along . . .

ANTONIO
Ed intanto a cavallo
Di galoppo a Siviglia andava il paggio.

ANTONIO
Meanwhile the page
was galloping off to
Seville?

FIGARO
Di galoppo o di passo, buon viaggio.
Venite, belle giovani.

FIGARO
Galloping or trotting, off he went.
Come along, my dears.

CONTE
(torna a ricondurlo in mezzo)
E a te la sua patente
Era in tasca rimasta . . .

COUNT
(again bringing him back)
And his commission
was left in your pocket . . .

FIGARO
Certamente.
Che razza di domande!

FIGARO
Yes indeed.
What a lot of questions!

ANTONIO
(a Susanna che fa dei moti a Figaro)
Via, non gli far più moti, ei non t'intende.
Ed ecco che pretende
Che sia un bugiardo il mio signor nipote.

ANTONIO
(to Susanna, who is making signs to Figaro)
Stop making signs to him, he doesn't understand.
Here's someone who claims
that my nephew-to-be
is a liar.

FIGARO
Cherubino!

FIGARO
Cherubino!

ANTONIO
(prende per mano Cherubino e lo presenta a Figaro)
Or ci sei.

FIGARO
(al Conte)
Che diamin canta?

CONTE
Non canta, no, ma dice
Ch'egli saltò stamane in sui garofani . . .

FIGARO
Ei lo dice! . . . sarà . . . se ho saltato io
Si può dare che anch'esso
Abbia fatto lo stesso.

CONTE
Anch'esso?

FIGARO
Perchè no?
Io non impugno mai quel che non so.
(Si ode una marcia spagnuola da lontano)

22. FINALE

FIGARO
Ecco la marcia . . . andiamo.
Ai vostri posti, o belle, ai vostri posti.
Susanna, dammi il braccio.

SUSANNA
Eccolo.
(Figaro prende per un braccio Susanna, partono tutti, eccettuati il Conte e la Contessa)

CONTE
(tra sé)
Temerari!

CONTESSA
(tra sé)
Io son di ghiaccio.

ANTONIO
(taking Cherubino by the hand and presenting him to Figaro)
There you are.

FIGARO
(to the Count)
What's this story of his?

COUNT
No story; but he says it was he who jumped on the carnations this morning . . .

FIGARO
He says so! . . . well, if I jumped down
it's possible that he too
could do the same.

COUNT
He too?

FIGARO
Why not?
I never dispute what I don't know.
(A Spanish march is heard in the distance)

22. FINALE

FIGARO
There's the march . . . let's go.
Take your places,
ladies.
Susanna, give me your arm.

SUSANNA
Here it is.
(Figaro takes Susanna's arm: exeunt omnes except the Count and Countess)

COUNT
(aside)
Such presumption!

COUNTESS
(aside)
I feel like ice.

CONTE
Contessa . . .

CONTESSA
Or non parliamo.
Ecco qui le due nozze:
Riceverle dobbiam; alfin si tratta
D'una vostra protetta.
Seggiamo.

CONTE
Seggiamo.
(tra sé)
E meditiam vendetta.

(siedono)

SCENA QUATTORDICESIMA

Cacciatori con fucili in spalla, contadini e contadine. Due giovinette che portano il cappello verginale con piume bianche. Due altre un bianco velo. Due altre i guanti e il mazzetto di fiori. Figaro con Marcellina. Bartolo con Susanna. Due giovinette incominciano il coro, che termina in ripieno. Bartolo conduce Susanna al Conte, e s'inginocchia per ricevere da lui il cappello, ecc. Figaro conduce Marcellina alla Contessa, e fa la stessa funzione

CORO
Amanti constanti,
Seguaci d'onor,
Cantate, lodate
Sì saggio signor.
A un diritto cedendo
Che oltraggia, che offende,
Ei caste vi rende
Ai vostri amator.

TUTTI
Cantiamo, lodiamo
Sì saggio signor.
(Susanna, essendo in ginocchio durante il coro, tira il Conte per l'abito, gli mostra il biglietto, dopo passa la mano dal lato degli

COUNT
My lady . . .

COUNTESS
Say no more now.
Here are the two couples:
we must receive them;
one especially has your protection.
Let us sit down.

COUNT
Let's sit.
(aside)
And plan my revenge.

(They sit)

SCENE 14

Hunters with rifles on their shoulders; villagers. Two young girls carrying a bridal hat with white feathers; two others, a white veil; two more, gloves and bouquet. Figaro with Marcellina, Bartolo with Susanna. Two girls begin the chorus, which the others take up. Bartolo leads Susanna to the Count, and she kneels to receive the hat etc. from him. Figaro leads Marcellina to the Countess: similar business

CHORUS
Faithful and
honourable girls,
sing praises
to our wise lord.
By renouncing a right
which outraged and offended,
he leaves you pure
for your lovers.

ALL
Let us sing praises
to our wise lord.
(Susanna, while kneeling during the chorus, pulls the Count's coat, shows him the letter, then lifts her hand on the audience's side to her head, where

spettatori alla testa, dove pare che il Conte le aggiusti il cappello, e gli dà il biglietto. Il Conte se lo mette furtivamente in seno. Susanna s'alza, gli fa una riverenza: Figaro viene a riceverla; si balla il fandango. Marcellina s'alza un po' più tardi. Bartolo viene a riceverla dalle mani della Contessa. Il Conte va da un lato, cava il biglietto, e fa l'atto d'uom che rimase punto al dito: lo scute, lo preme, lo succhia, e vedendo il biglietto sigillato colla spilla, dice, gittando la spilla a terra)

the Count takes it under cover of adjusting her hat. He puts it furtively in his breast pocket.
Susanna rises, making him a curtsey.
Figaro comes to receive her,
and a fandango is danced.
Marcellina rises slightly after;
Bartolo comes to receive
her from the Countess's hands.
The Count moves aside, takes out the letter, and pricks his finger; he shakes it, presses it, sucks it;
seeing the letter sealed with
a pin, he throws the pin down,
saying)

CONTE
Eh già, solita usanza,
Le donne ficcan gli aghi in ogni loco.
Ah! ah! capisco il gioco.

COUNT
Just like a woman,
to stick a pin in
everywhere.
Ha, ha! I see her meaning.

FIGARO
(vede tutto e dice a Susanna)
Un biglietto amoroso
Che gli die' nel passar qualche galante,
Ed era sigillato d'una spilla
Ond'ei si punse il dito;
(Il Conte legge, bacia il biglietto, cerca la spilla, la trova e se la mette alla manica del saio)
Il Narcisso or la cerca, oh che stordito!

FIGARO
(who is watching it all, to Susanna)
Some flirt, in passing,
has slipped him a billet
doux
sealed with a pin,
on which he's pricked his finger.
(The Count reads the letter, kisses it, looks for the pin, finds it and puts it in his sleeve)
Our Narcissus is looking for it—what fun!

CONTE
Andate, amici, e sia per questa sera
Disposto l'apparato nuziale
Colla più ricca pompa. Io vo' che sia
Magnifica la festa; e canti e fochi,
E gran cena e gran ballo: e ognuno impari
Com'io tratto color che a me son cari.

COUNT
Now go, friends, and let the wedding
celebration be arranged for this evening
with the richest ceremony. I wish there
to be a splendid entertainment, with
singing
and fireworks, a grand banquet
and ball.
You shall see how I treat those dear
to me.

(Il coro e la marcia si ripetono, e tutti partono)

(The chorus and march are repeated: exeunt omnes)

ATTO QUARTO ACT IV

SCENA PRIMA

Giardino

Barbarina sola

23. CAVATINA

BARBARINA
(cerca qualche cosa per terra)
L'ho perduta . . . me meschina! . . .
Ah chi sa dove sarà?
Non la trovo . . . e mia cugina . . .
E il padron cosa dirà?

SCENA SECONDA

Barbarina, Figaro e Marcellina

RECITATIVO

FIGARO
Barbarina, cos'hai?

BARBARINA
L'ho perduta, cugino

FIGARO
Cosa?

MARCELLINA
Cosa?

SCENE 1

The garden

Barbarina alone

23. CAVATINA

BARBARINA
(searching for something on the ground)
Oh dear me, I've lost it . . .
Oh, wherever can it be?
I can't find it . . . my cousin
and my lord . . . what will they say?

SCENE 2

Barbarina, Figaro and Marcellina

RECITATIVE

FIGARO
What's the matter, Barbarina?

BARBARINA
Oh cousin, I've lost it.

FIGARO
What?

MARCELLINA
What?

BARBARINA
La spilla
Che a me diede il padrone
Per recar a Susanna.

BARBARINA
The pin
his lordship gave me
to take back to Susanna.

FIGARO
A Susanna? la spilla?
(in collera)
E così tenerella
Il mestiero già sai . . .
(tranquillo)
Di far tutto si ben quel che tu fai?

FIGARO
To Susanna? the pin?
(angrily)
Even at your age
you know the practices . . .
(calmly)
of doing everything as well as you do?

BARBARINA
Cos'è? vai meco in collera?

BARBARINA
Why are you getting angry with me?

FIGARO
E non vedi ch'io scherzo?
osserva . . . questa
(cerca un momento per terra, dopo aver destramente cavata una spilla dall'abito o dalla cuffia di Marcellina e la dà a Barbarina)
È la spilla che il Conte
Da recare ti diede alla Susanna,
E servia di sigillo a un bigliettino.
Vedi s'io sono istrutto?

FIGARO
Can't you see I'm joking?
Look . . . this
(searching the ground for a moment, after having dexterously taken a pin from Marcellina's dress or cap and giving it to Barbarina)
is the pin the Count gave you
to take back to Susanna:
it was used to seal a note, wasn't it?
You see, I know all about it.

BARBARINA
E perchè il chiedi a me quando sai tutto?

BARBARINA
Then why ask me if you know it all?

FIGARO
Avea gusto d'udir come il padrone
Ti die' la commissione.

FIGARO
I wanted to hear how his lordship
sent you on this errand.

BARBARINA
Che miracoli!
«Tieni, fanciulla, reca questa spilla
Alla bella Susanna, e dille: questo
È il sigillo de' pini.»

BARBARINA
Nothing remarkable!
"Here, my girl, take this pin
to pretty Susanna, and say
this is the seal of the pine-grove".

FIGARO
Ah, ah! de' pini!

FIGARO
Aha! The pine-grove!

BARBARINA
È ver ch'ei mi soggiunse:
«Guarda che alcun non veda!»
Ma tu già tacerai.

BARBARINA
Oh yes, and then he added:
"Take care no one sees you!"
But you won't tell?

FIGARO
Sicuramente

FIGARO
Trust me.

BARBARINA
A te già niente preme.

BARBARINA
It can't concern you at all.

FIGARO
Oh niente, niente.

FIGARO
Oh, not at all.

BARBARINA
Addio, mio bel cugino:
Vo da Susanna e poi da Cherubino.

BARBARINA
Well, goodbye, cousin:
I'm going to Susanna and then to Cherubino.

(parte saltando)

(she dances off)

SCENA TERZA

SCENE 3

Marcellina e Figaro

Marcellina and Figaro

FIGARO
(quasi istupidito)
Madre.

FIGARO
(almost stupefied)
Mother . . .

MARCELLINA
Figlio.

MARCELLINA
My son?

FIGARO
Son morto.

FIGARO
All is over.

MARCELLINA
Càlmati, figlio mio.

MARCELLINA
Calm yourself, my son.

FIGARO
Son morto, dico.

FIGARO
All is over, I say.

MARCELLINA
Flemma, flemma e poi flemma; il fatto è serio
E pensarci convien. Ma guarda un poco,
Che ancor non sai di chi si prenda gioco.

MARCELLINA
Patience, patience and yet more patience;
things are serious and we must think them out.
But wait, you don't know whom the joke is on.

FIGARO
Ah! quella spilla, o madre, è quella stessa
Che poc'anzi ei raccolse.

FIGARO
Oh mother, that pin was
the one
he picked up a little while ago.

MARCELLINA
È ver . . . ma questo

MARCELLINA
I know . . . but this only

Al più ti porge un dritto
Di stare in guardia, e vivere in
sospetto:
Ma non sai se in effetto . . .

FIGARO
All'erta, dunque, il loco del
congresso
So dov'è stabilito.

MARCELLINA
Dove vai, figlio mio?

FIGARO
A vendicar tutti i mariti. Addio.

(parte infuriato)

SCENA QUARTA

MARCELLINA
(sola)
Presto, avvertiam Susanna . . .
Io la credo innocente. Quella
faccia . . .
Quell'aria di modestia . . . E caso
ancora
Ch'ella non fosse? Ah! quando il
cor non ciurma
Personale interesse,
Ogni donna è portata alla
difesa
Del suo povero sesso,
Da quest'uomini ingrati a torto
oppresso.

24. ARIA

MARCELLINA
Il capro e la capretta
Son sempre in amistà,
L'agnello all'agnelletta
La guerra mai non fa.
Le più feroci belve
Per selve e per campagne
Lascian le lor compagne
In pace e libertà.
Sol noi povere femmine,
Che tanto amiam quest' uomini,
Trattate siam dai perfidi
Ognor con crudelta.

justified you being on your guard
and keeping your eyes
open:
but you don't know if in fact . . .

FIGARO
I'll be on the alert!
I know
where the meeting has been arranged for.

MARCELLINA
Where are you going, my son?

FIGARO
To avenge all husbands. Farewell.

(exit furiously)

SCENE 4

MARCELLINA
(alone)
Quick, Susanna must be warned . . .
I think she's innocent. Her
face . . .
her modest air . . .
And yet
suppose she's not? Ah, when
the interest
of her own heart is not threatened,
every woman is bound to come to the
defence
of her own poor sex,
so put upon by these ungrateful
men.

24. ARIA

MARCELLINA
The billy-goat and she-goat
always live in amity,
the lamb never fights
with his mate.
The fiercest beasts
of woods and countryside
leave their fellows
in peace and liberty.
Only we poor women,
who love these men so much,
are always perfidiously
treated with cruelty.

(parte)

SCENA QUINTA

Folto giardino, con due padiglioni, l'uno a dritta e l'altra a sinistra

Barbarina sola, con un po' di frutta e di dolce

RECITATIVO

BARBARINA
Nel padiglione a manca, ei così disse, è questo.
E poi se non venisse! Oh, ve', che brava gente!
A stento darmi un arancio, una pera,
E una ciambella. «Per chi, madamigella?»
Oh per qualcun, signore. «Già lo sappiam»,
Ebbene, il padron l'odia, ed io gli voglio bene,
Però costommi un bacio, e cosa importa,
Forse qualcun me'l renderà.
(sente arrivare qualcuno)
Son morta!

(fugge spaventata nel padiglione a sinistra)

SCENA SESTA

Figaro solo con mantello e lanternino notturno; poi Bartolo, Basilio, e truppa di lavoratori

FIGARO
(tra sé)
È Barbarina.
(forte)
Chi va là?

BASILIO
Son quelli
Che invitasti a venir.

(exit)

SCENE 5

The depths of the garden, with two pavilions, one on the left, one on the right

Barbarina alone, with some fruit and sweetmeats

RECITATIVE

BARBARINA
In the left-hand pavilion, he said: this is it.
Suppose he doesn't come? Oh, these tiresome people!
I could hardly get them to give me an apple,
a pear and a pastry. 'Who's it for, my dear? '
'It's for someone, sir.' 'We know that'.
Oh well, his lordship hates him, but I love him:
it cost me a kiss, but what does it matter?
Someone's bound to pay it back.
(she hears someone coming)
Mercy on us!

(She flees in fright into the left pavilion)

SCENE 6

Figaro alone, with a cloak and dark lantern; then Bartolo, Basilio and a group of workmen

FIGARO
(aside)
That's Barbarina.
(aloud)
Who goes there?

BASILIO
Those whom
you invited to come.

BARTOLO
Che brutto ceffo!
Sembri un cospirator: che diamin sono
Quegli infausti apparati?

FIGARO
Lo vedrete tra poco.
In questo stesso loco
Celebrerem la festa
Della mia sposa onesta
E del feudal signor . . .

BASILIO
Ah, buono, buono!
Capisco come egli è.
(tra sé)
Accordati si son senza di me.

FIGARO
Voi da questi contorni
Non vi scostate: intanto
Io vado a dar certi ordini
E torno in pochi istanti:
A un fischio mio correte tutti quanti.

(partono tutti, eccetuati Bartolo e Basilio)

SCENA SETTIMA

Basilio e Bartolo

BASILIO
Ha i diavoli nel corpo!

BARTOLO
Ma cosa, quanti?

BASILIO
Nulla. Susanna piace al Conte;
Ella d'accordo gli diè un appuntamento,
Ch'a Figaro non piace.

BARTOLO
E che? Dunque dovria soffrirlo in pace?

BARTOLO
Why are you scowling?
You look like a conspirator;
what on earth is all this mystery about?

FIGARO
You'll soon see.
In this very spot
there'll be celebrated the union
of my virtuous bride
and our feudal lord . . .

BASILIO
Aha, I understand!
I see now how it is.
(aside)
They've settled it without me.

FIGARO
Do not go away
from hereabouts: meanwhile
I must go and give some instructions;
I'll be back very shortly;
when I whistle, all of you rush out.

(exeunt all save Bartolo and Basilio)

SCENE 7

Basilio and Bartolo

BASILIO
He has the devil in him!

BARTOLO
But what for?

BASILIO
Nothing. Susanna pleases the Count;
she agrees to give him an assignation,
which doesn't please Figaro.

BARTOLO
Well? Should he then take it calmly?

BASILIO
Quelche soffrono tanti, ei soffrir non potrebbe?
E poi sentite, che guadagno può far?
Nel mondo, amico, l'accozzarla con grandi
Fu pericolo ognora;
Dan novanta percento e han vinto ancora.

25. ARIA

BASILIO
In quegli anni, in cui val poco
La mal pratica ragion,
Ebbi anch'io lo stesso foco,
Fui quel pazzo ch'or non son.
Ma col tempo e coi perigli,
Donna Flemma capitò:
E i capricci ed i puntigli
Dalla testa mi cavò.
Presso un picciolo abituro,
Seco lei mi trasse un giorno,
E togliendo giù dal muro
Dal pacifico soggiorno
Una pelle di somaro,
Prendi, disse, o figlio caro,
Poi disparve e mi lasciò.
Mentre ancor tacito guardo quel dono,
Il ciel s'annuvola,
Rimbomba il tuono,
Mista alla grandine scroscia la piova.
Ecco le membra coprir mi giova
Col manto d'asino che mi donò.
Finisce il turbine, io fo due passi,
Che fiera orribile dianzi a me fassi;
Già mi tocca, l'ingorda bocca,
Già di difendermi speme non ho.
Ma il fiuto ignobile del mio vestito
Tolse alla belva sì l'appetito,
Che disprezzandomi si rinselvò.
Cosi conoscere mi fè la sorte
Ch'onte, pericoli, vergogna e morte
Col cuojo d'asino fuggir si può.

(partono)

BASILIO
Why should he not endure what so many endure?
And then again, what good would it do?
In this world, my friend, it always
was dangerous to rub shoulders with the great:
they can give away ninety per cent and still win.

25. ARIA

BASILIO
In youthful years, when reason,
little exercised, prevails but little,
I too felt that same fire,
I was the fool I am no longer.
But with time and experience
I came to know Dame Patience;
and whims and fancies
she drove from my head.
Near a small hovel
she led me one day,
and taking off the wall
of that peaceful dwelling
an ass's skin, she said,
'Take this, dear boy',
then vanished and left me.
While I still was looking,
silently,
at her gift, the sky grew dark,
the thunder roared,
and hail and rain poured down.
So I made use of the ass's skin
she gave me to cover myself.
The storm once over, I was setting off again
when suddenly a ferocious beast stood before me;
its greedy maw was already upon me,
and I had no hope of defending myself.
But the horrid stench of my covering
so took away the beast's appetite
that it took to the woods in disgust.
So fate taught me
that disgrace, danger, shame and death
can be avoided under a donkey's hide.

(exeunt)

SCENA OTTAVA	SCENE 8
26. RECITATIVO ED ARIA	26. RECITATIVE AND ARIA
FIGARO	FIGARO
(solo, con mantello)	*(alone, in a cloak)*
Tutto è disposto: l'ora	Everything is ready; the hour
Dovrebbe esser vicina, io sento	must be at hand; I heard
gente . . .	someone . . .
È dessa . . . non è alcun . . . buia	Is it she? . . . no, no one . . .
è la notte . . .	it's very dark
Ed io comincio omai	tonight . . . and now I begin
A fare il scimunito	to learn the foolish art
Mestiere di marito . . .	of being a husband.
Ingrata! nel momento	Traitress! at the very moment
Della mia cerimonia . . .	of our wedding . . .
Ei godeva leggendo, e nel vederlo	He reading with pleasure, and I,
Io rideva di me senza	watching him, unwittingly laughing at
saperlo.	myself.
Oh Susanna, Susanna,	Oh Susanna, Susanna,
Quanta pena mi costi!	what anguish you have cost me!
Con quell'ingenua faccia . . .	With that sweet face
Con quegli occhi innocenti . . .	and those innocent eyes . . .
Chi creduto l'avria! . . .	Who would have believed it!
Ah che il fidarsi a donna è ognor	Ah, to trust women is sheer
follia.	folly.
Aprite un po' quegli occhi,	Just open your eyes,
Uomini incauti e sciocchi,	you rash and foolish men,
Guardate queste femmine,	and look at these women;
Guardate cosa son.	see them as they are,
Queste chiamate Dee	these goddesses, so called
Dagli ingannati sensi,	by the intoxicated senses,
A cui tributa incensi	to whom feeble reason
La debole ragion.	offers tribute.
Son streghe che incantano	They are witches who cast spells
Per farci penar,	for our torment,
Sirene che cantano	sirens who sing
Per farci affogar;	for our confusion,
Civette che allettano	night owls who fascinate
Per trarci le piume,	to pluck us,
Comete che brillano	comets who dazzle
Per toglierci il lume.	to deprive us of light.
Son rose spinose,	They are thorned roses,
Son volpi vezzose,	alluring vixens,
Son orse benigne,	smiling she-bears,
Colombe maligne	malign doves,
Maestre d'inganni,	masters of deceit,
Amiche d'affanni	friends of distress
Che fingono, mentono,	who cheat and lie,
Che amore non sentono,	feel no love
Non senton pietà.	and have no pity.

Il resto nol dico,
Già ognuno lo sa.

(si ritira)

SCENA NONA

Susanna e la Contessa, travestite, Marcellina, e Figaro in disparte

RECITATIVO

SUSANNA
Signora, ella mi disse
Che Figaro verravvi.

MARCELLINA
Anzi, è venuto;
Abbassa un po' la voce.

SUSANNA
Dunque un ci ascolta, e l'altro
Dee venir a cercarmi.
Incominciam.

MARCELLINA
Io voglio qui celarmi.

(entra dove entrò Barbarina)

SCENA DECIMA

I suddetti, meno Marcellina

SUSANNA
Madama, voi tremate, avreste
freddo?

CONTESSA
Parmi umida la notte . . . io mi
ritiro.

FIGARO
(tra sé)
Eccoci della crisi al grande istante.

SUSANNA
Io sotto queste piante,
Se madama il permette,
Resto a prendere il fresco una

The rest I need not say,
for everyone knows it already.

(he retires)

SCENE 9

Susanna and the Countess, both in disguise, Marcellina, and Figaro to one side

RECITATIVE

SUSANNA
Marcellina told me, my lady,
that Figaro would be coming.

MARCELLINA
He's here already;
lower your voice a little.

SUSANNA
So one's listening, the other
should be coming to find me.
We can begin.

MARCELLINA
I'll hide myself in here.

(enters where Barbarina went)

SCENE 10

The above, without Marcellina

SUSANNA
Madam, you are trembling; are you
cold?

COUNTESS
The night is rather chilly . . . I'll
go in.

FIGARO
(aside)
Now comes the climax of the drama.

SUSANNA
If your ladyship will allow me,
I'll stay among the pine-trees
to take the air for half an

mezz'ora.

FIGARO
(tra sé)
Il fresco, il fresco!

CONTESSA
Restaci, in buon'ora.

SUSANNA
(sottovoce)
Il birbo è in sentinella.
Divertiamoci anche noi.
Diamogli la mercè de' dubbi suoi.

27. RECITATIVO ED ARIA

SUSANNA
Giunse alfin il momento
Che godrò senza affanno
In braccio all'idol mio; timide cure,
Uscite dal mio petto,
A turbar non venite il mio diletto.
Oh come par che all'amoroso foco
L'amenità del loco,
La terra e il ciel risponda!
Come la notte i furti miei seconda!

Deh vieni, non tardar, o gioio bella,
Vieni ove amore per goder t'appella,
Finchè non splende in ciel notturna face
Finchè l'aria è ancor bruna e il mondo tace.
Qui mormora il ruscel, qui scherza l'aura,
Che col dolce sussurro il cor ristaura.
Qui rodono i fioretti e l'erba è fresca;
Ai piaceri d'amor qui tutto adesca.
Vieni, ben mio, tra queste piante ascose
Ti vo' la fronte incoronar di rose.

SCENA UNDECIMA

I suddetti e Cherubino, poi il Conte

RECITATIVO

hour.

FIGARO
(aside)
To take the air!

COUNTESS
Stay, and take your time.

SUSANNA
(aside)
The rascal's watching,
so we'll have some fun.
We'll reward him for his doubts.

27. RECITATIVE AND ARIA

SUSANNA
At last comes the moment
when, without reserve, I can rejoice
in my lover's arms: timid scruples,
hence from my heart, and do not
come to trouble my delight.
Oh how the spirit of this place,
the earth and the sky, seem
to echo the fire of love!
How the night furthers my stealth!

Come, do not delay, oh bliss,
come where love calls thee to joy,
while night's torch does not shine in the sky,
while the air is still dark and the world quiet.
Here murmurs the stream, here sports the breeze,
which refreshes the heart with its sweet whispers.
Here flowers smile and the grass is cool:
here everything invites to the pleasures of love.
Come, my dearest, and amid these sheltered trees
I will wreathe thy brow with roses.

SCENE 11

The above and Cherubino, later the Count

RECITATIVE

FIGARO
Perfida! e in quella forma
Meco mentia? Non so s'io veglio
o dormo.

CHERUBINO
(cantarellando)
La la la . . .

CONTESSA
(tra sé)
Il piccol paggio!

CHERUBINO
Io sento gente: entriamo
Ove entrò Barbarina.
Oh, vedo qui una donna!

CONTESSA
Ahime meschina!

CHERUBINO
M'inganno! A quel cappello
Che nell'ombra vegg'io, parmi
Susanna.

CONTESSA
(tra sé)
E se il Conte ora vien? Sorte
tiranna!

28. FINALE

CHERUBINO
(tra sé)
Pian pianin le andrò più presso,
Tempo perso non sarà.

CONTESSA
(tra sé)
Ah se il Conte arriva adesso
Qualche imbroglio accaderà!

CHERUBINO
(alla Contessa)
Susannetta . . . non risponde . . .
Colla mano il volto asconde . . .
Or la burlo, in verità.
(La prende per la mano, l'accarezza, la Contessa cerca liberarsi)

FIGARO
The traitress! this is how
she was deceiving me. Am I awake
or dreaming?

CHERUBINO
(enters singing)
La la la . . .

COUNTESS
(aside)
The page!

CHERUBINO
I hear someone: I'll go
where I can find Barbarina.
Ah, I see a woman!

COUNTESS
Woe is me!

CHERUBINO
Surely not! By that hat I thought
I recognised Susanna in the
darkness.

COUNTESS
(aside)
If my lord should come now! Cruel
fate!

28. FINALE

CHERUBINO
(aside)
Very softly I'll approach her.
my time will not be wasted.

COUNTESS
(aside)
Oh, if the Count should arrive now
what confusion there will be!

CHERUBINO
(to the Countess)
Dear Susanna . . . she doesn't answer . . .
She hides her face with her hand . . .
Now I'll really tease her.
(He takes her hand and caresses it, while the Countess tries to free herself)

CONTESSA
(alterando la voce)
Arditello, sfacciatello,
Ite presto via di qua.

CHERUBINO
Smorfiosa, maliziosa,
Io già so perchè sei qua.

CONTE
(da lontano, in atteggiamento d'uno che guarda)
Ecco qui la mia Susanna.

SUSANNA E FIGARO
(lontani l'uno dall'altro)
Ecco qui l'uccellatore.

CHERUBINO
Non far meco la tiranna!

SUSANNA, CONTE E FIGARO
(tra sé)
Ah, nel sen mi batte il core!
Un altr'uom con lei si sta.

CONTESSA
(sottovoce a Cherubino)
Via, partite, o chiamo gente.

CHERUBINO
(sempre tenendola per la mano)
Dammi un bacio, o non fai niente.

SUSANNA, CONTE E FIGARO
(tra sé)
Alla voce, è quegli il paggio.

CONTESSA
Anche un bacio! che coraggio!

CHERUBINO
E perchè far io non posso
Quel che il Conte ognor farà!

SUSANNA, CONTESSA, CONTE E FIGARO
(ciascuno tra sé)
Temerario!

COUNTESS
(disguising her voice)
Impudent fellow,
be off from here at once.

CHERUBINO
Affected flirt,
I know why you're here.

COUNT
(from afar, in the attitude of a watcher)
There is my Susanna.

SUSANNA AND FIGARO
(distant one from the other)
Here's the bird-catcher.

CHERUBINO
Don't be so hard on me!

SUSANNA, COUNT AND FIGARO
(aside)
How my heart beats in my breast!
Another man is there with her.

COUNTESS
(softly to Cherubino)
Go away, or I'll call for help.

CHERUBINO
(still holding her hand)
Give me a kiss, or you'll do nothing.

SUSANNA, COUNT AND FIGARO
(aside)
By his voice, that's the page.

COUNTESS
What, a kiss? What insolence!

CHERUBINO
And why can't I do
what the Count does all the time?

SUSANNA, COUNTESS, COUNT AND FIGARO
(each aside)
What effrontery!

CHERUBINO
Oh ve' che smorfie!
Sai ch'io fui dietro il sofà.

SUSANNA, CONTESSA,
CONTE E FIGARO
(come sopra)
Se il ribaldo ancor sta saldo,
La faccenda guasterà.

CHERUBINO
Prendi intanto . . .
(Il paggio vuol dare un bacio alla Contessa, il Conte si mette in mezzo e riceve il bacio egli stesso)

CONTESSA E CHERUBINO
Oh ciel! il Conte.
(Il paggio entra da Barbarina)

FIGARO
Vo' veder cosa fan là.

CONTE
Perchè voi nol ripetete,
Ricevete questo qua.
(Il Conte vuol dare uno schiaffo a Cherubino, Figaro in questo s'appressa e lo riceve egli stesso)

FIGARO
Ah! ci ho fatto un bel guadagno
Colla mia curiosità.
(ritira)

SUSANNA, CONTESSA E CONTE
Ah! ci ha fatto un bel guadagno
Colla sua temerità.
(Susanna, che ode lo shiaffo, ride)

CONTE
(alla Contessa)
Partito è alfin l'audace,
Accostati, ben mio.

CONTESSA
Giacchè così vi piace,
Eccomi qui, signor.

CHERUBINO
Don't be so prudish!
You know I was behind the sofa.

SUSANNA, COUNTESS,
COUNT AND FIGARO
(as above)
If the wretch persists in being obstinate,
he will ruin all our plan.

CHERUBINO
Take a kiss then . . .
(He tries to kiss the Countess, but the Count intervenes and receives the kiss himself)

COUNTESS AND CHERUBINO
Oh heavens! the Count.
(The page goes into the pavilion with Barbarina)

FIGARO
I must see what's going on there.

COUNT
Since you won't behave,
take that, then.
(He goes to slap Cherubino, but Figaro approaches at this moment and receives it himself)

FIGARO
Ah! That's the reward
my curiosity has brought me.
(retires)

SUSANNA, COUNTESS AND COUNT
Ah! That's the reward
his temerity has brought him.
(Susanna, who has seen the slap, laughs)

COUNT
(to Countess)
At last that impudent fellow's gone;
come nearer, my dear.

COUNTESS
As you wish.
Here I am, my lord.

FIGARO
(tra sé)
Che compiacente femmina!
Che sposa di buon cor!

FIGARO
(aside)
What an obliging girl!
What an open-hearted bride!

CONTE
Porgimi la manina.

COUNT
Give me your little hand.

CONTESSA
Io ve la do.

COUNTESS
Here it is.

CONTE
Carina!

COUNT
My dearest!

FIGARO
Carina?

FIGARO
His dearest?

CONTE
Che dita tenerelle!
Che delicata pelle!
Mi pizzica, mi stuzzica,
M'empie d'un nuovo ardor.

COUNT
What slender fingers,
what delicate skin!
They pierce me through and through
and fill me with new ardour.

SUSANNA, CONTESSA E FIGARO
La cieca prevenzione
Delude la ragione,
Inganna i sensi ognor.

SUSANNA, COUNTESS AND FIGARO
His blind infatuation
deludes his reason
and deceives all his senses.

CONTE
Oltre la dote, o cara,
Ricevi anche un brillante,
Che a te porge un amante
In pegno del suo amor.
(le dà un anello)

COUNT
Besides your dowry, my dearest,
take this jewel too,
which a lover gives you
as token of his love.
(gives her a ring)

CONTESSA
Tutto Susanna piglia
Dal suo benefattor.

COUNTESS
Susanna owes everything
to her benefactor.

SUSANNA, CONTE E FIGARO
(tra sé)
Va tutto a maraviglia!
Ma il meglio manca ancor.

SUSANNA, COUNT AND FIGARO
(aside)
Everything is going splendidly!
But the best is yet to come.

CONTESSA
(al Conte)
Signor, d'accese fiaccole
Io veggio il balenar.

COUNTESS
(to Count)
My lord, I see the glow
of kindled torches.

CONTE
Entriam, mia bella Venere.

COUNT
Come then, my Venus,

Andiamoci a celar.

let us conceal ourselves in here.

SUSANNA E FIGARO
(tra sé)
Mariti scimuniti,
Venite ad imparar.

SUSANNA AND FIGARO
(aside)
Foolish husbands,
come and learn your lesson.

CONTESSA
Al buio, signor mio?

COUNTESS
In the dark, my lord?

CONTE
È quello che vogl'io:
Tu sai che là per leggere
Io non desìo d'entrar.

COUNT
That's what I would have:
you know I'm not going there
in order to read.

FIGARO
La perfida lo seguita,
È vano il dubitar.

FIGARO
Now she's followed him,
I cannot doubt her deceit.

SUSANNA E CONTESSA
I furbi sono in trappola,
Comincia ben l'affar.
(Figaro passa, il Conte con voce alterata)

SUSANNA AND COUNTESS
The rogues are in the trap;
the play has begun well.
(Figaro passes; the Count disguises his voice)

CONTE
Chi passa?

COUNT
Who's there?

FIGARO
(con rabbia)
Passa gente.

FIGARO
(angrily)
What's it to you?

CONTESSA
(sottovoce al Conte)
È Figaro, men vo.

COUNTESS
(softly to the Count)
That's Figaro; I'm going.

CONTE
Andate: io poi verrò.
(Il Conte si disperde nel folto, la Contessa entra nel padiglione a destra)

COUNT
Go on: I'll rejoin you soon.
(He retires among the trees; the Countess goes into the pavilion on the right)

FIGARO
Tutto è tranquillo e placido:
Entrò la bella Venere:
Col vago Marte prendere,
Nuovo Vulcan del secolo,
In rete li potrò.

FIGARO
All is quiet and peaceful;
fair Venus has gone in;
to take her with her lover Mars,
like a modern Vulcan
I'll catch them in my net.

SUSANNA
(con voce alterata)

SUSANNA
(disguising her voice)

Ehi, Figaro tacete!

FIGARO
Oh questa è la Contessa . . .
A tempo qui giungete . . .
Vedrete là voi stessa . . .
Il Conte e la mia sposa . . .
Di propria man la cosa
Toccar io vi farò.

SUSANNA
(Susanna si scorda di alterare la voce)
Parlate un po' più basso:
Di qua non muovo passo,
Ma vendicar mi vo'.

FIGARO
(tra sé)
Susanna!
(forte)
Vendicarsi?

SUSANNA
Sì.

FIGARO
Come potria farsi?
(tra sé)
La volpe vuol sorprendermi,
E secondarla vo'.

SUSANNA
(tra sé)
L'iniquo io vo' sorprendere,
Poi so quel che farò.

FIGARO
(con comica affettazione)
Ah, se madama il vuole!

SUSANNA
Su via, manco parole.

FIGARO
(come sopra)
Eccomi ai vostri piedi . . .
Ho pieno il cor di foco.
Esaminate il loco . . .
Pensate al traditor.

Hey, Figaro! Keep quiet!

FIGARO
Ah, that is the Countess . . .
you came in time.
There you'll see for yourself
the Count and my bride;
you can touch them
with your own hand.

SUSANNA
(forgetting to change her voice)
Speak a little softer:
I shall not stir from here,
but I will be avenged.

FIGARO
(aside)
Susanna!
(aloud)
Be avenged?

SUSANNA
Yes.

FIGARO
How can you do this?
(aside)
The vixen wants to trap me,
I'll lead her on.

SUSANNA
(aside)
I'll trap the villain,
then I'll know what to do.

FIGARO
(with comic exaggeration)
Ah, if my lady wishes it!

SUSANNA
Go on, don't waste words.

FIGARO
(as above)
Here I kneel at your feet,
my heart full of fire.
Look at this spot,
and think how you were betrayed.

SUSANNA
(tra sé)
Come la man mi pizzica,
Che smania! che furor!

SUSANNA
(aside)
How my hand tingles
with impatience and fury!

FIGARO
Come il polmon mi s'altera!
Che smania! che calor!

FIGARO
How my bosom heaves
with impatience and fire!

SUSANNA
(alterando la voce un poco)
E senza alcun affetto? . . .

SUSANNA
(altering her voice a little)
Without any love?

FIGARO
Suppliscavi il rispetto.
Non perdiam tempo invano,
Datemi un po' la mano . . .

FIGARO
Let my indignation be sufficient.
Let's waste no more time in vain;
give me your hand . . .

SUSANNA
Servitevi, signor.
(Gli dà uno schiaffo parlando in voce naturale)

SUSANNA
Take it, sir.
(Speaking in her own voice, she slaps his face)

FIGARO
Che schiaffo!

FIGARO
What a blow!

SUSANNA
E ancora questo
E questo, e poi quest'altro.

SUSANNA
And that too,
and that, and that as well.

FIGARO
Non batter così presto.

FIGARO
Don't beat me so fast.

SUSANNA
E questo, signor scaltro,
E poi quest'altro ancor.

SUSANNA
And that, you rascal,
and that again.

FIGARO
Oh schiaffi graziosissimi!
Oh mio felice amor!

FIGARO
How sweet these blows!
How happy is my love!

SUSANNA
Impara, impara, o perfido,
A fare il seduttor.

SUSANNA
That'll teach you, false one,
to play the seducer.

FIGARO
(si mette in ginocchio)
Pace, pace, mio dolce tesoro:
Io conobbi la voce che adoro,
E che impressa ognor serbo nel cor.

FIGARO
(kneeling)
Now peace, my dearest treasure:
I recognised the voice I love
and which keeps my heart in thrall.

SUSANNA
(ridendo e con sorpresa)
La mia voce?

FIGARO
La voce che adoro.

SUSANNA E FIGARO
Pace, pace, mio dolce tesoro,
Pace, pace, mio tenero amor.

CONTE
(entrando)
Non la trovo, e girai tutto il bosco.

FIGARO E SUSANNA
Questi è il Conte, alla voce il conosco.

CONTE
(parlando verso il padiglione dove entrò la Contessa; apre la nicchia)
Ehi, Susanna . . . sei sorda . . .
sei muta?

SUSANNA
(sottovoce a Figaro)
Bella, bella! non l'ha conosciuta!

FIGARO
(sottovoce a Susanna)
Chi?

SUSANNA
(c.s.)
Madama.

FIGARO
(c.s.)
Madama?

SUSANNA E FIGARO
(c.s.)
Madama.
La commedia, idol mio, terminiamo,
Consoliamo il bizzarro amator.

FIGARO
(ad alta voce, si mette ai piedi di Susanna)

SUSANNA
(laughing, in surprise)
My voice?

FIGARO
The voice I adore.

SUSANNA AND FIGARO
Then peace, my dearest treasure,
peace, my sweetest love.

COUNT
(entering)
I can't find her, though I've been through all the wood.

FIGARO AND SUSANNA
That's the Count, I recognise his voice.

COUNT
(Calling towards the pavilion into which the Countess went; he opens the door)
Susanna . . . are you deaf . . .
are you dumb?

SUSANNA
(softly to Figaro)
Oh lovely! he didn't recognise her!

FIGARO
(softly to Susanna)
Who?

SUSANNA
(as above)
My lady.

FIGARO
(as above)
My lady?

SUSANNA AND FIGARO
(as above)
My lady.
Let's end this comedy, my dearest,
and console this strange lover.

FIGARO
(aloud, throwing himself at Susanna's feet)

Sì Madama, voi siete il ben mio.	Yes, my lady, you are my love.
CONTE *(tra sé)* La mia sposa: ah, senz'arme son io!	COUNT *(aside)* My wife; and I unarmed!
FIGARO Un ristoro al mio cor concedete.	FIGARO Grant some solace to my heart.
SUSANNA Io son qui, faccio quel che volete.	SUSANNA Here I am: do what you will.
CONTE Ah ribaldi!	COUNT How dare they!
SUSANNA E FIGARO Ah corriamo, mio bene, E le pene compensi il piacer.	SUSANNA AND FIGARO Let us hasten, love, and let pleasure make up for our pain.
(vanno verso il padiglione a sinistra)	*(They go towards the pavilion on the left)*
SCENA ULTIMA	FINAL SCENE
CONTE Gente, gente, all'armi, all'armi.	COUNT Ho there! Bring your swords!
FIGARO Il padrone! son perduto! *(Susanna entra nel padiglione, Figaro finge eccessiva paura)*	FIGARO The master! I'm lost! *(Susanna goes into the pavilion; Figaro feigns extreme fright)*
CONTE Gente, gente, aiuto, aiuto!	COUNT Ho there, I say! Help!
I suddetti, Antonio, Basilio e Bartolo. Coro con fiaccole accese	*The above, Antonio, Basilio and Bartolo. Chorus with lit torches*
CURZIO, BASILIO, ANTONIO E BARTOLO Cosa avvenne?	CURZIO, BASILIO, ANTONIO AND BARTOLO What's amiss?
CONTE Il scellerato: M'ha tradito, m'ha infamato, E con chi, state a veder.	COUNT The scoundrel: he's betrayed me, he has shamed me, and with whom, you shall see.
CURZIO, BASILIO, ANTONIO E BARTOLO Son stordito, sbalordito. Non mi par che ciò sia ver.	CURZIO, BASILIO, ANTONIO AND BARTOLO I'm astounded, I'm bewildered, I can't believe it's true.

FIGARO
Son storditi, sbalorditi:
Oh che scena, che piacer!

FIGARO
They're astounded, they're bewildered.
What a scene! oh what joy!

CONTE
Invan resistete,
Uscite, Madama,
Il premio or avrete
Di vostra onestà.
(Il Conte tira pel braccio Cherubino, che fa forza per non uscire, nè si vede che per metà; dopo il Paggio, escono Barbarina, Marcellina e Susanna, vestita cogli abiti della Contessa, si tiene il fazzoletto sulla faccia, s'inginocchia ai peidi del Conte)

COUNT
In vain you resist:
come forth, my lady,
and receive the reward
of your virtue.
(The Count pulls out by the arm Cherubino, who attempts to resist and is only half seen: then follow Barbarina, Marcellina and Susanna, who, dressed in the Countess's clothes and holding a handkerchief to her face, kneels at the Count's feet)

CONTE
Il paggio!

COUNT
The page!

ANTONIO
Mia figlia!

ANTONIO
My daughter!

FIGARO
Mia madre!

FIGARO
My mother!

CURZIO, BASILIO, ANTONIO E BARTOLO
Madama!

CURZIO, BASILIO, ANTONIO AND BARTOLO
My lady!

CONTE
Scoperta è la trama,
La perfida è qua.

COUNT
The plot is discovered,
the traitress is here.

SUSANNA
Perdono, perdono.
(S'inginocchiano tutti ad uno ad uno)

SUSANNA
Forgive me, forgive me.
(All kneel, one after the other)

CONTE
No, no, non sperarlo.

COUNT
No, no, do not hope for it.

FIGARO
Perdono, perdono.

FIGARO
Forgive me, forgive me.

CONTE
No, no, non vo' darlo.

COUNT
No, no I will not.

TUTTI
Perdono, perdono.

ALL
Forgive us, forgive us.

CONTE
(con più forza)
No, no, no, no, no.
(Esce la Contessa dall' altro padiglione. Vuol inginocchiarsi. Il Conte nol permette)

COUNT
(more forcefully)
No, no, no, no.
(The Countess emerges from the other pavilion tries to kneel, but the Count prevents her)

CONTESSA
Almeno io per loro
Perdono otterrò.

COUNTESS
At least let me plead
forgiveness for them.

CURZIO, BASILIO, CONTE, ANTONIO E BARTOLO
Oh cielo! che veggio!
Deliro! vaneggio!
Che creder non so.

CURZIO, BASILIO, COUNT, ANTONIO AND BARTOLO
Heavens! What do I see?
A delusion, a vision,
that I can't believe.

CONTE
(in tono supplichevole)
Contessa, perdono.

COUNT
(in tones of supplication)
My Countess, forgive me.

CONTESSA
Più docile io sono,
E dico di sì.

COUNTESS
I am kinder:
I will say Yes.

TUTTI
Ah! tutti contenti
Saremo così.
Questo giorno di tormenti,
Di capricci e di follia,
In contenti e in allegria
Solo amor può terminar.
Sposi, amici, al ballo, al gioco,
Alle mine date foco,
Ed al suon di lieta marcia
Corriam tutti a festeggiar.

ALL
Then let us all
be happy.
This day of torment,
of caprices and folly,
love can end
only in contentment and joy.
Lovers and friends, let's round
things off in dancing and pleasure,
and to the sound of a gay march
let's hasten to the revelry.

Così Fan Tutte

libretto by

Lorenzo da Ponte

Dramatis Personae

FIORDILIGI
DORABELLA — *sisters from Ferrara, living in Naples*

GUGLIELMO, *in love with Fiordiligi*
FERRANDO, *in love with Dorabella* — *officers*

DESPINA, *a maid*

DON ALFONSO, *an elderly philosopher*

CHORUS of soldiers, sailors, servants, etc.

The scene is set in Naples

Synopsis

ACT I

A coffee house. The cynical Don Alfonso taunts Ferrando and Guglielmo into a wager on the virtue of Fiordiligi and Dorabella: are they indeed paragons of constancy as the officers suppose, or merely like all other women? For their part of the bargain, the men must obey Don Alfonso's instructions implicitly for a whole day, a condition they accept eagerly.

A garden by the sea. Don Alfonso comes upon the sisters in rapt contemplation of their lovers' portrait miniatures, and tells them that the officers have been called on active service. The following ensemble of farewell is marked by desperate grief on the part of the sisters and sublime confidence on that of the officers. Don Alfonso is much amused.

A room in the sisters' house. The maid Despina is amazed by her mistresses' wildly distracted behaviour, particularly as the cause seems to her quite trivial. She urges them to take as much advantage of their lovers' absence as their lovers' themselves undoubtly are.

With the aid of a gold piece Alfonso enlists Despina's aid in part of his plot: she is to urge Fiordiligi and Dorabella to accept consolation at the hand of two rich Albanian suitors, but without knowing that they are Ferrando and Guglielmo in disguise.

At first sight of them the sisters are outraged, and even when Don Alfonso introduces them as old friends of his they remain obdurate to their advances and sweep out. The officers offer to let Alfonso off half his wager, but he bids them bide their time.

The garden. The Albanians burst in on the sisters singing of their sadness, swallow 'arsenic' before their very eyes and fall senseless to the ground. The sisters are urged by Don Alfonso to show some consideration to these men in their last moments on earth, and they go so far as to take pulses and feel fevered brows. Despina arrives, disguised as a doctor, and draws the 'poison' from the bodies with Doctor Mesmer's magnet. The Albanians become extremely amorous–the effects of the poison–but Fiordiligi and Dorabella, though starting to weaken, draw the line at a kiss.

ACT II

A room. Despina bombards the sisters with earthy peasant wisdom and urges them to give in to their new suitors. Fiordiligi and Dorabella are afraid of a scandal, so Despina suggests that the world could be told that the Albanians are paying court to *her.* The sisters agree that no harm could come from being at least polite, and Dorabella decides to choose the dark one (Guglielmo) and Fiordiligi the fair one (Ferrando). Don Alfonso summons them to the garden, where the rich Albanians have prepared a *festa.*

The garden by the sea. After a serenade and much encouragement from Alfonso and Despina, who tactfully retire, the stilted conversation gradually becomes more free and the two couples walk arm in arm. The ardour of Guglielmo's advances soon melts Dorabella's resistance, and almost without knowing it she has exchanged her miniature of Ferrando for Guglielmo's token of a jewelled heart. Fiordiligi, however, firmly dismisses Ferrando, and when left alone she begs her absent lover's forgiveness for a moment of weakness.

When the officers return to compare notes, Ferrando is deeply disturbed by the proof of Dorabella's faithlessness: it has revealed to him the depth of his love for her. They are now ready to bring the game to an end, but Don Alfonso reminds them that they are his to command for a day.

A room. In great distress Fiordiligi admits to Despina and Dorabella that she loves the fair Albanian, but she is quite determined not to give in to her desires. She orders Despina to bring Guglielmo's uniform so that she and Dorabella may join their lovers at the front. But Ferrando enters, and his disillusion naturally makes him redouble his efforts to win over Guglielmo's beloved; Guglielmo himself witnesses the scene from the next-door room. At last Fiordiligi gives in.

The three men meet, and Don Alfonso urges the young officers to accept their womenfolk as they are: after all, he makes them repeat after him–'*così fan tutte,* thus do they all'. Despina tells the Albanians that her mistresses have agreed to marry them.

A brilliantly lit salon. A notary (Despina in disguise again) draws up the contract, but just as the sisters have signed, the march heralding their lovers' return is heard off-stage. The Albanians disappear, the officers return, Despina is unmasked and the contract discovered. The officers find the Albanians' clothes and taunt the sisters, who promise to make good their lapse. All end by agreeing that happy is the man who lets reason be his guide in all things.

ATTO PRIMO

ACT I

SCENA PRIMA

Bottega di caffè

Ferrando, Don Alfonso e Guglielmo

1. TERZETTO

FERRANDO
La mia Dorabella
Capace non è;
Fedel quanto bella
Il cielo la fe'.

GUGLIELMO
La mia Fiordiligi
Tradirmi non sa;
Uguale in lei credo
Costanza e beltà.

DON ALFONSO
Ho i crini già grigi,
Ex cathedra parlo,
Ma tali litigi
Finiscano qua.

FERRANDO E GUGLIELMO
No, detto ci avete
Che infide esser ponno;
Provar cel' dovete
Se avete onestà.

DON ALFONSO
Tai prove lasciamo.

SCENE 1

A coffee-house

Ferrando, Don Alfonso and Guglielmo

1. TRIO

FERRANDO
My Dorabella couldn't
do such a thing:
Heaven made her
as faithful as she's fair.

GUGLIELMO
My Fiordiligi simply
couldn't betray me:
I believe her constancy
equals her beauty.

DON ALFONSO
My hair is already grey,
I speak with authority;
but let's have done
with argument.

FERRANDO AND GUGLIELMO
No, you've told us
they could be faithless;
if you're honest
you will prove it.

DON ALFONSO
Let's not trouble with proof.

FERRANDO E GUGLIELMO
(metton mano alla spada)
No, no, le vogliamo:
O fuori la spada,
Rompiam l'amistà.

DON ALFONSO
O pazzo desire,
Cercar di scoprire
Quel mai che, trovato,
Meschini ci fa.

FERRANDO E GUGLIELMO
Sul vivo mi tocca
Chi lascia di bocca
Sortire un accento
Che torto le fa.

RECITATIVO

GUGLIELMO
Fuor la spada: scegliete
Qual di noi più vi piace.

DON ALFONSO
(placido)
Io son uomo di pace
E duelli non fo,
Se non a mensa.

FERRANDO
O battervi,
O dir subito
Perchè d'infedeltà le nostre amanti
Sospettate capaci.

DON ALFONSO
Cara semplicità, quanto mi piaci!

FERRANDO
Cessate di scherzar,
O giuro al cielo . . .

DON ALFONSO
Ed io giuro alla terra.
Non scherzo, amici miei;
Solo saper vorrei
Che razza d'animali
Son queste vostre belle,
Se han come tutti noi carne, ossa
e pelle,

FERRANDO AND GUGLIELMO
(setting their hands to their swords)
No, no, we demand it:
or out with your sword
and we'll break up this friendship.

DON ALFONSO
O what folly
to try to discover
the wrong which will make us wretched
when we've found it!

FERRANDO AND GUGLIELMO
He strikes at my honour
who allows his lips
to utter a word
which does her wrong.

RECITATIVE

GUGLIELMO
Draw your sword!
Choose which of us you'd prefer.

DON ALFONSO
(calmly)
I'm a peaceable man
and don't touch steel
except at table.

FERRANDO
Either fight,
or say at once
why you suspect our sweethearts
could possibly be untrue.

DON ALFONSO
Sweet simplicity, how I love it!

FERRANDO
A truce to your jests,
or I swear, by heaven . . .

DON ALFONSO
And I swear by this world.
My friends, I'm not jesting;
I'd only like to know
what kind of creatures
are these beauties of yours,
if they're flesh and blood and bone
like us,

Se mangian come noi, se veston gonne,
Alfin, se dee, se donne son . . .

if they eat like us, and wears skirts,
if, in fact, they're goddesses or women . . .

FERRANDO E GUGLIELMO
Son donne, ma son tali . . .

FERRANDO AND GUGLIELMO
They're women, but the like of them . . .

DON ALFONSO
E in donne pretendete
Di trovar fedeltà?
Quanto mi piaci mai, semplicità!

DON ALFONSO
And in woman you expect
to find fidelity?
How I love such simplicity!

2. TERZETTO

2. TRIO

DON ALFONSO
È la fede delle femmine
Come l'araba fenice,
Che vi sia ciascun lo dice,
Dove sia nessun lo sa.

DON ALFONSO
Woman's constancy
is like the Arabian Phoenix;
everyone swears it exists,
but no one knows where.

FERRANDO
La fenice è Dorabella.

FERRANDO
The phoenix is my Dorabella.

GUGLIELMO
La fenice è Fiordiligi.

GUGLIELMO
The phoenix is my Fiordiligi.

DON ALFONSO
Non è questa, non è quella,
Non fu mai, non vi sarà.

DON ALFONSO
It's neither one nor the other.
It never existed, and never will.

RECITATIVO

RECITATIVE

FERRANDO
Sciocchezie di poeti!

FERRANDO
Poets' nonsense!

GUGLIELMO
Scempiaggini di vecchi!

GUGLIELMO
Old men's drivel!

DON ALFONSO
Or bene, udite,
Ma senza andar in collera:
Qual prova avete voi, che ognor costanti
Vi sien le vostre amanti;
Chi vi fe' sicurtà, che invariabili
Sono i lor cori?

DON ALFONSO
Well then, listen,
but without flying into a rage:
what proof have
you
that your loves are always true to you?
what makes you so sure
that their hearts are steadfast?

FERRANDO
Lunga esperienza . . .

FERRANDO
Long acquaintance . . .

GUGLIELMO
Nobil educazion . . .

FERRANDO
Pensar sublime . . .

GUGLIELMO
Analogia d'umor . . .

FERRANDO
Disinteresse . . .

GUGLIELMO
Immutabil carattere . . .

FERRANDO
Promesse . . .

GUGLIELMO
Proteste . . .

FERRANDO
Giuramenti . . .

DON ALFONSO
Pianti, sospir, carezze, svenimenti.
Lasciatemi un po' ridere!

FERRANDO
Cospetto!
Finite di deriderci!

DON ALFONSO
Pian, piano;
E se toccar con mano
Oggi vi fo che come l'altre sono?

GUGLIELMO
Non si può dar!

FERRANDO
Non è!

DON ALFONSO
Giochiam!

FERRANDO
Giochiamo!

DON ALFONSO
Cento zecchini.

GUGLIELMO
Their noble upbringing . . .

FERRANDO
Their sublime thoughts . . .

GUGLIELMO
Kindred feelings . . .

FERRANDO
Unselfishness . . .

GUGLIELMO
Steadfast characters . . .

FERRANDO
Their promises . . .

GUGLIELMO
Their protests . . .

FERRANDO
Their oaths . . .

DON ALFONSO
Tears and sighs, caresses, swoons.
Excuse me if I laugh!

FERRANDO
Confound you!
Stop taunting us!

DON ALFONSO
Gently, gently; what if I prove
conclusively to you today
that they're just like the others?

GUGLIELMO
It couldn't be!

FERRANDO
Impossible!

DON ALFONSO
Shall we bet on it?

FERRANDO
We're on!

DON ALFONSO
A hundred sequins.

GUGLIELMO
E mille, se volete.

DON ALFONSO
Parola!

FERRANDO
Parolissima!

DON ALFONSO
E un cenno, un motto, un gesto,
Giurate di non far di tutto questo
Alle vostre Penelopi.

FERRANDO
Giuriamo.

DON ALFONSO
Da soldati d'onore?

GUGLIELMO
Da soldati d'onore.

DON ALFONSO
E tutto quel farete
Chi'io vi dirò di far?

FERRANDO
Tutto.

GUGLIELMO
Tuttissimo.

DON ALFONSO
Bravissimi!

FERRANDO E GUGLIELMO
Bravissimo,
Signor Don Alfonsetto.

FERRANDO
A spese vostre or ci divertiremo.

GUGLIELMO
(a Ferrando)
E de' cento zecchini che
faremo?

3. TERZETTO

GUGLIELMO
A thousand, if you like.

DON ALFONSO
My hand on it!

FERRANDO
Both hands!

DON ALFONSO
Swear not to give a sign, a whisper,
a hint of all this
to your Penelopes.

FERRANDO
We swear.

DON ALFONSO
On your honour as soldiers?

GUGLIELMO
On our honour as soldiers.

DON ALFONSO
And you'll do
Everything I tell you to?

FERRANDO
Everything!

GUGLIELMO
Even more!

DON ALFONSO
Well done!

FERRANDO AND GUGLIELMO
And well done,
dear Don Alfonso!

FERRANDO
We'll make merry at your expense.

GUGLIELMO
(to Ferrando)
What shall we do with the hundred
sequins?

3. TRIO

FERRANDO
Una bella serenata
Far io voglio alla mia dea.

GUGLIELMO
In onor di Citerea
Un convito io voglio far.

DON ALFONSO
Sarò anch'io de' convitati?

FERRANDO E GUGLIELMO
Ci sarete, sì, signor.

FERRANDO, GUGLIELMO
E DON ALFONSO
E che brindis replicati
Far vogliamo al dio d'amor.

(partono)

SCENA SECONDA

Giardino sulla spiaggia del mare

Fiordiligi e Dorabella, che guardano ciascùna un medaglione

4. DUETTO

FIORDILIGI
Ah, guarda, sorella,
Se bocca più bella,
Se aspetto più nobile
Si può ritrovar.

DORABELLA
Osserva tu un poco,
Osserva, che foco
Ha ne' sguardi,
Se fiamma, se dardi
Non sembran scoccar.

FIORDILIGI
Si vede un sembiante
Guerriero ed amante.

DORABELLA
Si vede una faccia
Che alletta e minaccia.

FERRANDO
I'll arrange a fine serenade
for my goddess.

GUGLIELMO
In honour of Venus
I will give a banquet.

DON ALFONSO
Shall I be invited?

FERRANDO AND GUGLIELMO
Yes, you shall be there.

FERRANDO, GUGLIELMO
AND DON ALFONSO
And many a toast we'll offer
to the god of love.

(exeunt)

SCENE 2

A garden by the seashore

Fiordiligi and Dorabella are both gazing at miniatures hanging round their necks

4. DUET

FIORDILIGI
Ah tell me sister,
if one could ever find
a nobler face,
a sweeter mouth.

DORABELLA
Just look,
see what fire
is in his eye,
if flames and darts
do not seem to flash forth!

FIORDILIGI
This is the face
of a soldier and a lover.

DORABELLA
This is a face
both charming and alarming.

FIORDILIGI E DORABELLA
Io sono felice!
Se questo mio core
Mai cangia desio,
Amore mi faccia
Vivendo penar.

FIORDILIGI AND DORABELLA
How happy I am!
If ever my heart
changes its affection,
may love make me
live in pain.

RECITATIVO

RECITATIVE

FIORDILIGI
Mi par, che stamattina volentieri
Farei la pazzerella: ho un certo foco,
Un certo pizzicor entro le vene.
Quando Guglielmo viene, se sapessi
Che burla gli vo' far!

FIORDILIGI
This morning I feel in the mood
for some mischief: I've a fire.
a tingling in my veins.
If Guglielmo knew what pranks
I'll play on him when he comes!

DORABELLA
Per dirti il vero,
Qualche cosa di nuovo
Anch'io nell'alma provo: io giurerei,
Che lontane non siam dagli Imenei.

DORABELLA
To tell the truth,
I also feel something new
stirring within me: I'd swear
that we're not far from the altar.

FIORDILIGI
Dammi la mano: io voglio astrologarti.
Uh, che bell'Emme! E questo è un Pi: va bene:
Matrimonio presto.

FIORDILIGI
Give me your hand: I want to read it.
Well, there's a clear M; and here's a P!
That's it–Marriage Prospects!

DORABELLA
Affè che ci avrei gusto!

DORABELLA
That suits me splendidly.

FIORDILIGI
Ed io non ci avrei rabbia.

FIORDILIGI
And I'll have no objections.

DORABELLA
Ma che diavol vuol dir che i nostri sposi
Ritardano a venir?
Son già le sei.

DORABELLA
But what the devil do our lovers mean by this
delay in coming?
It's six o'clock already.

SCENA TERZA

SCENE 3

Le suddette e Don Alfonso

The above and Don Alfonso

FIORDILIGI
Eccoli!

FIORDILIGI
There they are!

DORABELLA
Non son essi: è Don Alfonso,
L'amico lor.

DORABELLA
No, it's not them:
it's their friend Don Alfonso.

FIORDILIGI
Ben venga
Il signor Don Alfonso!

FIORDILIGI
Welcome,
Don Alfonso!

DON ALFONSO
Riverisco!

DON ALFONSO
Your servant!

DORABELLA
Cos'è? Perchè qui solo? Voi piangete?
Parlate, per pietà: che cosa è nato?
L'amante . . .

DORABELLA
What is it? Why are you alone?
You shed a tear? Speak, for pity's sake:
what has happened? My lover . . .

FIORDILIGI
L'idol mio . . .

FIORDILIGI
My dearest . . .

DON ALFONSO
Barbaro fato!

DON ALFONSO
O cruel fate!

5. ARIA

DON ALFONSO
Vorrei dir, e cor non ho:
Balbettando il labbro va.
Fuor la voce uscir non può,
Ma mi resta mezza quà.
Che farete? Che farò?
Oh, che gran fatalità!
Dar di peggio non si può.
Ho di voi, di lor pietà!

5. ARIA

DON ALFONSO
I would speak, but my courage fails:
my lips stammer.
I cannot say the words,
which stay locked inside me.
What will you do? What shall I?
O dire misfortune!
It could not be worse.
I grieve for you and for them!

RECITATIVO

FIORDILIGI
Stelle! Per carità, signor Alfonso,
Non ci fate morir.

DON ALFONSO
Convien armarvi,
Figlie mie, di constanza.

DORABELLA
Oh Dei! Qual male
È addivenuto mai, qual caso rio?
Forse è morto il mio bene?

RECITATIVE

FIORDILIGI
Mercy! For pity's sake,
Don Alfonso, do not torment us so.

DON ALFONSO
You will need to summon
all your courage, my dears.

DORABELLA
O heaven! What harm has befallen them?
What disaster?
Is my beloved killed?

FIORDILIGI È morto il mio?	FIORDILIGI Is mine dead?
DON ALFONSO Morti non son, ma poco men che morti.	DON ALFONSO No, not dead, but nearly as bad.
DORABELLA Feriti?	DORABELLA Wounded?
DON ALFONSO No.	DON ALFONSO No.
FIORDILIGI Ammalati?	FIORDILIGI Sick?
DON ALFONSO Neppur.	DON ALFONSO Not that either.
FIORDILIGI Che cosa, dunque?	FIORDILIGI Well, what then?
DON ALFONSO Al marzial campo Ordin regio li chiama.	DON ALFONSO The royal command has called them to the battlefield.
FIORDILIGI E DORABELLA Ohimè, che sento!	FIORDILIGI AND DORABELLA Alas, what do I hear?
FIORDILIGI E partiran?	FIORDILIGI And they are going?
DON ALFONSO Sul fatto.	DON ALFONSO At once.
DORABELLA E non v'è modo d'impedirlo?	DORABELLA Is there no way of stopping them?
DON ALFONSO Non v'è.	DON ALFONSO None.
FIORDILIGI Nè un solo addio?	FIORDILIGI Not a single farewell?
DON ALFONSO Gl'infelici non hanno Coraggio di vedervi; Ma se voi lo bramate, Son pronti.	DON ALFONSO The poor fellows hadn't the courage to see you; but if you wish it, they are willing.

DORABELLA
Dove son?

DON ALFONSO
Amici, entrate.

SCENA QUARTA

I suddetti. Ferrando e Guglielmo (in abito da viaggio)

6. QUINTETTO

GUGLIELMO
Sento, oh Dio, che questo piede
È restio nel girle avante.

FERRANDO
Il mio labbro palpitante
Non può detto pronunziar.

DON ALFONSO
Nei momenti più terribili
Sua virtù l'eroe palesa.

FIORDILIGI E DORABELLA
Or che abbiam la nuova intesa,
A voi resta a fare il meno;
Fate core, a entrambe in seno
Immergeteci l'acciar.

FERRANDO E GUGLIELMO
Idol mio, la sorte incolpa
Se ti deggio abbandonar.

DORABELLA
(a Guglielmo)
Ah, no, no, non partirai!

FIORDILIGI
(a Ferrando)
No, crudel, non te n'andrai!

DORABELLA
Voglio pria cavarmi il core!

FIORDILIGI
Pria ti vo' morire ai piedi!

FERRANDO
(piano a Don Alfonso)

DORABELLA
Where are they?

DON ALFONSO
Come in, my friends!

SCENE 4

The above, Ferrando and Guglielmo (in travelling clothes)

6. QUINTET

GUGLIELMO
I feel, O God . . . my steps falter
in their progress towards you.

FERRANDO
My trembling lips
cannot utter the words.

DON ALFONSO
In moments of the greatest stress
a hero calls up all his strength.

FIORDILIGI AND DORABELLA
Now that we have heard the news,
one detail remains for you to perform:
be brave, and plunge your blade
into this heart.

FERRANDO AND GUGLIELMO
My love, blame fate
if I must abandon you.

DORABELLA
(to Guglielmo)
No, no, do not go!

FIORDILIGI
(to Ferrando)
Cruel one, do not leave me!

DORABELLA
I would sooner tear my heart out!

FIORDILIGI
I would sooner die at your feet!

FERRANDO
(aside, to Don Alfonso)

Cosa dici?	What do you say to that?
GUGLIELMO *(c.s.)* Te n'avvedi?	GUGLIELMO *(aside, to Don Alfonso)* Do you see now?
DON ALFONSO *(piano)* Saldo, amico; Finem lauda!	DON ALFONSO *(aside)* Patience, friend; we've not reached the end yet!
TUTTI Il destin così defrauda Le speranze de' mortali. Ah, chi mai, fra tanti mali, Chi mai può la vita amar?	ALL Thus destiny confounds our mortal hopes. Ah who, amid such sorrow, can ever more delight in life?
RECITATIVO	RECITATIVE
GUGLIELMO Non piangere, idol mio!	GUGLIELMO Do not weep, my darling!
FERRANDO Non disperarti, Adorata mia sposa!	FERRANDO Do not despair, my dearest love!
DON ALFONSO Lasciate lor tal sfogo. È troppo giusta La cagion di quel pianto.	DON ALFONSO Leave them that comfort. They have only too good cause to grieve.
FIORDILIGI Chi sa s'io più ti veggio!	FIORDILIGI Who knows if we shall ever meet again!
DORABELLA Chi sa se più ritorni! *(Si abbracciano teneramente.)*	DORABELLA Who knows if you will ever return! *(They embrace tenderly.)*
FIORDILIGI Lasciami questo ferro: ei mi dia morte Se mai barbara sorte In quel seno a me caro . . .	FIORDILIGI Leave me this dagger: may it bring me death if ever cruel fate in that bosom dear to me . . .
DORABELLA Morrei di duol, D'uopo non ho d'acciaro.	DORABELLA I should die of grief, even without a dagger.
FERRANDO E GUGLIELMO Non farmi, anima mia, Quest'infausti presagi!	FERRANDO AND GUGLIELMO My love, do not make such gloomy predictions!

Proteggeran gli Dei
La pace del tuo cor ne' giorni miei.

Heaven will assure your peace of mind
so long as I live.

7. DUETTINO

7. DUET

FERRANDO E GUGLIELMO
Al fato dàn legge
Quegli occhi vezzosi;
Amor li protegge
Nè i loro riposi
Le barbare stelle
Ardiscon turbar.
Il ciglio sereno,
Mio bene, a mi gira;
Felice al tuo seno
Io spero tornar.

FERRANDO AND GUGLIELMO
Those lovely eyes
dictate to fate;
Love protects them
though the cruel stars
dare to disturb
their peace.
Turn a calm gaze,
my dearest, on me;
I hope to return
in happiness to your bosom.

RECITATIVO

RECITATIVE

DON ALFONSO
(da sé)
La commedia è graziosa e tutti due
Fan ben la loro parte.
(Si sente un tamburo.)

DON ALFONSO
(to himself)
The comedy is delightful,
and both are playing their parts well.
(A drum is heard.)

FERRANDO
Oh cielo! Questo
È il tamburo funesto
Che a divider mi vien dal mio
tesoro!

FERRANDO
O heavens!
That is the fatal drum that comes
to tear me from my
treasurer!

DON ALFONSO
Ecco amici la barca.

DON ALFONSO
Friends, here is the boat.

FIORDILIGI
Io manco!

FIORDILIGI
I'm fainting!

DORABELLA
Io moro!

DORABELLA
I'm dying!

SCENA QUINTA

SCENE 5

Arriva una barca alla sponda. Durante la marcia seguente, entra nella scena una truppa di soldati, accompagnati da uomini e donne. I suddetti.

A boat arrives at the shore. During the following march, a troop of soldiers enters accompanied by men and women. The above.

8. CORO

8. CHORUS

SOLDATI
Bella vita militar!
Ogni dì si cangia loco;
Oggi molto, doman poco,
Ora in terra ed or sul mar.
Il fragor di trombe e pifferi,
Lo sparar di schioppi e bombe
Forza accresce al braccio e
all'anima
Vaga sol di trionfar.
Bella vita militar!

RECITATIVO

DON ALFONSO
Non v'è più tempo, amici; andar
conviene
Ove il destino,
Anzi il dover v'invita.

FIORDILIGI
Mio cor!

DORABELLA
Idolo mio!

FERRANDO
Mio ben!

GUGLIELMO
Mia vita!

FIORDILIGI
Ah, per un sol momento . . .

DON ALFONSO
Del vostro reggimento
Già è partita la barca;
Raggiungerla convien coi pochi
amici
Che su legno più lieve
Attendendo vi stanno.

FERRANDO E GUGLIELMO
Abbaracciami, idol mio!

FIORDILIGI E DORABELLA
Muoio d'affanno!

9. QUINTETTO (E CORO)

SOLDIERS
A soldier's life for me!
Every day a change of scene;
plenty today, little tomorrow,
now on land and now on sea
The sound of trumpets and fifes,
the din of guns and shells
lend strength to our arms and our
spirits,
longing only for victory.
A soldier's life for me!

RECITATIVE

DON ALFONSO
There's no more time,
friends:
you must go where both
fate and duty call you.

FIORDILIGI
My love!

DORABELLA
My idol!

FERRANDO
My dearest!

GUGLIELMO
My life!

FIORDILIGI
Ah, for just a moment . . .

DON ALFONSO
Your regiment's ship
has already left;
you'll have to
join it
with a few friends who await you
on a smaller boat.

FERRANDO AND GUGLIELMO
Embrace me, my love!

FIORDILIGI AND DORABELLA
My heart is breaking!

9. QUINTET (AND CHORUS)

FIORDILIGI
(piangendo)
Di scrivermi ogni giorno
Giurami, vita mia!

FIORDILIGI
(weeping)
Swear that you'll write me
every day, my love!

DORABELLA
(piangendo)
Due volte ancora tu scrivimi, se puoi.

DORABELLA
(weeping)
Write me twice as often, if you can.

GUGLIELMO
Non dubitar, mio bene!

GUGLIELMO
Never doubt me, my dear!

FERRANDO
Sii certa, o cara!

FERRANDO
Rest assured, my love!

DON ALFONSO
(da sè)
Io crepo se non rido!

DON ALFONSO
(to himself)
I'll burst if I don't laugh!

FIORDILIGI
Sii costante a me sol!

FIORDILIGI
Be true to me alone!

DORABELLA
Serbati fido!

DORABELLA
Remain faithful!

FIORDILIGI, DORABELLA, FERRANDO E GUGLIELMO
Addio!
Mi si divide il cor, bell'idol mio!
Addio! Addio! Addio!

FIORDILIGI, DORABELLA, FERRANDO E GUGLIELMO
Farewell!
My heart is rent in twain, my love.
Farewell! Farewell! Farewell!

(Mentre si ripete il coro, Ferrando e Guglielmo entrano nella barca che poi s'allontana. I soldati partono, seguiti dagli uomini e dalle donne)

(During the repetition of the chorus, Ferrando and Guglielmo board the boat which then moves away. The soldiers march off, followed by the people)

SCENA SESTA

SCENE 6

Fiordiligi, Dorabella e Don Alfonso

Fiordiligi, Dorabella and Don Alfonso

RECITATIVO

RECITATIVE

DORABELLA
(in atto di chi rinviene da un letargo)
Dove son?

DORABELLA
(as if recovering from a swoon)
Where are they?

DON ALFONSO
Son partiti.

DON ALFONSO
They've gone.

FIORDILIGI
Oh dipartenza
Crudelissima amara!

DON ALFONSO
Fate core,
Carissime figliuole;
Guardate: da lontano vi fan cenno
Con mano i cari sposi.

FIORDILIGI
Buon viaggio, mia vita!

DORABELLA
Buon viaggio!

FIORDILIGI
Oh Dei! Come veloce
Se ne va quella barca! Già sparisce!
Già non si vede più! Deh, faccia il cielo
Ch'abbia prospero corso!

DORABELLA
Faccia che al campo giunga
Con fortunati auspici!

DON ALFONSO
E a voi salvi gli amanti
E a me gli amici.

10. TERZETTINO

FIORDILIGI, DORABELLA
E DON ALFONSO
Soave sia il vento,
Tranquilla sia l'onda
Ed ogni elemento
Benigno risponda
Ai vostri desir.

(Fiordiligi e Dorabella partono.)

SCENA SETTIMA

RECITATIVO

DON ALFONSO
Non son cattivo comico; va bene;
Al concertato loco i due campioni
Di Ciprigna, e di Marte

FIORDILIGI
O most cruel,
bitter parting!

DON ALFONSO
Have courage,
dearest ladies;
look; in the distance
your lovers are waving.

FIORDILIGI
God speed you, my love!

DORABELLA
God speed you!

FIORDILIGI
O heavens! How swiftly their boat
disappears! It's gone already!
It's out of sight! Heaven grant it
a safe voyage!

DORABELLA
May Heaven protect them too
on the field of battle!

DON ALFONSO
Preserve your lovers
and my friends.

10. TRIO

FIORDILIGI, DORABELLA
AND DON ALFONSO
Gentle be the breeze,
calm be the waves.
And every element
smile in favour
on their wish.

(Exeunt Fiordiligi and Dorabella.)

SCENE 7

RECITATIVE

DON ALFONSO
I'm not a bad actor! Now then;
the two champions
of Venus and Mars

Mi staranno attendendo; or senza indugio
Raggiungerli conviene. Quante smorfie,
Quante buffonerie!
Tanto meglio per me,
Cadran più facilmente;
Questa razza di gente è la più presta
A cangiarsi d'umore. Oh poverini!
Per femmina giocar cento zecchini!
«Nel mare solca
E nell'arena semina
E il vago vento
Spera in rete accogliere
Chi fonda sue speranze
In cor di femmina.»

await me at the appointed place;
I must join them without delay.
What grimaces, what affectations!
All the better for me,
they'll fall more easily;
people of that kind are the first
to change their minds. Poor fools,
to wager a hundred sequins on a woman!
"He who builds his hopes
on a woman's heart
ploughs the sea
and sows on sand
and hopes to snare
the wild wind in a net".

SCENA OTTAVA

SCENE 8

Camera con diverse sedie, un tavolino, ecc. Tre porte: due laterali, una di mezzo.

A room with various chairs, a table etc. Three doors: two at the sides, one centre.

RECITATIVO

RECITATIVE

DESPINA
(che sta frullando il cioccolatte)
Che vita maledetta
È il far la cameriera!
Dal mattino alla sera
Si fa, si suda, si lavora, e poi
Di tanto, che si fa, nulla è per noi.
È mezz'ora che sbatto;
Il cioccolatte è fatto, ed a me tocca
Restar ad odorarlo a secca bocca?
Non è forse la mia come la vostra?
O garbate signore,
Che a voi dessi l'essenza, e a me l'odore!
Per Bacco, vo' assaggiarlo.
(Lo assaggia.)
Com'è buono!
(Si pulisce la bocca.)
Vien gente!
Oh cielo, son le padrone!

DESPINA
(who is whipping the chocolate)
What a wretched life
a lady's maid leads!
From morning till night working,
sweating and toiling, and after all
one's done there's nothing for oneself!
I've been beating this for half an hour,
and now the chocolate's ready; yet though my tongue's
hanging out, must I just stand and smell it?
Aren't my tastes just like yours?
O dearest ladies, you have the
substance and I only the smell!
Dammit, I'm going to try it.
(She tastes it.)
Delicious!
(She wipes her mouth.)
Someone's coming!
Goodness, it's my ladies!

SCENA NONA

SCENE 9

La suddetta; Fiordiligi e Dorabella (ch'entrano disperatamente. Despina presenta il cioccolatte sopra una guantiera)

RECITATIVO

DESPINA
Madame, ecco la vostra colazione.
(Dorabella gitta tutto a terra.)
Diamine, cosa fate?

FIORDILIGI E DORABELLA
(Si cavano entrambe tutti gli ornamenti donneschi.)
Ah! Ah!

DESPINA
Che cosa è nato?

FIORDILIGI
Ov'è un acciaro?

DORABELLA
Un veleno, dov'è?

DESPINA
Padrone, dico!

DORABELLA
Ah, scostati! Paventa il tristo effetto
D'un disperato affetto!
Chiudi, quelle finestre; odio la luce,
Odio l'aria che spiro, odio me stessa.
Chi schernisce il mio duol, chi mi consola?
Deh, fuggi; per pietà, lasciami sola!

11. ARIA

DORABELLA
Smanie implacabili
Che m'agitate,
Entro quest'anima
Più non cessate,
Finchè l'angoscia
Mi fa morir.

The above, Fiordiligi and Dorabella (who enter distractedly. Despina offers the chocolate on a tray)

RECITATIVE

DESPINA
Here's your breakfast, ladies.
(Dorabella flings it all to the ground.)
Jiminy! What are you doing?

FIORDILIGI AND DORABELLA
(Both stripping off all their ornaments.)
Ah! Ah!

DESPINA
What's happened?

FIORDILIGI
Where is a dagger?

DORABELLA
Where is the poison?

DESPINA
Ladies, I beg you!

DORABELLA
Ah leave me! Flee the dread effect
of a distracted love!
Close those windows; I hate the light,
I hate the air I breathe, I hate myself.
Who mocks at my grief: Who consoles me?
Ah fly; leave me alone, for pity's sake!

11. ARIA

DORABELLA
Implacable pangs
which torment me,
do not subside
within my being
until my anguish
brings me death.

Esempio misero
D'amor funesto
Darò all'Eumenidi,
Se viva resto
Col suono orribile
De'miei sospir.

If I remain alive
I will furnish the Furies
with a wretched example
of tragic love
with the dreadful sound
of my sighs.

RECITATIVO

RECITATIVE

(Si mettono a sedere in disparte, da forsennate)

(the ladies sit distractedly)

DESPINA
Signora Dorabella,
Signora Fiordiligi,
Ditemi: che cos'è stato?

DESPINA
My lady Dorabella,
my lady Fiordiligi,
tell me: what has happened?

DORABELLA
Oh terribil disgrazia!

DORABELLA
O dreadful disaster!

DESPINA
Sbrigatevi in buon'ora!

DESPINA
Get on with it!

FIORDILIGI
Da Napoli partiti
Sono gli amanti nostri.

FIORDILIGI
Our lovers
have left Naples.

DESPINA
(ridendo)
Non c'è altro?
Ritorneran.

DESPINA
(laughing)
Is that all?
They'll be back.

DORABELLA
Chi sa!

DORABELLA
Who knows!

DESPINA
Come, chi sa?
Dove son iti?

DESPINA
What do you mean, who knows?
Where have they gone?

DORABELLA
Al campo di battaglia!

DORABELLA
To the field of battle!

DESPINA
Tanto meglio per loro:
Li vedrete tornar carchi
d'alloro.

DESPINA
So much the better for them:
you'll see them return crowned with
laurel.

FIORDILIGI
Ma ponno anche perir!

FIORDILIGI
But they might be killed!

DESPINA
Allora poi
Tanto meglio per voi.

FIORDILIGI
(sorge arrabbiata)
Sciocca, che dici?

DESPINA
La pura verità: due ne perdete,
Vi restan tutti gli altri.

FIORDILIGI
Ah, perdendo Guglielmo,
Mi pare ch'io morrei!

DORABELLA
Ah, Ferrando perdendo,
Mi par che viva a seppellirmi
andrei!

DESPINA
Brave! Vi par, ma non è ver;
ancora
Non vi fu donna che d'amor sia
morta.
Per un uomo morir! Altri ve n'hanno
che compensano il danno.

DORABELLA
E credi che potria
Altr'uom amar chi s'ebbe per
amante
Un Guglielmo, un Ferrando?

DESPINA
Han gli altri ancora
Tutto quello ch'han essi.
Un uom adesso amate,
Un altro n'amerete;
Uno val l'altro,
Perchè nessun val nulla.
Ma non parliam di ciò;
Sono ancor vivi
E vivi torneran,
Ma son lontani,
E piuttosto che in vani
Pianti perdere il tempo,
Pensate a divertirvi.

DESPINA
Why then,
so much the better for you.

FIORDILIGI
(rises angrily)
Fool, what are you saying?

DESPINA
The simple truth: you lose these two
but all the rest are left.

FIORDILIGI
Ah, without Guglielmo,
I think I'd die!

DORABELLA
Ah, without Ferrando
I think I'd bury myself
alive!

DESPINA
Splendid! That's what you think, but
you wouldn't;
no woman yet has ever died for or
love.
Die for a man? There's lots more
where he came from.

DORABELLA
And do you believe anyone could love
another man who once had
for a lover a
Guglielmo, a Ferrando?

DESPINA
The others have everything
that these have.
You love this man now;
so you'd love another:
one's as good as the other
since neither's worth a thing.
But we won't go into that;
they're still alive
and will come back alive;
but they're far away,
and rather than
waste time in idle tears,
think about enjoying yourselves.

FIORDILIGI
(con trasporto di collera)
Divertirci?

DESPINA
Sicuro! E, quel ch'è meglio,
Far all'amor come assassine, e come
Faranno al campo i vostri cari amanti.

DORABELLA
Non offender così quell'alme belle,
Di fedeltà, d'intatto amore esempi.

DESPINA
Via, via! Passaro i tempi
Da spacciar queste favole ai bambini.

12. ARIA

DESPINA
In uomini, in soldati
Sperare fedeltà?
(ridendo)
Non vi fate sentir, per carità!
Di pasta simile
Son tutti quanti;
Le fronde mobili,
L'aure incostanti
Han più degli uomini
Stabilità.
Mentite lagrime,
Fallaci sguardi,
Voci ingannevoli,
Vezzi bugiardi,
Son le primarie
Lor qualità.
In noi non amano
Che il lor diletto;
Poi ci dispregiano,
Neganci affetto,
Nè val da' barbari
Chieder pietà.
Paghiam, o femmine,
D'ugual moneta
Questa malefica
Razza indiscreta;
Amiam per comodo,

FIORDILIGI
(in a transport of rage)
Enjoying ourselves?

DESPINA
Certainly! And what's more,
making love furiously,
as your
dear gentlemen will be doing on active service!

DORABELLA
Don't insult those pure souls like this,
those models of fidelity and
perfect love.

DESPINA
Go on with you! The time are past
for spinning such tales even to babies!

12. ARIA

DESPINA
You look for fidelity
in men, in soldiers?
(laughing)
Don't tell me that, for pity's sake!
All of them
are made of the same stuff;
the quivering leaves,
the inconstant breezes
have more stability
than men.
Crocodile tears,
lying looks,
deceiving words,
false endearments
are the basis
of their tricks.
In us they only prize
their own pleasure;
then they despise us,
deny us affection,
and from such tyrants
there's no mercy to be had.
We woman should pay out
this hurtful,
impudent breed
in their own coin;
let's love them

Per vanità!

(Tutte partono.)

SCENA DECIMA

Don Alfonso, poi Despina

RECITATIVO

DON ALFONSO
Che silenzio! Che aspetto di tristezza
Spirano queste stanze! Poverette!
Non han già tutto il torto:
Bisogna consolarle; infin che vanno
I due creduli sposi,
Com'io loro commisi,
A mascherarsi,
Pensiam cosa può farsi.
Temo un po' per Despina; quella furba
Potrebbe riconoscerli; potrebbe
Rovesciarmi le macchine. Vedremo
Se mai farà bisogno
Un regaletto a tempo; un zecchinetto
Per una cameriera è un gran scongiuro.
Ma per esser sicuro, si potria
Metterla in parte a parte del secreto.
Eccellente è il progetto;
La sua camera è questa.
(batte)
Despinetta!

DESPINA
Chi batte?

DON ALFONSO
Oh!

DESPINA
Ih!
(esce dalla sua stanza)

DON ALFONSO
Despina mia, di te

to suit our convenience and our vanity!

(All go out.)

SCENE 10

Don Alfonso, later Despina

RECITATIVE

DON ALFONSO
How silent! What an air of sorrow
these rooms wear! Poor dears!
It's not really their fault;
they need consolation;
until their two credulous lovers
appear disguised,
as I instructed them,
let's see what can be done.
I'm a bit worried about Despina;
that little baggage might recognise them.
She could upset the apple-cart.
Let's see–now's the time,
if ever, to grease her palm;
a tip works wonders with a ladies' maid.
But to be certain, it might be best
to let her into a part of the secret.
That's a splendid idea!
Here's her room.
(he knocks)
Despina dear!

DESPINA
Who's that?

DON ALFONSO
Oh!

DESPINA
Ih!
(she comes out)

DON ALFONSO
Despina my dear,

Bisogno avrei.	I have need of you.
DESPINA Ed io niente di lei.	DESPINA Well, I haven't of you.
DON ALFONSO Ti vo' fare del ben.	DON ALFONSO I mean you well.
DESPINA A una fanciulla Un vecchio come lei non può far nulla.	DESPINA An old man like you can do nothing for a girl.
DON ALFONSO *(mostrandole una moneta d'oro)* Parla piano ed osserva.	DON ALFONSO *(showing her a gold coin)* Drop your voice and look here!
DESPINA Me la dona?	DESPINA Are you giving me it?
DON ALFONSO Sì, se meco sei buona.	DON ALFONSO Yes, if you'll do what I ask.
DESPINA E che vorrebbe? È l'oro il mio giulebbe.	DESPINA And what do you want? Gold is my undoing.
DON ALFONSO Ed oro avrai, Ma ci vuol fedeltà.	DON ALFONSO And you shall have it if I can trust you.
DESPINA Non c'è altro? Son qua.	DESPINA Is that all? I'm ready.
DON ALFONSO Prendi ed ascolta. Sai che le tue padrone Han perduti gli amanti.	DON ALFONSO Take it, then; now listen. You know your mistresses have lost their lovers.
DESPINA Lo so.	DESPINA I know.
DON ALFONSO Tutti i lor pianti, Tutti i deliri loro ancor tu sai.	DON ALFONSO And you know of all their weeping and wailing.
DESPINA So tutto.	DESPINA I know it all.
DON ALFONSO Or ben: se mai	DON ALFONSO All right:

Per consolarle un poco
E trar, come diciam,
Chiodo per chiodo,
Tu ritrovassi il modo
Da metter in lor grazia
Due soggetti di garbo
Che vorrieno provar, già mi capisci,
C'è una mancia
per te
Di venti scudi,
Se li fai riuscir.

if, to console them
a little and, as they say,
to replace like with like,
you were to find a way
of bringing to their favour
two presentable fellows
who are anxious
to try—
you take my meaning—there's another
twenty scudi for you
if you bring it off.

DESPINA
Non mi dispiace
Questa proposizione.
Ma con quelle buffone . . . basta, udite:
Son giovani? Son belli? E, sopra tutto,
Hanno una buona borsa
I vostri concorrenti?

DESPINA
I've nothing against this proposition.
But with those sillies . . .
Well, listen: these suitors of yours,
are they young? Are they handsome?
And, above all,
have they plenty of money?

DON ALFONSO
Han tutto quello
Che piacer può alle donne di giudizio.
Li vuoi veder?

DON ALFONSO
They have everything
which could please ladies
of taste.
Do you want to see them?

DESPINA
E dove son?

DESPINA
Where are they?

DON ALFONSO
Son lì;
Li posso far entrar?

DON ALFONSO
Just here:
shall I call them in?

DESPINA
Direi di sì.

DESPINA
That's all right with me.

SCENA UNDECIMA

SCENE 11

I suddetti, Ferrando e Guglielmo; poi Fiordiligi e Dorabella

The above, Ferrando and Guglielmo; later Fiordiligi and Dorabella

Don Alfonso fa entrar gli amanti, che son travestiti

Don Alfonso brings in the lovers, who are disguised

13. SESTETTO

13. SEXTET

DON ALFONSO
Alla bella Despinetta

DON ALFONSO
I present you, my friends,

Vi presento, amici miei;
Non dipende che da lei
Consolar il vostro cor.

to pretty Miss Despina;
the consolation of your heart
lies in her hands alone.

FERRANDO E GUGLIELMO
(con tenerezza affettata)
Per la man, che lieto io bacio,
Per quei rai di grazia pieni,
Fa che volga a me sereni
I begli occhi il mio tesor.

FERRANDO AND GUGLIELMO
(with feigned tenderness)
By those hands, which with joy I kiss,
by that smile so full of charm,
make my treasure turn on me
her clear and lovely eyes.

DESPINA
(ridendo, da sè)
Che sembianze! Che vestiti!
Che figure! Che mustacchi!
Io non so se son Valacchi
O se Turchi son costor.

DESPINA
(laughing, to herself)
What sights! What clothes!
What faces! What moustaches!
I wonder what they are–
Wallachians or Turks?

DON ALFONSO
(piano, a Despina)
Che ti par di
quell'aspetto?

DON ALFONSO
(aside, to Despina)
What do you think of their
appearance?

DESPINA
Per parlarvi schietto schietto,
Hanno un muso
Fuor dell'uso,
Vero antidoto d'amor.

DESPINA
To be quite frank,
they're exceptional
in their ugliness,
enough to make one renounce love.

FERRANDO, GUGLIELMO
E DON ALFONSO
(sottovoce)
Or la cosa è appien decisa;
Se costei non ci ravvisa,
Non c'è più nessun timor.

FERRANDO, GUGLIELMO
AND DON ALFONSO
(sotto voce)
Now the plan is quite decided;
if she doesn' recognise us,
there's no more need to fear.

FIORDILIGI E DORABELLA
(di dentro)
Ehi, Despina! Olà, Despina!

FIORDILIGI AND DORABELLA
(from within)
Oh Despina! Despina!

DESPINA
Le padrone!

DESPINA
The ladies!

DON ALFONSO
(a Despina)
Ecco l'istante!
Fa con arte; io qui m'ascondo.
(Si ritira.)

DON ALFONSO
(to Despina)
Now's the moment!
Use your wits: I'll hide in here.
(He hides.)

FIORDILIGI E DORABELLA
(Escono dalla loro stanza)

FIORDILIGI AND DORABELLA
(coming out of their rooms)

Ragazzaccia tracotante,
Che fai lì con simil gente?
Falli uscire immantinente,
O ti fo pentir con lor.

Impudent baggage!
What are you doing with those people?
Turn them out at once,
or you'll be as sorry for it as they.

DESPINA, FERRANDO
E GUGLIELMO
(Tutti i tre s'inginocchiano)
Ah, madame, perdonate!
Al bel piè languir mirate
Due meschin, di vostro merto
Spasimanti adorator.

DESPINA, FERRANDO
AND GUGLIELMO
(All three kneel)
Ah, ladies, pardon!
See at your lovely feet
two wretches languishing,
tortured with love by your beauty.

FIORDILIGI E DORABELLA
Giusti numi! Cosa sento?
Dell'enorme tradimento,
Chi fu mai l'indegno autor?

FIORDILIGI AND DORABELLA
Great heavens! What do I hear?
Who was the shameless instigator
of this vile betrayal?

DESPINA, FERRANDO
E GUGLIELMO
Deh, calmate quello sdegno!

DESPINA, FERRANDO
AND GUGLIELMO
Pray calm your indignation!

FIORDILIGI E DORABELLA
Ah, che più non ho ritegno!
Tutta piena ho l'alma in petto
Di dispetto
E di terror!

FIORDILIGI AND DORABELLA
I can contain myself no more!
My heart within my breast
is filled with outrage
and with fear!

DESPINA E DON ALFONSO
(da sè)
Mi dà un poco di sospetto
Quella rabbia e quel furor.

DESPINA AND DON ALFONSO
(aside)
I'm a bit suspicious
of this rage and fury!

FERRANDO E GUGLIELMO
(da sè)
Qual diletto
È a questo petto
Quella rabbia e quel furor!

FERRANDO AND GUGLIELMO
(aside)
What balm
to this heart
is all this rage and fury!

FIORDILIGI E DORABELLA
(da sè)
Ah, perdon, mio bel diletto;
Innocente è questo cor.

FIORDILIGI AND DORABELLA
(aside)
Forgive me, beloved;
this heart of mine is innocent.

RECITATIVO

RECITATIVE

DON ALFONSO
(dalla porta)
Che sussurro! Che strepito!
Che scompiglio è mai questo!
Siete pazze,

DON ALFONSO
(from the doorway)
What a commotion! What a din!
Whatever's this confusion? My
dear ladies,

Care le mie ragazze?
Volete sollevar il
vicinato?
Cos'avete? Ch'è nato?

have you taken leave of your senses?
Do you want to rouse the
neighbourhood?
What's the matter? What is it?

DORABELLA
(con furore)
Oh ciel! Mirate:
Uomini in casa nostra.

DORABELLA
(angrily)
Heavens! See:
men in our house!

DON ALFONSO
(senza guardarli)
Che male c'è?

DON ALFONSO
(not looking at them)
What's wrong with that?

FIORDILIGI
(con fuoco)
Che male?
In questo giorno?
Dopo il caso funesto?

FIORDILIGI
(with spirit)
What's wrong?
On this day,
after our tragic loss?

DON ALFONSO
Stelle! Sogno, o son desto!
Amici miei, miei dolcissimi amici!
Voi qui? Come? Perchè? Quando?
In qual modo?
Numi! Quanto ne godo!
(piano a Ferrando e Guglielmo)
Secondatemi.

DON ALFONSO
Gracious! Am I awake or dreaming?
My friends, my dearest friends!
You here? What? Why?
When? How?
Ye gods! I'm delighted!
(aside, to Ferrando and Guglielmo)
Play up to me.

FERRANDO
Amico Don Alfonso!

FERRANDO
Our friend Don Alfonso!

GUGLIELMO
Amico caro!
(Si abbracciano con trasporto.)

GUGLIELMO
Our dear friend!
(They embrace eagerly.)

DON ALFONSO
Oh bella improvvisata!

DON ALFONSO
What a pleasant surprise!

DESPINA
Li conoscete voi?

DESPINA
Do you know them?

DON ALFONSO
Se li conosco?
Questi sono i più dolci amici
Ch'io mi abbia in questo mondo
E vostri ancor saranno.

DON ALFONSO
Know them?
They are the dearest friends
I have in this world,
and will be yours too.

FIORDILIGI
E in casa mia che fanno?

FIORDILIGI
But what are they doing in my house?

GUGLIELMO
Ai vostri piedi
Due rei, due delinquenti, ecco, Madame!
Amor . . .

GUGLIELMO
Here at your feet, ladies, are two miscreants, two culprits!
It was love . . .

DORABELLA
Numi, che sento!

DORABELLA
Ye gods, what do I hear?

FERRANDO
Amor, il nume
Sì possente per voi, qui ci conduce.
(le donne si ritirano; essi le inseguono.)

FERRANDO
It was love, that powerful god, who drew us here in search of you.
(the ladies draw back; the officers pursue them.)

GUGLIELMO
Vista appena la luce
Di vostre fulgidissime pupille, . . .

GUGLIELMO
No sooner having glimpsed the light of your dazzling eyes . . .

FERRANDO
. . . che alle vive faville, . . .

FERRANDO
. . . than at their bright sparks . . .

GUGLIELMO
. . . farfallette amorose agonizzanti, . . .

GUGLIELMO
. . . like moths tormented by desire . . .

FERRANDO
. . . vi voliamo davanti . . .

FERRANDO
. . . we flew before you . . .

GUGLIELMO
. . . ed ai lati ed a retro . . .

GUGLIELMO
. . . and round you and behind you . . .

FERRANDO E GUGLIELMO
. . . per implorar pietade in flebil metro.

FERRANDO AND GUGLIELMO
. . . to implore your pity in plaintive accents.

FIORDILIGI
Stelle! Che ardir!

FIORDILIGI
Heavens, what presumption!

DORABELLA
Sorella, che facciamo?

DORABELLA
Sister, what shall we do?

FIORDILIGI
Temerari! Sortite!
Fuori di questo loco!
(Despina sorte impaurita)
E non profani
L'alito infausto degli infami detti

FIORDILIGI
Begone, bold creatures!
Leave this house!
(Despina goes out, in a fright)
And with the unwelcome breath of base words
do not profane our hearts,

Nostro cor, nostro orecchio e nostri affetti!
Invan per voi, per gli altri, invan si cerca
Le nostr'alme sedur; l'intatta fede
Che per noi già si diede ai cari amanti,
Saprem loro serbar infino a morte
A dispetto del mondo e della sorte.

our ears and our affections!
In vain do you, or others, seek to seduce
our souls; the unsullied faith which
we plighted to our dear loves
we shall know how to preserve for them
until death, despite the world and fate.

14. ARIA

FIORDILIGI
Come scoglio immoto resta
Contra i venti e la tempesta,
Così ognor quest'alma è forte
Nella fede e nell'amor.
Con noi nacque quella face
Che ci piace,
E ci consola,
E potrà la morte sola
Far che cangi affetto il cor.
Rispettate,
Anime ingrate,
Quest'esempio di costanza
E una barbara speranza
Non vi renda audaci ancor!
(Van per partire. Ferrando la richiama, Guglielmo richiama l'altra)

14. ARIA

FIORDILIGI
Like a rock standing impervious
to winds and tempest,
so stands my heart ever strong
in faith and love.
Between us we have kindled
a flame which warms
and consoles us,
and death alone could
change my heart's devotion.
Respect this example
of constancy,
you abject creatures,
and do not let a base hope
make you so rash again!
(The ladies make to go. Ferrando detains one, Guglielmo the other)

RECITATIVO

FERRANDO
Ah, non partite!

GUGLIELMO
(a Dorabella)
Ah, barbara, restate!
(sottovoce a Don Alfonso)
Che vi pare?

DON ALFONSO
(sottovoce)
Aspettate.
Per carità, ragazze:
Non mi fate più far trista figura.

RECITATIVE

FERRANDO
Ah, do not go!

GUGLIELMO
(to Dorabella)
Cruel one, stay!
(sotto voce to Don Alfonso)
What do you say now?

DON ALFONSO
(sotto voce)
Just wait.
In charity to me, my dears,
don't put me more out of countenance.

DORABELLA
(con fuoco)
E che pretendereste?

DON ALFONSO
Eh, nulla! Ma mi pare . . .
Che un pochin di dolcezza . . .
Alfin son galantuomini
E sono amici miei.

FIORDILIGI
Come! E udire dovrei . . .?

GUGLIELMO
Le nostre pene e sentirne
pietà!
La celeste beltà degli occhi vostri
La piaga aprì nei nostri,
Cui rimediar può solo
Il balsamo d' amore:
Un solo istante il core aprite, o
belle,
A sue dolci facelle; a voi davanti
Spirar vedrete i più fedeli
amanti.

15. ARIA

GUGLIELMO
Non siate ritrosi,
Occhietti vezzosi;
Due lampi amorosi
Vibrate un po' qua.
Felici rendeteci;
Amate con noi,
E noi felicissime
Faremo anche voi.
Guardate,
Toccate,
Il tutto osservate:
Siam due cari matti,
Siam forti e ben fatti,
E come ognun vede,
Sia merto, sia caso,
Abbiamo bel piede,
Bell'occhio, bel naso,
Guardate bel piede, osservate
bell'occhio,
Toccate bel naso, il tutto osservate:
E questi mustacchi
Chiamare si possono

DORABELLA
(angrily)
And what do you expect?

DON ALFONSO
Oh, nothing! But it seems to me . . .
that a scrap of courtesy . . .
after all, they are gentlemen
and they are friends of mine.

FIORDILIGI
So! And I should listen . . .?

GUGLIELMO
To our sufferings, and take pity
on them!
The heavenly beauty of your eyes
opened a wound in ours
that the salve of love
alone can cure.
Open your heart for a
moment
to its sweet words, my beauties; you'll
see before you the most faithful of
lovers.

15. ARIA

GUGLIELMO
Be not wayward,
dear beguiling eyes;
let two loving lightning flashes
strike for a moment here.
Make us happy,
and love with us;
and we will make you in return
the happiest of women.
Look at us,
touch us,
take stock of us:
we're crazy but we're charming,
we're strong and well made,
and as anyone can see,
whether by merit or by chance,
we've good feet,
good eyes, good noses.
Look, good feet; note, good
eyes;
touch, good noses; take stock of us;
and these moustaches
could be called

Trionfi degli uomini,
Pennacchi d'amor.

(Fiordiligi e Dorabella partono con collera)

manly triumphs,
the plumage of love.

(Fiordiligi and Dorabella exeunt angrily)

SCENA DODICESIMA

Ferrando, Guglielmo e Don Alfonso

SCENE 12

Ferrando, Guglielmo and Don Alfonso

16. TERZETTO

16. TRIO

FERRANDO E GUGLIELMO
(Appena soli con Don Alfonso, ridono)

FERRANDO AND GUGLIELMO
(No sooner alone with Don Alfonso than they burst into laughter)

DON ALFONSO
E voi ridete?

DON ALFONSO
So you're laughing?

FERRANDO E GUGLIELMO
Certo, ridiamo.

FERRANDO AND GUGLIELMO
Of course we're laughing.

DON ALFONSO
Ma cosa avete?

DON ALFONSO
But what's the matter?

FERRANDO E GUGLIELMO
Già lo sappiamo.

FERRANDO AND GUGLIELMO
Oh, we know.

DON ALFONSO
Ridete piano.

DON ALFONSO
Don't laugh so loudly.

FERRANDO E GUGLIELMO
Parlate invano.

FERRANDO AND GUGLIELMO
You can save your breath.

DON ALFONSO
Se vi sentissero,
Se vi scoprissero,
Si guasterebbe
Tutto l'affar.

DON ALFONSO
If they heard you,
if they found you out,
the whole thing
would be ruined.

FERRANDO E GUGLIELMO
Ah, che dal ridere
L'alma dividere . . .
Ah, che le viscere
Sento scoppiar!

FERRANDO AND GUGLIELMO
How can I
keep from laughing . . .
I feel as though
I'm going to burst!

DON ALFONSO
Mi fa da ridere
Questo lor ridere,
Ma so che in piangere

DON ALFONSO
Their laughter
makes me laugh too,
though I know

Dee terminar.

RECITATIVO

DON ALFONSO
Si può sapere un poco
La cagion di quel riso?

GUGLIELMO
Oh cospettaccio!
Non vi pare che abbiam giusta ragione,
Il mio caro padrone?

FERRANDO
(scherzando)
Quanto pagar volete
E a monte è la sommessa?

GUGLIELMO
(scherzando)
Pagate la metà.

FERRANDO
Pagate solo
Ventiquattro zecchini

DON ALFONSO
Poveri innocentini!
Venite qua, vi voglio
Porre il ditino in bocca.

GUGLIELMO
E avete ancora
Coraggio di fiatar?

DON ALFONSO
Avanti sera
Ci parlerem.

FERRANDO
Quando volete.

DON ALFONSO
Intanto
Silenzio e ubbidienza
Fino a doman mattina.

GUGLIELMO
Siam soldati
E amiam la disciplina.

it's bound to end in tears.

RECITATIVE

DON ALFONSO
And may I ask to know
the reason for this laughter?

GUGLIELMO
Oh what a face!
Don't you think, my dear sir,
that we have good cause?

FERRANDO
(mockingly)
How much will you pay,
and we'll drop our wager?

GUGLIELMO
(mockingly)
Pay half.

FERRANDO
We'll let you off with
twenty-four sequins.

DON ALFONSO
Poor little innocents!
Come here; I'll give you
my little finger to suck on.

GUGLIELMO
And you still have
the courage to go on?

DON ALFONSO
Before evening
we'll talk of this.

FERRANDO
Whenever you like.

DON ALFONSO
Meanwhile
silence and obedience.
until tomorrow morning.

GUGLIELMO
We are soldiers
and accept discipline.

DON ALFONSO
Or bene: andate un poco
Ad attendermi entrambi in
giardinetto;
Colà vi manderò gli ordini miei.

DON ALFONSO
Very well: both of you go
and wait for me in the
garden:
there I'll give you your orders.

GUGLIELMO
Ed oggi non si mangia?

GUGLIELMO
But don't we eat today?

FERRANDO
Cosa serve?
A battaglia finita
Fia la cena per noi più saporita.

FERRANDO
What's it matter?
When the battle's over
our supper will taste the better.

17. ARIA

17. ARIA

FERRANDO
Un'aura amorosa
Del nostro tesoro
Un dolce ristoro
Al cor porgerà.
Al cor che, nudrito
Da speme d'amore,
D'un'esca migliore
Bisogno non ha.

FERRANDO
A breath of love
from our treasures
will afford our hearts
sweet sustenance.
A heart nourished
on the hope of love
has no need
of greater inducement.

(Ferrando e Guglielmo partono)

(Exeunt Ferrando and Guglielmo)

SCENA TREDICESIMA

SCENE 13

Don Alfonso solo, poi Despina

Don Alfonso, later Despina

RECITATIVO

RECITATIVE

DON ALFONSO
Oh, la saria da ridere! Sì poche
Son le donne costanti in questo
mondo
E qui ve ne son due!
Non sarà nulla.
(Entra Despina)
Vieni, vieni, fanciulla, e dimmi
un poco
Dove sono e che fan le tue
padrone.

DON ALFONSO
It's quite absurd! There are
so few constant women in this
world
and here are two of them!
It can't be.
(Enter Despina)
Come here, child, and
tell me
where your mistresses are and what
they're doing.

DESPINA
Le povere buffone
Stanno nel giardinetto
A lagnarsi coll'aria e colle mosche
D'aver perso gli amanti.

DESPINA
The poor fools
are standing in the garden
bewailing the loss of their lovers
To the breezes and the mosquitos.

DON ALFONSO
E come credi
Che l'affar finirà? Vogliam sperare
Che faranno giudizio?

DON ALFONSO
And how do you think
this will end? Can we hope
they'll come to their senses?

DESPINA
Io lo farei;
E dove piangon esse io riderei.
Disperarsi, strozzarsi
Perchè parte un amante!
Guardate che pazzia!
Se ne pigliano due, s'uno va via.

DESPINA
Well, I would;
where they weep, I'd laugh.
To choke with despair
because a lover goes away!
Have you ever seen such folly!
If one goes, take two others.

DON ALFONSO
Brava! Questa è prudenza.
(da sè)
Bisogna impuntigliarla.

DON ALFONSO
Well said! That's sense.
(to himself)
I'd better compliment her.

DESPINA
È legge di natura
E non prudenza sola.
Amor cos'è?
Piacer, comodo, gusto,
Gioia, divertimento,
Passatempo, allegria; non è più amore
Se incomodo diventa,
Se invece di piacer nuoce e tormenta.

DESPINA
It's a law of nature, and not merely sense.
What is love?
Pleasure, convenience, taste,
enjoyment, amusement,
pastime, fun; it's no longer love
if it becomes a burden and
instead of pleasure brings pain and torment.

DON ALFONSO
Ma intanto quelle pazze . . .

DON ALFONSO
But meanwhile our sillies . . .

DESPINA
Quelle pazze
Faranno a modo nostro.
È buon che sappiano
D'essere amate da color.

DESPINA
They'll do
what we say.
It's good that they should know
they're loved by them.

DON ALFONSO
Lo sanno.

DON ALFONSO
They know it.

DESPINA
Dunque riameranno.
Diglielo si suol dire
E lascia fare al diavolo.

DESPINA
Then they'll re-admit them,
they'll spin the usual tale,
and devil take the hindmost!

DON ALFONSO
E come far vuoi perchè ritornino
Or che partiti sono, e che li

DON ALFONSO
But how can you bring them back
now they've gone, and

sentano
E tentare si lascino
Queste tue bestioline?

make
these tiger-cats of yours listen to them again and let themselves be tempted?

DESPINA
A me lasciate
La briga di condur tutta la macchina.
Quando Despina macchina una cosa
Non può mancar d'effetto; ho già menati
Mill'uomini pel naso:
Saprò menar due femmine. Son ricchi
I due monsieurs mustacchi?

DESPINA
Leave me the bother
of running the show.
When Despina runs something
it can't fail: I've already led
a thousand men by the nose:
I should know how to manage two women.
Are your two whiskered monsieurs rich?

DON ALFONSO
Son ricchissimi.

DON ALFONSO
Rolling in it.

DESPINA
Dove son?

DESPINA
Where are they?

DON ALFONSO
Sulla strada
Attendendomi stanno.

DON ALFONSO
In the street,
waiting for me.

DESPINA
Ite e sul fatto
Per la picciola porta
A me riconduceteli; v'aspetto
Nella camera mia.
Purchè tutto facciate
Quel ch'io v'ordinerò, pria di domani
I vostri amici canteran vittoria
Ed essi avranno il gusto, ed io gloria.

DESPINA
Then off you go
and bring them to me here
by the little door;
I'll wait for you in my room.
If you'll do all I tell you,
Before tomorrow your friends
will win the day: they'll have their way,
and I'll have the glory.

(partono)

(Exeunt)

SCENA QUATTORDICESIMA

SCENE 14

Giardinetto gentile. Due banchi d'erba ai lati.

A pretty garden. Two grassy banks at the sides.

18. FINALE

18. FINALE

FIORDILIGI E DORABELLA
Ah, che tutta in un momento
Si cangiò la sorte mia!
Ah, che un mar pien di tormento
È la vita omai per me!
Finchè meco il caro bene
Mi lasciar le ingrate stelle,
Non sapea cos'eran pene,
Non sapea languir cos'è.

FIORDILIGI AND DORABELLA
Ah, how my lot has changed
all in a moment!
Ah, what a sea of torment
is life henceforth for me!
So long as the cruel stars
left my dear one with me,
I knew not what grief was,
I knew not what it was to pine.

SCENA QUINDICESIMA

Le suddette; Ferrando, Guglielmo, Don Alfonso; poi Despina

SCENE 15

The above; Ferrando, Guglielmo, Don Alfonso; later Despina

FERRANDO E GUGLIELMO
(di dentro)
Si mora, sì, si mora
Onde appagar le ingrate.

FERRANDO AND GUGLIELMO
(off-stage)
Let us die, yes, let us die
and thus melt their hard hearts.

DON ALFONSO
(di dentro)
C'è una speranza ancora;
Non fate, oh Dei, non fate!

DON ALFONSO
(off-stage)
There is yet a hope:
I beg you, do not do it!

FIORDILIGI E DORABELLA
Stelle, che grida orribili!

FIORDILIGI AND DORABELLA
Goodness, what terrible cries!

FERRANDO E GUGLIELMO
Lasciatemi!

FERRANDO AND GUGLIELMO
Let me be!

DON ALFONSO
Aspettate!
(Ferrando e Guglielmo, portando ciascuno una boccetta, entrano seguiti da Don Alfonso.)

DON ALFONSO
Wait!
(Ferrando and Gugliemo, each carrying a phial, enter followed by Don Alfonso.)

FERRANDO E GUGLIELMO
L'arsenico mi liberi
Di tanta crudeltà!
(Bevono e gittan via le boccette, nel voltarsi, vedono le due donne)

FERRANDO AND GUGLIELMO
May arsenic set me free
from such cruelty!
(They drink and throw down the containers; the two women turn and see them)

FIORDILIGI E DORABELLA
Stelle, un velen fu quello?

FIORDILIGI AND DORABELLA
Heavens, was that poison?

DON ALFONSO
Veleno buono e bello,
Che ad essi in pochi istanti
La vita toglierà!

DON ALFONSO
Poison good and proper,
that in a few moments
will deprive them of their lives!

FIORDILIGI E DORABELLA
Il tragico spettacolo
Gelare il cor mi fa.

FERRANDO E GUGLIELMO
Barbare, avvicinatevi;
D'un disperato affetto
Mirate il triste effetto
E abbiate almen pietà.

TUTTI
Ah, che del sole il raggio
Fosco per me diventa!
Tremo, le fibre e l'anima
Par che mancar mi senta,
Nè può la lingua o il labbro
Accenti articolar!
(Ferrando e Guglielmo cadono sopra i banchi d'erba)

DON ALFONSO
Giacchè a morir vicini
Sono quei meschinelli,
Pietade almeno a quelli
Cercate di mostrar.

FIORDILIGI E DORABELLA
Gente, accorrete, gente!
Nessuno, oh Dio, ci sente!
Despina!

DESPINA
(di dentro)
Chi mi chiama?

FIORDILIGI E DORABELLA
Despina!

DESPINA
(entrando)
Cosa vedo!
Morti i meschini io credo
O prossimi a spirar!

DON ALFONSO
Ah, che purtroppo è vero!
Furenti, disperati,
Si sono avvelenati!
Oh, amore singolar!

FIORDILIGI AND DORABELLA
The tragic sight
turns my heart to ice.

FERRANDO AND GUGLIELMO
Draw near, cruel ones;
see the dire effect
of despairing love
and at least pity us.

ALL
May the sun's rays
be darkened for me!
I tremble, I feel
the very fibres of my being failing,
and my tongue and lips
cannot form a word.
(Ferrando and Guglielmo fall on the grassy banks)

DON ALFONSO
Since these unfortunates
are near to death,
at least try to show them
a little pity.

FIORDILIGI AND DORABELLA
Help, someone, come quickly!
O Heaven, can no one hear!
Despina!

DESPINA
(off-stage)
Did someone call?

FIORDILIGI AND DORABELLA
Despina!

DESPINA
(entering)
What do I see?
I fear the poor things are dead,
or very near to dying!

DON ALFONSO
Alas, only too true!
Distraught, despairing,
they have taken poison!
Oh strange love!

DESPINA
Abbandonar i miseri
Saria per voi vergogna.
Soccorrerli bisogna.

DESPINA
It would be shameful of you
to forsake these unhappy wretches.
You must aid them.

FIORDILIGI, DORABELLA
E DON ALFONSO
Cosa possiam mai far?

FIORDILIGI, DORABELLA
AND DON ALFONSO
Whatever can we do?

DESPINA
Di vita ancor dan segno;
Colle pietose mani
Fate un po' lor sostegno.
(a Don Alfonso)
E voi con me correte:
Un medico, un antidoto
Voliamo a ricercar.
(Despina e Don Alfonso partono)

DESPINA
They still show signs of life;
give them a little comfort
from your kindly hands.
(to Don Alfonso)
You hurry away with me
and we'll seek
a doctor and an antidote.
(Despina and Don Alfonso exeunt)

FIORDILIGI E DORABELLA
Dei, che cimento è questo!
Evento più funesto
Non si potea trovar!

FIORDILIGI AND DORABELLA
What a tribulation!
No more dreadful situation
could ever be imagined!

FERRANDO E GUGLIELMO
(da sè)
Più bella commediola
Non si potea trovar!
(ad alta voce)
Ah!

FERRANDO AND GUGLIELMO
(aside)
No more farcical comedy
could ever be imagined!
(aloud)
Ah!

FIORDILIGI E DORABELLA
(stanno lontano dagli amanti)
Sospiran gl'infelici!

FIORDILIGI AND DORABELLA
(standing away from the men)
The poor dears are sighing!

FIORDILIGI
Che facciamo?

FIORDILIGI
What shall we do?

DORABELLA
Tu che dici?

DORABELLA
You suggest something.

FIORDILIGI
In momenti
Sì dolenti
Chi potriali abbandonar?

FIORDILIGI
At a moment
so painful
who could forsake them?

DORABELLA
(accostandosi un poco)
Che figure interessanti!

DORABELLA
(approaching a little)
Their faces are quite interesting!

FIORDILIGI
(c.s.)
Possiam farci un poco avanti.

FIORDILIGI
(approaching a little)
We could go a little further.

DORABELLA
Ha freddissima la testa.

DORABELLA
His head is very cold.

FIORDILIGI
Fredda fredda è ancora questa.

FIORDILIGI
This one's cold as ice.

DORABELLA
Ed il polso?

DORABELLA
And his pulse?

FIORDILIGI
Io non gliel' sento.

FIORDILIGI
I can't feel it.

DORABELLA
Questo batte lento lento.

DORABELLA
This one's beating very slowly.

FIORDILIGI E DORABELLA
Ah, se tarda ancor l'aita,
Speme più non v'è di vita!

FIORDILIGI AND DORABELLA
Oh, if help is long in coming,
there'll be no more hope of life!

FERRANDO E GUGLIELMO
(sottovoce)
Più domestiche e trattabili
Sono entrambe diventate;
Sta a veder che lor pietade
Va in amore a terminar.

FERRANDO AND GUGLIELMO
(softly)
Both have become
calmer and more gentle;
we shall see if their pity
will turn into love.

FIORDILIGI E DORABELLA
Poverini! La lor morte
Mi farebbe lagrimar.

FIORDILIGI AND DORABELLA
Poor dears! Their death
would fill me with grief.

SCENA SEDICESIMA

SCENE 16

I suddetti; Despina travestita da medico, Don Alfonso

The above; Despina disguised as a doctor, Don Alfonso

DON ALFONSO
Eccovi il medico,
Signore belle!

DON ALFONSO
Here's the doctor,
gentle ladies!

FERRANDO E GUGLIELMO
(fra loro)
Despina in maschera!
Che trista pelle!

FERRANDO AND GUGLIELMO
(aside)
Despina dressed up!
How heavily she's disguised!

DESPINA
«Salvete, amabiles
Bonae puellae!»

DESPINA
"Salvete, amabiles
Bonae puellae!"

FIORDILIGI E DORABELLA
Parla un linguaggio
Che non sappiamo.

DESPINA
Come comandano,
Dunque, parliamo.
So il greco e l'arabo,
So il turco e il vandalo;
Lo svevo e il tartaro
So ancor parlar.

DON ALFONSO
Tanti linguaggi
Per sè conservi;
Quei miserabili
Per ora osservi:
Preso hanno il tossico;
Che si può far?

FIORDILIGI E DORABELLA
Signor dottore,
Che si può far?

DESPINA
(toccando il polso e la fronte all'uno ed all'altro)
Saper bisognami
Pria la cagione
E quinci l'indole
Della pozione:
Se calda o frigida,
Se poca o molta,
Se in una volta
Ovvero in più

FIORDILIGI, DORABELLA E DON ALFONSO
Preso han l'arsenico,
Signor dottore;
Qui dentro il bevvero.
La causa è amore
Ed in un sorso
Sel mandar giù.

DESPINA
Non vi affannate,
Non vi turbate;
Ecco una prova
Di mia virtù.

FIORDILIGI AND DORABELLA
He speaks a language
we do not understand.

DESPINA
Let's speak, then
as you command me.
I know Greek and Arabic,
Turkish and the Vandal tongue;
and I can speak
Swabian and Tartar too.

DON ALFONSO
Keep all these languages
for yourself, sir;
for the moment,
look at these poor fellows;
they've taken poison;
what can be done?

FIORDILIGI AND DORABELLA
Yes, doctor,
what can be done?

DESPINA
(feeling the pulse and forehead of each)
First I must know
the nature of this potion
and the reason it was taken;
whether it was swallowed
hot or cold,
a little or much,
in one draught
or in several.

FIORDILIGI, DORABELLA AND DON ALFONSO
They took arsenic,
good doctor,
and drank it here.
The cause was love
and they swallowed it
in a single gulp.

DESPINA
Don't worry,
don't be afraid;
here is an earnest
of my skill.

FIORDILIGI E DORABELLA
Egli ha di un ferro
La man fornita.

DESPINA
Questo è quel pezzo
Di calamita:
Pietra mesmerica,
Ch'ebbe l'origine
Nell'Alemagna,
Che poi sì celebre
Là in Francia fu.
(Tocca con un pezzo di calamita la testa ai finti infermi e striscia dolcemente i loro corpi per lungo)

FIORDILIGI, DORABELLA E DON ALFONSO
Come si muovono,
Torcono, scuotono!
In terra il cranio
Presto percuotono.

DESPINA
Ah, lor la fronte
Tenete su.

FIORDILIGI E DORABELLA
Eccoci pronte!

DESPINA
Tenete forte.
Corraggio! Or liberi
Siete da morte.

FIORDILIGI, DORABELLA E DON ALFONSO
Attorno guardano,
Forze riprendono.
Ah, questo medico
Vale un Perù!

FERRANDO E GUGLIELMO
(sorgendo in pedi)
Dove son? Che loco è questo?
Chi è colui? Color chi sono?
Son di Giove innanzi al trono?
Sei tu Palla o Citerea?
(Ferrando a Fiordiligi e Guglielmo a Dorabella)

FIORDILIGI AND DORABELLA
He's taken a piece
of iron in his hand.

DESPINA
This is
a piece of magnet,
the stone which the great
Doctor Mesmer discovered
in Germany
and then became
so famous in France.
(She touches the heads of the feigned invalids with the magnet and gently draws it the length of their bodies)

FIORDILIGI, DORABELLA AND DON ALFONSO
Look, they're moving,
twisting, shaking!
They'll hit their heads
on the ground in a moment.

DESPINA
Ah, hold their foreheads
steady, will you?

FIORDILIGI AND DORABELLA
We're standing ready!

DESPINA
Hold tight.
Courage! Now you
are safe from death.

FIORDILIGI, DORABELLA AND DON ALFONSO
They're looking round
and recovering their strength.
Ah, this doctor's
worth all the gold in Peru!

FERRANDO AND GUGLIELMO
(rising to their feet)
Where am I? What place is this?
Who is he? Who are they?
Am I before Jove's throne?
Are you Pallas or Cytherea?
(Ferrando to Fiordiligi and Guglielmo to Dorabella)

No, tu sei l'alma mia dea!
Ti ravviso
Al dolce viso
E alla man ch'or ben conosco
E che sola è il mio tesor.
(Abbracciano le amanti teneramente e bacian loro la mano)

No, you are my fair goddess!
I recognise you by
that sweet face,
and by that hand I now know so well;
it is my only treasure.
(They embrace the girls tenderly and kiss their hands)

DESPINA E DON ALFONSO
Sono effetti ancor del tosco;
Non abbiate alcun timor.

DESPINA AND DON ALFONSO
It's the effect of the poison still;
don't be afraid.

FIORDILIGI E DORABELLA
Sarà ver, ma tante smorfie
Fanno torto al nostro onor.

FIORDILIGI AND DORABELLA
That may be so, but such liberties
do violence to our reputation.

FERRANDO E GUGLIELMO
(a Fiordiligi e Dorabella)
Per pietà, bell'idol mio!
Volgi a me le luci liete.

FERRANDO AND GUGLIELMO
(to Fiordiligi and Dorabella)
I beg you, my adored one,
turn your lovely eyes on me.

FIORDILIGI E DORABELLA
Più resister non poss'io!

FIORDILIGI AND DORABELLA
I can resist no longer!

DESPINA E DON ALFONSO
In poch'ore, lo vedrete,
Per virtù del magnetismo
Finirà quel parossismo,
Torneranno al primo umor.

DESPINA AND DON ALFONSO
Very soon now you'll see,
by virtue of magnetism's power,
the end of this paroxysm,
and they'll be as they were before.

FERRANDO E GUGLIELMO
(da sè)
Dalla voglia ch'ho di ridere
Il polmon mi scoppia or or.
(forte)
Dammi un bacio, o mio tesoro;
Un sol bacio, o qui mi moro.

FERRANDO AND GUGLIELMO
(aside)
My lungs are bursting
with the need to laugh.
(aloud)
Give me a kiss, my treasure,
one single kiss, or else I die.

FIORDILIGI E DORABELLA
Stelle, un bacio?

FIORDILIGI AND DORABELLA
Heavens, a kiss?

DESPINA
Secondate
Per effetto di bontate.

DESPINA
Agree,
as an act of kindness.

FIORDILIGI E DORABELLA
Ah, che troppo si richiede
Da una fida onesta amante!
Oltraggiata è la mia fede,
Oltraggiato è questo cor!

FIORDILIGI AND DORABELLA
This is too much to ask
of a chaste and faithful woman!
It's an outrage to my love,
it's an outrage to my heart!

DESPINA, FERRANDO, GUGLIELMO E DON ALFONSO
(ognuno da sè)
Un quadretto più giocondo
Non si vide in tutto il mondo;
Quel che più mi fa da ridere
È quell'ira e quel furor.

DESPINA, FERRANDO, GUGLIELMO AND DON ALFONSO
(aside)
A more amusing picture
can't be found in all the world
that which makes me laugh the most
is their rage and fury.

FIORDILIGI E DORABELLA
Disperati,
Attossicati,
Ite al diavol quanti siete;
Tardi inver vi pentirete
Se più cresce il mio furor!

FIORDILIGI AND DORABELLA
Despairing or poisoned,
go to the devil,
the lot of you;
truly you'll repent too late
if you anger me more!

FERRANDO E GUGLIELMO
(da sè)
Ma non so se vera o finta
Sia quell'ira e quel furor,
Nè vorrei che tanto foco
Terminasse in quel d'amor.

FERRANDO AND GUGLIELMO
(aside)
I don't know if their rage
and fury are feigned or real,
but wouldn't wish this fire
to end in the fire of love.

DESPINA E DON ALFONSO
(da sè)
Io so ben che tanto foco
Cangerassi in quel d'amor.

DESPINA AND DON ALFONSO
(aside)
I know full well this fire
will change to that of love.

ATTO SECONDO ACT II

SCENA PRIMA

Camera
Fiordiligi, Dorabella e Despina

RECITATIVO

DESPINA
Andate là, che siete
Due bizzarre ragazze!

FIORDILIGI
Oh cospettaccio!
Cosa pretenderesti?

DESPINA
Per me nulla.

FIORDILIGI
Per chi dunque?

DESPINA
Per voi.

DORABELLA
Per noi?

DESPINA
Per voi.
Siete voi donne o no?

FIORDILIGI
E per questo?

DESPINA
E per questo

SCENE 1

A room
Fiordiligi, Dorabella and Despina

RECITATIVE

DESPINA
Upon my word, you're
the strangest pair of creatures!

FIORDILIGI
You jade!
What are you after?

DESPINA
For me, nothing.

FIORDILIGI
For whom, then?

DESPINA
For you.

DORABELLA
For us?

DESPINA
For you.
Are you women or not?

FIORDILIGI
What do you mean?

DESPINA
I mean,

Dovete far da donne.

DORABELLA
Cioè?

DESPINA
Trattar l'amore en bagatelle,
Le occasioni belle
Non negliger giammai; cangiar
a tempo,
A tempo esser costanti,
Conquetizzar con grazia,
Prevenir la disgrazia sì comune
A chi si fida in uomo,
Mangiar il fico, e non gittare il
pomo.

FIORDILIGI
Che diavolo! Tai cose
Falle tu, se n'hai voglia.

DESPINA
Io già le faccio,
Ma vorrei che anche voi
Per gloria del bel sesso
Faceste un po' lo stesso; per
esempio;
I vostri Ganimedi
Son andati alla guerra; infin che
tornano,
Fate alla militare: reclutate.

DORABELLA
Il cielo ce ne guardi.

DESPINA
Eh, che noi siamo in terra e non
in cielo!
Fidatevi al mio zelo. Giacchè
questi forestieri v'adorano,
Lasciatevi adorar. Son ricchi,
belli,
Nobili, generosi, come fede
Fece a voi Don Alfonso; avean
coraggio
Di morire per voi; questi son
merti
Che sprezzare non si denno
Da giovani qual voi, belle e
galanti,
Che pon star senza amor, non

you should act like women, then.

DORABELLA
And how is that?

DESPINA
Treat love lightly,
never neglect an opportunity;
change at the right moment,

sometimes be constant,
flirt with charm,
foresee the misfortune so common
to those who trust in men,
have your cake and eat it
too.

FIORDILIGI
You minx! That's what
you'd do if you had the chance.

DESPINA
That's what I do now,
but I wish that you too
would do the same
for the glory of the fair
sex;
for example, your gallants
have gone off to the wars, till
they return,
act like the army: go recruiting!

DORABELLA
Heaven protect us.

DESPINA
Oh, we're on earth and not in
heaven!
Trust in my zeal.
Since these strangers adore you,
let them do so. They're rich,
handsome,
Well-born, generous, as Don
Alfonso guaranteed you;
they had the courage
to die for you; these are
virtues
not to be despised by ladies
such as you, of beauty and
fashion,
who can do without love but

senza amanti.
(da sè)
Par che ci trovin gusto.

FIORDILIGI
Perbacco, ci faresti
Far delle belle cose;
Credi tu che vogliamo
Favola diventar degli oziosi?
Ai nostri cari sposi
Credi tu che vogliam dar tal
tormento?

DESPINA
E chi dice che abbiate
A far loro alcun torto?

DORABELLA
Non ti pare
Che sia torto bastante
Se noto si facesse
Che trattiamo costor?

DESPINA
Anche per questo
C'è un mezzo sicurissimo:
Io voglio sparger fama
Che vengono da me.

DORABELLA
Chi vuoi che il creda?

DESPINA
Oh bella! Non ha forse
Merto una cameriera
D'aver due cicisbei? Di me
fidatevi.

FIORDILIGI
No, no; son troppo audaci
Questi tuoi forestieri,
Non ebber la baldanza
Fin di chieder dei baci?

DESPINA
(da sè)
Che disgrazia!
(forte)
Io posso assicurarvi
Che le cose che han fatto

not without lovers.
(to herself)
I think they're coming round.

FIORDILIGI
Indeed, you'd have us
acting very strangely.
Do you think we want to be
the talk of all the gossips?
Do you think we want to cause
such anguish to our loved
ones?

DESPINA
And who says
you'd be doing them any harm?

DORABELLA
Don't you consider
it would be harm enough
if word got round
that we were entertaining them?

DESPINA
As for that, there's
a perfectly safe method:
I'll spread it abroad
that they're after me.

DORABELLA
Who'd believe that?

DESPINA
Oh thank you! Hasn't a maid
the right to have a couple of
followers?
You can trust in me.

FIORDILIGI
No, no; these strangers of yours
are too bold.
Didn't they even go so far
as to ask for kisses?

DESPINA
(to herself)
How shocking!
(aloud)
I can assure you
that all the things they did

Furo effetto del tossico che han preso:
Convulsionsi, deliri,
Follie, vaneggiamenti;
Ma or vedrete come son discreti,
Manierosi, modesti e mansueti.
Lasciateli venir.

were the fault of the poison they took:
Convulsions, deliriums,
Delusions, ravings:
but now you'll see how mild they are,
well-behaved, modest and gentle.
Let them come back.

DORABELLA
E poi?

DORABELLA
And then?

DESPINA
E poi?
Caspita, fate voi.
(da sè)
L'ho detto che cadrebbero.

DESPINA
And then?
Bless us, get on with it.
(to herself)
I said they'd fall!

FIORDILIGI
Cosa dobbiamo far?

FIORDILIGI
What should we do?

DESPINA
Quel che volete.
Siete d'ossa e di carne,
O cosa siete?

DESPINA
Whatever you want.
Are you flesh and blood,
or what?

19. ARIA

DESPINA
Una donna a quindici anni
Dee saper ogni gran moda,
Dove il diavolo ha la coda,
Cosa è bene e mal cos'è.
Dee saper le maliziette
Che innamorano gli amanti,
Finger riso, finger pianti,
Inventar i bei perchè.
Dee in un momento
Dar retta a cento,
Colle pupille
Parlar con mille,
Dar speme a tutti,
Sien belli, o brutti,
Saper nascondersi
Senza confondersi,
Senza arrossire
Saper mentire
E, qual regina
Dall'alto soglio,
Col posso e voglio
Farsi ubbidir.
(da sè)

19. ARIA

DESPINA
At fifteen a woman
should know the ways of the world,
where the devil keeps his tail,
what's right and what is wrong.
She should know the wiles
that ensnare lovers,
how to feign laughter or tears
and to make up good excuses.
At one and the same moment
she must listen to a hundred
but speak with her eyes
to a thousand,
hold out hope to all,
be they handsome or plain,
know how to hide things
without getting flustered,
know how to tell lies
without ever blushing.
And, like a queen
on her lofty throne,
get her own way
with 'I can' and 'I will'
(aside)

Par ch'abbian gusto
Di tal dottrina;
Viva Despina
Che sa servir.

(parte)

SCENA SECONDA

Fiordiligi e Dorabella

RECITATIVO

FIORDILIGI
Sorella, cosa dici?

DORABELLA
Io son stordita
Dallo spirto infernal di tal ragazza.

FIORDILIGI
Ma credimi: è una pazza.
Ti par che siamo in caso
Di seguir suoi consigli?

DORABELLA
Oh certo, se tu pigli
Pe! rovescio il negozio.

FIORDILIGI
Anzi io lo piglio
Per il suo vero dritto:
Non credi tu delitto
Per due giovani omai promesse spose
Il far di queste cose?

DORABELLA
Ella non dice
Che facciamo alcun mal.

FIORDILIGI
È mal che basta
Il far parlar di noi!

DORABELLA
Quando si dice
Che vengon per Despina!

FIORDILIGI
Oh, tu sei troppo larga di coscienza!

It seems they're taking
to this doctrine;
hooray for Despina,
she knows how to do it.

(exit)

SCENE 2

Fiordiligi and Dorabella

RECITATIVE

FIORDILIGI
Sister, what do you say?

DORABELLA
I'm dumbfounded
at the fiendish ideas of that girl.

FIORDILIGI
Believe me, she's crazy.
Do you think that we could possibly
follow her counsel?

DORABELLA
Of course, if you stood everything
upside down.

FIORDILIGI
On the contrary, I'm standing things
the right way up:
Don't you think it wrong
for two young women who are
betrothed
to do such things?

DORABELLA
She's not saying
we should do any harm.

FIORDILIGI
It's bad enough
getting ourselves talked about!

DORABELLA
But if it's said
they've come to see Despina!

FIORDILIGI
Your conscience is too elastic!

E che diran gli sposi nostri?

What will our menfolk say?

DORABELLA
Nulla;
O non sapran l'affare,
Ed è tutto finito,
O sapran qualche cosa,
E allor diremo
Che vennero per lei.

DORABELLA
Nothing;
either they'll not know about it
and it's all over and done with,
or they'll hear something,
and then we'll say
they came to see her.

FIORDILIGI
Ma i nostri cori?

FIORDILIGI
But our hearts?

DORABELLA
Restano quel che sono;
Per divertirsi un poco, e non
morire dalla malinconia,
Non si manca di fè,
Sorella mia.

DORABELLA
Will stay as they are;
to amuse ourselves a little
and not to die of boredom
is not to be false,
my dear sister.

FIORDILIGI
Questo è ver.

FIORDILIGI
That's true.

DORABELLA
Dunque?

DORABELLA
So?

FIORDILIGI
Dunque fa un po'tu:
Ma non voglio aver colpa
Se poi nasce un imbroglio.

FIORDILIGI
So you go ahead:
but I don't want to be involved
if there should be a scandal.

DORABELLA
Che imbroglio nascer deve
Con tanta precauzion? Per
altro, ascolta,
Per intenderci bene:
Qual vuoi sceglier per te de' due
Narcisi?

DORABELLA
How can there be a scandal
when we're taking such
precautions?
However, listen, let's come to
an agreement.
Which of these two Narcissi do you
fancy yourself?

FIORDILIGI
Decidi tu, sorella.

FIORDILIGI
You choose, sister.

DORABELLA
Io già decisi.

DORABELLA
I've already chosen.

20. DUETTO

20. DUET

DORABELLA
Prenderò quel brunettino,
Che più lepido mi par.

DORABELLA
I'll take the dark one,
who seems to me more fun.

FIORDILIGI
Ed intanto io col biondino
Vo' un po' ridere e burlar.

DORABELLA
Scherzosetta, ai dolci detti
Io di quel risponderò.

FIORDILIGI
Sospirando, i sospiretti
Io dell'altro imiterò.

DORABELLA
Mi dirà:
Ben mio, mi moro!

FIORDILIGI
Mi dirà:
Mio bel tesoro!

FIORDILIGI E DORABELLA
Ed intanto che diletto,
Che spassetto
Io proverò!

SCENE TERZA

Le suddette e Don Alfonso

RECITATIVO

DON ALFONSO
Ah, correte al giardino,
Le mie care ragazze!
Che allegria! Che musica!
Che canto!
Che brillante spettacolo! Che
incanto!
Fate presto, correte!

DORABELLA
Che diamine esser può?

DON ALFONSO
Tosto vedrete.

(partono)

FIORDILIGI
And meantime I'll laugh
and joke a bit with the fair one.

DORABELLA
Playfully I'll answer
his sweet words.

FIORDILIGI
Sighing, I'll imitate
the other's sighs.

DORABELLA
He'll say to me:
My love, I'm dying!

FIORDILIGI
He'll say to me:
My dearest treasure!

FIORDILIGI AND DORABELLA
And meanwhile
what sport and pleasure
I shall have!

SCENE 3

The above and Don Alfonso

RECITATIVE

DON ALFONSO
Come, make haste to the garden,
dear young ladies!
What fun! What music! Such
singing!
What a brilliant sight!
What magic! Come along,
quickly!

DORABELLA
Whatever's going on?

DON ALFONSO
You'll soon see.

(exeunt)

SCENA QUARTA

Giardino alla riva del mare con sedili d'erba e due tavolini di pietra. Alla sponda, una barca ornato di fiori.
Ferrando e Guglielmo, con suonatori e cantanti nella barca; Despina nel giardino; Fiordiligi e Dorabella, accompagnate da Don Alfonso, vengono da una lato. Servi riccamente vestiti, ecc.

21. DUETTO (CON CORO)

FERRANDO E GUGLIELMO
Secondate, aurette amiche,
Secondate i miei desiri,
E portate i miei sospiri
Alla dea di questo cor.
Voi, che udiste mille volte
Il tenor delle mie pene,
Ripetete al caro bene
Tutto quel che udiste allor.

RECITATIVO

DON ALFONSO
(ai servi che portano bacili con fiori)
Il tutto deponete
Sopra quei tavolini, e nella barca
Ritiratevi, amici.

FIORDILIGI E DORABELLA
Cos'è tal mascherata?

DESPINA
(agli amanti)
Animo, via coraggio: avete perso
L'uso della favella?
(La barca s'allontana dalla sponda)

FERRANDO
Io tremo e palpito
Dalla testa alle piante.

GUGLIELMO
Amor lega le membra a vero amante.

SCENE 4

A garden by the seashore, with garden seats and two small stone tables. At the landing stage is a barge decorated with flowers.
Ferrando and Guglielmo, in the barge, with singers and musicians; Despina in the garden; Fiordiligi and Dorabella, accompanied by Don Alfonso, come in from one side. Richly attired servants, etc.

21. DUET (WITH CHORUS)

FERRANDO AND GUGLIELMO
Ye friendly breezes,
help, o help my desires
and carry my sighs
to the goddess of my heart.
Repeat, you who a thousand times
have heard the tenor of my griefs,
all that you have heard
to my beloved.

RECITATIVE

DON ALFONSO
(to the servants carrying baskets of flowers)
Set all those down
on these tables, my lads,
and then return to the barge.

FIORDILIGI AND DORABELLA
What is this masquerade?

DESPINA
(to the suitors)
Come now, courage!
Have you lost your tongues?
(The barge leaves the shore)

FERRANDO
I tremble and quake
from head to foot.

GUGLIELMO
Love binds the limbs of a true lover.

DON ALFONSO
(alle donne)
Da brave, incoraggiateli.

FIORDILIGI
(agli amante)
Parlate.

DORABELLA
Liberi dite pur quel che bramate.

FERRANDO
Madama!

GUGLIELMO
Anzi, Madame!

FERRANDO
Parla pur tu.

GUGLIELMO
No, no, parla pur tu.

DON ALFONSO
Oh, cospetto del diavolo!
Lasciate tali smorfie
Del secolo passato. Despinetta,
Terminiam questa festa;
Fa tu con lei, quel ch'io farò
con questa.

22. QUARTETTO

DON ALFONSO
(prendendo per mano Dorabella; Despina prende Fiordiligi.)
La mano a me date,
Movetevi un po'!
(agli amanti)
Se voi non parlate,
Per voi parlerò.
(alle donne)
Perdono vi chiede
Un schiavo tremante;
V'offese, lo vede,
Ma solo un istante;
Or pena, ma tace . . .

FERRANDO E GUGLIELMO
Tace . . .

DON ALFONSO
(to the ladies)
Give them a word of encouragement.

FIORDILIGI
(to the suitors)
Speak then.

DORABELLA
Say frankly what it is you want.

FERRANDO
My lady!

GUGLIELMO
Rather, my ladies!

FERRANDO
You do the talking.

GUGLIELMO
No, no, you do it.

DON ALFONSO
The devil take it!
Do stop this absurd
old-fashioned nonsense.
Despina, let's get this over;
You act for one side while I act
for the other.

22. QUARTET

DON ALFONSO
(taking Dorabella by the hand; Despina takes Fiordiligi.)
Give me your hand,
and come this way a little.
(to the suitors)
If you won't speak,
I'll speak up for you.
(to the ladies)
A trembling slave
implores your pardon;
he offended you, he sees,
though only for a moment;
now he repents in silence . . .

FERRANDO AND GUGLIELMO
In silence . . .

DON ALFONSO
Or lasciavi in pace . . .

FERRANDO E GUGLIELMO
In pace . . .

DON ALFONSO
Non può quel che vuole,
Vorrà quel che può.

FERRANDO E GUGLIELMO
Non può quel che vuole,
Vorrà quel che può.

DON ALFONSO
Su, via rispondete;
Guardate e ridete?

DESPINA
(alle signore)
Per voi la risposta
A loro darò.
Quello che è stato, è stato
Scordiamci del passato.
Rompasi amai quel laccio,
Segno di servitù.
A me porgete il braccio,
Nè sospirate più.

DESPINA E DON ALFONSO
(sottovoce a parte)
Per carità, partiamo;
Quel che san far veggiamo,
Le stimo più del diavolo
S'ora non cascan giù.

(partono)

SCENA QUINTA

Fiordiligi, Dorabella, Ferrando e Guglielmo

RECITATIVO

FIORDILIGI
Oh che bella giornata!

FERRANDO
Caldetta anzi che no.

DON ALFONSO
Now he leaves you in peace . . .

FERRANDO AND GUGLIELMO
In peace . . .

DON ALFONSO
He can't do what he wants to,
he would do what he can.

FERRANDO E GUGLIELMO
He can't do what he wants to,
he would do what he can.

DON ALFONSO
Now come, give them an answer.
You just look on and laugh?

DESPINA
(to the ladies)
I'll give them an answer
for you.
What's done is done
Least said, soonest mended.
So let the knot, the sign
of servitude, be broken.
Give me your arm,
and sigh no more.

DESPINA AND DON ALFONSO
(softly, aside)
Let's go, for mercy's sake;
we'll watch what they will do.
I'll rank them higher than the devil
if they don't give way now.

(exeunt)

SCENE 5

Fiordiligi, Dorabella, Ferrando and Guglielmo

RECITATIVE

FIORDILIGI
What a lovely day!

FERRANDO
Perhaps a trifle hot.

DORABELLA
Che vezzosi arboscelli!

GUGLIELMO
Certo, certo, son belli;
Han più foglie che frutti.

FIORDILIGI
Quei viali
Come sono leggiadri!
Volete passeggiar?

FERRANDO
Son pronto, o cara,
Ad ogni vostro cenno.

FIORDILIGI
Troppa grazia!

FERRANDO
(sottovoce a Guglielmo, nel passare)
Eccoci alla gran crisi!

FIORDILIGI
Cosa gli avete detto?

FERRANDO
Eh, gli raccomandai
Di divertirla bene.

DORABELLA
(a Guglielmo)
Passeggiamo anche noi.

GUGLIELMO
Come vi piace
(passeggiano)
Ahimè!

DORABELLA
Che cosa avete?

GUGLIELMO
Io mi sento sì male,
Sì male, anima mia,
Che mi par di morire.

DORABELLA
(da sè)

DORABELLA
What pretty bushes!

GUGLIELMO
Yes, yes, very pretty;
They've more leaves than fruit.

FIORDILIGI
How charming
these paths are!
Shall we take a stroll?

FERRANDO
Your slightest wish
is my command.

FIORDILIGI
You are too kind!

FERRANDO
(aside to Guglielmo, as he passes)
This is the big moment!

FIORDILIGI
What did you say to him?

FERRANDO
Er . . . I told him
to keep her entertained.

DORABELLA
(to Guglielmo)
Let us go for a stroll too.

GUGLIELMO
Just as you please.
(they stroll)
Oh dear!

DORABELLA
What's the matter?

GUGLIELMO
I feel so bad,
my dearest one,
that I think I'm going to die.

DORABELLA
(to herself)

Non otterrà nientissimo.
(forte)
Saranno rimasugli
Del velen che beveste.

GUGLIELMO
(con fuoco)
Ah, che un veleno
Assai più forte io bevo
In que' crudi e focosi
Mongibelli amorosi!

(Fiordiligi parte con Ferrando)

DORABELLA
Sarà veleno calido;
Fatevi un poco fresco.

GUGLIELMO
Ingrata, voi burlate
Ed intanto io mi moro.
(da sè)
Son spariti;
Dove diamin son iti?

DORABELLA
Eh via, non fate.

GUGLIELMO
Io mi moro, crudele, e voi
burlate?

DORABELLA
Io burlo?

GUGLIELMO
Dunque datemi qualche segno.
Anima bella, della vostra pietà.

DORABELLA
Due, se volete;
Dite quel che far deggio e lo
vedrete.

GUGLIELMO
(da sè)
Scherza, o dice davvero?
(forte)
Questa picciola offerta
D'accettare degnatevi.

This simply won't do.
(aloud)
It'll be the after-effects
of the poison that you drank.

GUGLIELMO
(fierily)
Ah, I drink in
a far stronger poison
from the cruel, fiery
volcanoes of love!

(Fiordiligi goes out with Ferrando.)

DORABELLA
It'll be a burning poison;
cool yourself a little.

GUGLIELMO
Unkind one, you mock me
while I'm dying.
(to himself)
They've vanished;
where the devil have they got to?

DORABELLA
Oh, don't do that.

GUGLIELMO
I'm dying, cruel one, and you
mock me?

DORABELLA
I mock you?

GUGLIELMO
Then give me, light of my life,
some token of your pity.

DORABELLA
Two, if you like.
Tell me what you'd have, and
we'll see.

GUGLIELMO
(to himself)
Is she joking or in earnest?
(aloud)
Deign to accept
this humble offering.

DORABELLA
Un core?

GUGLIELMO
Un core:è simbolo di quello
Ch'arde, languisce e spasima per voi.

DORABELLA
(da sè)
Che dono prezioso!

GUGLIELMO
L'accettate?

DORABELLA
Crudele,
Di sedur non tentate un cor fedele.

GUGLIELMO
(da sè)
La montagna vacilla;
Mi spiace, ma impegnato
E l'onor di soldato.
(a Dorabella)
V'adoro!

DORABELLA
Per pietà!

GUGLIELMO
Son tutto vostro!

DORABELLA
Oh Dei!

GUGLIELMO
Cedate, o cara!

DORABELLA
Mi farete morir.

GUGLIELMO
Morremo insieme,
Amorosa mia speme.
L'accettate?

DORABELLA
A heart?

GUGLIELMO
Yes, a heart, the symbol of that one
which burns, pines and longs for you.

DORABELLA
(to herself)
What a precious gift!

GUGLIELMO
Will you accept it?

DORABELLA
Cruel man,
do not seek to tempt a faithful heart.

GUGLIELMO
(to himself)
The mountain is weakening.
I don't like this, but I've pledged
my honour as a soldier.
(to Dorabella)
I adore you!

DORABELLA
I beg of you!

GUGLIELMO
I am all yours.

DORABELLA
O Heavens!

GUGLIELMO
Give in, my dear one!

DORABELLA
You'll drive me to my death!

GUGLIELMO
We'll die together then,
my hope and love.
Will you accept it?

DORABELLA
(dopo breve intervallo, con un sospiro)
L'accetto.

GUGLIELMO
(da sè)
Infelice Ferrando!
(forte)
Oh che diletto!

23. DUETTO

GUGLIELMO
Il cor vi dono,
Bell'idolo mio;
Ma il vostro vo' anch'io:
Via, datelo a me.

DORABELLA
Mel date, lo prendo,
Ma il mio non vi rendo;
Invan me'l chiedete,
Più meco ei non è.

GUGLIELMO
Se teco non l'hai,
Perchè batte qui?

DORABELLA
Se a me tu lo dai,
Che mai balza li?

DORABELLA E GUGLIELMO
E' il mio coricino
Che più non è meco;
Ei venne a star teco,
Ei batte così.

GUGLIELMO
(vuol metterle il cuore dove ha il ritratto di Ferrando)
Qui lascia che il metta.

DORABELLA
Ei qui non può star.

GUGLIELMO
T'intendo, furbetta.
(Le torce dolcemente la faccia

DORABELLA
(after a brief pause, with a sigh)
I accept.

GUGLIELMO
(to himself)
Poor Ferrando!
(aloud)
Oh what joy!

23. DUET

GUGLIELMO
This heart I give you,
my adored one;
but I want yours in return:
come, give it me.

DORABELLA
You've given it and I take it,
but mine I cannot give;
in vain you ask it of me,
it is no longer mine.

GUGLIELMO
If you no longer own it,
why does it beat here?

DORABELLA
If you gave me it,
what is still beating there?

DORABELLA AND GUGLIELMO
It is my own dear heart
that is no longer mine;
it's come to lodge with you,
and that's what's beating so.

GUGLIELMO
(trying to put the heart where she has the miniature of her lover)
Let me put it here.

DORABELLA
There it cannot stay.

GUGLIELMO
I understand, you little rogue.
(He gently turns her face away,

dall'altra parte, le cava il ritratto e vi mette il cuore)

DORABELLA
Che fai?

GUGLIELMO
Non guardar.

DORABELLA
(da sè)
Nel petto un Vesuvio
D'avere mi par!

GUGLIELMO
(da sè)
Ferrando meschino!
Possibil non par.
(forte)
L'occhietto a me gira.

DORABELLA
Che brami?

GUGLIELMO
Rimira,
Se meglio può andar.

DORABELLA E GUGLIELMO
Oh, cambio felice
Di core e d'affetti!
Che nuovi diletti,
Che dolce penar!
(Partono abbracciati)

SCENA SESTA

Entra Fiordiligi agitata, seguita da Ferrando

RECITATIVO

FERRANDO
Barbara! Perchè fuggi!

FIORDILIGI
Ho visto un aspide,
Un'idra, un basilisco!

FERRANDO
Ah crudel, ti capisco!

takes out the miniature and puts in the heart)

DORABELLA
What are you doing?

GUGLIELMO
You're not to look.

DORABELLA
(to herself)
I feel I have
a volcano in my bosom!

GUGLIELMO
(to himself)
Poor Ferrando!
It doesn't seem possible!
(aloud)
Now turn your pretty eyes on me.

DORABELLA
What do you want?

GUGLIELMO
See,
doesn't that look better?

DORABELLA AND GUGLIELMO
Oh happy exchange
of hearts and affections!
What new delights!
What sweet pain!
(They go out arm in arm)

SCENE 6

Fiordiligi enters in agitation, followed by Ferrando

RECITATIVE

FERRANDO
Unkind one! Why do you fly me?

FIORDILIGI
I've seen an asp,
an hydra, a basilisk!

FERRANDO
Ah, cruel one, I understand you!

L'aspide, l'idra, il basilisco
E quanto i Libici deserti
Han di più fiero in me solo tu vedi.

FIORDILIGI
È vero, è vero!
Tu vuoi tormi la pace.

FERRANDO
Ma per farti felice.

FIORDILIGI
Cessa di molestarmi!

FERRANDO
Non ti chiedo che un guardo.

FIORDILIGI
Partiti!

FERRANDO
Non sperarlo,
Se pria gli occhi men fieri a me non giri.
O ciel! Ma tu mi guardi e poi sospiri?

24. ARIA

FERRANDO
(lietissimo)
Ah, io veggio, quell'anima bella
Al mio pianto resister non sà:
Non è fatta per esser rubella
Agli effetti di amica pietà.
In quel guardo, in quei cari sospiri
Dolce raggio lampeggia al mio cor:
Già rispondi a miei caldi desiri,
Già tu cedi al più tenero amor.
Ma tu fuggi, spietata tu taci,
Ed invano mi senti languir?
Ah cessate, speranze fallaci,
La crudel mi condanna a morir.

(parte)

SCENA SETTIMA

The asp, the hydra, the basilisk
and all that's fiercest in the Libyan desert
you see in me alone.

FIORDILIGI
Ah yes, it's true!
You would rob me of my peace.

FERRANDO
Only to make you happy.

FIORDILIGI
Molest me no further!

FERRANDO
I ask but for a glance.

FIORDILIGI
Leave me!

FERRANDO
How can I, until you turn on me
an eye less haughty?
Oh Heaven! But you look at me
and sigh?

24. ARIA

FERRANDO
(very cheerfully)
Ah, I see that this lovely creature
could not resist my pleading:
she is not made to be obdurate
to the expression of kindly pity.
In that glance, in those dear sighs
a sweet ray penetrates my heart:
already you respond to my hot
desires, already you yield to my
most tender love.
But you flee, silently and without pity:
will you hear me languish in vain?
Ah, have done, deceitful hopes;
cruelly she condemns me to die.

(exit)

SCENE 7

RECITATIVO

FIORDILIGI
(sola)
Ei parte . . . senti . . . ah no!
Partir si lasci,
Si tolga ai sguardi miei l'infausto oggetto
Della mia debolezza. A qual cimento
Il barbaro mi pose! Un premio è questo
Ben dovuto a mie colpe!
In tale istante
Dovea di nuovo amante
I sospiri ascoltar? L'altrui querele
Dovea volger in gioco? Ah, questo core
A ragione condanni, o giusto amore!
Io ardo, e l'ardor mio non è più effetto
D'un amor virtuoso; è smania, affanno,
Rimorso, pentimento,
Leggerezza, perfidia e tradimento!

25. RONDO

FIORDILIGI
Per pietà, ben mio, perdona
All'error d'un alma amante;
Fra quest'ombre e queste piante
Sempre ascoso, oh Dio, sarà.
Svenerà quest'empia voglia
L'ardir mio, la mia costanza,
Perderà la rimembranza
Che vergogna e orror mi fa.
A chi mai mancò di fede
Questo vano ingrato cor?
Si dovea miglior mercede,
Caro bene, al tuo
candor!

(parte)

SCENA OTTAVA

Ferrando e Guglielmo

RECITATIVE

FIORDILIGI
(alone)
He's left me . . . listen . . . Ah no!
Let him go,
let my sight be free of the unlucky object
of my weakness. To what a pass
this cruel man has brought me!
This is just a reward for my sins!
Was this the time
for me to heed the sighs
of a new lover, to make sport
of another's sighs? Ah, rightly
you condemn this heart, o just love!
I burn, and my ardour is no longer
the outcome of a virtuous love:
it is madness,
anguish, remorse, repentance,
fickleness, deceit and
betrayal!

25. RONDO

FIORDILIGI
In pity's name, my dearest,
forgive the misdeed of a loving soul;
Oh God, it shall evermore be
hidden among these shady bushes.
My courage, my constancy
will drive away this dishonourable
desire and banish the memory
which fills me with shame and horror.
And who is it whom
this unworthy heart has betrayed?
Dear heart, your trust deserved
a better reward!

(exit)

SCENE 8

Ferrando and Guglielmo

RECITATIVO

FERRANDO
(lietissimo)
Amico, abbiamo vinto!

GUGLIELMO
Un ambo o un terno?

FERRANDO
Una cinquina, amico; Fiordiligi
È la modestia in carne.

GUGLIELMO
Niente meno?

FERRANDO
Nientissimo; sta attento
E ascolta come fu.

GUGLIELMO
T'ascolto, di' pur su.

FERRANDO
Pel giardinetto,
Come eravam d'accordo,
A passeggiar mi metto;
Le do il braccio, si parla
Di mille cose indifferenti; alfine
Viensi all'amor.

GUGLIELMO
Avanti.

FERRANDO
Fingo labbra tremanti,
Fingo di pianger, fingo
Di morir al suo piè.

GUGLIELMO
Bravo assai per mia fè!
Ed ella?

FERRANDO
Ella da prima ride, scherza,
Mi burla.

GUGLIELMO
E poi?

RÉCITATIVE

FERRANDO
(in high spirits)
We've won my boy!

GUGLIELMO
Two of a kind?

FERRANDO
A straight flush!
Fiordiligi is modesty incarnate.

GUGLIELMO
Not a crack?

FERRANDO
Not one: just wait
and listen to what happened.

GUGLIELMO
I'm listening: tell me.

FERRANDO
We went for a stroll
in the garden,
as we'd agreed:
I gave her my arm,
we chatted of nothing in particular;
at last we came to the subject of love.

GUGLIELMO
Go on.

FERRANDO
I feigned a stammer,
I pretended to weep,
I swore I'd die at her feet.

GUGLIELMO
Very clever, I grant.
And she?

FERRANDO
At first she laughed,
joked and teased me.

GUGLIELMO
And then?

FERRANDO
E poi,
Finge d'impietosirsi.

FERRANDO
Then she pretended
to melt a little.

GUGLIELMO
Oh cospettaccio!

GUGLIELMO
Oh, did she!

FERRANDO
Alfin scoppia la bomba;
Pura come colomba
Al suo caro Guglielmo ella si serba;
Mi discaccia superba,
Mi maltratta, mi fugge,
Testimonio rendendomi e messaggio
Che una femmina ell'è senza paraggio.

FERRANDO
Then the bomb exploded.
She was keeping herself pure as a dove
for her dear Guglielmo:
haughtily she repulsed me,
upbraided me, fled me,
giving me evidence and proof
that she's a woman without equal.

GUGLIELMO
Bravo tu, bravo io,
Brava la mia Penelope!
Lascia un po' ch'io ti abbracci
Per sì felice augurio,
O mio fido Mercurio!
(si abbracciano)

GUGLIELMO
Good for you, good for me,
good for my Penelope!
Let me embrace you
for your happy tidings,
my faithful Mercury!
(they embrace)

FERRANDO
E la mia Dorabella?
Come s'è diportata?
Ah, non ci ho neppur dubbio.
(con trasporto)
Assai conosco
Quella sensibil alma.

FERRANDO
And my Dorabella,
how did she behave?
Oh, I haven't a doubt of her.
(enthusiastically)
I know so well
her sensitive soul.

GUGLIELMO
Eppur un dubbio,
Parlandoti a quattr'occhi,
Non saria mal, se tu l'avessi.

GUGLIELMO
Well, just between ourselves,
if you had a doubt
it might not be such a bad thing.

FERRANDO
Come?

FERRANDO
What?

GUGLIELMO
Dico così per dir!
(da sè)
Avrei piacere d'indorargli la pillola.

GUGLIELMO
Oh, don't take me seriously.
(to himself)
I'd like to gild the pill for him.

FERRANDO
Stelle! Cesse ella forse

FERRANDO
Speak out! Did she perhaps

Alle lusinghe tue? Ah, s'io potessi Sospettarlo soltanto!	fall for your flatteries? Ah, if I could even suspect it!
GUGLIELMO E sempre bene Il sospettare un poco in questo mondo.	GUGLIELMO In this world it's always wise to be a bit suspicious.
FERRANDO Eterni dei! Favella! A foco lento Non mi far qui morir; ma no, tu vuoi Prenderti meco spasso; ella non ama, Non adora che me.	FERRANDO Ye immortal gods! speak out! Don't roast me on a slow fire; but no, you're making sport of me; she loves me, adores me alone.
GUGLIELMO Certo! Anzi in prova Di suo amor, di sua fede, Questo bel ritrattino ella mi diede.	GUGLIELMO Certainly! And so in proof of her love and devotion she gave me this little picture.
FERRANDO *(furente)* Il mio ritratto! Ah, perfida! *(vuol partire)*	FERRANDO *(in a fury)* My portrait! The traitress! *(he makes to go)*
GUGLIELMO Ove vai?	GUGLIELMO Where are you going?
FERRANDO A trarle il cor dal scellerato petto *(furente)* E a vendicar il mio tradito affetto.	FERRANDO To tear her heart from her wicked bosom *(in a fury)* and avenge the betrayal of my love.
GUGLIELMO Fermati!	GUGLIELMO Stop!
FERRANDO *(risoluto)* No, mi lascia!	FERRANDO *(with determination)* No, let me go!
GUGLIELMO Sei tu pazzo? Vuoi tu precipitarti Per una donna che non val due soldi? *(da sè)* Non vorrei che facesse	GUGLIELMO Are you raving? Would you ruin yourself for a worthless woman? *(to himself)* I wouldn't want him

Qualche corbelleria!

FERRANDO
Numi! Tante promesse,
E lagrime, e sospiri, e giuramenti,
In sì pochi momenti
Come l'empia obliò?

GUGLIELMO
Perbacco, io non lo so.

FERRANDO
Che fare or deggio?
A qual partito,
A qual idea m'appiglio?
Abbi di me pietà, dammi consiglio.

GUGLIELMO
Amico, non saprei
Qual consiglio a te dar.

FERRANDO
Barbara! Ingrata!
In un giorno! In poch'ore!

GUGLIELMO
Certo un caso quest'è da far stupore.

26. ARIA

GUGLIELMO
Donne mie, la fate a tanti,
Che, se il ver vi deggio dir,
Se si lagnano gli amanti
Li comincio a compatir,
Io vo'bene al sesso vostro,
Lo sapete, ognun lo sa;
Ogni giorno ve lo mostro,
Vi do segno d'amistà.
Ma quel farla a tanti e tanti,
M'avvilisce in verità.
Mille volte il brando presi
Per salvar il vostro onor;
Mille volte vi difesi
Colla bocca e più col cor.
Ma quel farla a tanti e tanti
E un vizietto seccator.
Siete vaghe, siete amabili,
Più tesori il ciel vi diè

to commit some folly!

FERRANDO
Ye gods! All those promises,
and tears, and sighs, and vows,
how could the inhuman creature
forget them so soon?

GUGLIELMO
I'm sure I don't know.

FERRANDO
What should I do now?
To what course,
what plan apply myself?
Take pity on me, give me your counsel.

GUGLIELMO
My friend, I don't know
how to advise you.

FERRANDO
Cruel! Heartless!
In a day! In a few hours!

GUGLIELMO
It's certainly something to wonder at.

26. ARIA

GUGLIELMO
Ladies, you treat so many thus
that, if I must speak the truth,
I begin to sympathise
when your lovers complain,
I adore the sex, you know,
everyone knows it;
each day I show it
and always take your part.
But such treatment of so many
discourages me, in truth.
A thousand times I've drawn my sword
to defend your honour.
A thousand times I've championed you
with my tongue and, still more, with my heart.
But such treatment of so many
is pernicious and a bore.
You're attractive, you are charming,

E le grazie vi circondano
Dalla testa sino ai piè.
Ma la fate a tanti e tanti
Che credibile non è,
Chè, se gridano gli amanti,
Hanno certo un gran perchè.

Heaven has given you treasures galore,
and graces envelop you
from head to foot.
But thus you treat so many
that it's difficult to believe,
and if your lovers complain
they have good reason indeed.

(parte)

(exit)

SCENA NONA

SCENE 9

Ferrando solo, poi Don Alfonso e Guglielmo che parlano in fondo

Ferrando alone, later Don Alfonso and Guglielmo talking in the background

RECITATIVO

RECITATIVE

FERRANDO
In qual fiero contrasto,
In qual disordine
Di pensieri e di affetti io mi ritrovo!
Tanto insolito e novo è il caso mio,
Che non altri, non io
Basto per consigliarmi . . .
Alfonso, Alfonso,
Quanto rider vorrai
Della mia stupidezza!
Ma mi vendicherò, saprò dal seno
Cancellar quell'iniqua . . .
Cancellarla?
Troppo, oh Dio, questo cor per lei mi parla.

FERRANDO
In what fierce strife,
in what confusion
of thoughts and affections I find myself!
So unusual and novel is my situation
that neither others nor I myself
suffice to give me counsel . . .
Oh, Alfonso,
how you must be laughing
at my stupidity!
But I'll be revenged, I'll banish
the traitress from my mind . . .
Banish her?
O Heaven, too loudly my heart intercedes for her.

27. CAVATINA

27. CAVATINA

FERRANDO
Tradito, schernito
Dal perfido cor,
Io sento che ancora
Quest'alma l'adora,
Io sento per essa
Le voci d'amor.

FERRANDO
Betrayed and scorned
by her faithless heart,
I still know
that my soul adores her,
I still hear
the voice of love for her.

RECITATIVO

RECITATIVE

DON ALFONSO
Bravo, questa è costanza.

DON ALFONSO
Bravo, that's true fidelity.

FERRANDO
Andate, barbaro,
Per voi misero sono.

DON ALFONSO
Via, se sarete buono
Vi tornerò l'antica calma.
Udite:
(mostrando Guglielmo)
Fiordiligi a Guglielmo
Si conserva fedel,
E Dorabella infedel a voi fu.

FERRANDO
Per mia vergogna.

GUGLIELMO
Caro amico, bisogna
Far delle differenze in ogni cosa;
Ti pare che una sposa
Mancar possa a un Guglielmo?
Un picciol calcolo,
Non parlo per lodarmi,
Se facciamo tra noi . . .
Tu vedi, amico,
Che un poco di più merto . . .

DON ALFONSO
Eh, anch'io lo dico.

GUGLIELMO
Intanto mi darete
Cinquanta zecchinetti.

DON ALFONSO
Volentieri;
Pria però di pagar, vo'che facciamo
Qualche altra esperienza.

GUGLIELMO
Come?

DON ALFONSO
Abbiate pazienza; infin domani
Siete entrambi miei schiavi; a me
voi deste parola da soldati,
Di far quel ch'io dirò. Venite, io
spero
Mostrarvi ben che folle è quel
cervello

FERRANDO
Get away, you tormentor.
It's through you I'm suffering.

DON ALFONSO
Come, if you're sensible
your old calm will return.
Listen:
(pointing to Guglielmo)
Fiordiligi has remained
faithful to Guglielmo.
but Dorabella's unfaithful to you.

FERRANDO
To my shame.

GUGLIELMO
Dear friend, one must
make distinctions in everything.
Do you imagine a woman could
fail a Guglielmo?
Speaking in all modesty,
make a small comparison
between us . . . you see, my friend,
there's a little extra something . . .

DON ALFONSO
Yes, that's what I say.

GUGLIELMO
So meantime you can pay me
those fifty sequins.

DON ALFONSO
Willingly;
but before I do so, I'd like us
to try another experiment.

GUGLIELMO
What's that?

DON ALFONSO
Have patience; until tomorrow
you are both at my command;
you gave me your words as soldiers
to do what I said. Come, I hope
to show you how foolish it is
to count your chickens before
they're hatched.

Che sulla frasca ancor vende
l'uccello.

(partono)

(exeunt)

SCENA DECIMA

SCENE 10

Camera con diverse porte, specchio e tavolini.

A room with several doors, a mirror and a table.

Dorabella e Despina, poi Fiordiligi.

Dorabella and Despina, later Fiordiligi.

RECITATIVO

RECITATIVE

DESPINA
Ora vedo che siete
Una donna di garbo.

DESPINA
Now I can see
you're a woman of sense.

DORABELLA
Invan, Despina,
Di resister tentai: quel demonietto
Ha un artifizio, un'eloquenza,
un tratto,
Che ti fa cader giù se sei di sasso.

DORABELLA
In vain, Despina, I tried to resist:
that little devil has such tricks,
such eloquence, such a way
with him,
that he'd melt the heart of a stone.

DESPINA
Corpo di satanasso!
Questo vuol dir saper! Tanto di
raro noi povere ragazze
Abbiamo un po' di bene,
Che bisogna pigliarlo allor ch'ei
viene.
Ma ecco la sorella.
Che ceffo!

DESPINA
Saints above!
That's really something!
It's so rarely we poor girls
get the chance of something good
that we must grab it when it
comes.
But here's your sister.
What a face she's pulling!

FIORDILIGI
Sciagurate!
Ecco per colpa vostra
In che stato mi trovo!

FIORDILIGI
You wretches!
See what a state I'm in,
and all through you!

DESPINA
Cosa è nato,
Cara madamigella?

DESPINA
What's the matter,
my poor madame?

DORABELLA
Hai qualche mal, sorella?

DORABELLA
Is something wrong, sister?

FIORDILIGI
Ho il diavolo, che porti me,
Te, lei, Don Alfonso, i forestieri

FIORDILIGI
The devil's in me; let him take me,
you two, Don Alfonso, the strangers

E quanti pazzi ha il mondo.

DORABELLA
Hai perduto il giudizio?

FIORDILIGI
Peggio, peggio,
Inorridisci: io amo, e l'amor mio
Non è sol per Guglielmo.

DESPINA
Meglio, meglio!

DORABELLA
E che forse anche tu se' innamorata
Del galante biondino?

FIORDILIGI
(sospirando)
Ah, purtroppo per noi!

DESPINA
Ma brava!

DORABELLA
Tieni,
Settantamila baci:
Tu il biondino, io il brunetto,
Eccoci entrambe spose!

FIORDILIGI
Cosa dici?
Non pensi agli infelici
Che stamane partir?
Ai loro pianti?
Alla lor fedeltà tu più non pensi?
Così barbari sensi
Dove, dove apprendesti?
Si diversa da te come ti festi?

DORABELLA
Odimi, sei tu certa
Che non muoiano in guerra
I nostri vecchi amanti? E allora?
Entrambe resterem colle
Man piene di
mosche.
Tra un ben certo e un incerto
C'è sempre gran divario.

and all the other fools in the world.

DORABELLA
Have you lost your senses?

FIORDILIGI
Worse, much worse,
Recoil from me: I'm in love,
and my love isn't just for Guglielmo.

DESPINA
That's better, much better!

DORABELLA
And perhaps you too have fallen
in love with the fair gallant?

FIORDILIGI
(sighing)
Ah, only too deeply!

DESPINA
Well, hooray!

DORABELLA
Take seventy thousand kisses:
you for the fair one,
I for the dark one,
and there we are, both married!

FIORDILIGI
What are you saying?
Don't you spare a thought for the
unfortunates
who left us this morning?
For their grief?
Have you forgotten their faithfulness?
Where, where did you learn
such barbarous feelings?
How have you so changed your
nature?

DORABELLA
Listen: are you sure
that our former lovers won't be
killed in the war? What then?
We'll both be left high and dry.
There's always a big difference
between one in the hand and
one in the bush.

FIORDILIGI
E se poi torneranno?

DORABELLA
Se torneran, lor danno!
Noi saremo allor mogli,
Noi saremo lontane mille miglia.

FIORDILIGI
Ma non so, come mai
Si può cangiar in un sol giorno
un core.

DORABELLA
Che domanda ridicola!
Siam donne!
E poi, tu com'hai fatto?

FIORDILIGI
Io saprò vincermi.

DESPINA
Voi non saprete nulla.

FIORDILIGI
Farò che tu lo veda.

DORABELLA
Credi, sorella, è meglio che tu
ceda.

28. ARIA

DORABELLA
È amore un ladroncello,
Un serpentello
È amor.
Ei toglie e dà la pace,
Come gli piace,
Ai cor.
Per gli occhi al seno appena
Un varco aprir si fa
Che l'anima incatena
E toglie libertà.
Porta dolcezza e gusto,
Se tu lo lasci far,
Ma t'empie di disgusto
Se tenti di pugnar.
Se nel tuo petto ei siede,
S'egli ti becca qui,
Fa tutto quel ch'ei chiede,

FIORDILIGI
And then if they come back?

DORABELLA
If they come back, too bad for them!
We'll be married by then
and far away from here.

FIORDILIGI
Well, I'd like to know how one can
change one's affections in a single
day.

DORABELLA
What a silly question!
We're women!
And how have you behaved?

FIORDILIGI
I can control myself.

DESPINA
You can't, I bet.

FIORDILIGI
I'll show you.

DORABELLA
Believe me, sister, you'd best
give in.

28. ARIA

DORABELLA
Love is a little thief,
a little serpent
is he,
According to his whim
the heart finds peace
or no.
Scarcely does he open a path
between your eyes and your bosom
than he chains your soul
and takes away your liberty.
He'll bring sweetness and content,
if you give him his way,
but will make your lot heavy
if you try to deny him.
If he visits your breast
and plucks at you there,
do all that he asks,

Che anch'io farò così.

(Dorabella e Despina partono)

SCENA UNDICESIMA

Fiordiligi sola, poi Guglielmo, Ferrando e Don Alfonso, che stanno in un'altra camera, che si vede per la porta della prima, poi Despina

RECITATIVO

FIORDILIGI
Come tutto congiura
A sedurre il mio cor! Ma no!
Si mora,
E non si ceda! Errai quando
alla suora
Io mi scopersi ed alla serva mia.
Esse a lui diran tutto, ed ei più
audace,
Fia di tutto capace; agli occhi miei
Mai più non comparisca! A tutti
i servi minaccerò il congedo
Se lo lascian passar; veder nol
voglio quel seduttor.

GUGLIELMO
Bravissima,
La mia casta Artemisia; la sentite?

FIORDILIGI
Ma potria Dorabella
Senza, saputa mia . . . piano, un
pensiero
Per la mente mi passa; in casa mia
Restar molte uniformi
Di Guglielmo e di Ferrando:
ardir!
Despina, Despina!

DESPINA
(entrando)
Cosa c'è?

FIORDILIGI
Tieni un po' questa chiave e senza
replica,
Senza replica alcuna,

as I will do too.

(Dorabella and Despina go out)

SCENE II

Fiordiligi alone, then Guglielmo, Ferrando and Don Alfonso in another room which can be seen through the door of the first, later Despina

RECITATIVE

FIORDILIGI
How everything conspires to tempt
my heart! But no! Let me die
rather than yield!
I was wrong to confess my feelings
to my sister and my servant.
They'll tell him all, and he'll
be bolder,
carrying all before him; my
eyes must not
fall on him again! I'll threaten
all the servants with dismissal
if they let him in; I will not see
that seducer.

GUGLIELMO
Well spoken, my chaste Diana!
Did you hear her?

FIORDILIGI
But perhaps Dorabella,
without my knowledge . . .
Softly a thought comes to mind;
in the house are several uniforms
of Guglielmo's and Ferrando's:
courage now!
Despina, Despina!

DESPINA
(entering)
What is it?

FIORDILIGI
Take this key, and without any
questions
or any back answers,

Prendi nel guardaroba, e qui mi porta
Due spade, due cappelli e due vestiti de' nostri sposi.

DESPINA
E che volete far?

FIORDILIGI
Vanne, non replicare.

DESPINA
(da sè)
Comanda in abregê donna Arroganza.
(parte)

FIORDILIGI
Non c'è altro; he speranza
Che Dorabella stessa
Seguirà il bell'esempio;
Al campo, al campo!
Altra strada non resta
Per serbarci innocenti.

DON ALFONSO
(da sè)
Ho capito abbastanza.
(a Despina, che ritorna)
Vanne pur, non temer.

DESPINA
Eccomi.

FIORDILIGI
Vanne.
Sei cavalli di posta
Voli un servo a ordinar; dì a Dorabella
Che parlarle vorrei.

DESPINA
Sarà servita.
(da sè)
Questa donna mi par di senno uscita.

(parte)

go to the wardrobe and bring me here
two swords, two helmets and two tunics of our lovers.

DESPINA
What do you want with them?

FIORDILIGI
Go on, and no back answers.

DESPINA
(to herself)
Milady's on her high horse!

(exit)

FIORDILIGI
There's nothing else to do:
I hope Dorabella herself
will follow a good example;
away, away!
No other way is left
for us to preserve our honour.

DON ALFONSO
(to himself)
I've heard enough.
(to Despina, who is returning)
Go on, don't be afraid.

DESPINA
Here I am.

FIORDILIGI
Now go.
Send a servant at once
to order six post-horses;
tell Dorabella I want to speak her.

DESPINA
Very good, ma'am.
(to herself)
I think she's out of her mind.

(exit)

SCENA DODICESIMA

Fiordiligi, poi Ferrando; Guglielmo e Don Alfonso restano nell'altra camera

RECITATIVO

FIORDILIGI
L'abito di Ferrando
Sarà buono per me; può Dorabella
Prender quel di Guglielmo. In
questi arnesi raggiungerem gli sposi
Nostri, al loro fianco pugnar
Potremo e morir, se fa d'uopo.
(Si cava quello che tiene in testa)
Ite in malora,
Ornamenti fatali, io vi detesto.

GUGLIELMO
(da sè)
Si può dar un amor simile a questo?

FIORDILIGI
Di tornar no sperate alla mia
fronte
Pria ch'io qui torni col mio ben;
In vostro loco porrò questo
cappello.
Oh, come ei mi trasforma le
sembianze e il viso!
Come appena io medesma or mi
ravviso!

29. DUETTO

FIORDILIGI
Fra gli amplessi in pochi istanti
Giungerò del fido sposo;
Sconosciuta a lui davanti
In quest'abito verrò.
Oh, che gioia il suo bel core
Proverà nel ravvisarmi!

FERRANDO
Ed intanto di dolore,
Meschinello io mi morrò.

FIORDILIGI
Cosa veggio? Son tradita!
Deh, partite!

SCENE 12

Fiordiligi, then Ferrando; Guglielmo and Don Alfonso remain in the other room

RECITATIVE

FIORDILIGI
Ferrando's uniform will fit me;
Dorabella can take Guglielmo's.
In these outfits
we'll join our sweethearts,
we can fight beside them
and die, if need be.
(She throws off her head-dress)
Out with you, fatal finery,
I despise you.

GUGLIELMO
(to himself)
Could there be a love like this?

FIORDILIGI
You shall never deck my head
again
till I return here with my true
love.
In your place I don this helmet.
How it transforms my whole
appearance!
I can hardly recognise myself!

29. DUET

FIORDILIGI
Very soon now I'll be enfolded
in the embraces of my true love;
unrecognised in these garments
I will come before him.
Oh, what joy will fill his heart
when he sees me again!

FERRANDO
And meanwhile, I, left wretched,
shall die of grief.

FIORDILIGI
What do I see? I am betrayed!
Oh leave me!

FERRANDO
Àh no, mia vita!
Con quel ferro di tua mano
Questo cor tu ferirai,
E se forza, oh Dio, non hai,
Io la man ti reggero.

FERRANDO
Ah no, dear heart!
With this sword in your hand
strike me to the heart,
and if you lack the strength,
by Heaven, I'll guide your hand myself.

FIORDILIGI
Taci, ahimè! Son abbastanza
Tormentata ed infelice!
(da sè)
Ah, che omai la mia costanza
A quei sguardi, a quel che dice,
Incomincia a vacillar!

FIORDILIGI
Alas, be silent! I am
tormented and unhappy enough!
(aside)
Ah, now my constancy
begins to falter
before his looks and his words!

FERRANDO
(da sè)
Ah, che omai la sua costanza
A quei sguardi, a quel che dice,
Incomincia a vacillar.

FERRANDO
(aside)
Ah, now her constancy
begins to falter
before my looks and my words!

FIORDILIGI
Sorgi, sorgi!

FIORDILIGI
Get up, I beg!

FERRANDO
Invan lo credi.

FERRANDO
It cannot be.

FIORDILIGI
Per pietà, da me che chiedi?

FIORDILIGI
In pity's name, what do you ask of me?

FERRANDO
Il tuo cor o la mia morte.

FERRANDO
Your heart or my death.

FIORDILIGI
Ah, non son, non son più forte!

FIORDILIGI
My strength is giving out!

FERRANDO
Cedi, cara!
(le prende la mano e gliela bacia)

FERRANDO
Yield, my dearest!
(taking her hand and kissing it)

FIORDILIGI
Dei, consiglio!

FIORDILIGI
Heaven, direct me!

FERRANDO
Volgi a me pietoso il ciglio.
In me sol trovar tu puoi
Sposo, amante e più, se vuoi.
(tenerissimamente)
Idol mio, più non tardar.

FERRANDO
Turn a merciful eye on me.
In me alone you'll find
husband, lover and more, if you wish.
(most tenderly)
Delay no longer, my adored one.

FIORDILIGI
(tremando)
Giusto ciel! Crudel, hai vinto;
Fa di me quel che ti par.

FIORDILIGI
(tremblingly)
Merciful heaven! Cruel man, you've won!
Do with me what you will.

(Don Alfonso trattiene Guglielmo che vorrebbe uscire)

(Don Alfonso holds back Guglielmo who tries to leap forward)

FERRANDO E FIORDILIGI
Abbracciamci, o caro bene,
E un conforto a tante pene
Sia languir di dolce affetto,
Di diletto
Sospirar!

FERRANDO AND FIORDILIGI
Embrace me, my dearest,
and may the consolation for our sorrows
be to spend our time in sweet affection, and sigh for joy!

(partono)

(exeunt)

SCENA TREDICESIMA

SCENE 13

Guglielmo e Don Alfonso, poi Ferrando, indi Despina.

Guglielmo and Don Alfonso, then Ferrando, later Despina.

RECITATIVO

RECITATIVE

GUGLIELMO
Oh poverretto me, cosa ho veduto!
Cosa ha sentito mai!

GUGLIELMO
Alas, poor me, what have I seen!
What have I heard!

DON ALFONSO
Per carità, silenzio!

DON ALFONSO
Keep quiet, for heaven's sake!

GUGLIELMO
Mi pelerei la barba,
Mi graffierei la pelle
E darei colle corna entro le stelle.
Fu quella Fiordiligi, la Penelope,
L'Artemisia del secolo! Briccona,
Assassina, furfante, ladra, cagna!

GUGLIELMO
I'll pluck out my beard,
I'll tear my flesh,
and charge the stars with my horns!
So that was Fiordiligi, my Penelope,
the chaste Diana of the age! Strumpet,
assassin, cheat, swindler, bitch!

DON ALFONSO
Lasciamolo sfogar.

DON ALFONSO
Let him get it off his chest.

FERRANDO
(entrando)
Ebben!

FERRANDO
(entering)
Well!

GUGLIELMO
Dov'è?

GUGLIELMO
Where is she?

FERRANDO
Chi? La tua Fiordiligi?

GUGLIELMO
La mia Fior, fior di diavolo,
Che strozzi lei prima e dopo me!

FERRANDO
Tu vedi bene:
V'han delle differenze in ogni cosa;
(ironicamente)
Un poco di più merto . . .

GUGLIELMO
Ah, cessa, cessa
Di tormentarmi ed una via
piuttosto
Studiam di castigarle
Sonoramente.

DON ALFONSO
Io so qual è: sposarle.

GUGLIELMO
Vorrei sposar piuttosto
La barca di Caronte!

FERRANDO
La grotta di Vulcano.

GUGLIELMO
La porta dell'inferno.

DON ALFONSO
Dunque restate celibi in eterno.

FERRANDO
Mancheran forse donne
Ad uomin come noi?

DON ALFONSO
Non c'è abbondanza d'altro.
Ma l'altre che faran,
Se ciò fer queste?
In fondo, voi le amate
Queste vostre cornacchie
spennacchiate.

GUGLIELMO
Ah, purtroppo!

FERRANDO
Who? Your Fiordiligi?

GUGLIELMO
My Fior . . . Furies of hell!
Strangle first her and then me!

FERRANDO
You see now;
there are distinctions in everything;
(ironically)
There's a little extra something . . .

GUGLIELMO
Stop it! Stop
taunting me, and instead
let's find a way
of punishing them soundly.

DON ALFONSO
I know what to do: marry
them.

GUGLIELMO
I'd rather marry
Charon's boat.

FERRANDO
Vulcan's smithy.

GUGLIELMO
The gates of hell.

DON ALFONSO
Then you'll stay bachelors for ever.

FERRANDO
Are there no women
Fit for men like us?

DON ALFONSO
There's not so many.
But what would they do,
if these act like this?
At bottom, you still love
these plucked birds.

GUGLIELMO
Alas, it's true!

FERRANDO
Purtroppo!

DON ALFONSO
Ebben, pigliatele
Com'elle son; natura non potea
Fare l'eccezione, il privilegio
Di creare due donne d'altra pasta
Per i vostri bei musi; in ogni cosa
Ci vuol filosofia. Venite meco;
Di combinar le cose
Studierem la maniera.
Vo'che ancor questa sera
Doppie nozze si facciano;
Frattanto un'ottava ascoltate:
Felicissimi voi se la imparate.

30. ANDANTE

DON ALFONSO
Tutti accusan le donne,
Ed io le scuso
Se mille volte al di cangiano
amore;
Altri un vizio lo chiama, ed altri
un uso,
Ed a me par necessità del core.
L'amante che si trova alfin deluso,
Non condanni l'altrui,
Ma il proprio errore,
Giacchè giovani, vecchie e belle
e brutte,
Ripetete con me:
Così fan tutte!

SCENA QUATTORDICESIMA

I suddetti; Despina

RECITATIVO

DESPINA
Vittoria, padroncini!
A sposarvi disposte
Son le care madame; a nome vostro
Loro io promisi che in tre giorni
circa
Partiranno con voi; l'ordin mi
diero di trovar un notaio
Che stipuli il contratto;

FERRANDO
Too true!

DON ALFONSO
Well then, take them as they are:
Nature can't make exceptions
and create two women of a
different stuff
just to suit your tastes: in such
matters
you must be philosophical.
Come along then; let's find a way
of putting things together.
Tonight I still want to see
a double wedding;
meanwhile listen to my song:
take heed, and you'll be happy.

30. ANDANTE

DON ALFONSO
Everyone blames women, but I forgive
them
if they change their love
a thousand times a day;
some call it a sin, others a habit.
But I say it's a necessity of
their heart.
The lover who finds that he's been
deceived should blame not others
but his own mistake;
whether they're young or old,
fair or plain –
Repeat with me:
Women are all the same!

SCENE 14

The above, Despina

RECITATIVE

DESPINA
Victory, gentlemen!
The dear ladies are disposed
to marry you; in your name
I promised that in about three
day's time
they'd go away with you:
they ordered me to find a notary
to draw up the contract;

alla lor camera
Àttendendo vi stanno.
Siete così contenti?

FERRANDO, GUGLIELMO
E DON ALFONSO
Contentissimi.

DESPINA
Non è mai senz'effetto
Quand'entra la Despina in un progetto.

(partono)

SCENA QUINDICESIMA

Sala ricchissima illuminata. Orchestra in fondo; tavola per quattro persone con doppieri d'argento. Quattro servi riccamente vestiti.

Despina, servitori e suonatori; poi Don Alfonso

31. FINALE

DESPINA
Fate presto, o cari amici,
Alle faci il foco date
E la mensa preparate
Con ricchezza e nobiltà.
Delle nostre padroncine
Gli imenei son già disposti
E voi gite ai vostri posti
Finchè i sposi vengon qua.

CORO DI SERVI E SUONATORI
Facciam presto, o cari amici,
Alle faci il foco diamo
E la mensa prepariamo
Con ricchezza e nobiltà.

DON ALFONSO
Bravi, bravi! Ottimamente!
Che abbondanza!
Che eleganza!
Una mancia conveniente
L'un a l'altro a voi darà.
Le due coppie omai s'avvanzano;

they're waiting for you in their room.
Are you satisfied with that?

FERRANDO, GUGLIELMO
AND DON ALFONSO
Most satisfied.

DESPINA
When Despina takes a job in hand
she always gets results.

(exeunt)

SCENE 15

A salon brilliantly lit. An orchestra in the background: a table laid for four persons, with silver candlesticks. Four richly clad servants.

Despina, servants and musicians; then Don Alfonso

31. FINALE

DESPINA
Be quick about it, friends,
light the torches
and prepare the table
in style for the nobility.
The marriage of our mistresses
is already arranged,
and you must take your places
as soon as the bridegrooms appear.

CHORUS OF SERVANTS AND MUSICIANS
Let's be quick about it, friends,
light the torches
and prepare the table
in style for the nobility.

DON ALFONSO
Well done! Splendid!
What abundance!
What elegance!
You'll all be given
a suitable reward.
Now the two couples are arriving;

Fate plauso al loro arrivo:
Lieto canto e suon giulivo
Empia il ciel d'ilarità.

applaud them as they enter:
let cheerful song and merry music
fill the air with gaiety.

DESPINA E DON ALFONSO
(piano, partendo per diverse porte)
La più bella commediola
Non s'è vista, o si vedrà!

DESPINA AND DON ALFONSO
(softly, leaving by different doors)
A prettier piece of comedy
there never was, nor ever will be!

SCENA SEDICESIMA

SCENE 16

I suddetti; Fiordiligi, Dorabella, Ferrando, Guglielmo

The above, Fiordiligi, Dorabella, Ferrando, Guglielmo

CORO
Benedetti i doppi coniugi
E le amabili sposine!
Splenda lor il ciel benefico,
Ed a guisa di galline
Sien di figli ognor prolifiche
Che le agguaglino in beltà.

CHORUS
Blessed be the two bridegrooms
and their lovely brides!
May a kindly heaven smile on them,
and, in the way that hens are,
may they be prolific
of progeny to equal them in beauty.

FIORDILIGI, DORABELLA,
FERRANDO E GUGLIELMO
Come par che qui prometta
Tutto gioia e tutto amore!
Della cara Despinetta
Certo il merito sarà.
Raddoppiate il lieto suono,
Replicate il dolce canto
E noi qui seggiamo intanto
In maggior giovialità.

FIORDILIGI, DORABELLA,
FERRANDO AND GUGLIELMO
Surely here's the promise
of every joy and perfect love!
And all the credit
goes to dear Despina.
Repeat that joyful music,
renew that lovely song,
and we will sit here
in highest mirth and glee.

(Il coro parte; restano quattro servitori per servire gli sposi che si mettono alla tavola)

(The chorus leaves; four servants remain to serve the couples, who seat themselves at the table)

FERRANDO E GUGLIELMO
Tutto, tutto, o vita mia,
Al mio foco or ben risponde.

FERRANDO AND GUGLIELMO
Everything now, my dearest,
accords with my desires.

FIORDILIGI E DORABELLA
Pel mio sangue l'allegria
Cresce, cresce e si diffonde.

FIORDILIGI AND DORABELLA
Joy grows and spreads
throughout my veins.

FERRANDO E GUGLIELMO
Sei pur bella!

FERRANDO AND GUGLIELMO
You are so beautiful!

FIORDILIGI E DORABELLA
Sei pur vago!

FIORDILIGI AND DORABELLA
You are so handsome!

FERRANDO E GUGLIELMO
Che bei rai!

FERRANDO AND GUGLIELMO
What lovely eyes!

FIORDILIGI E DORABELLA
Che bella bocca!

FIORDILIGI AND DORABELLA
What an attractive mouth!

FERRANDO E GUGLIELMO
Tocca e bevi!

FERRANDO AND GUGLIELMO
Clink glasses and drink!

FIORDILIGI E DORABELLA
Bevi e tocca!

FIORDILIGI AND DORABELLA
Drink and clink glasses!

FIORDILIGI, DORABELLA E FERRANDO
E nel tuo, nel mio bicchiero
Si sommerga ogni pensiero
E non resti più memoria
Del passato ai nostri cor.

FIORDILIGI, DORABELLA AND FERRANDO
In your glass and mine
may every care be drowned,
and let no memory of the past
remain in our hearts.

GUGLIELMO
(da sè)
Ah, bevessero del tossico,
Queste volpi senza onor!

GUGLIELMO
(to himself)
Would that we were drinking poison,
the dishonourable jades!

SCENA DICIASSETTESIMA

I suddetti; Don Alfonso; poi Despina da notaio

SCENE 17

The above, Don Alfonso, then Despina disguised as a notary

DON ALFONSO
Miei signori, tutto è fatto:
Col contratto nuziale
Il notaio è sulle scale
E ipso fatto qui verrà.

DON ALFONSO
Everything is ready, friends;
the notary is coming up the stairs
with the marriage contract
and ipso facto he'll be here.

FIORDILIGI, DORABELLA, FERRANDO E GUGLIELMO
Bravo, bravo. Passi subito!

FIORDILIGI, DORABELLA, FERRANDO AND GUGLIELMO
Splendid! Let him in at once!

DON ALFONSO
Vo a chiamarlo. Eccolo qua.

DON ALFONSO
I'll go and call him. Here he is.

DESPINA
(con voce nasale)
Augurandovi ogni bene,
Il notaio Beccavivi
Coll'usata a voi sen viene
Notariale dignità.
E il contratto stipulato
Colle regole ordinarie
Nelle forme giudiziarie,

DESPINA
(in a nasal voice)
Wishing you every happiness,
the notary Beccavivi
comes to you with his usual
notarial dignity.
And first coughing,
then sitting down,
in a clear voice he will read

Pria tossendo,
Poi sedendo,
Clara voce leggerà.

FIORDILIGI, DORABELLA, FERRANDO E GUGLIELMO
Bravo, bravo in verità!

DESPINA
Per contratto
Da me fatto,
Si congiunge in matrimonio
Fiordiligi con Sempronio
E con Tizio Dorabella,
Sua legittima sorella;
Quelle, dame ferraresi,
Questi, nobili albanesi.
E per dote e contradote . . .

FIORDILIGI, DORABELLA, FERRANDO E GUGLIELMO
Cose note, cose note!
Vi crediamo,
Ci fidiamo;
Soscriviam, date pur qua.

(solamente le due donne sottoscrivono)

DESPINA E DON ALFONSO
Bravi, bravi in verità!

(La carta vesta in mano di Don Alfonso. Si sente un gran suono di tamburo)

CORO
(di dentro)
Bella vita militar!
Ogni di si cangia loco,
Oggi molto e doman poco,
Ora in terra ed or sul mar.

FIORDILIGI, DORABELLA, DESPINA, FERRANDO E GUGLIELMO
Che rumor, che canto è questo?

the stipulated contract
with the normal provisions
in judicial form.

FIORDILIGI, DORABELLA, FERRANDO AND GUGLIELMO
Excellent, in truth!

DESPINA
By this contract
drawn up by me,
the following are joined in matrimony:
Fiordiligi with Sempronio,
and with Tizio Dorabella,
her legitimate sister;
the ladies, natives of Ferrara,
the gentlemen, Albanian nobles
and in dowry and settlement . . .

FIORDILIGI, DORABELLA, FERRANDO AND GUGLIELMO
We know all that!
We believe you,
we trust you:
give it here, and we'll sign.

(only the two ladies sign)

DESPINA AND DON ALFONSO
Excellent, in truth!

(The paper is in Don Alfonso's hand. The sound of drums is heard.)

CHORUS
(off-stage)
A soldier's life for me!
Every day a change of scene;
plenty today and little tomorrow,
now on land and now on sea.

FIORDILIGI, DORABELLA, DESPINA, FERRANDO AND GUGLIELMO
What's that noise? What's that singing?

DON ALFONSO
State cheti; io vo a guardar.
(va alla finestra)
Misericordia!
Numi del cielo!
Che caso orribile!
Io tremo! Io gelo!
Gli sposi vostri . . .

DON ALFONSO
Keep quiet: I'll go and see.
(he goes to the window)
Mercy on us!
God in Heaven!
Disaster is upon us!
I tremble! My blood runs cold!
Your former lovers . . .

FIORDILIGI E DORABELLA
Lo sposo mio . . .

FIORDILIGI AND DORABELLA
My former lover . . .

DON ALFONSO
In questo istante
Tornaro, oh Dio!
Ed alla riva
Sbarcano già!

DON ALFONSO
Are returning, oh heaven,
at this moment,
and are now disembarking
on the shore!

FIORDILIGI, DORABELLA,
FERRANDO E GUGLIELMO
Cosa mai sento!
Barbare stelle!
In tal momento
Che si farà?
*(I servi portono via la tavola,
e i suonatori partono in furia)*

FIORDILIGI, DORABELLA,
FERRANDO AND GUGLIELMO
What do I hear?
Ye cruel stars!
What's to be done
at this dire moment?
*(The Servants carry the table away,
the musicians leave in a rage)*

FIORDILIGI E DORABELLA
Presto partite,
Presto fuggite:
Là, là celatevi,
Per carità!

FIORDILIGI AND DORABELLA
Go at once,
quickly, fly;
conceal yourselves,
for pity's sake!

DESPINA, FERRANDO,
GUGLIELMO E DON ALFONSO
Ma se ci (li) veggono?
Ma se ci (li) incontrano?

DESPINA, FERRANDO,
GUGLIELMO AND DON ALFONSO
Suppose they see us (them)?
Suppose we (they) meet them?

(Don Alfonso conduce Despina in una camera; Fiordiligi e Dorabella conducono gli amanti in un'altra. Gli amanti escono non veduti e partono)

(Don Alfonso leads Despina into a room. Fiordiligi and Dorabella show the men into another. The men escape unseen and go off)

FIORDILIGI E DORABELLA
Numi, soccorso!
Numi, consiglio!
Chi dal periglio
Ci salverà?

FIORDILIGI AND DORABELLA
Heaven help us!
Heaven guide us!
Who will save us
from this peril?

DON ALFONSO
Rasserenatevi,
Ritranquillatevi;
In me fidatevi,
Ben tutto andrà.

DON ALFONSO
Be reassured,
keep calm,
trust in me,
and all will be well.

FIORDILIGI E DORABELLA
Mille barbari pensieri
Tormentando il cor mi vanno
Se discoprono l'inganno
Ah, di noi che mai sarà!

FIORDILIGI AND DORABELLA
A thousand cruel thoughts
are tormenting my heart;
if they discover the deception
whatever will become of us?

SCENA ULTIMA

FINAL SCENE

Fiordiligi e Dorabella, Ferrando e Guglielmo con mantelli e cappelli militari, Despina in camera, e Don Alfonso

Fiordiligi and Dorabella, Ferrando and Guglielmo in military cloaks and caps, Despina in a room, Don Alfonso.

FERRANDO E GUGLIELMO
Sani e salvi, agli amplessi amorosi
Delle nostre fidissime amanti
Ritorniamo di gioia esultanti
Per dar premio alla lor fedeltà!

FERRANDO AND GUGLIELMO
Safe and sound, exulting with joy,
We return to the loving embraces
of our faithful sweethearts
to crown them for their constancy!

DON ALFONSO
Giusti Numi! Guglielmo!
Ferrando!
Oh, che giubilo! Qui! Come e
quando?

DON ALFONSO
Great heaven! Guglielmo,
Ferrando!
What joy! You here? How and
when?

FERRANDO E GUGLIELMO
Richiamati da regio contrordine,
Pieno il cor di contento e di
gaudio,
Ritorniamo alle spose adorabili,
Ritorniamo alla vostra amistà.

FERRANDO AND GUGLIELMO
Recalled by royal countermand,
our hearts full of contentment and
joy,
we've returned to our adorable
sweethearts,
we've returned to your friendship.

GUGLIELMO
(a Fiordiligi)
Ma cos'è quel pallor, quel
silenzio?

GUGLIELMO
(to Fiordiligi)
But why this pallor, this
silence?

FERRANDO
(a Dorabella)
L'idol mio perchè mesto si sta?

FERRANDO
(to Dorabella)
Why is my love so sad?

DON ALFONSO
Dal diletto confuse ed attonite
Mute mute si restano là.

DON ALFONSO
Their tongues are tied
with confusion and overwhelming joy.

FIORDILIGI E DORABELLA
(da sè)
Ah, che al labbro le voci mi mancano;
Se non moro un prodigio sarà.

FIORDILIGI AND DORABELLA
(aside)
My tongue has forsaken me;
if I don't die it will be a miracle.

(I servi portano un baule)

(The servants bring in a trunk)

GUGLIELMO
Permettete che sia posto
Quel baul in quella stanza.
Dei, che veggio!
Un uom nascosto!
Un notaio! Qui che fa?

GUGLIELMO
Allow me to have
this trunk brought into that room.
Heavens, what do I see!
A man hidden here!
A notary! What's he doing here?

DESPINA
(esce senza cappello)
No, signor, non è un notaio;
E Despina mascherata
Che dal ballo or è tornata
E a spogliarsi or venne qua.

DESPINA
(comes out without a hat)
No, sir, it's not a notary:
It's Despina in fancy dress
who's just back from a ball
and come in here to change.

FERRANDO E GUGLIELMO
(da sè)
Una furba uguale a questa
Dove mai si troverà?

FERRANDO AND GUGLIELMO
(aside)
Could so clever a rogue
ever be found?

DESPINA
(da sè)
Una furba che m'agguagli
Dove mai si troverà?

DESPINA
(aside)
Could they ever find
anyone as smart as me?

FIORDILIGI E DORABELLA
La Despina? La Despina?
Non capisco come va.

FIORDILIGI AND DORABELLA
Despina? Despina?
I don't begin to understand.

(Don Alfonso lascia cadere accortamente il contratto sottoscritto dalle donne)

(Don Alfonso cunningly lets fall the contract signed by the women)

DON ALFONSO
(piano agli amanti)
Già cader lasciai le carte;
Raccoglietele con arte.

DON ALFONSO
(quietly to the men)
I've just dropped the papers:
pick them up neatly.

(Ferrando raccoglie il contratto)

(Ferrando picks up the contract)

FERRANDO
Ma che carte sono queste?

FERRANDO
But what are these papers?

GUGLIELMO
Un contratto nuziale!

FERRANDO E GUGLIELMO
Giusto ciel! Voi qui scriveste,
Contraddirci omai non vale!
Tradimento, tradimento!
Ah, si faccia il scoprimento
E a torrenti, a fiumi, a mari
Indi il sangue scorrerà!

(Vanno per entrare nell'altra camera; le donne li arrestano)

FIORDILIGI E DORABELLA
Ah, signor, son rea di morte
E la morte io sol vi chiedo;
Il mio fallo tardi vedo;
Con quel ferro un sen ferite
Che non merita pietà!

FERRANDO E GUGLIELMO
Cosa fu?

FIORDILIGI E DORABELLA
(additando Despina e Don Alfonso)

Per noi favelli
Il crudel, la seduttrice!

DON ALFONSO
Troppo vero è quel che dice
E la prova è chiusa lì!

(Accenna la camera dov'erano entrati prima gli amanti. Ferrando e Guglielmo entrano in camera)

FIORDILIGI E DORABELLA
Dal timer io gelo, io palpito;
Perchè mai li discopri!

(Ferrando e Guglielmo escono dalla camera, senza capelli, senza mantelli e senza mustacchi, ma coll'abito finto e burlano in modo ridicolo le amanti e Despina)

FERRANDO
(a Fiordiligi)

GUGLIELMO
A marriage contract!

FERRANDO AND GUGLIELMO
Merciful heaven! You've signed here,
don't try to deny it!
Treachery, treachery!
Let us find the villains
and their blood shall flow
in torrents, rivers, oceans!

(They make to enter the other rooms; the women prevent them)

FIORDILIGI AND DORABELLA
Ah, my love, my sin is mortal
and death alone I seek now;
too late I see my error;
with your sword pierce this bosom
that deserves no pity!

FERRANDO AND GUGLIELMO
Tell us all.

FIORDILIGI AND DORABELLA
(pointing to Despina and Don Alfonso)
Let them speak for us,
that pander and that procuress!

DON ALFONSO
Too true is what she says,
and the proof is shut in there!

(He indicates the room by which the men first entered. Ferrando and Guglielmo go into it)

FIORDILIGI AND DORABELLA
I freeze, I shiver with fright;
why did he give them away?

(Ferrando and Guglielmo come out of the room, without caps, cloaks and without moustaches, but in the false lovers' clothes, and burlesque their antics with Despina)

FERRANDO
(to Fiordiligi)

A voi s'inchina,
Bella damina,
Il cavaliere dell'Albania!

GUGLIELMO
Il ritrattino
Pel coricino
Ecco, io le rendo, signora mia!

FERRANDO E GUGLIELMO
(a Despina)
Ed al magnetico signor dottore
Rendo l'onore
Che meritò!

FIORDILIGI, DORABELLA E DESPINA
Stelle, che veggo!

FERRANDO, GUGLIELMO E DON ALFONSO
Son stupefatte!

FIORDILIGI, DORABELLA E DESPINA
Al duol non reggo!

FERRANDO, GUGLIELMO E DON ALFONSO
Son mezze matte!

FIORDILIGI E DORABELLA
(accennando Don Alfonso)
Ecco là il barbaro
Che c'ingannò!

DON ALFONSO
V'ingannai, ma fu l'inganno
Disinganno ai vostri amanti,
Che più saggi amai saranno,
Che faran quel ch'io vorrò.
Qua le destre, siete sposi.
Abbracciatevi e tacete.
Tutti quattro ora ridete,
Ch'io già risi e riderò.

FIORDILIGI E DORABELLA
Idol mio, se questo è vero,
Colla fede e coll'amore

Lovely lady,
a noble of Albania
bows before you!

GUGLIELMO
The miniature
exchanged for the little heart
I return herewith, madame!

FERRANDO AND GUGLIELMO
(to Despina)
And to the magnetic doctor
I give the honour
which he merited!

FIORDILIGI, DORABELLA AND DESPINA
Heavens, what do I see?

FERRANDO, GUGLIELMO AND DON ALFONSO
They're stupefied!

FIORDILIGI, DORABELLA AND DESPINA
I cannot bear this torment!

FERRANDO, GUGLIELMO AND DON ALFONSO
They're half crazy!

FIORDILIGI AND DORABELLA
(pointing to Don Alfonso)
That is the cruel man
who deceived us!

DON ALFONSO
I deceived you, but my deception
undeceived your lovers,
who henceforth will be wiser
and will do as I wish.
Give me your hands, now you're united,
embrace each other and say no more.
All four of you can laugh now
as I have laughed and shall do again.

FIORDILIGI AND DORABELLA
My love, if this is true,
with fidelity and with love

Compensar saprò il tuo core,
Adorarti ognor saprò.

I will make good what I have done
and adore you evermore.

FERRANDO E GUGLIELMO
Te lo credo, gioia bella,
Ma la prova far non vo'.

FERRANDO AND GUGLIELMO
I believe you,my fair one,
but I won't put it to the test.

DESPINA
Io non so se veglio o sogno,
Mi contondo, mi vergogno;
Manco mal, se a me l'han fatta,
Ch'a molt'altri anch'io la fo.

DESPINA
I don't know if I'm awake or
dreaming.
I'm confused, I feel ashamed;
I'm slipping badly if they can do to
me what I have done to many others.

TUTTI
Fortunato l'uom che prende
Ogni cosa pel buon verso
E tra i casi e le vicende
Da ragion guidar si fa.
Quel che suole altrui far piangere
Fia per lui cagion di riso
E del mondo in mezzo ai turbini
Bella calma troverà.

ALL
Happy is the man who looks
at everything on the right side
and through trials and tribulations
makes reason his guide.
What always makes another weep
will be for him a cause of mirth
and amid the tempests of this world
he will find sweet peace.

Discography

(All English disc numbers are given in roman type; *all USA numbers in italic type)*

LE NOZZE DI FIGARO

Complete sets

	SET A	SET B	SET C
COUNT	Bacquier	Wächter	Schöffler
COUNTESS	Söderström	Schwarzkopf	Jurinac
FIGARO	Evans	Taddei	Berry
SUSANNA	Grist	Moffo	Streich
CHERUBINO	Berganza	Cossotto	Ludwig
BARTOLO	Langdon	Vinco	Czerwenka
BASILIO	Hollweg	Ecolani	Majkut
MARCELLINA	Burmeister	Gatta	Malaniuk
Ensemble	New Philharmonia	Philharmonia	Vienna Opera
Conductor	Klemperer	Giulini	Böhm
Disc Nos.	SLS 955	SAX2381/4	SFL14012/4
		*Ang.*S3608	*Ep.*SC6022
Highlights		ColSAX2573	
		*Ang.*S35640	

	SET D	SET E	SET F
COUNT	Fischer-Dieskau	Poell	Bruscantini
COUNTESS	Janowitz	della Casa	Gatti
FIGARO	Prey	Siepi	Tajo
SUSANNA	Mathis	Güden	Noni
CHERUBINO	Troyanos	Danco	Gardino
BARTOLO	Lagger	Corena	Corena
BASILIO	Vantin	Dickie	Mercuriali
MARCELLINA	Johnson	Rossl-Majdan	Truccato-Pace
	Berlin Opera	Vienna Opera	Radio Roma
	Böhm	Kleiber	Previtali
	2711007	GOS 585/7	ITALY Cet.1219
	" " "	*Lon.*1402	*Ev./Cet.S424-3*
Highlights	DGG 136283	AOD SDD 237	*Ev./Cet. 7424*
		Lon.25045	

SET G

COUNT	Henderson
COUNTESS	Rautawaara
FIGARO	Domgraf-Fassbänder
SUSANNA	Mildmay
CHERUBINO	Helletsgruber
BARTOLO	Allin & Tajo
BASILIO	Nash
MARCELLINA	Willis
Ensemble	Glyndebourne 1934-5
Conductor	Busch
Disc Nos.	CFP 117/8 *Turn.4114/6*

Also available *(in German)* in USA (Ser.S6002) and Germany: Prey; Berry; Rothenberger; Gueden, etc. Dresden opera, Suitner.

Additional and now obsolete complete recordings include:
GERMANY, GB and USA: DGG 138697/9
Fischer-Dieskau; Stader; Seefried; Capecchi; Töpper; Benningsen, etc. Berlin Radio, Fricsay.
USA: EJS118 (recorded from Radio transmission)
Pinza; Rethberg; Novotna; Brownlee; Sayão. Metropolitan Opera, New York, Panizza. 9 March 1940.
GB: HMV ASD275/7 (also in Italy)
Calabrese; Jurinac; Bruscantini; Sciutti; Stevens; Wallace, etc. Glyndebourne Festival, Gui.
FRANCE: Pathé DTX206/8 (also on *OPBX-165* in USA)
Stich-Randall; Streich; Lorengar; Panerai; Rehfuss; Cuénod; Cortis. Aix-en-Provence Festival, Rosbaud.
GB: SER4508/11 (also on *LSC-6408* in USA)
Della Casa; London; Tozzi; Peters; Corena; Elias. Vienna Opera, Leinsdorf.
GB: CX1007-9. USA: SL114
London; Schwarzkopf; Kunz; Seefried; Jurinac; Hongen; Rus. Vienna State Opera, Karajan.

COSÌ FAN TUTTE

Complete sets

	SET A	SET B	SET C
FIORDILIGI	della Casa	Schwarzkopf	L.Price
DORABELLA	Ludwig	Ludwig	Troyanos
FERRANDO	Dermota	Kraus	Shirley
GUGLIELMO	Kunz	Taddei	Milnes
ALFONSO	Schöffler	Berry	Flagello
DESPINA	Loose	Steffek	Raskin
Ensemble	Vienna Philharmonic	Philharmonic	New Philharmonic
Conductor	Böhm	Böhm	Leinsdorf
Disc Nos.	GOS 543-5	SAN 103-6	SER 5575-8
	Rich.63508	*S3631*	*LSC 6416*
Highlights	SDD 208	ASD 2265	
	Lond.25047	*S36167*	

	SET D	SET E	SET F
FIORDILIGI	Seefried	Sovez	Stich-Randall
DORABELLA	Merriman	Helletsgruber	Sciutti
FERRANDO	Häfliger	Nash	Kmentt
GUGLIELMO	Prey	Domgraf-Fassbänder	Berry
ALFONSO	Fischer-Dieskau	Brownlee	Ernster
DESPINA	Koth	Eisinger	Malaniuk
Ensemble	Berlin Philharmonic	Glyndebourne	Vienna Opera
Conductor	Jochum	Busch	Moralt *(in Germa*
Disc Nos.	2709012	GERMANY	EUROPE A00417/
	" " "	E80681/3	
		Turn 4120/2	*PHC 3-005*

Additional and now obsolete complete recordings include:
GB: Nixa PLP555-1/3. USA: Classic C6142-4 (also on Remington and Period)
Hassler; Plumacher; Weikenmeier; Hoppe; Kelch. Stuttgart Ensemble, Dunnwald.
USA: Columbia SL122 *(in English)*
Steber; Thebom; Peters; Guarrera; Alvary. Metropolitan Opera New York, Stiedry.
GB: Columbia CX1262-4. USA: Angel 35164-6
Schwarzkopf; Merriman; Otto; Simoneau; Panerai; Bruscantini. Philharmonia; Karajan.

GB: Columbia CX1262-4. USA: Angel 35164-6
Schwarzkopf; Merriman; Tucker; Otto; Simoneau; Panerai; Bruscantini. Philharmon Karajan.
A single LP of highlights, also obsolete, is historically important:
USA: LM1126 (only on 78 rpm in GB)
Jurinac; Thebom; Lewis; Kunz; Borrielo. Glyndebourne Festival, Busch.